ALSO BY ANDRE DUBUS III

The Cagekeeper and Other Stories
Bluesman
House of Sand and Fog

THE GARDEN OF LAST DAYS

ANDRE DUBUS III

WILLIAM HEINEMANN: LONDON

Published by William Heinemann, 2008

2 4 6 8 10 9 7 5 3 1

Copyright © Andre Dubus III, 2008

Grateful acknowledgement is made to the following for permission to reprint
previously published material:

Collected Poems 1909–1962 copyright © 2002 by the Estate of T. S. Eliot and
reprinted by permission of Faber and Faber Ltd.

Andre Dubus III has asserted his right under the Copyright, Designs
and Patents Act, 1988, to be identified as the author of this work

This book is sold subject to the condition that it shall not, by way of trade
or otherwise, be lent, resold, hired out, or otherwise circulated without the
publisher's prior consent in any form of binding or cover other than that in which
it is published and without a similar condition, including this condition, being
imposed on the subsequent purchaser.

First published in the United States in 2008 by W. W. Norton & Company, Inc

First published in Great Britain in 2008 by
William Heinemann
Random House, 20 Vauxhall Bridge Road,
London SW1V 2SA

www.rbooks.co.uk

Addresses for companies within The Random House Group Limited can be
found at: www.randomhouse.co.uk/offices.htm

The Random House Group Limited Reg. No. 954009

A CIP catalogue record for this book
is available from the British Library

ISBN 9780434019205 (Hardback)
ISBN 9780434019212 (Trade Paperback)

Penguin Random House is committed to a sustainable future for
our business, our readers and our planet. This book is made from
Forest Stewardship Council® certified paper.

Printed and bound in Great Britain by Clays Ltd, Elcograf S.p.A.

Book design by Chris Welch Design

FOR LARRY BROWN

THE GARDEN OF LAST DAYS

LATE SUMMER, '01

THURSDAY

APRIL DROVE NORTH on Washington Boulevard in the late-afternoon heat. She passed housing developments behind acacia and cedar trees, Spanish moss hanging from their limbs like strings of dead spiders. Between her legs was the black coffee she'd bought at the Mobil station on the way out of town and it was too hot to drink, the sun still shining bright over the Gulf and blinding her from the side like something she should've seen coming, like Jean getting laid up and now there's no one to watch Franny and no calling in sick at the Puma. And little Franny was strapped in her car seat in the back, tired and happy with no idea how different tonight will be, how strange it could be.

But even in September, Thursday was a big money night, seven to eight hundred take-home, and that's what April concentrated on as she drove, Franny's chin starting to loll against her chest—April made herself think of that fat roll of tens and twenties she'd have at closing, how she'd fold it into the front pocket of her jeans then go to the house mom's office off the dressing room and give Tina a hundred before she found Franny in her pj's on Tina's brown vinyl couch, and she'd try not to think of the walls above Tina's desk covered with dancers' schedules and audition Polaroids of naked women, some of them under postcards from girls who came and went. In the corner were a small TV and VCR where once Louis kept playing a porno starring Bobbie Blue, who used to dance at the Puma as Denise, though the name her mother gave her was Megan.

But Tina would be sure no tapes like that were around. She'd let Franny watch Disney videos as long as she wanted. Bring her chicken fingers and fries from the kitchen. Play cards with her or give her the back of an old schedule she could draw on with a Puma pen. And if the noise from the club got too loud—the rock and roll numbers the DJ blasted, the constant clink of bottles and glasses from the bar, all the men's hooting and hollering, Tina would turn up *Aladdin* or *Cinderella* or *The Little Mermaid* and pull the sliding door halfway shut so she could keep the right girls on rotation at the right time because it was all just a show, April told herself now, it was just a different kind of show business and Franny'd have to be backstage just this one time and she'd be fine. She was only three and she wouldn't know what she was seeing and she'd be fine.

April passed the industrial park, acres of one-story buildings behind hurricane fences, barbed wire coiled along the top, the sky an endless coral haze. She checked Franny in the rearview mirror. There was a ring of grape around her mouth from the Slush Puppie she'd let her have at the Mobil. April had put sunblock all over her in Jean's garden. Jean, with her heavy body and aging face, she always looked embarrassed to take April's rent and had never taken a penny all these months to babysit Franny. But nothing's for free and you should never count on anything that is and April wanted to know how she could have fallen so easily into thinking that Jean and her kindness was a sure thing she could trust? How could she not have found at least one backup babysitter in all the months she'd been here, just in case? And

Jean sounding so guilty on the phone from the hospital. Two days of tests. A bunch of tests for her heart.

Up ahead on the southbound side of the boulevard was the neon sign for the Puma Club. Thirty feet high and always on, it was two silhouettes of naked women, one standing, the other sitting with a knee drawn up to her breast. Just seeing it, something hot and hard gathered in April's stomach because even when she'd auditioned for Louis back in March, when she'd done her routine to a ZZ Top song out on the floor of the empty club at eight in the morning, she hadn't brought Franny inside with her; instead she'd parked the Sable under the trees and she'd locked her into the car with coloring books and crayons, a chocolate milk and two powdered doughnuts. She'd checked the doors twice and told Franny through the glass to lie down on her belly and eat and draw, and as she walked toward the club she'd tried to ignore the muffled cry of her daughter calling her from the car. April told herself it was in the shade and was hard to see unless you were looking for it, that it was all locked up anyway and what else could she do? Leave her alone back in the motel? They'd been here only three weeks and knew no one. She'd be done in less than thirty minutes anyway, though it turned out to be forty-five, and when she'd run to the car and unlocked it, it was full of heated air and Franny was sweating and it looked like she'd cried awhile. April had wiped her face and made her drink the rest of her chocolate milk, though it was warm, and she swore she'd never do anything even close to that ever again and took them to a lunch and matinee they couldn't afford.

April slowed for the illegal U-turn through the median strip, a patch of gravel she steered onto too fast, rocking her Sable, splashing hot coffee through her jeans onto her thigh. "*Shit.*" She turned and checked Franny. Her chin had swung to her other shoulder but she was still asleep. April edged up to the southbound boulevard and waited for a Winnebago to lumber by. Her thigh burned. She reached for the box of tissues and pressed one on the spill. Barely cool air blew in her face and at this moment she hated this car and her ex-husband for buying it, she hated Jean and her weak heart, she hated

Tina the house mom for being the one to watch over her Franny, she even hated Florida and its Gulf Coast that Stephanie up north had told her she'd love; but more than anything, she hated herself, April Marie Connors, for doing what she was about to do, for breaking the one rule she swore she'd never break, pulling out onto the macadam, then driving into the crushed-shell lot of the Puma Club for Men, her daughter Franny right there in the car with her.

It was not quite six yet, but parked up against the split-rail fence were pickup trucks and station wagons, a Mercedes next to three motorcycles next to a gray Lexus with gold trim. Always all kinds of men. It didn't matter if they were in the trades or gave orders in a high-rise office, if they were married and had children or lived alone and had nobody—men were men and soon enough, it seemed, every one of them would find their way to the Puma or places like it. Most nights she felt nothing about them whatsoever; they were simply the objects of her work and she worked them. But tonight, she hated them too.

Under the fake-Puma-skin canopy leading to the front door, two regulars in shirts and ties talked and laughed. One of them glanced over at her as she drove by and she accelerated past them, her rear tires spinning in the crushed shells. She steered around the club to where the employees parked up against the oak and acacia trees. Twenty or thirty cars were there already in the late-day sun. She saw Lonnie's red Tacoma and pulled alongside it. A lot of the floor hosts wore tight Puma Club T-shirts and drove big SUVs, anything to show off just how much room they could take up themselves. Lonnie wasn't big like the rest of them, but he had a knockout punch and when he talked to her during her shift he always looked right into her face and not at her naked breasts. The way the others did, like it was their right. Like it was another kind of tip.

"Franny?" April sipped her coffee. Still too hot. She ran a finger down the side of her daughter's forehead and cheek. Her skin was warm, her chin sticky. "Wake up, sweetie." April checked her watch—

four minutes to sign-in. She balanced her coffee in her other hand and opened the glove compartment for the box of Wetnaps and began to wipe off the purple ring from around Franny's mouth. Franny turned her face away and whimpered and April had to press harder to get the syrup off.

"*Mama, don't.*"

"Wake up, honey. You're gonna see some *movies.*"

Franny pushed at April's hand. She opened her eyes, a little bloodshot, green as Glenn's.

"Don't you want to see *The Little Mermaid?*" April opened her door, dumped her coffee. She unbuckled Franny's car seat and grabbed her pink starfish backpack that held her toothbrush and toothpaste wrapped in foil, her pj's and two books, a Berenstain Bears and *Stellaluna.*

Outside it was hot and smelled like the trees but also the Dumpster near the kitchen door, bar trash and kitchen trash, and next to it the steel barrel of rancid Frialator oil. April carried Franny with both arms, the backpack hanging from her fingers and bouncing off her leg as she walked over the crushed shells for the kitchen door. It was always hard to walk in them in her flip-flops but harder now, holding Franny, her arms around her neck, her cheek resting on April's shoulder.

April reached for the door handle. She could hear music coming from the front of the club, someone spraying dishes. A cool sweat beaded up across her forehead and upper lip and there was a sickening pull in her belly and she breathed deeply, pulled open the screen door, and carried Franny over the greasy linoleum, a fine mist rising on the other side of the big dishwashing machine and its short conveyor belt on her right, somebody new working there, an old man with brown skin spraying a rack of bar glasses. He looked up at them and nodded his head, then looked away. A Cuban probably, an old Cuban who didn't speak English.

To her left, past the chrome racks glowing orange under the foodwarming lights, Ditch's back was to her. He was slicing up ribbons of steak on the greased hot top, the steam and smoke rising off the bell peppers and onions he flipped with his spatula. Someone had left the hatch to the ice machine open, and she moved past it and the battered swinging door the waitresses used, Renée's Foreigner song blaring out there in the darkness behind it. For a second, hearing this meant nothing. Then it did, that Renée was already into her ice queen act, shedding her icicle costume one silvery fringe at a time, and unless Tina'd changed the rotation, April was less than two numbers from having to be onstage herself.

She stepped quickly into the dark hallway lit only by the crooked sconce over the dressing room door. Franny lifted her head. Zeke sat on the stool against the wall with his glass of iced Coke, all shoulders and blond crew cut, that strip of whiskers down the center of his chin. Franny squeezed April's neck and Zeke leaned over in the dark noise to open the dressing room door, a long bright room full of naked and half-dressed women, most of them talking and smoking as they got ready, and it was stupid of her to only tell Franny she'd watch movies with a nice lady like Jean, that she hadn't mentioned all the women they'd have to walk through right now, most of them bitches April had nothing to do with—they smiled right at you while they tried to steal your customer for a private, they paid the minimum to everybody in the house from the DJ to Tina, and a few of them were into Oxy and Ecstasy and went back to hotels with big-spending clients and gave the rest of them a bad name.

But now they smiled for Franny; they sat or stood at the long makeup mirror under the lights, all hair and naked backs. A few waved at Franny in the reflection, some turned and came closer with their smoking cigarettes and naked breasts and big smiles for her daughter, but April kept moving, heading for Tina's office straight ahead, the door wide open. Tina was leaning over her desk whiting out something on the wall schedule. April squeezed behind her and dropped Franny's backpack on the couch.

Tina turned around, the bottle of Wite-Out in her hand, the whole office smelling like it. "Rachel's history and Lucy just got bumped to days so now my rotation's all fucked up. You're on after Renée, Spring. Sorry." She fixed her eyes on Franny standing on the couch, leaning against April and gripping her T-shirt. "Jesus, I forgot." She capped the bottle, her one-inch nails a bright orange. She'd been in the business for years and had her boobs done before anybody and they were massive and hard-looking. April grabbed the sign-in pen hanging by its string near the clipboard.

"So you're Annie."

"Franny." April wrote: *Spring—5:58 P.M.* She wanted to ask Tina why she hadn't called her in earlier, but Tina was asking Franny about her starfish backpack, if she had anything yummy in there to play with, and Franny being quiet wasn't a good sign but April was thinking how she didn't even have time for makeup now and she quickly signed into the pickup log, wrote: *Spring—drove self. Sable.*

"Mama?"

Renée was already into her second number, a heavy metal song she ended with her ass in the air.

"Your mama's gotta work now, sweets. Show me what's in your bag. Are you hungry?" There was an edge to Tina's voice and April knew it was to get her moving, though it was scaring Franny, her face so still and about to take a bad turn, her arms held out, and April wanted to pick her up and hold her just a second but then Franny wouldn't let go and April was due out on the floor in less than two minutes.

"Mama."

"I'll be right back." She blew Franny a kiss and stepped by Tina, moving fast by all the girls who could take their time getting ready, and she hurried to the wall of gray metal lockers across from the mirror and had her shirt off before she got to number 7, Franny beginning to cry, a long shriek and wail, calling her. April lifted the padlock and spun the dial right to 11, then left to 17, then right again to 6, but she stopped two marks past it and now it wouldn't open and she had to do it again, slower this time.

"Mama!"

Tina's office door slid shut. Behind the walls to the club Renée's number was in the final crash of guitars. The padlock dropped open and one of the girls behind her, Wendy or Marianne, asked about Franny, asked if that little doll was hers. April didn't answer and could give a shit if they were offended or not. The music ended and a half-full house clapped, a few of them letting out a whoop or a yell. April knew Renée was on her hands and knees now, scooping up bills, show-ing her ass to whoever wanted to toss more before she had to make her exit. And April only had on her white halter top, buttoning the three buttons up the middle. No time to get into her T-back, nylons, garters, and skirt. She started to pull down her jeans, but no, she wouldn't make it—she'd just have to do a blue jean act with heels.

She jerked her black stilettos out of her locker and pushed in one foot at a time and leaned over to cinch the straps. There were just men's voices now. Two of them laughed, she could hear them clearly as Renée came whisking into the dressing room naked, clutching her ice queen costume and a fistful of cash. Franny's crying was louder now and April couldn't get the metal pin in the hole of the strap and her Melissa Etheridge song had started and Tina stuck her head out her office doorway. "Get out there, Spring!"

"Mama! *Mama!*" It was almost too much. April's face was hot, her chest tight with trapped air, and she took a breath and found the hole and didn't bother threading the strap any farther. She moved by Renée standing there in heels and silver glitter and pathetic white frosted eyeliner, counting her money. Franny kept calling her, and out in the club a man called for her, too, then another, and Tina looked hard down at her jeans as April passed the office and didn't look in, her daughter's cry the only sound she heard as she stepped into the darkness of the hallway heading for the blue glow of the backstage hall and the three carpeted steps she climbed. She told herself her daughter would be fine. She would. She'd be fine. She waited behind the main curtain for her cue, for Etheridge's voice she heard now, but shit, how was she going to get her jeans off past her stilettos with-out taking them off first? And Louis didn't allow bare feet on the stage—everything else but not the feet. And when she got her jeans off, it'd be *her* underwear she pulled down for them. Not Spring's, but April's. Etheridge started singing about coming through the window, and men were calling for her now, calling for Spring, and she put on her nightworld smile, parted the curtain, and stepped into the amber glow of the stage.

A few regulars let out a yell. A few more clapped. She smiled and smiled and her hips started to do what they did. She swung her head back and looked hard down into the darkness of the tables, smiling like nothing would ever make her happier than what she was doing right now. Men sat back with their drinks and bottles of beer. They stared at her face, her crotch, her breasts. A college kid in a white cap smiled up at her but he couldn't look her in the eye, and that's the one she'd come back to, that's the one she'd unsnap her jeans for first, the one that made her feel this was her show, that *she* controlled *them* and always would, that she'd be fine—this was her show and she'd be just fine. She and Franny both.

∨ ∨ ∨

B ASSAM WATCHES HIMSELF drive the Neon along the water in the setting sun. At the place called Mario's-on-the-Gulf, he sat among the kufar and ate a small basket of onion rings and drank one glass of beer and two vodkas over ice. Living so haram all these months, he has become fond of this feeling the drinking gives him, as if he is a spirit floating loosely behind his own skin. Inside the open envelope beside him are 160 one-hundred-dollar bills. Some of them are new, some are old, and the kafir woman at the bank insisted for his own security he accept a check, but no, he preferred cash.

She was young and plump, but even with a blemish upon her chin she was pretty the way these mushrikoon are pretty, showing their bare arms and legs, their throats, their painted faces. This is what has surprised him most—that the kufar are largely asleep in the evil they do.

He steers away from the sun and passes a small park, its palm and thorn trees which remind him of home. But nothing else does. In the sun's last rays, its light the color of fires against shops and restaurants, he passes men and women sitting at outdoor tables, laughing and smoking and drinking. He passes a young couple walking side by side holding hands. The man is young and thin and wears a baseball Nike hat like Karim in Khamis Mushayt who is lost but does not believe it. The woman is blond, an American whore, but still Bassam looks twice more at her in his rearview mirror, his heart pushing hungrily inside his chest, his mouth suddenly dry for he knows where he is going.

Do not forget, Bassam, it was the Egyptian, the man who hates all women, not simply the kufar, who took you there. It was Amir, certain they were being followed, who drove you. Would he have done this if they had not permitted him to fly alone and afterward, in his joy, he had not asked all his questions about the weight limits of the single-engine? Was there a hold for cargo and a release to dump it? The instructor had narrowed his eyes upon them, and Amir had seen his mistake and as he drove away from the airfield he continued looking into the rear mirrors of the Neon and he ordered you to light a cigarette and blow smoke out the window, to turn on the radio and move your head. Amir, who never smiles, who always watches the money and wears too much cologne and never smokes, he drove them both into the parking area of this club for men. He rose quickly out of the auto and studied the road, but there was no one. Still, he said, "We go in, but say a supplication of place. Say it now."

Bassam is still surprised by his cell phone call this morning from the northern city, not that there is additional money to wire back to Dubai, but that he has asked *him* to do it, Bassam al-Jizani, the one he has monitored so closely here. It has been their primary task all these months: Do not draw attention. Live like the kufar when you are among them. Smoke cigarettes in public. Drink alcohol moderately. Wear short pants on hot days and never carry the Book upon your person. Never speak of the Creator or all we know is holy. The polytheists will see it. It will strike fear into the mushrikoon and bring suspicion upon you.

But Bassam, living like the kufar has weakened you and, you must admit this, it began immediately, that one night in Dubai before flying west, the taxi driver as old as your father and uncles, laughing at you and Imad and Tariq in his rear seat, the dark happiness in his eyes as he drove slowly by the hotels, their bright electric signs and then, like stumbling upon a hill of insects in the sand, so very many uncovered women in the side walking areas and in the street, calling to you.

Your breathing seemed to stop, and the driver laughed more loudly and slowed the taxi. "These Russians call them night butterflies." And he explained to you and your brothers from Asir things you did not wish to know. These whores from Uzbekistan and Ukraine, Georgia, Chechnya, and Azerbaijan, the first uncovered women you had ever seen, and not simply the arms but their legs as well, their bellies and half of their nuhood, their faces painted heavily, cheap jewelry hanging from their ears, their lips dark and glistening.

"Don't look, brothers," said Imad. "Do not look at these jinn."

But you did, Bassam. You looked at their nuhood and their backsides, you heard their talk and their laughter and you watched them walk in their high shoes, and surely this was the first of many temptations from Shaytan himself. But you were steadfast. In your rented room, you three performed your ablutions at the bath sink and you determined the qiblah and prayed the Isha prayer and you tried to ignore the noise outside the walls, the passing autos and their radio music, the shout of a man, the laughter of uncovered women who in the kingdom would be stoned to death.

Here it has only grown worse. All these months, in every leased room, Amir has kept the windows covered. He has pulled down shades and drawn curtains. He has lit incense in mabakhir and placed the Qur'an on a small table on the east wall they faced daily for the five prayers, and Bassam would make himself forget the young women beyond that wall, driving their topless autos in the sun, walking so uncovered into and out of shops and malls, sitting on blankets on sand reading books and magazines and talking and laughing, their

long blond hair, their bare legs and feet, their uncovered faces looking directly at whomever they wished to, including him. He made
himself think of the companions reserved for him and his brothers in
Jannah, Insha'Allah, not these dirty kufar who would laughingly pull
him between their legs straight to the eternal fire.

Yet now he drives north when he should be driving west. He told
Imad and Tariq he would be back before the final prayer, Allah willing. And tomorrow is too important and the first business is to wire
this money to Dubai. Already he has spent some of it, though he
did not leave the young bartender anything extra, something which
pleased Bassam as he walked away from Mario's-on-the-Gulf, this
feeling of hardening himself once more, of turning his back on these
people who should fear him but do not.

Soon this will change, Allah willing. Very soon.

And as the tall yellow sign of naked whores rises up ahead, Bassam
looks in the rearview mirror and sees the empty road behind him. But
how does he know he has not brought suspicion upon himself with
all the money he pulled from his pocket at the bar? He should do as
the Egyptian did, should he not? Go into the evil place one last time
where he will appear harmless? Where he will appear as just another
man? Normal in his hunger for what these whores will show him? A
normal man?

This Neon is inexpensive and plain and slow because Amir leased
it, and Bassam parks it beside a pickup truck. He silences the engine.
From the bank envelope he pulls the 160 hundred-dollar bills. He
divides the stack into two thick halves, folding each one, pushing one
into his front right pocket, the other into his left. He needs cigarettes
and remembers the machine in the pink entrance. Pink, a color he
fears for it is the color of seduction and the color of lies, and he takes
his cell phone and pushes it under the money in his left pocket.

The woman who had danced for him once before. Her long dark
hair and eyes that looked straight into him as he watched her. If the
Egyptian had not been beside him, holding his cranberry juice, enduring the filth of their visit here, already beyond this world, then Bas-

sam would have paid her for private time. He would have paid for her as any kafir would. It's only right that he do that now, that he deflect suspicion and appear this way, one last time.

He closes his eyes, the keys in his sweating hand. *O Lord, I ask You the best of this place, and ask You to protect me from its evils. You are more dear than all Your creation. O Lord, protect me from them as You wish.*

Y Y Y

A T FIRST SHE'D thought it was a toothache.

April had taken Franny to the beach, and Jean, in her loose sundress, had uncoiled the hose from under the stairs and was watering the ixora and allamanda, showering them with a fine spray. She'd had a particularly sweet morning with Franny, and she was thinking of her as she turned the water away from the red star clusters of the ixora to the bougainvillea hanging like an undone necklace from the trunk of the palm.

This morning she'd made herself and Franny silver-dollar pancakes, cooking them in melted butter on the griddle while she sipped her coffee and peeled a kiwi for garnish. Franny sat at the peninsula on two gardening books on her stool near the window, and today she drew with a dull purple crayon, talking with that impossibly high voice of hers. Even now, after six months, Jean couldn't stop staring at her, this tiny three-year-old human being with her curly hair that was already darkening to her mother's color, her round cheeks and surprisingly graceful neck. Her deep green eyes. Whenever Franny listened, she'd sit completely still and raise her chin and tilt her face up. And the child got excited to do the most mundane chores, like feed the cat or rinse the dishes for the machine or squat on the floor and hold the dustpan with both hands while Jean swept into it.

The first few weeks of taking care of her, it had been that, Franny leaping with unguarded hope and wonder into every suggestion Jean made, which pierced Jean where she believed she'd long ago stopped feeling much at all. This morning was one of those times, though Jean couldn't point to any one thing that did it: the early-morning light coming over the east wall into the window across Franny's face and arms; or that voice as she talked to Jean without a break, telling her dream of starfish and Teletubbies and a garden like theirs that could fly—the fact she referred to Jean's garden as *theirs;* maybe it was the warm-yeast smell of the buttermilk pancakes steaming on the griddle, the taste of chicory coffee with cream and too much sugar, the bright, nearly translucent green of the kiwi she sliced—all this *life*, she didn't know; all she did know is that in that moment she felt so full, so blessed, that her eyes welled up and she had to turn to the griddle so Franny wouldn't see her because how do you explain joy making you cry? How could she explain it even to herself? This opening up inside her that seemed to fill from the bottom with unspeakable love for this child and everything under her own nose in this one and only day given her?

Just before eleven, April walked down the outside stairs in her robe and flip-flops, carrying her coffee in a tall mug. It was a sound and image Jean had come to dread for they signaled the end of her morning with Franny, and nearly always it was the same: she'd hear the screen door above swing open and shut, then the dull *thwock-thwock* of her tenant's flip-flops on the outside steps. Through the window she'd see April's feet and bare calves, the hem of her robe. Some mornings April would pause and lean over the railing and peer into one of the front windows of Jean's house. But even if she saw Franny drawing, or painting, or watching some PBS, she would keep going down and out into the garden and sit in one of the Adirondack chairs in the shade of the mango. She'd sit there and sip her morning coffee in Jean's walled garden where no one could see her.

The first week or so of looking after Franny, if she wasn't near the window Jean would call her over and point out her mother. But the little girl always dropped whatever she was doing and ran outside and that would be it; Jean's time with her would be over. She'd stand there at her door and watch Franny climb up onto April's lap where Jean couldn't see her anymore. Standing there watching them, her time had never felt shorter; she could feel each slipping moment; she was seventy-one years old and came from a family line where no one made it past seventy-four. Not her mother or father. Not a grandparent, aunt, or uncle. And she was a large woman who labored heavily. Sweated a lot. Got dizzy. In her lonelier, weaker moments she saw the terrible unfairness of this: she had so little time left and she was finding this feeling only *now*? Did April know how fortunate she was to be given it so young? This was a question rooted in envy, Jean knew, and she was ashamed of herself for even asking it.

But then one Friday morning, just as April was raising her mug to her lips, Franny ran out and jumped into her mother's lap and the coffee spilled and she pushed her daughter away from it and stood quickly, swatting at her robe, Franny sitting on the ground, her hair in her face, silent only a second before she let out a howl, then began crying. April picked her up right away. Jean ran cold water over a dish towel and rushed outside, April holding Franny close, explaining how hot the coffee was and how she didn't want her to get burned and that's why Mama pushed you away. That's why.

April's long dark hair was tied up loosely in the back. In the tiny crow's feet of her eyes was just the trace of the foundation she wore to her work. April began humming softly and Jean reached over and patted Franny's small back, felt the pencil-sized ribs under her fingers, her shaky breath, but it was as if she were standing between two people in an intimate conversation and she pulled her hand away. Stood there feeling useless, the wet dish towel in her hand.

After that she stopped telling Franny her mother was in the garden. She told herself she did this to give April some morning solitude, to protect her daughter from hot coffee, but she knew she was really doing it to prolong her time with Franny.

They'd both been gone only a few minutes today when the pain began in her jaw. A bad molar? But then it was in her left upper arm, and this seemed strange to her at the time because she was spraying the hibiscus with her right so why would that one hurt? She shook it in the air, the flesh there waggling the way it did. The pain didn't go away but she shrugged it off and turned the hose to the frangipani along the wall. She could still see the two girls as they'd looked when they'd left, Franny in her bathing suit under a Cinderella halter, her curly hair held back with a sun visor. She wore flip-flops like her mother, who held her hand and looked so young and lovely in her khaki shorts and purple T-shirt, her sunglasses and smiling face, her long shining hair. She carried a woven bag that held their towels and sand toys and probably a snack and water, and seeing her you'd never know she spent her nights doing what she did. Jean began to worry about her again. Both of them. What kind of life were they going to have, after all?

At the gate they'd turned and waved at her, and that image was still behind her eyes when the pain increased and a sharp pinch shot up her arm into her shoulder and jaw. She was not ignorant of these things. Now a weight began to press on her chest and a cold sweat broke out on her forehead and upper lip. She let go of the nozzle and hose, dropping them into the tangled red of the ixora. She walked carefully through the shade of the mango, her eyes on the door ahead of her. *Her* door. A French door she'd hired a man to put in so she could better see her garden and let in the light. Now she saw the door so clearly, clearer than when she'd spent two days painting it; it no longer looked lovely to her but more like a cold and distant piece of machinery she would have to learn to operate to get help, and all the love she'd felt that morning with Franny had now turned upside down inside her and become a terrible crushing weight on her chest.

This was surely it. She would die as Harold had. Alone in his office back in Oak Park, Chopin's nocturnes on the record player. She saw him as she'd seen him. Slumped in his favorite diamond-tufted chair, his nearly handsome face pointed downward and blue. *Blue.* His tongue stuck out stiffly and she'd felt a vague mortal disgust and sudden and permanent grief, but now it was her turn and she refused to go; she wanted to stay, stay with her two girls, who were not hers but should have been. Her survivors.

Then she was inside, her door somehow behind her, the cordless phone she rarely used in her hand. Her plump, liver-spotted hand. She had a hard time breathing and a malevolent force was pressing a thousand pounds to her chest and it was terrible to die this way. To suffocate alone in the late-morning brightness, the lush and verdant brightness of her and poor Harry's Sarasota home.

❯ ❯ ❯

TINA'S OFFICE DOOR was slid all the way open when April came around the corner naked and barefoot. She was hugging her stilettos and balled-up jeans, her underwear and halter. The clapping had stopped and Wendy's number came on, Wendy brushing by her in her negligee and heels. April clutched a wad of bills that should be thicker but wasn't because there was no garter belt for customers to slip their money into and she had to leave her panties on so they'd use that, but most of them didn't. And there was Franny sitting on Tina's brown couch watching the TV, her pink flip-flops barely reaching the edge of the cushion. Tina's desk lamp was off and in the shifting colored light of the screen Franny's lips were parted, her cheeks glistened, she needed to blow her nose, and who the hell was looking after her?

April hurried to her locker and dropped her clothes and shoes on the floor. The dressing room was empty except for the makeup artist at her perch in the corner reading a book. "Where's Tina?" She kept her voice down. Donna didn't look up. She was a big woman, her kit laid out on the counter under the mirror. She knew her stuff, though April never used her.

"Donna, where's Tina? She's supposed to be watching my kid."

"She went to get her something from the kitchen. I'm watching her." Donna went back to her book, a novel about vampires, and April knew she'd expect at least a ten now before the night was over.

At her locker she counted her bills: eighteen ones and a five. The act was never where the money was, but still, if Tina had called her she could've gotten in early enough to dress right and make more. She noticed she still had her watch on. She took it off, picked up her jeans, and stuck her watch into one of the front pockets. Through the plywood walls of the club, Michael Bolton was singing how he can't live anymore and there was also the music of *The Lion King*, African drums and the high-throated wail of some talking, singing animal. April could hear the deep voice of the actor who played Mufasa, the sweet way he was talking to his son, Simba. And she wanted to get dressed quickly and go see Franny. Maybe she could sit with her a few minutes while her daughter ate.

On the floor of her locker was a zippered vinyl pouch she bought at Walgreen's in the school supplies section. It was supposed to hold pencils and pens but she liked that it was purple and she stuck her money into it and was zipping it shut when the door opened and Louis walked in, Zeke pulling the door shut behind him.

Louis had wiry red hair and pink freckled skin and spent as much time on his boat as possible. Tonight he was wearing his aquamarine contacts that went with his Tommy Bahama silk shirt and pleated pants. On his freckled wrist was a turquoise and silver watchband and a silver bracelet, and any other man dressed like this would look elegant, but Louis was too petty to look that way, too convinced everybody's actions were designed to rob him. He stood there staring at her. She dropped her money pouch into her locker and began stepping into her T-back.

"What's with the act tonight, Spring?"

"Ask Tina."

"I'm asking you."

She could feel his stare as she pulled up her G-string, and it was always like being naked again when Louis looked at you. Out in the club Michael Bolton was really screaming now, the way he did, and the house was loud and happy for Wendy's act. From Tina's office came another Disney song, and April just hoped Louis wouldn't notice and go back there.

"Her rotation got changed. I don't know, I guess she didn't have time to call me." She cupped herself into her T-back and snapped the front snaps. She picked her blouse up off the floor, turned it right side out, found the armholes. "I didn't have time to get ready."

"Know how much I pay for liability, Spring? Do you?"

April pulled her garter halfway up her thigh, then stepped into the other one, a frayed yellow floral she'd been meaning to replace for a while now, and she stayed quiet because with Louis any answer was the wrong answer if it didn't come from him first, so you waited.

"Will you look at me when I'm talking to you, please?"

She turned to him, saw his watery, aquamarine eyes move from her bare ass to her face. Donna turned a page of her book lightly, quietly.

"More than you make in a month, easy. I don't care what your fucking problem is. Next time you leave the shoes *on*, all right? Just leave 'em on and shake your tits or I'll find somebody else because there's always somebody else. All *right*?"

"Yes." She stepped into her skirt, cinched it snugly over her hips. Louis was done now, though he wasn't moving. She could hear *The Lion King* and so must he, her heart thumping against her ribs, not because Louis cared about Tina babysitting but because he was Louis and she couldn't have him even seeing Franny, looking at her with his fake eyes, sizing her up.

He started walking toward Tina's office.

"Louis, my kid's in there and she finally calmed down." She smiled at him. It was her nightworld smile and it knew when to come and maybe even Louis believed it; he didn't smile back but his face changed; now he was a man in front of a woman, his insurance policies back in a drawer for now. He jiggled the change in his pocket.

"Since when do you have a kid?"

"Three years. She just turned three." These were dayworld words and she couldn't smile through them and had to look away. She grabbed her brush and makeup.

"What, you think I'll spook her?"

"Not on purpose." She moved past him to the makeup mirror, let her bare arm touch his, and she hoped he'd do what he did, turn to watch her lean over the counter toward her reflection because nobody touched Louis, especially after what happened with Denise, but that's all it took.

Wendy's second number had started, a Celine Dion song she thought was classy though it ended with her on her hands and knees, and it was time for April to get out on the floor, Louis just standing there like a big pink reptile in the sun, his eyes on April's ass in her skirt. The dressing room door opened. Tina walked in carrying a tray of food—hamburger and fries, a glass of watered-down milk from the bar. Franny wouldn't eat the bun, and there was no knife and fork to cut up the burger.

"Nice schedule tonight, Tina."

"Don't give me any of your shit, Louis. You know what you did."

"You could've bumped Wendy in the rotation."

"*Right.*"

Tina was already to her office, sliding the door shut, the only one who could talk to him like that because they lived together years ago after his divorce and he seemed to need her around like some men need their mothers or sisters. But he didn't like her to talk like that in front of anyone, and now he called to her through the door. "I want you upstairs, Tina. You hear me? First chance you fucking get."

"She's in a bad mood, Louis. It's nobody's fault."

He stood there studying April in the mirror. And her smile smiled back. He nodded once, his fake contacts looking pathetic, the only color in his face that wasn't pink and sun-damaged and dried-out and mean. Then he smiled like he'd never really seen her before, a smile that harbored a secret he was convinced only he and April shared, and it was as if a fine invisible net had just blossomed from his flabby belly and shot out over her, his new prize.

The dressing room door opened. Retro walked in in her red heels and red leather hot pants and red lace bra, her brown skin glowing. "Hi, Lou." Retro pretended she was happy to see him in here, smiling as she headed straight for her locker. She unsnapped her bra in the front with two long fingers. Louis watched her only a second or two, then his attention was back on April as she brushed her hair. She knew she'd have to avoid him now and she wanted him to leave; in *The Lion King* the part that scared Franny was coming soon, brother killing brother, Mufasa's terrified lion's face as he falls into the ravine below. April needed to tell Tina to fast-forward through that.

Louis's coins jingled in his pocket, but she was done smiling at him or talking to him. She leaned close to the mirror to apply her lipstick and it was always hard not to look at Retro, that brown skin, her long back and legs as she stepped out of her shorts. She reached inside her locker for her gown, one of the only girls to do a formal act, satin gloves and everything. Celine Dion was on her last breath now, her siren's voice slicing through all the clapping and hollering.

April hooked in her earring. "How's the VIP?"

"Not bad for September."

Retro stepped into her gown, real ivory satin that needed stitching at the hem, though it was nothing customers ever noticed. April hooked in her other hoop and started brushing on some blush, and Louis was still standing there like a boy who needed just one more sign to be sure. Tina's door slid open. "Spring?"

Franny was crying again, a sound that spilled into the room and hit April dully in the bones. *The Lion King* was muted or off.

"I'll be in the office, Tina. Don't make me wait."

"I'll get there when I get there, Louis. Spring?"

Franny began shrieking, but she'd have to wait two more seconds, just two more, because once cash started to go into the purple bag, you could never leave your locker unlocked though April knew she was late in saving Franny from what scared her; she was late for that, and even later for the VIP.

∨ ∨ ∨

From the Amazon Bar three steps higher than the main floor, Lonnie Pike could see out over the crowd to the other side of the club where Paco sat at the VIP bar and Little Andy guarded the black curtains to the Champagne Room. Tiny purple lights were strung along the half wall between here and the VIP and in the orange light of the stage Spring danced in blue jeans, which was strange, and the DJ had the music cranked so loud Lonnie could feel the ice vibrate in his glass. It was September, the low season, but the place was filling up, and he leaned back against the bar with his ginger ale and scanned the club for pockets, those dark human spaces in the room where something has just changed: above the music a man lets out an appreciative yell when before he was quiet; one of the dancers out on the floor laughs a little too hard or steps back too fast; a chair leg scrapes the carpet—something Lonnie can't hear, just feels, a shift of objects in the space there, this change in the air, a pocket of possible trouble.

Two of the girls climbed the steps from the main floor, their hips swaying. They moved by him to work the men at the bar, only four of them, but they were in shirts and ties and one of them had on a gold Rolex. Spring danced and he didn't watch. Let all the others watch because out on the floor were seventeen girls working it for their one-on-ones. He counted them and counted them again. Seventeen women in their floor costumes, none of them the same. Some moved from table to table in heels and short shorts and Puma T-shirts cut just below their breasts. Others wore business skirts and blouses and had their hair up because it was Thirsty Thursday and they knew the office boys would pay to see them take off the same clothes the women at work wore. Some of the real young ones came out in hardly anything, just a garter, G-string, and see-through negligee so you could see their breasts and ass, and sometimes this worked against them and nobody paid for what they were getting for free anyway. But on busy nights in the high season, when the drinks were selling and everybody was whooping it up and it was one big party, all they had to do was smile and shake what they had and they scored seven or eight privates in the VIP before they were due for their act back onstage.

Lonnie glanced over there. Spring's top was off, her back to him, her long hair swishing over her skin. She rocked her hips from side to side, both hands on her button and zipper. Between acts she'd work the floor in a cotton skirt and half-buttoned blouse, her hair shiny and brushed. She'd wear silver hoop earrings and smile at you like she was your best friend's sister you'd always wanted and this was the night she was coming to tell you she'd always wanted you, too. And it was her smile the men liked because she was always smiling and it never looked phony.

Except now. She was at the apron of the stage, her hair covering one of her nipples as she reached down to pull off her right high heel. She lost her balance and came down hard on her barefoot, both breasts bouncing out of time to the music. Two or three men laughed though it wasn't a sound Lonnie heard, just saw and felt. Spring smiled at them, but it wasn't a real smile, not her professional one anyway. Lonnie had never seen it before.

Another pocket opened out on the floor. A tall regular stood to go back to the VIP with one of the short-shorts girls whose name started with an M, though Lonnie couldn't remember the rest. Names didn't matter. Just their bodies. Keep track of the bodies and make sure nobody touched them.

The club was more than half full now, all four bartenders working fast and without a break. There was the thump of the bass guitar and drums, the woman singer's backstreet voice; there was the clink and scrape of ice, the talk and laughter of men and a few women, and Spring was starting her night out badly, kicking her jeans off behind her now, dancing in a pair of panties, just panties, not a G-string or crotchless, and another pocket began to show itself off to the right, a big man in a Miami Dolphins cap sitting back and tossing a wadded bill at her. It hit Spring in a rib and she ignored it, turned and started pushing down her panties, letting them all glimpse her ass before she pulled them back up again. Other pockets kept opening at the entrance, new customers coming in in twos or threes, parting the curtains and letting in the pink light of the front hallway where Big Scaggs and Larry T sat on stools.

Dolphins Cap tossed another one. Spring moved to the other side of the stage. She'd rolled the sides of her panties up high onto her hips and was dancing at the edge now, holding her hair up with her hands. Lonnie stood away from the bar, watched the man crumple another one in his fist. Behind the man's ear was an unlit cigarette. In front of him was a scotch or bourbon on the rocks and he wore the mustache and goatee so many men did now, and you could bet if they had one, they were not near as tough as they wanted to look. Out on the floor another pocket opened up, then another and another, but they were just customers hooked on the line of the VIP, and Dolphins Cap tossed one that missed Spring and landed in the tables on the other side of the stage, just a few bills folded into her panties, her second number almost over, time to give them everything.

And Dolphins Cap didn't deserve it.

Lonnie took the steps lightly, moving between the tables like a mist. He was aware he had a heartbeat, that his adrenal glands had just secreted some juice, but he wouldn't need much of it; he was relaxed and clear of everything. Dolphins yelled out something ugly and Lonnie didn't hear the actual words, just felt them rip the pocket open wider, and he stepped sideways between occupied chairs on his toes in his Nikes, and if he brushed up against someone's shoulder or head, he didn't feel that because all there was now was Dolphins Cap sitting back in the pocket he created, raising his arm to toss another wadded insult. Paco or Little Andy would grab that arm and twist it till he dropped whatever he held. But Lonnie preferred the soft touch, the quiet approach; they were always more surprised then.

He stepped past the last table. Dolphins didn't even look over, just snapped his wrist toward Spring, and Lonnie's arm left his side and there were the soft corners of a crumpled dollar in his hand, the lip of the stage at his back. Dolphins Cap looked up at him with eyes small and dark and so deeply instinctual it appeared he'd bite his own flesh. Was he looking for it? Or surprised? And if he was surprised, was it a good surprise or a bad one? But what Lonnie saw in those small eyes above that clichéd goatee was a man used to having his amusement thwarted, a man trying to decide, at this very moment, just how much more he was going to take. And so Lonnie would make it easy for him; he lifted his hand, wagged his finger at him, and shook his head. Behind him, in the air around him, the song was in its last measures, which meant Spring was naked and collecting folded bills from men who knew how to behave, but Dolphins Cap hadn't moved, nor had he stopped looking into Lonnie's eyes, and this, Lonnie knew, is where he came out ahead, because he was tall and lean with none of the beef Louis's other boys had. All he had was what his hands had been able to do for a long time now.

The music ended and there was clapping and a few hoots. Then the man broke his stare just long enough to watch Spring's lovely ass disappear behind the curtain. He looked back at Lonnie, but it was clear it was over, and Lonnie placed the crumpled bill on the table and stepped sideways back into the darkness of the crowd. He looked behind him once but this pocket was now closed, Dolphins Cap sipping his drink and looking hard at the curtains, as if the dancers somewhere behind it, and not Lonnie Pike, had stopped his fun.

Three-quarters of the tables were filled now, mainly with men, though there were a few women too, wives or girlfriends who maybe got turned on by the dancers or were lesbians or just women who liked to sit in the dark and drink themselves into a warm bed of the brain where seeing a woman dance for them put them somewhere they rarely went—on top, no longer the server but the served.

But it was the men Lonnie watched. The quiet ones, the loud ones, those who traveled in packs, and those who came in alone. The loners were more dangerous; they were here because they couldn't stay away. And right now in the club there were five of them: Dolphins Cap probably. And a thin man two tables over. On the other side of the stage were three more, including Gordon, a longtime regular with a neatly trimmed white mustache who wore silk ties and starched shirts. The girls said he sold his company and in the last six months alone had spent over fifty thousand dollars in the Champagne Room on Wendy. That was the trouble right there. A lone dog fell in love.

At first he'd come in only once or twice a week. He'd get a table on the main floor and hold on to his money and watch all the acts. Every now and then one of the girls would approach him for a private, but for a while—most of a night or an entire week—he'd smile and shake his head and stay put. But then one would come up to him he couldn't say no to and he'd let her lead him back to the VIP for a one-on-one, and once he started to go there, he'd keep going, at twenty bucks a dance, again and again. Sometimes he fell for that one. Sometimes it was another. Then, each night, he'd wait for her. Like the man three tables over from Gordon waited now. He sat there and drank and said no to all the other girls because he was waiting for his girl and when she finally came back out on the floor he wanted her to come to him only, and when she didn't, his pocket could open with all kinds of trouble. But even when he got his girl, when she moved right to his table and he paid her to take him back to the easy chairs of the VIP, he didn't want her to dance for him anymore—he wanted to talk; at twenty dollars a song, he just wanted to sit and talk. Like the man in the VIP now, the fourth lone dog in the club, sitting with Marianne, who hadn't taken off a thing.

For weeks he'd chosen her, her hair dyed so black it looked purple on stage. Her blue eyes and pouty lips and fake breasts, her nipples stretched wide as a silver dollar. She couldn't be more than twenty-two or -three and spoke with an accent that was east Texas, her voice high in her throat and nose. She laughed hard and often at nothing and, despite everything, had the naïve, too-friendly gaze of a child.

But this one liked her. He had bright blond hair and heavy shoulders and he leaned forward with his elbows on his knees, his hand opening and closing, gesturing this way and that. Marianne leaned forward too, nodding her head with an overly enthusiastic but feigned interest, and onstage, Retro's gown was off as her second number began, a Luther Vandross that made the whole place feel like somebody's carpeted fuck van. In the smoky recessed light, five or six dancers had their customers happily seated in easy chairs and they stripped for them to Retro's number. Marianne's boy still had his elbows on his knees, one hand illegally holding hers as he made point after point with the other. His eyes were on his eight-dollar Budweiser, and as he talked, he shook his head as if he'd been deeply wronged. Marianne's face was stuck in a half smile. She kept glancing behind her toward Paco standing in the blue light of the VIP bar talking to a regular, missing it all, seeing none of it.

Lonnie hit the steps. It was Paco's station for the night, but still, a pocket was a pocket and it had to be zipped shut.

Retro's number was on its last seconds, Luther done now, just a hundred synthesized strings in the air as the crowd applauded and the pack yelled it up. Retro's long legs were spread wide, and leaning back on one hand, she lightly touched herself with the other. Lonnie hit the steps and moved through the crowd for the VIP. The air was heavy with cigar and cigarette smoke, perfume and cologne, hot French fries from the kitchen. Lonnie had to step by a waitress balancing a tray and just as he got to the half wall and was about to leap over it, Paco moved to what he should've seen earlier. Half-Cuban, half-Chinese, with his thick forearms and big hands, Paco stepped between them and gripped his fingers around Lone Dog's wrist and twisted and it was as if an electric current had just shot into his easy chair, his torso straightening right up, his legs kicking out under the table.

Marianne pulled her arm away and stood.

Retro's number ended with a tinkling of falling electronic chimes and in the air were just dozens of voices and bar sounds, the kitchen door opening and swinging shut, the high whimper of Marianne's customer gripping Paco's hand with his own. A few seconds passed before a Hank Jr. song charged out of the speakers, all drums and piano and lead guitar, and even though her LD's eyes were squeezed shut, his wet cheek pressing against Paco's knuckles, Marianne just stood there, her silicone breasts round and hard-looking. She was supposed to get the money up front but it was clear to Lonnie she hadn't; she was staring down at her hurting customer. Paco eased up and she leaned over and said something. Then she straightened, rested one hand on her hip, and held out the other to get paid.

$$\vee \quad \vee \quad \vee$$

APRIL HELD FRANNY in the darkness of Tina's office. She twisted slowly from side to side, humming a nameless tune. She kissed the top of Franny's head, could smell the beach in her hair, the salt and sun, the watermelon shampoo from yesterday when they'd taken a bath together before supper. She tried to ignore the rowdy country song out on the floor Sadie danced to in boots and a cowboy hat, and she stroked Franny's hair, felt beneath her forearm the vertebrae of her three-year-old's spine.

It was so wrong to have her here at all. There was no way she could leave now, though, not after pissing off, then distracting Louis. If she left, he'd find a way to take it personally and make it harder for her to make money. No help from Glenn ever. Their five months on the third floor above the old Woolworth's that'd been sold and turned into a remnant carpet shop. You could smell the rugs all the way up the creaking stairs, the dusty weaves and that new chemical smell, though they'd had a big three-room apartment with a view over the naval yard to the Piscataqua River and the bridge, the big ships that Glenn always stared out at. He'd hand her Franny, still in his shirt and tie from the shop at the mall where he sold computer games all day to isolated teenagers or lonely men. Glenn would lean against the windowsill and smoke his daily joint, blowing his smoke out the window, his back wide and his hips narrow because he took care of himself, the first thing she'd noticed when they'd met at the pub a year earlier, his thick arms and broad shoulders, his skin soft as a woman's, but it was his green eyes that got her, so bright with flecks of blue in them, like they were lit from the inside, and when he finally looked at her and smiled, it was as if he was smiling right into her.

Probably the same thing that got the new one too. And he was probably with someone else after that one now, working a different shitty mall job in a different town. Going to the gym, smoking his joints, looking out a window at whatever he saw there, maybe thinking about the ships he never had the balls to get on. And not one dollar from him after the first couple of months. Just gone.

She should hate him but she didn't. Instead, she found herself thinking of his eyes those first months, how he seemed to take all of her in, how he seemed to love all of her.

April kept humming, turning from side to side. She put her back to the muted TV and hoped Franny might start watching the new movie Tina had put in before she left. In her small dark office, the club on the other side was loud and pulsing and April knew the place was filling up and every minute she wasn't out there she was losing money. Sadie was already into her second number, the third dancer in the rotation to do her act since April's. She stopped humming, said into Franny's ear: "Want some ice cream?"

"I want to go home."

"We will. We will." April reached back for Franny's fingers, gently pried them away from her hair. "Chocolate or vanilla?"

Franny didn't answer, her eyes on Neptune and his mermaid daughter swimming side by side deep at the bottom of the sea. April could taste the coffee she'd had on the way in, knew she'd have to get a mint from her locker before going out to the tables, her mind already there, her heart and face and body gearing itself up for the nightsmile that had to come from all of her. She let go of Franny's hands but didn't stand just yet. She'd wait till this cartoon movie had her attention completely. Another few seconds, that's all it would take.

She turned up the volume on *The Little Mermaid*, then unzipped Franny's backpack and pulled out her pajamas, her pink cotton pants and shirt with buttons. She lifted Franny's flip-flops off her feet, had her lie back so she could get her shorts off, too.

"We going, Mama?"

"Soon." She gathered up the hems of both pajama legs, pushed them over Franny's feet, and pulled them up over her underwear. It was Jean who'd potty trained her. Not her mother, but Jean.

"Arms up."

Franny lifted them slowly, a tentative smile on her face as another silly number began to play. April could hear the crowd out on the floor, could feel the bass notes from the speakers in the air around her. She pulled off her daughter's top, working her left arm into the sleeve, then her right, buttoning it up. She kissed her on the forehead, whispered, "Love you." Then she folded her clothes and placed them into the backpack, rising slowly and backing out of Tina's office, the manufactured colored light of the TV spilling over Franny, her small face, her hair needing combing, her lips parted as she got pulled yet again into another made-up story, a scary part coming there too. This time April would tell Tina to fast-forward through it before it was too late. She'd tell her to bring Franny a bowl of ice cream and to make sure she used the bathroom before she got sleepy, to put a toilet cover on the seat.

Then April would become Spring; she'd place a mint on her

tongue, smooth her skirt, and finally walk out into the dark noise of the floor and all the men there, her smile and hair and body taking her from the tables to the VIP and back again till each garter was stuffed, stuffed with every single reason why, she kept telling herself, she was here at all.

                                   ⌄ ⌄ ⌄

J EAN LAY IN her private room on the ninth floor overlooking
      the Gulf of Mexico. Earlier she'd watched the sun set into it,
      leaving behind a bright rim of green. Now the sky and water
were one black mass distinguished only by the lights of an oil tanker
out there. Under her johnny, taped to her upper chest, were two
wires connected to the heart monitor beside her. Every thirty or forty
minutes a cheerful, condescending nurse would come in and study it
briefly, take her blood pressure, record information on a clipboard,
then ask Jean in loud, overly enunciated words if she was comfortable.
Did she want her to reposition the bed for her or turn on the TV?

   Jean answered no and smiled politely but was relieved to see her go;
why, when one was laid up in some way, was it automatically assumed
you'd lost half your hearing and your mind too? She shouldn't even
be here; her EKG had come back normal and so had her blood test.
She was only lying in this bed, trapped in this place and not taking

care of Franny, because she'd thought she was dying and had made the mistake of telling the cardiologist about all the heart attacks in her family, her high blood pressure and cholesterol, her true age. They'd given her aspirin and something to calm her, but all it did was knock her out for a few hours and now she wanted to get up and leave.

Tomorrow morning they'd release her anyway, make her come back later to discuss losing weight and getting her cholesterol and blood pressure down, things she'd been trying to do for years to no avail really, and what was the use? What happened to her today is how it would happen when it finally came; it's how the people in her family went—even Harold—tall fit Harry. Him, too.

She missed him acutely right now, knew if he were still here he'd be sitting in the chair by the window, keeping an eye on the monitor as if he understood what he was seeing. His long legs would be crossed at the knees, his glasses perched at the tip of his hooked nose. He'd grill the nurse on medication frequency, fluid intake, rest, the possible contraindications of drugs. Eventually she'd assume he was a physician, though he knew next to nothing about medicine. Except for sales pitches and boats, he knew next to nothing about most things, but had always read daily and widely and so knew a little about quite a lot. She'd watch as experts in their fields got fooled by him—from the roofer working on their old house in Oak Park, to the dentist recommending an expensive crown, to the cable TV installer who'd come to upgrade their service, Harry always asked questions with just the right terminology to wake them up and keep them honest. He said he did it because he was interested in everything, but she had always thought it came from years of selling all those water filtration systems, replacement windows, forklifts for heavy industrial use, residential security systems, even eggs. He said he had the gift of gab, but what he really meant was he knew how to establish common ground with all kinds of people, to use what little he knew to make them think he knew more than that: their days and their nights, the very lives they were living, and, therefore, what they needed most. He made her feel that way, too. She missed that about him more than anything, that he had her best interests in mind at all times and she could leave the practicalities to him: car and house maintenance; banking, investments, and insurance, all those services that left her feeling surrounded by firm, deep cushions. At least that's what she'd thought until he died in his office lined with top sales awards—she'd believed it was *what* he'd done that made her feel secure, yet weeks after his funeral, lying in the dark in their half-empty bed, angry at him for abandoning her, she pictured him at his desk in front of his computer talking on the phone to some agent or advisor, peering through his glasses at a figure, his calculator within reach, a pen between his long fingers, and her eyes welled up, for *that's* what had made her feel so taken care of, not knowing he was tending to their business but actually seeing and hearing him do it.

It was everything else, too: it was having him there to deal with anyone who came to their door—the UPS man, Jehovah's Witnesses, trick-or-treaters, neighborhood fund-raisers. She'd listen from the living room or kitchen as he engaged each of them, asking them knowledgeable-sounding questions before he wished them luck and sent them away with nothing. When she and he hosted dinner parties, she would prepare the appetizers and the meal but she could count on him to be the central engine for the entire evening, to mix drinks and make everyone comfortable, to ask the right questions.

In the thirty-five years they were married, she'd never had even one panic attack. Nervousness, yes. But nothing like these past months since he'd been gone. Nothing like today's.

Sometimes they would come with no warning and no seeming origin; she'd be driving past the lovely shops of St. Armand's Circle looking for a parking place, watching from her air-conditioned cocoon all the brightly dressed tourists walking along the sidewalks or crossing the streets with their shopping bags and sodas, their melting ice cream cones, and she'd feel that weight begin to press against her chest; she'd break out in a sweat and could no longer breathe the air all the way into her lungs. Everything would begin to appear as if from a dream—a young boy looking past her and her car like they weren't there, the sway of a purse from an old woman's hand, the green of the palm fronds as they hung precariously off the tops of their long, gray trunks. The thought of actually stopping her car and stepping outside terrified her and it was as if she were a witness to something horrible only she could see.

She would drive straight home and lock her car and gate behind her, take refuge in her walled garden in her chair under the mango with a full glass of Cabernet. Soon her breathing would return to normal and she'd begin to get that sideways perspective the wine gave, the ability to retrace her steps, then walk beside herself; she'd see that looking for a parking space had started it, that tiny lack of assurance that she'd find one simply opened up into a black chasm of no assurance of anything: continued good health, money, human kindness, God, a hereafter; she began to wonder if she'd find any help or comfort or meaning in this world at all before she was dust no one would remember or speak of or even think about in passing while reaching for the butter or unlocking the door.

But today. What could've triggered it today? She closed her eyes, saw again the water spraying over the small white flowers of the frangipani against the wall. There was the way Franny had waved at the gate, a loving I'll-miss-you gesture that made Jean miss her. That's when she began to worry about them again, to wonder how long April could do what she did without corrupting Franny's life. How long before April began to sell more than just an open view of her body? For all Jean knew, she may already do that.

I'll just have to take her.

Jean kept hearing April's voice over the phone when she'd called her from her new bedside, already drowsy from what they'd given her. At first, April had sounded genuinely concerned, asking if she was all right and did she need anything, but then a distracted tension came into her voice.

"Do you know anyone who can watch Franny? I can't call in sick. I just can't."

"No. Not really." There was the woman who'd sold her the house, the man who advised her on gardening supplies, there was her new dentist out on Longboat Key, the somber owner behind the cash register at the wine and cheese shop, four or five teenagers and housewives who rang up her purchases at the grocery store, there was the young man Teddy, who pumped the gas into her car, and the occasional waiter or waitress when she would treat herself to a dinner out. Did she know anyone? Yes. And no.

She hung up, ashamed of herself for not being home to care for Franny, but more, for not knowing anyone she could call. It's how she'd thought she wanted it, so damn tired of being treated like a widow in Illinois, she was content to be just *her* for a while. She knew other people, mainly women, who could not leave the house they'd shared with their mates all those years for it was too full of shrines to their dead: the framed family photographs spanning decades, closets full of clothes and shoes, favorite books and a chair, a garage littered with tools. But for Jean, what had filled their house with so much life was Harry himself, and when he was gone, so was the feeling that it was her home.

Old friends came by to try and fill the void: Lindsey and Bob Andersen, Mary Ann and Dick Hall, Joan and Larry Connorton—they'd bring food and make themselves the drinks Harry would have; they'd sit across from Jean or stand close to her, already hesitant to talk about him. As if it would make her feel worse when the opposite was true. Instead they'd talk about their kids or local politics, a class one of them was taking, a car that needed trading in. They'd make sure she ate what they brought her, and they tended to drink more than usual or not much at all.

Sometimes Jean would nod her head at a point one of them was making and say, "Harry would get the price down." Or "Harry hated that one." Or "Harry always wanted to sell and move to Florida for good." And at the mention of him, her friends would glance at each other or smile sadly or both, nodding their heads respectfully. For a while Jean thought they didn't talk about him much because they didn't want to rub it in her face, his permanent and lifelong—and maybe longer—absence from her. But after the first month or so, when the calls and the visits came less frequently, she began to suspect it was something else entirely: Harold Hanson was the first in their group to go. Harry, who golfed twice a week and walked briskly thirty minutes every night before dinner. Harry, who had never smoked and knew when to quit a cocktail. Harry, who could wear the same pants he'd graduated from Loyola in; *he* had dropped dead on an ordinary Tuesday afternoon and if it could happen to him it most certainly could happen to them, too; why come around and get constantly reminded of *that*?

Meanwhile, living alone in the house that had always been just hers and Harry's began to feel unnatural, as if she were riding a bicycle with two seats, the one in front of her now forever vacant.

Jean raised her arm and peered at her watch. It was hard to see in the dim light of the headboard, her glasses back home on the kitchen counter. It looked like nine- or ten-thirty. If it were the former she would've tucked Franny in a half hour ago into the bedroom she'd made her. She would've pulled the blue sheets up over her shoulders, covered her feet and lower legs with the quilt she'd sewn—nothing ornate, just patches of Franny's favorite colors: red, pink, and yellow, some square, others diamond, all surrounded by a border of dancing figurines Jean had cut from mail-order fabric. She'd bought a pine dresser and hung lemon curtains, and on the walls she'd tacked a Teletubbies poster and a large print of a child's hand reaching into the sunshine.

She'd been taking care of Franny only a week when she decided to give her her own room; she hated to see her mother wake her up on the couch at three or four every night, pick her up, and carry her upstairs. Jean watched her in the morning anyway, so why not let her sleep downstairs? But the few days it took to decorate the spare room, there was the feeling she was doing something slightly wrong and inappropriate. This wasn't her child after all but this striking woman who'd knocked on her door last March dressed in jeans and a light sweater, holding Franny on her hip, April smiling widely and with an air of earnestness that bordered on the desperate. Her daughter had looked directly into Jean's face as if she were going to interview *her*. They were the first to answer her ad and when she saw them she knew she'd wanted a tenant not for the money, which she still had plenty of and would for a long time, but for the company.

Where was Franny now? In some smoky club for men? April had said the house mom, whoever that was, would take care of her, but *how*? And where? Where on earth in a place like that would a child feel safe and be able to sleep? Why not stay *home*? April certainly didn't need the money for babysitting because Jean had never had the inclination to charge her; it would feel wrong to take money for the joy Franny gave her.

The nurse walked in smiling widely and holding a Dixie cup. She came around to the heart monitor, studied it a moment, then put two tiny pills and the cup of water on Jean's bed tray. "Your heart rate's up. How do you feel?" She pressed two fingers to Jean's wrist.

"Fine. I just need to go home. I have things to do."

"It'll have to wait. Here, your doctor's prescribed something to help you rest." The nurse brushed the pills into the palm of her hand and placed them into Jean's.

"I'd rather not."

"C'mon, now." She smiled even wider, handing Jean the paper cup of water. She turned to reach for the blood pressure cuff behind her and Jean lifted her hip, wedged the pills and a fold of sheet under her rear, and drank down the water. Her deception made her heart go faster. Her nurse opened the cuff, pausing to look at the monitor.

"Are you upset about something?"

"I have a granddaughter. I really need to get home."

"Oh, you will. Just not tonight, okay?" She cinched the cuff around Jean's upper arm and began to squeeze the bulb, the cuff tightening like a serpent. "You need to calm yourself. Those pills will help."

Slowly she let the air out of the cuff, and Jean looked at her. She was younger than she'd thought, her skin smooth and unblemished, her lips pursed in concentration. Her watch was thin and gold but there were no rings on her fingers. No real human complications yet.

That's how she'd always put it to herself when it was long clear she and Harry would never have kids of their own, that it freed her life up to be less complicated, that they'd be freer than their friends ever would. But free of what? This dark, urgent pull inside her that she was needed badly right now by someone precious?

‎ᵛ ᵛ ᵛ

H E SEES HER. She leads men one at a time to the soft chairs. Her face is raised, and each kafir pays for one song, or two. Bassam sees only her back as she dances, her long hair, her hips. He looks away. He drinks his vodka, so new to him but already so old. He is ready to leave it behind. But not yet. Not yet.

Many whores come to him. Their eyes and teeth and warm skin he can smell, but he waves them away. He will wait. He will watch those on the stage and he will wait for her to come to him and if she does not he will accept this as what is deemed to happen, Insha'Allah.

The bills push tightly against both his legs. It makes him feel he has enough fuel for a long trip when, in fact, this trip is nearly over. This is not something he thinks but feels. An end approaching. And a beginning. Everyone here in a shadow world.

This dancing woman upon the stage wears nothing but the hat of cowboys. He sits far enough away she does not attempt to seduce any

bills from him, just the kufar seated near her. Her qus is shaved and
she spreads her knees apart and Bassam can see it, her folds opening slightly, and he should look away for a yearning rises in him that
leaves him only alone. He no longer sees the sin that will condemn
her. He sees only the flowering herbs and dusty streets of Khamis
Mushayt, feels again the nothing he was as Bassam, son of Ahmed
al-Jizani, brother to Khalid and fourteen more, brother to two sisters
whose eyes smiled at him from behind their abayas. Good girls, good
Muslims. Not like he was. Not like Khalid was, though they lived
across from the mosque built by their father and his many workers
from Yemen and Sudan, each day the five calls to prayer from the
loudspeakers. So many times during the day, working as a stock boy
like any Arab, not a Saudi, not an al-Jizani, working in the housewares
shop behind Al Jazeera Paints, he had to handle and store cheaply
made incense burners, rolled carpets, lamps, crates of dishware and
tea glasses, even having to clean away the reddish dust from the street
that settled upon everything, having to bear the commands of Ali al-
Fahd, who smelled of body odor and the hunger for nothing but more
and more riyals, his thawb stretching across his belly, his breath old
cardamom and coffee, then Bassam would use the Dhuhr and 'Asr
prayers not to pray to the Creator but to escape the shop and Ali al-
Fahd, who stayed in his office to pray. Other workers too, the sales-
men who treated Bassam as if he were not the son of Ahmed al-Jizani,
they would pray to the wall facing Makkah, but Bassam would walk
to the open-air souq closed for prayer and he would sit under a tent
and smoke an American cigarette. If his father asked why he was not
in the mosque he built, he would lie to him, tell him he prayed in the
shop with the other men. But sometimes Ali al-Fahd would lock his
office and walk with others to the mosque, and Bassam would have to
go, but he did not take the proper time for his ablutions, and when
he stood barefoot inside with the men, facing the imam's back and
Makkah, he would perform the raka'ats but his mind was not with the
Sustainer and Provider, it wandered to idle time with his brother and

friends; it wandered to all they did in their nothingness he did not yet know was nothing.

After Bassam's work they would drive Khalid's Grand Am to Highway 15. His older brother, with his university degree, had no work and spent his days at the caffe in Abha playing billiards and balot, smoking apple tobacco in the water pipe or his Marlboros, paying to sit at computer screens made by the kufar. His face, always handsome, had taken a yellowish color and through the black market he had acquired a cassette player for the Grand Am and he installed it beneath the driver's seat and he only played the forbidden music when he and Bassam were racing on the Road of Death, passing Imad and Karim in their Le Mans, passing Tariq in his blue Duster with the 440 engine they left far behind on the hot highway, Khalid leaning into the wheel, kufar music filling the inside no one could hear.

Such a strange sound it was. Such happy, angry noise. And the singer David Lee Roth, an American Jew, he wore a cowboy hat like this whore, and he filled their heads with a nothingness that only made Khalid drive faster, faster. Always winning, always victorious.

"Another drink, honey?" The kafir serving woman leans close, her hair brushing his arm, and he pulls away. "Yes." He points to the bills on the table and she nods and takes twenty dollars for the drink he has not yet received but he does not care. Tomorrow, Insha'Allah, he and Imad and Tariq travel north, Amir and the others there now, and there is the feeling he has already left, like being home again in the national park in Asir, viewing the valley from atop Mount Souda—above everything, beyond everything, nothing below can touch him.

Except that which has weakened him.

A new whore dances now. Her legs and arms are pale and thin but her nuhood sways heavily and puts him in mind of an animal and he looks once more behind him for the other. She dances for a kafir seated before her. The man wears eyeglasses and he smiles approvingly and Bassam looks back at this new one. She has taken off everything very fast and she seems young and stupid about these things.

He looks once more to the women dancing alone for the seated kufar. And there she is still, Bassam, and it is difficult not to stare at her bare back, her hair swaying against it. Under the low light, there are more dancers now, and in the dark corner, a fat kafir guards a private room, its entry covered with black draping.

"Here you go, hon." The hand of the server, his drink leaving her tray, the bills she leaves there hoping he will instruct her to keep them.

"Please," Bassam points to the guarded room and the fat kafir. "That area, what is this?"

She follows his arm, his finger. "Champagne Room. Big money for that, hon. Three hundred to the club, two to the dancer. One hour."

"Thank you." He waves her away. He waves her away and feels like a king. The power of a man in this world who cares about this world, the things of it, its things.

At the Venice airfield they allowed for the first time Amir to fly alone. Bassam sat beside him as they flew over the water, the same greenish brown and dark blue of the Red Sea. For moments and moments they were silent. The land and cities of the far enemy were below to the east and Amir pulled up the nose of the plane, the weight of the earth pulling Bassam's head back against the seat, above them only the deep blue of where they would rise, and he felt afraid.

"Allahu Akbar," Amir said softly. The Egyptian was smiling then, his eyes upon the invisible doors to Jannah, Bassam never the pilot or driver, always the passenger, Khalid alone when the speeding Grand Am hit the sand blown onto the highway and perhaps Khalid jerked the steering wheel, the auto of forbidden music turning over once, twice, three times, his body thrown so many meters to the west, away from Makkah, the American Jew still singing inside the crushed chassis.

A man stands closely to the stage holding a bill for the young whore lying on her back. The music is too loud. In Khamis Mushayt there was only talk on the street, the hawking of wares in the souqs, passing autos and minibuses, the calls to prayer. But here, in the land of the al-Adou al-Baeed, there is nothing but noise—music from auto radios and stereos, televisions in cafés, in shop windows, in airport and bus terminals and malls, from the open windows of every single home talk, talk, talk, the horns of impatient mushrikoon, the loud engines of motorcycles, the spinning blades of helicopters above to report the squeezing traffic, small planes over the beach trailing banners to make the kufar spend their dirty money on more needless things. And the flesh of women. Exposed on all of them. Even the old wear dresses above their knees, the young in short short pants that can only tempt men. They are nearly naked on the covers of every magazine, on books, on television even when only selling beer or watches or pickup trucks—and alcohol wherever you want it. In bars and restaurants on every street corner. In stores for selling food. Even in small fuel stations, you can buy them as well as your cigarettes and magazines, the tiny bottles you can drink while driving home to your television. And these churches and synagogues, these stone and brick buildings of false idols for these polytheists to worship, Bassam would rig them with plastique and explode them to hell.

A woman's hands on his shoulders, her breath hot in his ear. "Wanna private, sweetie? Just you and me?"

"No."

"Honey, c'mon, one dance. You and me." She smells of perfume and now she shows him her face. She is from China or Japan or Cambodia, her hands on his chest, her eyes shining with hunger for his money.

Enough. He stands and leaves her the bills on the table and he goes in search of the one he came here for, the one with the eyes that seemed to see Bassam, son of Asir, son of the Ghamdi clan of the Qahtan tribe, chosen by Abu Abdullah himself, Bassam. Mansoor Bassam al-Jizani.

v v v

ONCE YOU HURT them you can't turn your back on them so they have to go. Louis's rule was for at least two floor hosts to do it, one on each side. Sometimes it took more, but Marianne's lone dog took only Paco, the LD's face a permanent wince as he held his bent wrist and Paco walked him through the smoky dark of the main floor between the tables. Lonnie knew Paco was promising more broken bones if he pulled any shit like that again, but if you didn't know this you might think Paco was comforting him, giving him words that might help him in the future. At the front entrance Paco parted the curtain and a pink light washed over them both and they disappeared.

The night was in full swing now, a big smoky machine. It was the time in the shift when whoever danced onstage was no longer the main attraction; there were other things happening, pockets opening and closing all over the floor, no trouble, just men rising one at a time for their trips to the VIP. It was almost full and Lonnie stayed at the half wall and watched both rooms till Paco came back. Little Andy had his eye on the VIP too, though he was slow to see anything. With his flat-top haircut and sloping bulk, his chest hard and bulbous and just a bit larger than his gut, Little Andy used to play football at FSU and told everyone who'd listen how he was heading for the NFL. Then he got hurt, jumping drunk off the second-story balcony of a motel, smashing both ankles on the concrete surrounding the pool he'd missed. Now he watched over the Champagne Room. He stared at the dancers more than he should, and he never saw a pocket till it'd opened all the way and other floor hosts were already there. But because he was unhappy, he was mean and a good closer, liked to be the one to take it to the parking lot and toss the customer face-first into the broken shells under the neon light of the Puma sign.

Spring seemed to be back on her game. Walking tall, her long hair brushing against her blouse and skirt, she led a tanned businessman back to his table and only had to tap his partner's shoulder to get him to follow her. On her way back to the VIP, she smiled through the crowd, careful to aim it at each man who happened to look up at her, and she was relaxed, her hoop earrings swaying, her makeup a little heavy but just right for this place. Whatever Lonnie had seen in her earlier seemed to be put away for now. She was back to being the pro she was, and at the end of the shift she'd look him in the eye and give him a genuine smile of gratitude, none of the hurried cash-toss and barely restrained tone of resentment he sometimes got from the others.

Paco was at the bar now. He nodded and winked at Lonnie, who turned and made his way through the noise of the main floor to the Amazon. He glanced back, saw Spring sit her customer down. He could see only her hair, ass, and legs, her hips swaying as she reached up and started to unbutton her blouse. Lonnie turned away and headed for his perch. Didn't know why—it was just always hard to watch her then. No one else. Only her. Undressing for just one. Her twenty-dollar one and only.

v v v

Some nights it was like reaching into a bin full of apples. She didn't have to act like she loved them, just smile and curl her finger at them to follow and they did. One or two always needed encouragement so she took their money, then guided them through the tables to the VIP, where all the easy chairs might be taken and she'd have to wait till the number was through and somebody's customer got up to leave. The whole time she'd talk to him, smiling. It'd be hard to hear anything so she'd have to let him put his wet mouth close to her ear, let him get that close just so he could piss her off by asking her real name. Like his twenty bucks entitled him to that. Like he was the first to ever have the balls and the heart, he thought, to ask that.

Most nights April used the music and shook her head as if she hadn't heard. Other nights she'd talk right through his question, ask if he wanted his private there in the private darkness at the blue-lit entry to the VIP. Just her and him in the shadows. Some nodded yes, their eyes already on her body she'd never stopped moving because you should never stop moving; if you did, you were just standing there talking, your body getting cold, the beat and rhythm leaving your muscles, but worse than that, it was harder to stay Spring if she stopped; if she stopped moving and started talking it was too easy for April to come out. To be her. Just April standing there in a smoky club in a skirt and blouse talking when she wasn't here to talk and hated it whenever that's what a man wanted in the VIP. Why not stay home and talk to his *wife*?

But if she just smiled and took their money and danced off her clothes, then she was Spring. Breasts and flat belly, ass and thighs and long swinging hair and big smile. Every one of them could look and look at *those* and she, April, could stay inside in that dark, quiet part of herself that wasn't here at all, had never been, was back home with her daughter, though tonight her Franny was in Tina's office, and as April danced now in the VIP for a fat man in a loosened tie, she was really with her baby on Tina's couch, the two of them eating ice cream and watching Ariel fall in love with a prince on land who would love her forever if only she'd come join him.

April could feel how close Franny was, knew she had to go there soon before climbing back onstage for her second act. When she was Spring and not April it was always easier to harden herself to everything—the *bend over*s and *come sit on this*, some of the men's faces so drunk and lonely, their eyes mean and dead-looking. But here in the smoky haze of the VIP under the dimmed light over the easy chair, this one kept smiling at her. He'd left his drink back at his table and he kept smiling and smiling. A big wide face with glasses and square teeth, his cheeks flushed. Her skirt and blouse were off, draped over the chair arms and his lap where she liked to put them. Make them feel they were special so they sometimes tipped a five on top of the twenty. And now her T-back. Other girls ripped free the Velcro all at once, letting themselves pop out sexy as toast from a toaster, saving their drama for their stage act, but not Spring; Spring had style all night long and now she rocked her hips from side to side, let him watch her do it slowly till her T-back was loose and she held it there with her fingers, watched him look hungrily from them to her still-covered breasts to her face, then back to her fingers, and that's when she lifted her left hand and let that cup fall and dangle, her right breast still covered, and it was funny how they always looked at the naked one only a second or two, their eyes on her hand now over her loosened cup over the other. This music was good. A man's voice singing high and hurt, guitar strings whining. And why didn't they ever look longer at the naked one? Why was the covered one more interesting now? It sometimes made her wonder why they came here at all.

Now the music changed, got harder and faster, the man's voice full of so much longing he was almost angry. She dropped her hand and let her bra fall open. Pulling one arm out of it, then the other, she dropped it onto his knee—silk pants she noticed just now, some money here, a banker or lawyer or bank's lawyer.

The song was almost over and it was time to give him bottoms too. She let her body move to the song whichever way it wanted. She put both hands behind her neck, lifting her hair, bringing her elbows in slightly, swaying in time, though there wasn't much time left. His eyes were on her belly, flat as it'd always been; she could eat anything and never worry because she was always moving and never staying still and this one was through with her breasts and had moved on to the next hidden thing, his eyes on her crotch. There were only a few seconds left in the song and when it ended she'd have her twenty already and didn't have to do more now, but this one had some cash—she could feel it—and it wouldn't take much, and she ran her fingers down along her ribs to her hips, hooking her thumbs into her G-string just as the number was ending, the singer's voice still lonely and riding out the last ringing guitar chord, and she noticed her customer was hard, something that usually happened with the young ones but not the busy busy men in the middle of their lives, this one with a short tent in his pants, her crotch close to his face, the song over now, but she showed him anyway, pushed her G-string down till her arms locked straight and she let him see the coarse hair there she didn't trim as closely as the other girls because they didn't have what she did, a scar from Franny. Her baby pulled out of the cut they made there, then sewed up badly, Glenn sitting stoned on a stool. He never touched her. Not a hand on her shoulder or forehead. Just sat there in the scrubs they made him put on, his eyes dark pools above his blue mask.

She pulled her G-string up and let it pop back into place. She smiled down at this fat banker with glasses, his shiny cheeks, though at this moment she didn't really care if he lived a long happy life or died right there in that chair. She picked her T-back and skirt off his knee. The next number had started and she was late, liked to be dressed again before that. Getting the clothes back on even more important than stripping them off. She stepped into her skirt and pulled it up, his eyes on her breasts still. She laughed a nightlaugh and told him he was getting a freebie now and if he wanted she'd do this number for him, too. He didn't answer her. And he wasn't reaching for any extra to give her either. His pants still a tent. His silk pants full of cash he wasn't going to do the right thing with.

She grabbed her blouse off the chair arm and put her back to him. She pulled on her T-back, snapped it closed, and walked fast out of the VIP, thinking, Fuck him. *Fuck* him. But it was wrong to get pulled into any kind of emotion at all. It would throw off the whole night.

"Everything cool?" Paco's voice floated briefly through the music and bar noise as she walked by him. She nodded and kept going. In the blue darkness at the half wall she pulled on her blouse and buttoned it. Onstage a new girl was only a quarter into her song and had her top off too soon, the crowd calling out things, a lot of young men tonight, drunk and smoking house cigars. April buttoned her last button as Retro walked by and winked at her, leading one of her regulars by his hand. He was a long-faced man in an out-of-fashion tie, and he was looking hard not at Retro's ass behind her red leather shorts but at the back of her head, like that's where he wanted to be—in Retro's *brain*. To see if she thought about him at all.

And now her fat banker was at the bar ordering a drink and looking straight ahead at his reflection in the mirror. His twenty was folded tightly into her garter with three others, and Renée was up after this new girl, this skinny redhead who had taken off everything way too fast so now the crowd was going to expect some floor action. Now they'd expect her to take them farther, to reach down and open her lips and show them some pink.

April was dressed again and ready to work, but her body wasn't moving. She could feel Franny in Tina's office somewhere behind her, her twenty-nine-pound daughter a wedge between being herself and being Spring. Tonight she was stuck somewhere between the two and right now she just wanted to walk through the dark crowded floor back to the dressing room to her baby. Maybe if she sat with her till she fell asleep, or at least till she had to do her act, it'd be better; she'd be able to see she was okay and finally let go completely into being Spring. Start dancing with no feelings about it either way.

It was too late for this song, but soon enough the second number began, a sugary hit by some country singer with high hair April'd seen on TV. The new girl was working the pole too much, hanging on it and snapping her hair out of time to the music. She had the whole song to work and nothing more to take off. Her legs were thin and white and she had a flat ass and made jerky movements that didn't come from the song and April knew Louis had only hired her for her breasts. They were huge and real, but because she danced so badly they swung around heavy as cow udders. April didn't have anything to do with these girls, but she'd have a talk with this one. Tell her to listen to the music. To work the apron of the stage more. Draw men up from their seats one at a time. And don't give them so much so soon. Don't do what the new girl began to do now, panic because she could see how much more they wanted before she was through and she was so new to this she thought she had to give it to them, lie down on her back and do a spread, then hump the air, her face pointed up at the lights, her eyes closed, probably praying for the DJ to speed up the song. A man in a white cap stood where he could see everything. He held a bill out to her like bait for a porpoise to jump for in those shows down in Miami, and now the new girl was smiling at him between her knees, reaching down to open herself up. The man leaned right over her with the bill. April was surprised they were letting him get that close.

She pushed herself from the wall and moved back into the smoke and darkness of the crowded main floor. More than half the tables were occupied and set with electric candles in a Puma glass. Up above the stage lights, close to the ceiling in the far wall, was the red glow of Louis's office window, him standing there, a black shadow watching them all make him money.

Men looked up at her as she passed, but more were watching the act than before. Watching this new girl raise the bar higher for all of them. Something she'd get talked to about by Tina. Or Marianne. If Wendy or Retro knew what this one was up to, they'd threaten her with a beating if she tried it again. Lonnie was coming down the steps from the Amazon Bar, his eyes on the man at the stage still waving his bill over the girl.

April's legs felt heavy, her upper body stiff. She shouldn't've stopped at all. Shouldn't've brought Franny. Should've taken her chances and taken the loss and called in sick; now she was moving just to move, to move back into Spring, and there, a few tables ahead, was one of Wendy's regulars smiling up at her. A tall man with big hands and a sweet face. Her nightsmile smiled and she brushed her hair back off her shoulder and sidestepped between two tables. There was still time to do this one and maybe even get him for a double before she had to change for her act. He looked back at the stage and craned his neck to see better. She'd have to work harder to hook him now and, because he was a regular, he knew he wouldn't get any pink in the VIP.

"Meese?"

A finger pressed her arm, then pulled away. A short man stood there, the amber light of the stage on his face. Young, her age probably, with deep eyes, and he was smiling at her, nodding his head. She glanced over at Wendy's regular but he'd forgotten her and she looked down at this short foreigner, Greek or Italian, and leaned close. "Want a private?"

"Yes, yes." An accent there, the smell of onions and cigarettes on his breath, and he was wearing a knockoff polo shirt and khakis. She led him through the tables to the VIP, walking fast to catch at least the last half of the number. She smiled at whoever looked up, though she hoped to nail this one for a double. The country singer's voice sang on and on and over it came the crash of something. It was behind April and she knew what it was and didn't want to take the time to see and maybe distract her customer, slow his momentum in following her, but in the blue light of the entry to the VIP, she turned and saw Lonnie standing with his back to the stage and the new girl, her legs together now, watching Scaggs and Larry T lift a man up off the floor, his eyes closed and his mouth hanging open.

She turned and led this foreign boy past the bar into the smells of cigar smoke and the dried glass rings on the tables of highballs and blender drinks and bottles of beer. She headed straight for an easy chair, Retro on the other side sitting on the cocktail table listening to her regular talk. Most of the other girls already had their tops off, dancing for their one-on-ones, running their hands over their hips, some turning around and bending over to watch the interruption on the main floor.

At the cocktail table in front of an empty easy chair, April let go of the man's hand and smiled at him to have a seat, her hips already moving, her fingers on her blouse button.

"No, please." He shook his head. He nodded in the direction of Little Andy in the corner. Andy hardly ever got off his stool, but right now he was standing there watching the other floor hosts carry the man out of the club.

"It's all right. He sits there all the time. Have a seat."

"No." He reached into his pants pocket and pulled out a thick roll of bills. He held it low in front of him like it was the answer to some kind of question she didn't need to ask. His eyes passed over her body—her breasts, belly, and hips. "Please, Champagne."

"The Champagne Room? You want to go to the Champagne?"

He nodded and peeled five hundreds off his roll, pressing two into her hand. Five and a half months at the Puma and only once had she gotten a high roller who wanted to go to the Champagne. She'd be off rotation and could stay back there as long as he wanted. Two hundred to her for just that one hour.

He was walking ahead of her with his cash toward Little Andy in his dark corner on his stool, and she had to follow him.

But Franny. First she had to go back. Check on her. He could wait five minutes, couldn't he?

But he was handing the three hundred to Little Andy, who stood and held open the black velvet curtain, looking at her, waiting for her. The foreigner, too; he stood there looking eager, his head cocked to the side, his eyes two dark holes. He'd pick another, she knew that. Now was the time he wanted, and if she turned and walked away and made him wait, he'd want his money back to give to Retro or Wendy or Marianne, so she had to, her body already taking her there, her nightsmile too, Franny back behind the narrow walls in Tina's office. It would only be for an hour anyway.

April stepped by the waiting foreigner and Little Andy. He smelled faintly like aftershave and bacon.

"You're gonna tell Tina I'm off rotation, right?"

"Yep." He let the heavy velvet drop behind her, the black-painted door in front of them, the red bulb above, her Champagne customer standing there with his intent eyes and fat roll of cash. She reached by him for the crystal knob and felt herself lift out of her body and back through the curtain to the bright dressing room and Tina's TV-lit office, her daughter on the couch waiting for her. April there with her now. The two of them snuggled on a single cushion. Only Spring turning the knob and stepping into the Champagne now. Not April. Just Spring.

         ᵛ ᵛ ᵛ

A T THE CORNER of the Amazon Bar, Lonnie pressed a dampened bar napkin to the base knuckle of his right middle finger. Dolphins Cap had gone down so easily, but under that thick beard he must have a snaggletooth or maybe his mouth had been open. Nobody touched the girls. Not out in the open anyway. And even the big spenders didn't get to do what Dolphins Cap did. Lean over the stage and brush his folded dollar along what this new dancer was showing, other men shouting him along, a brushfire that had to be tamped. And when Lonnie got there, the new one, this young skinny redhead with big breasts, didn't know she could dance away from that, and she just lay there spreading herself open. Dolphins Cap saying *cunt*. Something else and *cunt*. At the apron in the stage light in front of them all, Lonnie tapped the new girl's ankle and shook his head. At first she didn't seem to know what he wanted, Dolphins Cap standing there with his dollar. But then she took in

Lonnie's Puma T-shirt, and her fake smile fell away and she sat up. Dolphins Cap stepped back, his eyes on Lonnie now. He was squinting hard at him and was half a foot taller and much heavier, but it was the hollering customers behind him Lonnie needed to show something. One of them motioned with his arm for Lonnie to move out of the way.

Lonnie pointed at Dolphins Cap's chest, then the door. He mouthed the word *go*, saw the wedge of pink light as the front curtain parted and Larry T came walking. Scaggs, too.

"*Go.*"

Dolphins Cap looked back down at the new girl, his silver belt buckle glinting in the stage light. The DJ had lowered the music some, but still the singer sang and Lonnie heard only that, saw the man's lips beneath his whiskers say *cunt* as he wadded up his bill and flicked it in her direction and the jolt was almost always a surprise, a hard thrust into his shoulder, a sting in his hand, his arm just a conduit between the two as Dolphins Cap fell backward onto the table of the loud boys and it flipped their rum and Cokes, vodka shots, and half-empty beer bottles, their ashtray full of cigar stubs raining down onto Dolphins Cap, though he didn't seem to notice or care; his eyes were closed and Lonnie watched Larry T and Scaggs haul him up and carry him out.

There were a few more chords left in the new girl's song, but she was on her knees gathering the curled bills on the dusty stage around her, her breasts swaying heavily. Louis sent over two waitresses to clean up the mess and bring a free round to the young men with no drinks. Some stood to the side to make room for Larry T, Scaggs, and what they carried. A couple of them looked Lonnie up and down and when their eyes met his they looked away and Lonnie turned and waited for the new girl to leave the stage. She held her outfit under one arm. In the shifting light—pink and white now for the next act—she paused at the curtain and glanced at him. A strand of hair hung in her face, and she looked embarrassed, relieved, and a little scared. The DJ skipped the pause between numbers and cranked the system

higher, a lot of bass for "You're as Cold as Ice," Renée rushing out
in her ice queen costume, her big fake breasts and white eyeliner.
Nobody hollered out to her. It would take a few minutes for the party
to get revved back up again the way it should, and Lonnie stepped by
the loud boys, who were quiet now, sitting at their clean table.

His knuckle stung. He found himself thinking of bacteria and tet-
anus shots and what a strange night it was becoming. Earlier he'd
known he'd have to confront Dolphins Cap again but not so soon, and
as he dipped a new bar napkin into his ice water and pressed it back
on his hand, he did what he often did after dropping one of them—he
went over it in his mind, asking himself if he'd done it because he had
to or just wanted to, and with this one it was both; he'd shut his filthy
mouth for him; he'd shut up the table behind him too.

His heart was just beginning to slow back to normal. Out in the
VIP the girls were doing a good night's business, naked and half-
naked bodies writhing in the dimmed lights at the easy chairs. Little
Andy held open the curtain to the Champagne Room for Spring and
a small man in a polo shirt. Lonnie watched them. Something began
to tick deep behind his ribs. He looked away, saw Paco in the blue
light of the VIP raise his Coke glass to him, his dark Asian face smiling wide. Lonnie nodded and scanned the main floor for more pockets. He'd have to keep his eye on the front entrance now. He opened
and closed his hand. Sometimes, especially when they were as drunk
as Dolphins Cap, he'd start to feel some remorse for hurting them
but not much. The truth is, he enjoyed doing it. Maybe it was how
other people felt swinging a bat and watching the baseball fly far
out over the field, or with a basketball, springing off the court, flicking the wrist, and hearing the swish of net. For him, it was putting
a bigger man to the ground, his chin and shoulders dropping as he
pivoted off his back foot, his torso following through, his fist just the
messenger boy.

Renée was swinging round and round on the pole. On her nipples
she'd stuck white pasties with foot-long silver threads. Nobody did
that anymore. Lonnie looked back at Little Andy sitting on his stool,

the curtain to the Champagne Room hanging still. He scanned the girls working the floor. Then he glanced back at Renée and for just a moment he watched her pasties sway and rotate and glitter. Spring was really no different from the rest of them, so why did it pain him to know she was alone in there with some little shit with cash to burn?

᭦ ᭦ ᭦

OUT HERE IT was quiet. He could only hear the club noise when somebody walked in or out. He sat behind the wheel of his pickup, his wrist hot and swollen, and she kept saying she wanted to but she was obviously lying and that big motherfucker may have broken his goddamned arm.

He kept seeing Marianne's face, those round blue eyes, her smile that at first tonight was warm and friendly like always. Then it got fake and she kept looking back for her bouncer when all he did was hold her goddamned hand. She'd let him hold it a bunch of times before, so why not now?

Nobody had to tell him. She'd been lying since day one, since his second week blowing a hundred bucks a night on just *her*. He knew. She didn't want to hear his plan because she'd been lying all along. Never once meant it when she said she'd meet him somewhere else. Never once meant it when she said she liked him and thought he was nice and nice-looking with nice manners when none of the others are ever that *nice*. She said she had to dance for them all, but he was the only one she'd like to sit down and talk to 'cause he was so nice, and oh yes, let's go someplace *nice* sometime.

Lying piece of trash.

And so he wouldn't let go of her. Couldn't. Then he must've started to squeeze. But did she give a good god*damn* how much money he'd wasted on her? Money he'd *bled* for? *She* could just try sitting in the cab of an open CAT eight, nine hours a day—the mosquitoes and diesel exhaust, no Walkman allowed so he had nine hours of hearing nothing but vibrating steel and the moaning gears of the arm and bucket, the rattling of the engine pan and all the useless shit in his head: bad tunes from high school ten years ago, his wife's nonstop whining as she lay there on the couch not doing a thing, her restraining order she thought could actually stop him from coming over whenever he goddamned *felt* like it. And little Cole. His baby Cole. Too young to even know his daddy's gone when he's good and well gone. Her idea, not his. Though he'll get him someday. He'll goddamn well pull up to his house in a thirty-five-ton CAT and *take* him, and that piece of paper won't do shit to keep him from it either.

Working along and thinking like that, sometimes the CAT's treads would sheer off on rock or a rusted chunk of iron from the old days when Florida was crawling with pirates and whores and Creole kings and naked slaves and everybody knew their place. Didn't do shit without knowing the sword, always thinking of the sword and the man big enough for him to reach for it and goddamn use it.

That Chinese sonofabitch walking him all the way to the lot. Telling him he could come back another day if he cooled his attitude. Fucker. He'd cool *his* fucking attitude. He rested his elbow out the window frame, but he could hardly move his hand up and down or right and left and how the hell was he going to work an excavator like this?

His side view mirror, in this light he could see a dent in the chrome there, the truck just two years old and he couldn't remember where or when that'd happened. Another thing taken from him when he wasn't looking. More men walking under the lighted canopy to see all the dancing, lying whores. Rich-looking boys. His age or older. All dressed up in their club clothes—their pressed pants and open shirts and glinting watches and rings. Business boys from far away. Just here long enough to sit in one of those new high rises on the Gulf he'd probably dug the foundation for, look out over the marinas and water and sell what they're selling, then go get drunk at clubs like this with lying whores like Marianne. Fly home. None of them stupid enough to stay. None of them stupid enough to come around like the women in there weren't a pack of lying, cheating bitches. All of them.

He started his truck, gunned the engine just to feel all eight cylinders fire. His wrist was almost as wide as his palm now, something broken in there for sure. He was going to have to call in sick over it. Was going to have to goddamned miss at least a day's work over it. And he owed two months for Cole already. Couldn't even see him and still she wanted all his money. Well goddamnit, tonight somebody else besides A.J. Carey would be paying. Somebody else, by God, was going to pay the godamned *bill*.

HIS CIGARETTES WERE on the cocktail table. Marlboros. He was sitting back in the corner of the love seat, his legs crossed at the knees, looking at her. He said something. The club's music was muted in here but still loud enough you had to raise your voice.

"I'm sorry, what did you say?"

"Smoke?" He nodded at his pack on the table in front of them.

"No thank you. I don't smoke." She smiled at him, but he didn't smile back, just nodded and took a drag. The champagne was going down cold and sweet, and she hadn't realized how thirsty she'd been, but it was strange to drink in the club, the Champagne Room the only place Louis allowed it, *expected* her to help finish off this bottle so the little foreigner would have to order more.

His eyes were on her earrings, her bare arms, her breasts behind her T-back and blouse. He probably wanted her to dance now. Renée's second number wasn't quite over yet, the lead singer shrieking into the microphone, the electric guitars like chain saws ripping through aluminum.

His lips moved. He nodded his head at her. She had to get closer to hear him. She scooted over a bit, could feel herself sink into the black vinyl love seat. She smiled. Saw the glint in his eye from the dimmed light in the ceiling she'd soon dance under. "What did you say?"

He leaned forward slightly. "Say to me your name."

"Spring."

"No."

"Excuse me?" She smiled at him, sipped from her glass. She could see his teeth were bad, tobacco and tea or coffee stains between each crooked tooth. He lifted his champagne and drank it down. He glanced at the bottle in the ice bucket. She filled his glass again, then hers, pushing the bottle deep into the crushed ice. Little Andy had brought the first one and it'd be up to her to go get more. Every fifteen minutes he was supposed to come down the hall and knock twice, make sure everything was all right, but he hadn't come yet and she could feel the little foreigner watching her.

"Why do you say this lie?"

"Excuse me?"

"I said to you why are you saying this lie?"

"How do you know I lie?"

He smiled, like he'd been around the world at least twice and couldn't she see that? Wendy's Michael Bolton number was up. April put her glass on the table, stood, and moved to the spot of light under the dimmer in the black plywood ceiling, all ten of these rooms nothing but plywood painted black. Each about the size of a large bathroom. Barely enough room to dance, but she did. She kept her feet together and swayed slowly, letting her hair swish from side to side. In the dark corner he drank his champagne and smoked his cigarette and watched her, his mouth open slightly, and she began with her blouse buttons, starting at the top and working down. He was in the shadows and she only had to look in the general direction of his face and she didn't like him. Even though she was making more here than in the VIP, at least there she could sometimes glance around the room at the other girls doing their one-on-ones, feel she was just one working part of a large and necessary machine. But in this black room under this single bulb over this tacky red carpet, it was just her and him and she danced off her blouse and let herself think of anything but this; there was this morning, how she'd gotten up just after ten, pulled on her robe and flip-flops, and carried her mug of coffee down the outside stairs to Jean's garden. The best part of living here, it was surrounded by a high stucco wall painted turquoise and peeling in places, a thin wire mesh showing through. All along the base Jean had planted frangipani shrubs, their white flowers so sweet-smelling, and in the far corners were a tall jacaranda and palm tree. A bougainvillea vine, thick with orange flowers, hung from its trunk and at the edge of the garden was a mango tree shading two chairs on terra-cotta tiles. That's where April sat and sipped her coffee and waited for Franny to come running out barefoot in her T-shirt and bathing suit, her curly-haired girl among the yellow hibiscus and pink allamanda shaped like trumpets, the white spider lilies and ixora, clusters of red star flowers that were so beautiful they were almost ugly. All of this Jean had taught her in her off-handed midwestern way. April uncinched her skirt and let it drop to her pumps. She stepped out of them and felt such a pang to go back and check on Franny she barely saw what the foreigner was doing, shaking his head and motioning with his hand for her to stop dancing, to stop and come back to the love seat where he was.

She hated that. Having to sit and talk in just her T-back and G-string, garters and heels. He lifted the bottle from the ice and topped off her glass. Michael Bolton was singing at his highest pitch how he couldn't live anymore if living is without you, and she wanted to pull her skirt back on but knew this one wouldn't like it. She smiled and squatted and picked it up, draping it over the cocktail table on her way to the love seat. He held her full glass out to her. "Please, you sit."

She took the champagne and sat at the edge of the cushion, her knees together. On the table was the empty bottle. He kept his eyes on hers as he drank, and she did too. The champagne was still cold. It was helping; she could feel it planing down some of the jagged edges of this shitty night where nothing had gone quite right yet. She wasn't much of a drinker, never had been.

Two loud knocks came through the door.

"We're good, Andy!"

"Why does he do this?"

"What?"

"Interrupting. I do not like it." He was sitting forward, both elbows resting on his knees, the smoke from his cigarette curling up into his face. His eyes moved from hers down along her ribs to her thighs. His shoulders were narrow as a girl's, his arms slender.

"He just wants to know about the champagne. Should I get some more?"

He leaned back and pulled out his money. It was an inch thick, and nothing but hundreds. *Hundreds.* "And brandy or cognac or what you call that." He handed her two bills. "Quickly."

Usually she wouldn't take a command like this from anyone; no please, no tease. But with this one she did. She didn't know why; she just did.

She took his money and the empty bottle and left their room without her skirt and blouse. The hallway corridor was dark, lit only by a string of tiny white Christmas lights tacked to the baseboards. The rest of the rooms were black and empty, their doors wide open. Wendy's act was just ending and she'd probably be back here with Gordon before long. April knew she was lucky to get into the Champagne at all, but her little foreign customer had a meanness in him she could feel and she opened the door and moved through the red light and the velvet curtains.

Little Andy glanced down at her from his stool. The VIP had been full before but now there were only three girls dancing. That happened. A bunch of men would go to the VIP all at once. Maybe because they could see all the others going. They'd sit for their private, spend their twenty, then back at their table they wanted to drink more and save their money for that. Most of them were low rollers. Family men. She probably *was* lucky to get this asshole and his hundreds he might spend more of. She'd get him what he wanted and check on Franny, too.

She walked through the smoky light of the VIP to the blue bar. A few men out at the tables watched her on her way. She didn't like walking through the club like this, giving them a peek at her naked ass for nothing. Retro was back onstage swaying in her formal gown to that soft, black music April had never really liked.

She moved behind Paco. He was leaning on his elbow talking to the fat banker she'd danced for earlier. The bartender was new, in his fifties somewhere with thinning hair that was oily and parted on the side. He wore glasses in thick frames and in the bright blue light of the bar he was reaching into the beer cooler, his eyes on her belly he didn't seem to see. He straightened and put two Budweisers on the waitress's tray, then turned to April, his eyes dropping to the empty champagne bottle.

"Another?"

"Yeah and two Rémys, please." She was about to ask his name and tell him hers, but he was ducking under the bar for the walk-in cooler. She had to cut through the main floor to see Franny and she didn't like all the looks she was getting from men at the tables, most of them regulars who'd only seen her work the floor in her skirt and blouse, looking classy and not for sale on the cheap like she must look right now.

The air had gotten thick with smoke, the young guys at the front drawing on their Portofinos while Retro slipped off her satin gown. At nearly every table was a girl working it for the VIP and April didn't look directly at any of the men as she passed. But some of them were standing, and when two or three of them glanced at her she smiled and kept moving, saw Lonnie watching her from the Amazon Bar as she rounded the corner of the stage, stepping to the side to let a waitress by, pushing open the swinging kitchen door into the darkness split with fluorescent light she stepped into, the curtain sliding off her shoulder and face, and now there were the smells of frying meat and dishwashing soap, and the old Cuban stood in the rising steam, lifting a tray of glasses off the conveyor belt. She was heading for the dressing room to her left but her right foot stuck itself to the floor and she fell, catching herself on the corner of the ice machine, her heel wedged between two rubber mats Louis must have just installed because they weren't here last night, damnit.

She leaned on the machine and pulled her stiletto out. Then the old Cuban's damp hands were on her elbow and hip, helping her up. She could smell his sweat and all the soapy steam on him, saw how yellow his eyes were, the deep lines in his face. An old man.

"Thank you."

He smiled and nodded, ducking slightly as he went back to his work. Ditch stood at the Frialator shaking hot grease from two baskets of fries and out in the club Retro's number ended. April was sure the new bartender had her order ready. She should really turn around and get back out there, but this was a thought that only trailed behind her as she stepped into the black hallway and Zeke opened the door for her and she had to blink at the brightness of the empty dressing room. She could feel the Moët-warmth in her neck and face, and she had to pee. Donna still reading in the corner.

Tina's office door was slid open a few inches. On the floor against the wall were the food tray and dirty dishes. Most of the fries were gone, just a few in a ketchup streak. The hamburger was missing its top bun and the meat only had three bites taken out of it, three little half-moons.

The bar noise was loud here. On the other side of the thin walls came Paco's voice over the music and banter and clinking ice, the thump of bass in the speakers, the crowd hollering for Retro.

April put her hands on the door and leaned into the narrow opening there. Franny lay asleep on the couch. A Puma Club linen was tucked under her for a sheet, another on top. April felt obscene in her garters and G-string and heels, and she turned and walked fast to Donna in the corner. "Where's Tina?"

"Louis's office. And she better be back soon 'cause there's no business for me tonight."

"*Shit.*" April moved fast to her locker, working the combination, swinging open the door. She pulled out her purple money bag and stuck in the two hundred. She pictured her customer back in the Champagne Room he was paying so much for, sitting alone, maybe smoking and glancing at his watch. Quickly, he'd said. *Quickly.*

She zipped the bag and locked up. "Tell Tina I don't appreciate her leaving this fucking room, Donna."

"You tell her." Donna didn't look up from her book, and she was right but April wanted to push her face into it. She hurried into the bathroom, peed and washed her hands. She glanced into the mirror as she passed, saw this tanned woman with long brown hair, her ass pale with a bikini line, her hoop earrings dangling.

ⱽ ⱽ ⱽ

R ETRO ALWAYS GAVE a good act. Tonight she was even better than usual and had to take up the whole pause between numbers to get her cash off the stage floor. The young men at the table kept up their hollering for her and she smiled and winked over at them on her knees. Now Hank Jr. was back in the air and Retro just barely scooped up her gown and underthings before Sadie came dancing onstage in her white Stetson, vest, and boots. A pocket opened up to Lonnie's left, the front curtain parting pink, two men leaving, three more coming in. The main floor was still crowded and loud and smoky, but only three girls danced in the VIP, and Hank Jr. going on about his family tradition took Lonnie to Austin where he was raised, their small framed house overlooking a culvert where bluebonnets grew along the cracked concrete, his happily drunk mother and ineffectual father who'd made a life out of watching over books at the university library. Cataloguing them. Keeping the mold off. Checking them out to thousands of people over the years. He was tall like Lonnie, but quiet, and would let anyone say anything to him in anger and do nothing, from his wife to a man in traffic out on MLK Boulevard. On his off-hours he listened to records—Bob Wills and the Texas Playboys, Waylon Jennings and Jerry Jeff Walker, Hank Sr. and Jr., and for Lonnie it was hard to hear the son without thinking of the father, his, though now Spring walked quickly from the kitchen and around the stage still half-dressed from the Champagne, her long hair swinging low just above her naked bottom. She walked tall as usual, but there was nothing usual about her being in the Champagne or having to leave half-dressed and Lonnie felt the steps under his feet as an afterthought. He moved between the tables and cut her off between the Portofino boys, the lights on Sadie flashing white in a rodeo strobe. He put his hand on Spring's shoulder. Smooth skin and warm muscle. She stopped and looked up into his face, hers beautiful but distracted. He leaned close to her ear, her hoop earring brushing his chin. "Everything okay?"

She said something.

"What?" He turned his ear to her and now he felt her nose against his temple, her warm breath.

"My daughter's sleeping in Tina's office, Lonnie. Can you keep an eye on her? Tina's upstairs."

He nodded, straightened, watched her go. *Daughter.* She was hurrying through the tables, not bothering to work them a bit on her way to the Champagne Room, and she held something in her hand. A cold cave opened up in his gut—Wendy, yes, and maybe Retro or Sadie or Marianne, if she ever got asked—but not the one woman in this club who really seemed to be above everything she did here. Tell me that's not a rubber in her hand. Tell me Spring did not go back to her locker for a fucking *skin*.

He stood there between full tables, knew he was blocking the view of customers behind him but he didn't move. Watched her rush into the blue light of the VIP bar, smile at Paco, and hand the bartender the cash she held in her hand—not a rubber, but *money*, Lonnie. Money.

He felt the cave close up and his lungs filled with smoky Puma Club air. One of the Portofino boys yelled louder than anyone had all night and Lonnie turned to say something to him but onstage Sadie was spinning her breasts in perfect clockwise circles, one hand in the air spinning an imaginary lasso, so let him yell. Let them all yell. Yell themselves right over the line where he'd be waiting.

He climbed back up to the Amazon Bar, but he could only think of the one waiting for Spring. The little high roller who had her all to himself in his little black plywood room.

∀ ∀ ∀

H E SHOULD NOT have come. They are in the final phase, and he should not have come.

But he cannot leave. Not yet.

On the worn carpet lies her top she removed for him. Her bottom robe lies across the table where she dropped it beside her empty glass, the pail of ice, his ashtray and glass, empty as well. He picks up this clothing and he folds it and places it beside him. He should not drink further. He should stop. Why then did he send her for more? Because he wants *her* to drink. He wants her to drink so she will speak truthfully to him, so she will forget for a moment her work. For just this hour or maybe two. It is not anything the Egyptian is required to know. Or Imad or Tariq, his brothers, waiting for him on the other coast.

But this kufar music, even through the walls it charges like a wild animal. Why did Khalid like it so much? His eyes upon the highway, he would turn the volume until the ashes in the tray shook, his head bouncing to it, laughing as he gave the engine all its fuel, Bassam afraid and grasping the door handle but laughing as well.

This David Lee Roth, if there was time Bassam would find him and kill him. For he worries. At his death Khalid was living like the kufar. He had not yet turned back to holiness and the Book. He had not visited the imam many evenings between the last two prayers, he had not sat upon the carpet looking into the sheikh's eyes that shone with wisdom and the light of iman as he revealed the nothingness inside them, the nothingness that made them race on the Road of Death and sneak away to Mount Souda to smoke tobacco and play music, some of the boys using their cell phones to call girls and talk and talk and talk.

The imam pointed in the direction of the air base of the Americans, the air base Ahmed al-Jizani helped to build, the air base their own king permitted in the Land of the Two Holy Places. "It is what they want. The further you fall from our faith, the stronger they become. The ways of the West, it is how Shaytan spreads confusion among the believers."

And Khalid's body was washed and wrapped in white and laid down on his right side facing Makkah.

Bassam began smoking more. He and Imad drove friends to Mount Souda and made fires. They sat around the flames, Tariq playing the oud, and they smoked cigarettes and talked of nothing but gossip— the mall in Abha where girls entered with a male guardian only to separate and meet their friends, their heads covered, their laughter, their eyes you could see seeing you. The chat rooms where you could have for hours a written conversation. The music allowed in other countries that made your heart beat more quickly and made you want to dance, something that was permitted outside the kingdom in night-clubs where men and women could go freely. And beer. Tariq wanted to taste beer. To taste the drunkenness he heard you could find in it. Your head becoming someone else's.

Bassam lay beside the fire. He listened to his friends and all their longing for more nothingness he was only beginning to feel was nothing. He lay there upon the hard ground and he watched the sparks rise to the stars in the blue-blackness above. A baboon began its howling cry. There he was under the moonlight in a thorn tree, his head tilted upward. *That is me. I am just a baboon in a thorn tree. I am nothing. All of us. We are nothing.*

Until the imam. Until the fasting whose thirst and hunger bring you closer to the Creator, the All-Knowing Sustainer and Provider, the teachings of their boyhood, that all beliefs other than our own are void and it is the plan of the Ahl al-shirk to separate us from our faith, to occupy us with their armies, to send us away from the One True God and Jannah. How could Bassam have forgotten his own king permitting the kufar onto the birthplace of the Prophet, peace be upon him? How could he have forgotten as a boy of fourteen years, the roaring sound of the American jets taking off to bomb their Muslim brothers in Iraq and Kuwait? It was the sound of Shaytan laughing at them. The air shook and you could not hear the mu-adhin's call to prayer. You could not hear the prayers of the imam inside the mosque built by Ahmed al-Jizani, only the jet engines of the kufar attacking our faith.

But remember too the American officers walking through the souq. Their uniforms pressed, their shoes dusty from the street. They talked too loudly and laughed too often. They pointed at goatskins of olive oil and made jokes. One picked up precious incense you burn for guests in your home, musk and myrrh and amber, and held it to his nose as if to judge its worthiness. You watched him, Bassam. You watched him, hungry and thirsty as you were from the fast of Ramadan and you saw inked into his arm the false idol cross that is haram, and you looked up and down the crowded street but there were no mu'taween to report to, and you cannot lie, there was something about these men you wanted to become. Tall and strong and afraid of nothing. Warriors. Above the rules. Living by rules from another world.

Khalid. That evening during Ramadan. There was a cold wind

from the mountains and he came home without his coat. He'd missed the nightly Iftar to break the fast, and many uncles and cousins were in the outer building with Ahmed al-Jizani, who called Khalid inside to eat.

Where is your coat?

I don't have it.

Where is it?

I gave it to the man in the souq.

Why?

He was cold. He did not have a coat.

But now you have no coat.

Yes, that is true. Khalid sat down and their father was smiling and in his eyes was the wet light of pride.

In only three days, Insha'Allah, they will shine brighter than ever before for the highest place in Jannah is reserved for the shahid, but also for the man who helps widows and the poor. The Prophet has said this, peace be upon him, and so Bassam will see Khalid again, yes? He must have faith that he will see him very soon. Allah willing, Insha'Allah.

"MRS. HANSON?" THE young nurse hurried into the room. She pressed a button on the monitor, and the beeping stopped. Jean moved past her to the short chest of drawers in the corner and pulled out her sundress.

"I'm going home."

A second nurse appeared in the doorway, tall and older, her hair pulled back in a tight French braid. "What seems to be the trouble?" Again, speaking too loudly, enunciating her words too damn clearly.

"No trouble," Jean said. She untied her johnny and let it drop to the floor. "I have to get home and I'm leaving." She found her bra in the drawer and put it on, hooking it together in front, then pulling it around and cupping her breasts into each one. She couldn't remember the last time she'd done that in front of anyone else—years. With Harry, years ago.

"Mrs. Hanson," the young nurse said. "You should really stay and rest."

"Thank you, but I have to go."

The other nurse was in the room now, leaning against the wall, her arms folded. "If something happens to you, we're not responsible. You do understand that, don't you?"

"Of course." She stuck her arms into the sleeves of her dress and didn't bother reaching up in back to struggle with the button. Franny did that for her sometimes, her tiny fingers against Jean's bare neck.

"I can't let you leave without signing a release."

"Fine." Her soiled tennis shoes were side by side on the floor and she pushed one foot in, then the other, sitting on the bed to tie them. She was breathing hard and sweating a bit, but it felt good to breathe, to move.

"Mrs. Hanson?" the young nurse said. "Your insurance probably won't pay for this now. You should know that."

For once her voice wasn't too loud or condescending. She simply sounded concerned, and Jean touched her hand briefly. "I have more money than I know what to do with, dear. Money's not my problem."

The nurse nodded and smiled, looking mildly embarrassed. "I hope someone's picking you up, though. You can't drive with the medication I gave you."

Jean glanced down at the bedsheet, the two pills lost in its folds somewhere. "I have to take a cab anyway. I appreciate your concern, dear. I really do."

Jean sat in the rear of the cab as the driver drove too fast up Tamiami. He was an older man, maybe ten years younger than she, and he wore a bandanna around his head, a short gray ponytail in back. He chewed gum and had turned on the radio as soon as they'd gotten under way, a jazz station. It sounded like Chet Baker. Harry had loved jazz, and if she recognized any of its music it was solely because of him.

How strange to be sitting in the back of a moving taxicab with nothing—no purse, no driver's license or credit cards, no cash, no car keys. She could be anyone going anywhere and when she got there who knows what would become of her? Her dress was still unbuttoned at the back of her neck and she let it stay that way; tonight her entire life felt unbuttoned. She couldn't remember if she'd ever done anything like she'd done just now, disobeyed people in charge of her, unhitched their tethers and just did what she damn well pleased.

Again, there was the resurfacing thought that she'd lived such a safe and small life, her years before Harry taken up with caring full-time for her ailing father, who, like her husband, had left her comfortable and in need of nothing. Until she met Harry at a symphony fundraiser when she was thirty-six, she'd filled her time serving on boards conserving trees and wildlife in far reaches of the country, establishing a fund for the widows of policemen and firefighters, building a new wing onto the Children's Hospital; she went to lunches with friends, read classic works from Proust to García Márquez; she spent occasional Sunday afternoons at the Chicago Museum of Art taking in what she could, though she was drawn largely to the Impressionists, especially Monet.

Baker's voice was high and melodious as a woman's. It was sweet to hear as they drove along the black water. On the other side of it, a quarter or half mile, were the lights of the houses on Siesta Key. Palm trees leaned out over lawns and lighted docks where boats were tied. Beyond these was the public beach where April took Franny nearly every day to play in sugar sand and swim in the Gulf. Franny had asked Jean many times to come with them and April had smiled and echoed her daughter's invitation but Jean had always declined, certain that April was just being polite and would rather she not come.

"Sir, when we get there, you'll have to wait while I run inside for my wallet."

He glanced in the rearview mirror at her, a flash of concern in his eyes.

"I took an ambulance. Didn't have time to grab anything."

He turned down the radio. "You all right?"

"Oh, I believe so. They told me themselves I hadn't had a heart attack."

"*Heart* attack?"

"Yes."

"You have chest pain?"

"Oh yes."

"It go up your arm and all that?"

"Yes, it did."

"You sure you didn't have a heart attack?"

"It was a different kind of attack. I get them sometimes."

Now on the radio were strings and a tenor saxophone, Charlie Parker, it sounded like. As they drove north the cabbie was studying her in his rearview mirror, and Siesta Key ran itself out into the black Gulf just before the southern tip of Lido Key, Rex's Marina there, its parking lot crowded with luxury cars, the entire nautical structure beyond lit up in a soft turquoise light. She and Harry had eaten there years earlier. She remembered the bottle of Pinot Grigio they'd shared, his shrimp scampi, her fettucine Alfredo.

"What's one of those like?"

"Excuse me?"

"Your attacks. Mind if I ask what they're like?"

"Oh. It's silly really. Every little detail gets big as a barn and it feels like they'll all just fall down on you and crush you to death."

He nodded. His curiosity seemed satisfied, and he slowed at the traffic light and turned right onto Buena Vista without signaling with his blinker. He flicked the radio back up, the horns and drums of a band of men from sixty years ago. Jean pressed her window button and let in the warm air. She could smell boat fuel and the Gulf and grilling meat from somewhere. She was suddenly famished, but eating would have to wait: she began to see herself driving to the place where April worked, walking in and finding that house mom, packing Franny up and taking her home. *Home.*

A PRIL HELD BOTH snifters in her left hand. She stuck the foreigner's change into her G-string, grabbed the chilled neck of the opened Moët, and made her way through the hazy lights of the VIP. Business had picked up a bit and she had to scoot by the new girl dancing badly for one of Sadie's regulars. There were other girls dancing for other men and April hurried past them all, the Rémy Martins sloshing gently in their snifters, the Moët cold against her leg.

Her customer sat forward on the sofa talking fast and loud on a cell phone he pressed to his ear with two fingers. In his other hand was a smoldering cigarette, its ash an inch long. His cash lay on the table. Two or three thousand easy. He barely looked at her as she placed the cognacs and change in front of him, and he shook his head and said something in a language that wasn't French or Italian or Greek, she knew that much. She stepped back out for the champagne she'd had

to put on the floor to get the door open, and because he was so preoc-
cupied she cut down the hall and pulled the front door shut too, the
music not so loud now, the air more muted than before.

He was still on the phone when she closed the door behind her. He
nodded at whatever was being said on the other end, his eyes on her
crotch and belly as she carried the full bottle, filled his flute and hers,
and wedged it into the ice. Her skirt and blouse were neatly folded
and lay across his arm of the couch. She didn't like customers touching her costume like that, especially this one, and she wanted them
back on her side of the sofa. He glanced up at her face. She smiled and
sat on the edge of the cushion and took a long, cool drink of her Moët
& Chandon.

He spoke more quietly on his phone now. So many of the sounds of
his language came from his throat. April thought of Morocco, Algiers,
Lebanon—places like that. He reached for his Rémy. She watched the
bubbles of his champagne rise to the surface. There was her boss,
Fuad, at the Subway shop in New Hampshire where she wore latex
gloves all day and made sandwiches for businessmen and construction workers and a few women from the Empire across the highway.
He was big and bald and would find an excuse to come behind the
counter and pretend to look for something, pressing himself against
her whenever he could. He knew she had Franny and was divorced,
something she told him in her interview because he'd asked.

"Why did you leave this father?"

"I didn't say I left him."

"But what man would leave *you*?" He looked long at her, at her
eyes, her hair, her breasts. He hired her at $7.50 an hour to work from
ten to six-thirty every day while her baby stayed with her mother, who
made it known she'd already raised her kids and wasn't up to raising
another. *This is just temporary, April, right?* And the strippers from the
Empire never liked to be called that but there was this nice one who
had to be thirty-five with the curves of a twenty-year-old—high fake
breasts, firm legs, and long blond hair, fake too. Whenever she came
in to eat, usually at five o'clock before her shift across the highway,

she smiled at April. She'd order turkey, lettuce, and tomato on a low-fat wrap with mustard—no mayo. She wore expensive gold rings and bracelets and she'd reach into a Gucci handbag to pay, always tipping April three dollars for a five-dollar meal. One afternoon in October she looked into her eyes as she handed her the money.

"I hope you know how pretty you are."

April smiled. She knew it and didn't know it. Not since Glenn and having the baby, and hearing it from this generous woman wearing so much gold, a woman it was hard not to stare at, felt good and she thanked her and went to making her sandwich. Fuad came out of his office then. He always did when the woman was there. He smelled like breath mints and he squeezed behind April to talk to the woman over the counter, his big body blocking April's route to the lighted bins of sliced turkey and shredded lettuce.

"Hallo, Summer. Very nice to see you again."

Summer chatted with him, smiling and brushing her hair back off her shoulder. April squeezed past Fuad to make the sandwich. He didn't move and she felt him against her ass, him and the keys and coins in his pocket. She made the sandwich quickly. Soon Summer sat at her table by the window, Fuad rubbed by April on his way to the office, and April left the prep area and served her turkey wrap.

April turned to leave, and the woman touched her wrist. "If you're gonna get treated like that, you should get paid for it, honey." She nodded in the direction of the office. "I get fifty up front before I let 'em get that close. And look at you; Jesus, you could make a ton over there. A *ton*."

It was dark already, the parking lot dimly lit by a few leaning street-lamps. On the concrete overpass was the speeding glare of headlights, and under it, on the other side of the highway, the purple neon glow of the club where Summer worked.

"What does your tag say?"

"April."

"Look, April, you'd make a bundle over there, honey." She bit into her wrap, chewed thoughtfully, shook her head. "More in one night than two weeks working for that one." She nodded in the direction of Fuad's office. The door was parted, the bright fluorescent tube over the prep area buzzing. "I'm serious."

April felt her face warming. She didn't know what to say and was grateful when a group of high school kids clambered in. She smiled down at Summer, who smiled back, dabbing away a fleck of mustard from the corner of her lip. "My real name's Stephanie. Think about it."

April couldn't *stop* thinking about it. What she'd said about money anyway. After her shift, she drove home to her mother's in South Hooksett to the same house on Rowe's Lane where she was raised. There used to be fields and woods on both sides of the road but now they were gone, sold off to developers who'd built dozens of houses there. All the same size and shape, two-and-a-half-story rectangular boxes with gable roofs, each with a round window centered under the front ridge, each sided with clapboards painted in shades that varied only slightly from gray to sage to steel blue. There was a deck built onto the rear of the houses which overlooked square yards seeded with green grass and surrounded by fences or hedges, and they were not ugly homes, April thought, but their exact sameness was and she'd always figured if she ever had the down payment to buy one that she'd paint it red, build a deck in the front, take out the round window and put in an oval, something—anything—to stand out more. And that night in October, driving past the new homes in what were once meadows of long grass and purple loosestrife and tall stands of pines behind three-hundred-year-old stone walls, she couldn't stop hearing that woman's voice in her head. *More in one night than two weeks working for that one.*

How much *was* that? Because before taxes, Fuad paid her three hundred dollars a week. Could she make twice that in one *night*? How could that be possible? How could anyone make that much money? But there was all that jewelry this Stephanie wore, her clothes and shoes and handbag, the new Acura she'd park out front where she could see it from the window.

The club was tucked away on the other side of an overpass: it could be a secret thing she did for just a short time. Just till she'd made enough to leave the house she'd had to return to, to leave her dried-up, bitchy old mother who'd never seemed to like being a mother in the first place. April thought of her dad, dead ten years—what would he say? Though he never did say much. He was big on praying at dinner and at bedtime, big on running his printing company and spending the weekend away from home doing whatever he did. If his spirit saw her in such a place, would he care?

Would she care herself? She didn't know. She'd never been inside a place like the Empire, just seen a few movies where there were scenes of women dancing naked onstage for men seated politely in tables below. The lights were always dimmed and the women moved up there like teasing cats, cash stuffed into their garter belts. She imagined herself up there. She'd had to wean Franny early so she could work, and her breasts had only just begun to lose their milk-heaviness. Her belly was flat again but with looser skin. She'd have to look better before she took off her clothes for strangers, a thought that turned her on a little bit—it did. Not about being naked but in breaking a rule flat out. Like doing something wrong just to do it. Like quitting high school and never going back. Getting shit jobs like this. Spending too much time in bars and pubs and sometimes waking up with someone at his place. And the money. How else could she get that kind of money?

But all these thoughts fell away when she pulled into her mother's driveway and in minutes was holding her baby in the kitchen, her mother washing dishes with her back to her. The TV on the table was turned up too loud, an infomercial for real estate. Franny held on to her tightly, her hair so fine. April felt dirty for even thinking what she'd been thinking.

She turned the TV down, sat at the table in front of an empty plate. She began tickling Franny, getting her to laugh, though her diaper needed changing; she could feel its warm mass against her knee. Franny's chin was smeared with tomato sauce.

Her mother said something from the sink.

"What, Ma?"

"I said that girl eats like a bird."

What she used to say about her, too. Her mother's plump back, her short practical haircut. Her cigarette burning in an ashtray on the windowsill. She was still living off her dead husband's life insurance and business and complained all the time of barely getting by, though once or twice a year she and her girlfriends went on a cruise.

April took a clean napkin and wiped her daughter's chin, made a game of it so Franny'd let her do it. She wanted to tell her mother that Franny ate plenty, that she was in the fiftieth percentile in weight for her age, and please stop smoking around her and how long has her diaper been this wet?

But she knew what she would get, nothing but bitching in return about how lucky she was she'd let her come back home in the first place, how ungrateful she was—*and you'd better not get used to this sweet little deal either. I don't know what you're gonna do, but you should've thought about that before, shouldn't you?*

"There's meatballs on the stove."

"Thank you." April carried Franny upstairs to her room, a room she once shared with her sister, Mary, who'd gone to the community college and married Andrew Thompson, the vice principal of a middle school now. They had three children and lived in a modern ranch house in a cul-de-sac in Connecticut. In their old room were all of Mary's childhood books: a series of stories about a girl's softball champion who worked on the sly as a private eye, *Little House on the Prairie*, Nancy Drew. April had never been much of a reader. On her side were the bare walls where she'd tacked posters of bands her sister hated: AC/DC, Dokken, KISS, though April wasn't drawn to their music, just their look, their wild hair and tight pants, their sinewy arms etched with tattoos, their deep, heavily made-up eyes that seemed to stare right out into the world like they didn't care what anybody in it thought about them or said about them or even felt about them because they were what nobody else had the balls to be: *free*.

And Stephanie driving what she did. Tipping like she'd just picked it off a vine. Wearing three-hundred-dollar outfits just because she felt like it. It's not what April would do with her money, but it was a picture of a woman she'd never really seen before, a woman who had so much she made on her own she could come and go as she pleased. If that wasn't free, what was?

The foreigner stopped talking. He closed his cell phone, placed it on the table next to his money. She smiled and tried to look straight at him but it was hard with this one. She looked down at the cigarette he'd dropped into the ashtray, at his money, so much of it.

"Want me to dance?"

"Please, say to me your name. The name your father gave for you."

Such an unoriginal and lame request. He pushed her Rémy closer to her, smiling with his bad teeth. His eyes seemed more sunken than before, like he didn't eat or sleep or do enough good things for himself.

"Tell me yours."

"Mike."

"*Mike?*"

"Yes, Mike. Drink." He handed her the cognac. She put down the Moët and sipped the Rémy. It burned its way over her tongue and down her throat and she chased it with cold sweet champagne, swallowing twice, knowing she'd get drunk if she kept this up.

"You do not like this, do you?" He held up the full snifter, then drank it down.

"*You* like it."

"Yes." His lips were wet. He reached for his champagne. "How many years have you?"

"Here?"

"No, how old?"

"Old enough, Mike."

"Twenty-four, yes? Twenty-five?"

She nodded. "And you?"

"I have twenty-six years."

She smiled at him. "Are you here for business, Mike? You go to school?"

"My name is not Mike."

"I know. Don't you want me to dance?"

"If I tell to you my name, you will say yours, yes?"

"Why? We don't need to know, do we, Mike? Let's just pretend."

"What does this mean?"

"Pretend. Act. Like playing a game."

"You mean lies."

"I don't lie, I pretend."

"No, you lie. All these girls, they lie too." He waved his hand in the air as if he were excusing her and was big and generous to do it.

"But you call yourself Mike." She stood. She glanced down at his money. More cash than she'd ever seen up close.

"You wish to have this?"

"Who wouldn't?"

"*I* would not." He lit up another Marlboro, squinted at her through the smoke.

I don't believe you. Those were the words in her head, the ones she wanted to say, would be able to say with some.

"But it's yours, right?"

"You say I take it?"

"No, I'm not saying that." You should never talk about money with them, Summer taught her that. Keep their eyes on you, on the body you're letting them see, and act like the money's a nice surprise, a sign of their generosity it would be rude to deny.

"You would like more?"

She sipped, shook her head, swallowed.

"Your name is Kelly."

She shook her head again, Sadie's song coming to a close on the main floor. The crowd's reaction was lukewarm, just some polite clapping. Maybe the place was clearing out or the VIP had filled back up again. She wanted to get back out there. Get back on rotation and check on Franny just before her act.

"Gloria."

"Nope."

"You see this?" He left his cigarette between his lips, leaned forward, and pulled a hundred-dollar bill from the rest. He laid it flat on the black cushion between them. "Give to me your name and I let you keep it."

Asshole. She liked it better when he was eyeing her breasts. Now he looked into her eyes, and his were dark and distant and deep in his head where who knows what went on.

"You do not want it?"

"Why don't I dance for you?"

"There is no music."

It was true; Sadie's act was over and they were in the quiet between girls. She sipped her champagne, put her glass on the table, turned to see him lay two more hundred-dollar bills, one next to the other. He was smiling at her with his ugly teeth.

"How would you know?"

"I will know."

"But how?"

"Because you will not look like an American girl any longer."

"Excuse me?"

"The truth is new to you. Your eyes will show it because it is new." He took a long drag off his cigarette, his eyes on the black ceiling, on something there and not there. Out on the floor more music was blaring away, a hard rock song she didn't recognize. Maybe the new girl's, she didn't know; she'd lost her bearings in the rotation, and on the other side of him were her blouse and skirt folded on the arm of the sofa. As if he planned to keep something of hers for himself, as if he planned to keep her here.

Two knocks sounded through the door. She shouted she was fine, though as soon as her hour was up she was going to get up and go. Still, three hundred on top just to tell him her first *name*? She didn't know what he was going on about truth for, but what would he do if she told him?

"That's it? I tell you and you give me that?" She nodded at his money, didn't name it. He was sitting forward now. He looked distracted, his elbows on his knees, the cigarette smoke rising.

"This fat man, does he think he can save you if I am going to hurt you? Why does he knocking if he can do nothing? He leaves too much time, you see? What is he going to do?"

Something cool flipped inside her, a deeper fear she hadn't really considered. But she smiled. "Catch you, I guess. I guess he'd just catch you."

"No, there will be no catching."

"I know."

"No, you do not." He motioned toward the three hundred dollars. "Now, do not lie, please."

She made herself look into his eyes. Into his drunk eyes. "April."

"Take it."

"You sure?"

"Yes."

She gathered up the bills, folded them once, slid them behind her garter, though she'd prefer to put them into the pocket of her blouse with the rest and not wear a reminder of what she'd just won. She wanted to ask him if she looked American or not, but he might hear it wrong. Or right.

"How did you know?"

"I have already said to you."

"Oh."

He rested his cigarette in the ashtray, pinched six or seven bills between his fingers, dropped them on the cushion. One of the hundreds brushed her bare skin like an insect.

"Explain to me why you do this and I give these to you as well."

"Don't you want me to dance? Your time is almost up."

He nodded slowly, as if she'd just said something he hadn't expected from her, something intelligent and useful to him, his eyes passing over her entire face: her eyes, cheeks, nose, and mouth. She sipped her Moët. She tried not to glance down at the bills and count them. Five hundred from him already.

"What do you want to know?"

"Please." He pointed to her bra. "Remove this."

"Want me to dance?"

"No."

She'd rather do this dancing; it felt less intimate then but she reached up and pulled apart the Velcro, let her T-back fall open, pulling out first one arm, then the other. These rooms were cooler than the club, the vent in the ceiling on for the smoke, an air conditioner going somewhere. Her nipples stiffened and she felt strange; she felt shy.

She felt naked.

***

B OTH OF THEM is who he wanted to fuck up, the big mother-fucker *and* Marianne, though now he could hardly make a fist with his left hand and it was hard to hold the wheel to sip from the Wild Turkey he'd gone back to town for. In the bright light of the store he'd had to hold his wallet open with two fingers for the man at the register, an old sonofabitch who didn't want to go into AJ's wallet but then saw him holding his hurt wrist in the air and fished out a ten for him. Over a dollar change and AJ just walked out and let him keep it so he didn't have to mess with it.

Now he drove up Washington Boulevard, steering with his knee for sips off the pint, his left hand useless, and all the man had to do was say *let go*. Let go of Marianne's hand and he would've. He knew the goddamned house rules better than anyone, but it was Marianne who broke 'em. *She* was the first one to reach over and squeeze *his* hand, two weeks ago Wednesday night when he'd told her about Cole. Told her how he'd never done a good goddamned thing but break his neck to pay all the bills and now he can't see his boy.

"I bet you're a nice daddy." *She* said it. Smiled at him and took his hand like she meant it, and hell yes, hearing that and feeling her warm hand in his was better than watching her shake her ass and titties, so he told her that and she said he was *nice*. Been saying it since then too.

Till tonight.

What, she think it was easy for him to ask her? She think he didn't know he wasn't the first one to do that? Goddamn all he said was the time and place when *she* was the one told him it'd be nice to go someplace nice with him, the nice damn daddy.

His F-150 kept lurching ahead into its own headlight path, his foot pressing down on the gas just thinking of her and the spic chink sonofabitch. He should just wait for the club to close and follow his ass home.

He was past the industrial park now, the boulevard a dark empty stretch through swamp grass, his rifle at home, not in the claustrophobic condo he lived in now with Mama, but at home, in his house. In his goddamned bedroom closet. Deena had changed the locks on him but he could still get in. Didn't she know that? Did they *all* think he was stupid?

On the southbound side a half mile ahead, the Puma Club sign was just a yellow spot and the Wild Turkey was going down smooth, a little something to dull the hot throbbing in his wrist and hand. He wedged the pint between his legs, turned off the AC, and pushed the window buttons. Ten o'clock at night in September and the air was still hot, smelling like cypress root and asphalt and alligator shit. Least that's what he thought. Loved the Everglades south of here. Had always wanted to live out in them. Get a boat and build his own cabin on piers. Teach Cole how to fish and hunt, the two of them swinging in a hammock behind mosquito netting, eating roasted gator and bobcat and manatee. Lounge around like naked warriors. And no women. No goddamned women.

But he couldn't stop thinking of Marianne, her high cheerful voice. Her sweet blue eyes and that soft waist and pear-shaped ass he could curl up against till he was old and beyond. Her tits were fake, but that's only because she didn't know her own beauty. Didn't know how much better she was than all the others. That's what he'd told her and meant it. And the way she'd looked at him is what did it to him. Convinced him he had a chance. Her blue eyes getting all moist in the corners and round, her mouth partway open like a little kid's.

He drank down some Turkey, liked the feel of its heat spreading out in his chest. He'd just started reading to baby Cole. Small cardboard books about a puppy and his friend Steve, the gator. AJ would lie on the bed with him, feel his son's small head against his arm while he read each and every word slow, trying to make the story last and last, trying to slow time. Sometimes Cole would point to the picture, try to repeat a word he'd just heard his daddy say. His hand was so small and soft, his whole body like that, his feet hardly reaching AJ's hip. He'd sneak a look at the side of Cole's face staring at the book, at his short blond hair and rounded forehead, that bump of a nose, his pink lips and smooth chin. Then AJ would hug him close and kiss him on the head, smell the baby shampoo his wife used on him. It almost hurt to feel this much love. He'd never felt anything close to it before, and it scared him; lying there with baby Cole, he'd wanted to cover him with his whole body. Build a steel and concrete house around him. Erect a twelve-foot hurricane fence around that. Drive him places in a tank, and never let anybody bad close enough to see him or call his name or even *know* it.

He was driving fast now, the white lines of the boulevard zipping under his truck. The Puma Club came and went off to his left and he barely glanced out the window at its yellow glow. What they all seemed to forget is he didn't do anything wrong. Nothing. All he gave Marianne was his affections and hard-earned money. He only gave his wife what she deserved, and that paper scrap from the court could tell him all it wanted about how far away he had to be from his own son and his own damn home—fifty yards or a hundred, he couldn't remember, and he didn't give a good goddamn because twelve miles and some change up this road was his house *he* paid for. It'd been five weeks since he'd even laid eyes on Cole. It was time to see him. High goddamn time to see him.

He pressed his knee to the wheel, reached for the pint between his legs. The glass was smooth and warm. He thought how that and his F-150 were his only companions tonight, the only ones he could count on.

ᵛ ᵛ ᵛ

THE NEW BOTTLE of Moët was almost gone. He was small and should be drunk and maybe he was, but he didn't seem it. She sat there next to him on the edge of the love seat in nothing but her G-string, garters, and heels. He barely glanced down at her body, instead kept his attention on her face, his eyes narrowed and tired-looking but lit up with an urgent curiosity. That's what it looked like to her—urgent.

"Why do you sell yourself?"

"You think I'm selling myself, Mike?"

"Yes, you sell yourself."

"Doesn't everyone?"

He lit up another cigarette. "No, April. No."

She didn't like how he'd just said her name. As if he knew her. It didn't even belong in the air of this place. Why had she told him?

"Did your father go to university?"

"I don't think so."

"You do not know?"

"Nope. What about your father?"

His forehead ridged up and he blew smoke out his nose and mouth at the same time. "Take off your bottom piece, please."

"I'm s'posed to dance."

"Why? Soon my hour with you will be over and I will give to this business three hundred dollars more. Do you think the owner cares what you do in this room?"

"You want another hour?"

"Please, I would like you to tell me why you do this. And do not say it is for money because that is a lie." He pulled the bottle from the ice and poured the rest of the Moët into her glass. He stood, scooped his cash up off the table, handed her two hundred dollars but left the seven hundred on the cushion next to her. "I will buy you for one hour more. When I return you will not be wearing your bottom piece and you will surprise me, yes?"

He smiled down at her, his bad teeth on display, his eyes hungry but distant, passing over her face and breasts and knees as if he wanted her but had also tired of her long ago. His back was narrow, his polo shirt wrinkled like he'd been driving for days. He walked steadily, didn't look back at her, and pulled the door shut behind him.

⌄ ⌄ ⌄

Behind Bassam whores dance for seated kufar and he stands at the bar in blue light, the music loudest here, the smoke hanging thickly. A big man is beside him, one of the whores' protectors. He has his back to him so rudely and his white T-shirt is stretched tightly across his muscled shoulders, but there, above the whiteness of his shirt, is his dark neck and of course this kafir could break Bassam's body in two pieces but not if he is struck first. Not if the kafir is struck when he expects nothing but more and more of the comfort he is in now.

Beneath Bassam's feet, the floor seems to have movement. His arms and legs are like liquid, his face a smiling mask he gives to the barman as he hears his voice ask for the French champagne.

"Moët?"

"Yes, that." How easy to thrust the blade into his throat. How easy to turn and reach up and plunge the razor just below the ear.

Why is he here? Why does he stay? He can feel her waiting for him. Uncovered and beginning to talk. His last chance with one, he is certain. His last opportunity.

He places a bill onto the bar and the barman takes it and pushes at him the bottle, and Bassam must hurry to the last woman who is the first woman. Hurry back to her and discipline himself to stay for one more hour only.

The bottle is cool and heavy and he does not wait for the change. He walks back through the naked whores and they writhe like snakes in the firelight and he feels weak for giving the barman such money. How many dollars? Fifty? Sixty? But no, let him be fooled by it. Let them all be fooled.

"Hey, little man. You drinking that yourself?"

A black kafir, so much of her skin showing between thin red garments. She is tall, smiling down at his eyes, and in Khamis Mushayt, the daughter of the Sudanese who mixed the mortar for the mosque built by Ahmed al-Jizani, how tall she was and fully covered in the black abaya and she would bring to her father water, and Bassam was a boy but he watched her, her body covered and her head but not her face, her eyes like this one, her brown skin like this one.

"You in the Champagne?"

"Come, please," he hears himself say to her. "I buy you too."

The pig at the curtain, she tells him words about rotation and she laughs and steps into the red light and opens the black door. The music so loud and crashing in his ears, so loud, the air too smoky, too crowded, the smell of sweating and fading perfumes, and this too must be a sign, the Holy One showing him what, Insha'Allah, he will avoid.

T HE NIGHT AIR blew warm against the side of AJ's face, and
he turned east onto Myakka City Road. His hand still hurt,
and he was going to do something about that sonofabitch, but
he'd been wound tight all day just getting up his nerve to tell Marianne where he'd take her, to ask her when she wanted to go, and even
though she'd made a goddamned fool of him, at least it was behind
him. At least his heart wasn't going all day when it shouldn't, giving
him the shits for this woman who was all wrong about him.

He sat back behind the wheel of his cruising Ford, his whole body
light and loose in the warm Wild Turkey air, and he could see it all just
a bit more clearly now, could get philosophical about it. She just didn't
know him, that's all. He'd made the mistake of not talking about himself enough. He'd asked her questions about her because he wanted
to know and because he wanted her to know he wanted to know. But
she never did tell him much. And all he told her about himself was

missing Cole and how dumb-luck beautiful she was, that it was *his*
dumb luck to find someone so beautiful and she'd smiled a real smile
and put her hand in his for the first time, felt the calluses there from
working the knobs of his CAT. She probably thought right then that's
all he was. She didn't know he'd always been good at math and numbers, that he'd been the night manager at the Bradenton Walgreen's
at *twenty-one*, that they wanted him to go to their training clinic up
north somewhere, Deena working Register 3, sweet and quiet, her
body nice to look at behind her Walgreen's apron, woman curves all
over, and she called him Mr. Carey, which made him feel good, and
one night she needed a ride home and he drove her and on the way
they stopped and bought a six-pack of cold Millers and he got her to
stop calling him Mister, told her a joke about the real manager, Simon
Blau, and they both laughed and then they were parked under an oak
somewhere, kissing and tearing at each other and then, like that, she
was pregnant and they were married and her old man was offering to
train AJ on heavy equipment for better pay, and now he hadn't seen
his boy in thirty-seven days and all the good months he and Deena
had had were just asphalt under his wheels as he drove beneath I-75,
thinking about how much she'd changed on him, how she didn't like
to have a good time anymore.

Didn't want to drink. Or play cards. Never wanted to fuck or even
let him hold her or touch her a little. Just read her damn magazines
about TV stars and the goddamn cars they drove and the houses they
lived in and the pretty people they left for prettier ones ahead. She'd
gotten fat and knew it, but instead of getting off her ass she'd work on
her nails, growing them out too long, painting them a different color
every week. And she was always restless about her hair, was never
happy with the way God gave it to her, straight and brown. She'd get
into their secondhand Corolla AJ'd paid for and drive into Bradenton
to have her hair dyed or curled or bleached or ironed or whatever the
hell it was they did. Then he'd come home, his shoulders and back
stiff and sore, coughing up dust, a buzzing in his ears from the diesel
engine and that steel bucket and all he'd made it do, and there she'd

be cooking in the kitchen fat and unhappy with her new hair—blonde or red, sometimes a little purple or green, sometimes straight, other times curly—standing there frying him a steak and onions, or chicken and hush puppies, feeding Cole in his high chair, her face all round and greasy, and he didn't know if he should cry for her, or laugh, or go over and hug her and tell her she was fine just the way she was, that she didn't have to do that, but he never did any of those things because he'd be too goddamned angry, feel it rise up in his blood and muscles and skin, this tightening up when all he wanted to do was unwind, and he'd shake his head at her and tell her she looked ridiculous and how much goddamn money did *that* cost? Because he knew it was at least two *hours* of his workday, wasn't it? Maybe three hours, *his* three hours, sitting in that cage, working the machinery in the fumes and dust and mosquito heat for them, for Deena and Cole, for the bank that held the note on their two-bedroom, for Caporelli Excavators he bled for so they could pocket their profit and toss him the crumbs. And—he had to admit—for him, for Alan James Carey, and his hard-earned self-respect that when he'd gotten into trouble with this girl he'd done the right thing by her and the baby, borrowed the down payment from his old mother in Bradenton and bought them their house off Myakka City Road, this abandoned cinder-block hut out in the wire grass and slash pine. But it had a well and electrical service, and nights and weekends he'd gutted it, built new partition walls, reinsulated it, hung Sheetrock, put in seven new windows, roofed it, and laid new floors. Deena hadn't had the baby yet and they lived with her folks out on Lake Manatee. Shared the room she was raised in, the walls still covered with posters of those goddamned boy bands, and lying there after working from seven to eleven he couldn't bear to look at them, hated being there at all, hated having to borrow money from her old man for most of the materials. But he could see how her father had grown to respect him. Saw how he could work and work and how fast he learned things. And her old lady was one of those too-cheerful-smiling-mice-of-a-woman you could never trust. He was glad Deena never laid it on thick like she did. Her mother always asking him questions about what he did all day, her smile nailed to her face, her eyes glazing over, looking right at him.

But Deena was good, her belly growing by the week. It'd be between ten-thirty and midnight and the front porch light would be on when he pulled up behind her old man's F-250 so goddamned tired he could hardly get himself to squeeze the door handle. Under the gutter at the north corner of the house was a bug zapper behind wire mesh, this four-foot dull blue glow, and he'd sit there a second or two and watch the moths and flies get it, see their tiny insect bodies spark and flash out of this world. Stupid fucking bugs. Couldn't they sense the others getting fried right in front of them? It unsettled him to think about it, and he felt his own fate was somehow married to theirs, and that could bring him down. Being that flat bone-tired always did that anyway. Made him feel like he was losing at everything, that it was all just too big for him—the massive machinery they trusted him with, the house, Deena and this almost-baby—that he was going to trip and fall and get crushed under all its weight.

But then the front screen would swing open and there'd be Deena standing in the light, holding out a cold Miller, smiling at him. She'd started wearing a yellow-flowered maternity gown to bed at night. It was thin and he could see her breasts and belly under it and he knew other men didn't like looking at a pregnant woman but those nights, reaching for that iced bottle of beer she'd put in the freezer for him a half hour earlier, feeling those heavy breasts and that hard belly against him, tasting her warm mouth, he couldn't imagine a woman looking more like a woman's supposed to look and that's when he knew it was all going to work out. Him and her and this child they'd made because they couldn't keep their hands off each other, even though they hardly knew who lived there behind each other's eyes.

AJ sipped off his pint, the Turkey warm and medicinal down his throat. The pain in his wrist wasn't completely gone, but he could live with it better than before. Out his open window he could smell the slash pines and the thick undergrowth of saw palmetto between the bare trunks that during the dry season would burn when the pines wouldn't. It'd taken them years and years to get that way, seventy to eighty feet of bare trunk with all their pine needles clustered at the top where no wildfire could ever get them. They gave off a sap scent he smelled now and it was the smell of home and he felt more hopeful than he had in a long while that Deena might forgive him because he'd never laid half a finger on Cole and he only did it to her twice. Two times. That's all. And didn't she know why? Didn't she know that she'd just goddamned *disappeared* on him? That their best time was when there was something ahead of them they could hardly wait to get to—him finishing the house, her having the baby, then the two of them being able to drink a beer together again, the two of them in their hurricaneproof house out in the wire grass he kept cut back, behind them a deep stand of longleaf pines. Out at the road he'd dug a hole and filled it with concrete and sunk a four-by-four post into it, built a mailbox in the shape of their own house, a corrugated gable on top at the same pitch, and he'd painted on the side: *The Careys.*

He had to take a leak. His turnoff wasn't more than a quarter mile away, but he didn't want to knock on his door needing to take a piss. And shit, he should've brought something for them. A toy for Cole. Something pretty for her, though he didn't know what that would be. A blouse? A big blouse?

He steered off the asphalt onto the grassy shoulder. His truck jerked forward and he saw it was in park already, his hand on the stick. More than half the pint was gone. Time to slow down. Couldn't remember the last time he drank anything hard. It'd be better if he weren't like this right now, smelling like a roadhouse when he saw her. He had some Tums in his console from all the worrying she'd put him through, the shits and the heartburn. Sometimes during the day, working or driving to work or back, he'd tally up how much more his life cost now than it used to: the child support and mortgage; the gas in his truck from the longer drive to and from his mother's place; his new and lonesome habit at the Puma Club. He still owed on his truck, but by God he'd paid off her old man for the house materials. Let him take it out of his check for seven months of steady payments, and now they were all square, and right after Deena pulled that order on him he quit her daddy and hired on with Caporelli's for six dollars more an hour. Still, none of it was enough and he'd started using his credit card for the Puma. Got cash advances just to drink eight-dollar beers and look at lying whores like Marianne.

He had to go worse than ever. He set the pint on the passenger seat and reached for his door handle. But his left hand was useless so he swiveled, got the door open with his right, stepped out stumbling into the night. He leaned against his open door and got his zipper down and freed himself. Hadn't ever known till right this second you use two hands to do that, not one.

Two is better than one.

Always would be for him. He'd never liked being alone. Standing there aiming for the blackness under his truck he could feel how tired he was, just how much he'd missed this road and that home he'd made up ahead. How much he hated his foldout bed in front of the TV at his mama's, their quiet meals together in front of whatever the hell was on. His wrist hurt and he was tired and a little drunk on the relief he deserved, but he was tired more than anything. Tired of working so hard for nothing but bad feelings in return.

Maybe tonight would be different. Maybe she missed him, too. Maybe she remembered when Cole was just a little baby and they'd all played together on a blanket in the grass. Lifted him up and kissed him and blew on his belly and made him laugh. How later, after he was down and asleep, they'd set out on lawn chairs up against the house with tall cold ones and watch the sun go down through the pines. And then there were stars.

How'd she get tired of that? Why'd she start bitching at him about everything?

He shook himself off and zipped up best he could. Some of the old bad feeling was coming up again, and he didn't want it. Nobody but him knew he wasn't proud of what he'd done, backhanding her and her expensive hair across the kitchen. All this weight on him and all she ever wanted to do was add more. Couldn't she see how goddamned hard he worked? Even at home? Keeping the grass cut, scraping and painting the window and door trim, repointing the cinder block wherever it needed it, on and goddamned on. And it must've been having Cole that changed everything 'cause before he was born he'd catch her looking at him when she didn't know he knew, see the shy pride in her eyes that she'd caught herself a good one, a man who *did* things. Grabbed a shovel and started *digging*. But that changed fast as her body did. They had their baby and moved into their small, solid house, and then what was there to look forward to but watching Cole grow, looking at each other over the kitchen table or across the couch in front of the TV or in those lawn chairs out back?

Maybe she should've gotten out of the house more. It wasn't his fault she got bored with Cole all day. That she didn't have any girlfriends and hated visiting her mother out on the lake, that she didn't have any damn hobbies she could work on when Cole was napping, that all she could do was watch those soaps full of actors better-looking than he'd ever be, wearing suits he'd never be able to buy or even wanted, carrying on in bedrooms bigger than their whole house, so, when he came home, he'd catch her looking at him differently; he'd be on the couch bouncing Cole on his knees and he'd glimpse her watching them. Sometimes she looked happy, but that was because she liked hearing Cole laugh the way he could make him do. And he didn't know what she saw when she stared at him, just what she looked like—that he was a disappointment to her. Nothing but a plain man who worked hard and wasn't good-looking or rich and never would be and he didn't even begin to know the secrets of her heart. Seeing that look, his hands splayed across Cole's back, he felt it and believed she was right.

He began to scoot back behind the wheel. A vise was squeezing his wrist again and there was his left hand on the door handle where he put it every time he climbed into his truck, the things you do without thinking how good it is you can do them till you're hurt. That's what he was banking on with Deena. That she was no goddamned prize herself and after all these weeks she must miss him the way he missed her. Curling up at night to nothing but a pillow. He must look a lot better to her now, even though he'd done what he did.

He grasped the wheel with his right and pulled himself up and in, then reached for the door and barely got it and almost fell out. Marianne's face. Those wide blue eyes. He could still feel the sweet way she held his hand and listened to him. All that warm skin she showed him, sure, but more than that was how she looked at him when he told her about his boy and the house he'd built him—not like he was a plain man and a nothing, but like he was strong and handsome and something else.

He righted himself, yanked the door shut. He wedged the pint carefully between his legs, put her in drive, and pulled away from the grassy shoulder. A pair of headlights had been coming his way for a while and now they were close and a horn honked long and loud as it passed, a beat-up El Camino that was already gone, and what the hell was his problem? There was this feeling in AJ's throbbing wrist and arm that he was an easy mark somehow. But he'd never taken any shit from anyone and he wasn't about to start now; there was Marianne holding her hand out to him for her money, the smell of that big Chinese who'd walked him outside—cologne and hair oil and Coke on his breath—the final shove he'd given AJ out from under the canopy and into the crushed shells. That wasn't called for. None of it.

His truck lights lit up the road high and far ahead. He drove slow, sipped from his pint, saw under his dash the single blue dot of his brights, and that's why that sonofabitch had given him the horn and couldn't cut him a little slack like *he* never forgot about his damn brights before.

A little slack. That's all. Couldn't everybody just ease up and give each other a little slack? Didn't he work hard enough to expect some of that?

And there ahead, lit up by his brights he wasn't about to flick off now, was that old sable palmetto at the turnoff to his road home, its palm fronds fanning out high on its scarred and scaling trunk. His lights swept past it, a beacon marking the fort just for him, and again,

he felt sure he was doing the right thing coming home. Tired and
beat up on. Lonely for what Marianne had promised but only Deena
could give.

The road was two tire tracks of packed clay his truck fit right into,
carried him forward to where now he could hardly wait to get. He
thought of being inside Deena again. That had never stopped feeling
good. Even with all the weight she'd put on. It was still a soft, warm
place to sink the better part of himself, his desire for her and what
they could make together. Him and this woman, the mother of his
son. He reached for the pint between his legs but thought better of
it and left it there. Steered with his knee and fished his Tums out of
the console and shook two or three into his mouth. A breeze swung
in from the east, pushing through the high wire grass on both sides
of the road. Years since there'd been a fire out here in the dry season
and now they were in the wet months again but it was only a matter
of time before lightning struck and all the wire grass would go up and
he hoped she'd kept it all cut away from the house, which would never
burn anyway—still, little Cole.

His and Deena's son. Cole.

‬ ‬ ‬

S HE'S CRYING. SHE'S hot and sweaty under this blanket and
she cries for Mama. Where is she? She sees the light on the little table and naked mamas in pictures on the wall. Loud sounds
and bad yelling in the loud music. Sometimes Mama turns on the
radio and they drive to the store. This music. Like that.

Mama?

She doesn't like this blanket and the floor. Her feet and no shoes.
Where are her flip-flops? No knob on the door and her fingers go
into the crack and everything is hard to see because she's crying and
where's Mama? She uses her hands and the crack gets bigger and a
naked lady is pulling up her dress and zipping up her dress and the
lady looks at her and there's black all around her eyes. Something
shiny on her face and Franny runs back into the crack and onto the
soft pillow. The lady with the hard bobbies. Where did she go?

Mama.

Her throat hurts. Everything hard to see. She doesn't want that naked lady to come inside. She wants Jean. Where's Jean? She's afraid of the crack to the room with the naked lady and she covers her eyes so she can't see her, but they're all wet and it's dark and she opens them. She wants Jean. The rug is dirty. The floor makes her feet cold. She wipes her eyes to see. She wants the other lady not there now. She wants her to be gone because Mama went through the crack into the big room.

Now the lady is gone away and she goes into the big room. A pretty mirror, but the lights are hurting her eyes. She smells smoke like Granma made with her mouth when they lived in Granma's house far away. The pretty mirror, so many lights and her hair is in the mirror. Her nose is stopped up and Jean makes her use tissues and she sees the box with one sticking out, a yellow one. Everything pretty here but messy. All the colors. The shiny necklaces and pretty bracelets. She can't reach the yellow box and her hand is in the mirror and it looks funny. She wishes she had the tissue for her nose like Jean gives to her all the time. A pretty scarf under makeup like Mama puts on. She pulls it to her nose and wipes her face and the music is loud but it feels good under these lights. Bright lights. Round bright lights.

Don't look into the sun, honey, Mama says. Don't look into the sun or you can't see. She's scared and blinks her eyes but the big room is foggy, then bright foggy, then bright and Mama must be in that door. Like the door to her room at home. The same kind. She walks over the floor that is very dirty. Dirt sticking to the bottoms of her feet. Where are her flip-flops?

The knob round and gold metal like at home but Jean has glass knobs downstairs in her house. Knobs like big jewelry. And this one is loose and she turns it with both of her hands and it pulls away from her so fast and it's dark and loud and a big man is looking down at her face.

"Where're *you* goin'?"

And she turns and runs. Run run fast into the crack and into the lady's room. A boom-boom-booming where her heart is and she crawls under the chair under the table with the light on it. She hugs her knees with her arms and waits for the man to come and her eyes are all wet again and she closes her mouth tight and hears the loud music and yelling and laughing.

Mama.

Is the man in the room now? Scratches on the wood under her toes. One is a letter from the alphabet—F—she knows them all. Gums sticking under the table where the lady puts her legs. Is he here? *Mama.* If she puts her head under the chair and looks, he will see her and that will be bad. She's not *little.* She's not. She goes pee on the toilet now and Jean says she's a big girl.

Because she's not even crying anymore and she peeks under the chair and out the crack and sees the closed door on the other side of the bright empty room. But a new naked lady is coming in from a different door. And she has high shoes like Mama's Franny put on one day and Mama laughed and then she didn't like it. The lady opens a door in the wall and puts money there and closes it and turns a round metal blue thing and she gets dressed but her clothes are shorts, shiny shorts, and a small shiny shirt and Franny likes it because they're the same color—they match.

This one is nice. She doesn't have black on her eyes. Nothing shiny on her cheeks and she has white, soft ribbons around her legs. But she can't talk to her. Mama will get mad. Like when she talked to that man in the store by the candy. Mama wasn't looking. She was putting food on the moving thing and she got mad.

Some grown-ups are mean, Franny.

Now the booming again. In her ear too, she can hear it. The loud loud music. It's a party. Mama's at a party and she thinks she's asleep but she'll surprise her. She can't see the lady anymore. Maybe she's at the big mirror with the hot lights. She wants to ask her where Mama is but Mama will get mad.

She waits. She's thirsty for water. At home Jean puts water by her bed in a blue cup with orange butterflies on it. Maybe the lady left some on the table by the couch. She looks. Sees the couch, the pillow and blanket, the TV. Now she sees the new lady in shiny shorts walk fast in her high shoes by the mirror to the door with the man behind it. She knocks and the door opens and the man smiles at the lady and says something and the lady is laughing and goes into the blue dark. Her hair bounces like after a bath and Franny's going to cry but she can't or the man will hear her and she feels scared again and wants a drink of cold water and her flip-flops. She pushes the chair and crawls out. The floor is dirty on her knees and hands and she has to find Mama but she doesn't like this dirt against her feet. She lifts the blanket. She looks at the floor by the wall, then turns and sees a high shelf by the door. A shelf with papers up there and big books for the phone and her backpack and flip-flops on top. She stands under and stretches on her toes and touches the air. Mama used the chair from the kitchen to hang pictures on the wall they bought at the store, a picture of the moon and ocean waves. Franny peeks out the crack in the door. Just the big room and no naked ladies and she hurries and squeezes the chair with her hands and pulls on it and it drags over the dirty floor. She's strong. She is a big girl.

You're such a big girl.

Jean's voice in her head. Her smell in her head too so it's in her nose. Jean's smell. Pretty perfume and coffee and sweating from working. Franny works too. Climbing onto the chair. A bumpy cushion there with buttons. She puts her foot on it, then the other, and her body slides a little but she doesn't fall. She reaches for her flip-flops but the chair is too far away so she gets down and pulls on it till the dark shelf is above her and she climbs back onto the chair. The cushion is soft. Her knees feel good on it, but she's afraid she will slide again and stands slowly, holding her arms out. And now she can touch her backpack. She can feel it all lumpy with her clothes. She tries to reach her flip-flops, but her fingers just touch the backpack and can't go higher.

The music is loud again and the grown-ups are yelling. She will go out to the party with her bare feet. It's okay, she thinks. I walk in Jean's garden with bare feet and it doesn't hurt. It doesn't.

It feels better to be off the chair. And she's used to the dirty floor under her toes. She sticks her head out the crack. Nobody there. No naked ladies. No big man. But she can't go back to his door. She will go the other way. The way the new naked lady came.

She's still thirsty. Mama will give her something when she finds her. Maybe Jean is here too. But why is the music so loud? Why do the men yell and everybody's laughing?

She sees a black curtain. Like the one at the haunted house Granma took her to last time and it had skeletons and spiderwebs and two ghosts and she didn't like it. But there's a blue crack between them. A pretty blue light.

She touches the curtain. It's soft and thick. Not like the curtain in the haunted house. Thin and scratchy and smelling like dogs. She makes the blue crack wider and steps inside it. But where is the party? She can hear it better but she can't see it. Everything dark blue. Her hands and her arms. Her bare feet. She touches the wall with her blue fingers and it's black and hard. No door.

A blue light is shining on the other side of her because it's not a room, it's a little hallway like at home. Mama's room is at the end of it and down in Jean's house her room is at the end of it too. The light is pretty blue. And round like a bright moon. She thinks of winter where Granma is. Sledding with Mama down the snowy hill behind Granma's house when it was almost night and Mama held her between her legs and the wind came cold and fast on her face and her eyes got watery, but it was fun and the snow looked blue. Like this.

She knows she fell asleep when the lady read her about Stellaluna but she misses Mama now like she didn't see her for a long long time and she walks to the steps under the blue light. One. Two. Three of them. The music and yelling are louder and at the top is another curtain. What if she can't find her? Or Jean? What if they're not there?

Her face feels funny. It's hard to swallow and she's crying again. She's crying but she climbs the steps and touches the soft curtain with her blue fingers because *just do your best. Always try to do your best.*

✌ ✌ ✌

Apil glanced down at the money, touched the bills lightly with her fingers. Would he give her that as easily as he'd given her the three hundred and then the two hundred for the new hour? Was she really going to make this much off just one customer in one night? The most she'd ever made was eight hundred and that was before having to pay the house and tip everyone.

She was cold. Louis had the air-conditioning cranked too high. Her nipples were hard buds and she began to rub her upper arms and legs. She sipped her Moët, a warm flurry inside her veins and head. She wasn't as nervous around her foreigner as she was before. Maybe because he was so small. Maybe because he was showing such an interest in her, she didn't know. She stood and wriggled out of her G-string, then picked up her folded skirt and blouse and rested them on the floor on her side, tucking her G-string between them. She sat back down. Felt awkward in just her garter belts and stilettos, not dancing at all. Back at the Empire, Summer had gotten shit from a drunk customer who'd dropped a dollar on her crotch, then tried to stick his finger in her, and she leaned back and kicked him in the face, her spiked heel ripping through his cheek. But most of the men weren't like that to dancers the floor hosts were paid to watch over anyway, and unless McGuiness was hard up for dancers, then every dancer started as a waitress first just to tease the regulars for weeks with you topless in a skirt and fishnets so the place would fill up your first night dancing.

McGuiness was young and bigger than most of his floor hosts. He had a shaved head and eyes that made her think of Glenn, soft blue, almost pretty, but they could turn on and off like a light. Her first night at the Empire carrying a tray, after she'd changed in the restroom on the concrete floor with the drain in it, the smells of toilet deodorizer and rusty pipes—the dressing room for dancers only—after she'd zipped up her tight denim skirt and pulled the wrinkles out of her fishnets and cinched the straps of the pumps she'd had to buy with her own money, she stood there and looked at her breasts. They were still heavy from the breast-feeding she'd stopped. She wished she'd worn a light necklace or something. The door opened without a knock and McGuiness came in out of the music, a pager in his hand, chewing gum, looking hard at her breasts, her legs, the slight lip of flesh over the waistband of her skirt.

"Get your hair off 'em."

She did, her face heating up, a tangle of wire uncoiling inside her. He told her to tie her hair back every night and to lose ten pounds, then he was gone.

She didn't know what to do with her clothes, her pocketbook. She couldn't go to her car in the parking lot like this and didn't want to walk out into the dark club with them like she had no idea what she was doing. In the corner under a Tampax machine was a tall chrome waste can. She stuck her pocketbook into the dusty space behind it, wedging her rolled jeans and halter top there too.

She stopped at the mirror, didn't look at her body, just her face, saw the expression she must've had as a girl whenever she'd do just what she was told not to. She could feel her heart tapping away, ready to go, and that same voice inside her head: *Make me. Just try and make me.*

The Champagne Room door swung open. A wave of club music rolled in with it, that and laughter, a woman's brown leg circled by a red satin garter up high, Retro's. She stepped in carrying a fresh bottle of Moët, winking down at April, then smiling over her shoulder at the little foreigner, who wasn't smiling, whose eyes were on April as he closed the door.

FRIDAY

WHEN JEAN GOT home the outdoor faucet was still dripping under the stairs. She'd had to step over a puddle on the inlaid stone and had gone inside for her purse and now she paid the jazz-loving cabbie through his window, tipping him five dollars.

He thanked her and shifted the car into reverse. "You take care of yourself now."

His headlights blinded her a moment, then he was gone and she stood there in her darkened driveway wondering what he thought of her: Did he see a fat old widow? She didn't usually think like this when it came to men, but when he'd told her to take care of herself, it was sincere, as if she were as precious as the little girl she was going to take care of now.

The hose connection at the wall had been emitting a fine spray against the house for hours. She stepped into the puddle, stuck her head under the outdoor stairs, and patted around till she grasped the wet knob and turned it off. All was quiet. The dark garden at her back felt like a benevolent presence. She could smell the bougainvillea and hibiscus. She was still hungry.

Inside the kitchen, she stood at the open fridge and allowed herself a plum. The number of the Puma Club for Men was taped to the side of her refrigerator. Maybe she should call ahead? Tell April she was on her way. But what if April tried to talk her out of it? Tried to convince her this house mom had everything taken care of?

Jean switched on the front and rear floodlights and backed the DeVille out of the driveway. It was the last car Harry had ever bought, and whenever she thought of selling it, she could see his face looking hurt, and now she steered it past the dimly lit stucco and tile homes of her neighbors, people she'd yet to meet.

It was 12:17 on her digital clock, the numbers glowing blue-green across her lap. She wished she'd thought to ask the cabdriver for the call numbers of the station he was listening to; the jazz had calmed her, but she no longer felt calm; she was breathing fast, and a band of sweat had come out on her forehead. Maybe she *had* had a heart attack and was completely foolish to have left the hospital like that.

At the end of the street she stopped at Heron Way, the traffic lights of downtown on her left, to her right the empty street lined with towering palms all the way to the Gulf. She turned left, her breath caught somewhere high in her chest: What was she going to do when she arrived at this place in the darkness north of here? Just walk in and wade through what she imagined would be a smoky room full of raucous men, their eyes on her dancing naked tenant?

She stopped at the intersection of Heron Way and Washington Boulevard, looked out her window at the lighted Mobil station and convenience store where she bought her gas. A gray sports car was at the self-service pumps, and it was full of young people talking and laughing with one another. The driver's seat was empty. A lovely young woman stood at the trunk, one hand on the gas nozzle trigger, the other wrapped around a cellular phone she held to her ear. She was smiling, her long hair straight and shiny, her jeans tight the way they wore them now. She had youth, beauty, and that air of physical confidence that came from money.

A horn sounded behind Jean. She accelerated and turned north onto Washington Boulevard, her headlights sweeping over the turquoise glow of a motel's lighted swimming pool, and she knew that one day, perhaps one day soon, she wouldn't be leaving the hospital at all, a thought that, strangely enough, didn't frighten her so much; what frightened her more was not doing enough before then. Enough for Franny.

Y Y Y

AJ's TRUCK LIGHTS glinted off his mailbox and the corrugated roof there. Clay dust coated the post but the letters of his family name stood out clear and black, just the way he'd painted them. Lights shone in the house. Deena's Corolla was parked close to the front steps, and the plastic John Deere Santa'd brought Cole was facing the road, its decals catching the light from AJ's truck.

He switched them off and edged slowly, quietly, he hoped, up behind the Corolla. Over its top and into the curtained window was the flicker of the TV, though he could see only some of Deena's leg on the couch, a leg that stood with the other one, and he killed the engine, opened the door with his left hand, a fire flaring up through the bones of his arm into his shoulder. And the pint. Goddamnit but it turned over and clattered to the ground and now his pants were wet and whatever the Tums in his mouth were supposed to do about the smell was useless now.

Deena peered between the curtains out into the driveway. It was lit only by the light from the TV room, and she couldn't see past her own car, he was sure. He didn't want to spook her. Left his door half-open and moved fast around the front, his bumper almost touching hers, his legs squeezing between both as he slid through and stepped past Cole's toy and up onto the brick steps he'd laid himself as she flicked on the outdoor light he'd wired, and now her voice through the door he'd hung. Her fat, scared voice.

"Who's that?"

"Me, hon." He bit down on the Tums, chewed quickly, swallowed.

"AJ?"

"I want to see you, Deen. No hard feelings, 'kay? I just want to visit."

He heard TV voices. A fan going.

"You can't. You know you can't."

His wrist hurt more hanging like it was, but he left it there. His pants were wet against his leg, and he breathed deep through his nose, felt more tired and alone than he had in a long time. Maybe since he was a boy. Maybe then.

"AJ?"

"Yeah?"

"You hear what I said?"

"I heard you."

"You gonna leave?" TV sounds. A siren. Fake sounds filling up his real house.

"I'm hurt, Deen."

She didn't say anything. He pictured her standing there with her arms crossed looking down at the floor he'd installed, at the threshold he'd cut and fit and nailed.

"Deena?"

"Hurt how?"

"A disagreement."

She was quiet again. Just that damn TV and the faint hum of the air conditioner he'd put in Cole's room. The only one in the house and it cooled it all. A Sears Coolsport.

"AJ, don't make me call the cops."

The tightening again. This time a cord that seemed to pull straight up from his balls. He didn't know how much more he could take, and now his throat swelled and his face felt funny. "Deen? I need to put some ice on this. Something. I don't know. I need to see my *family*." His eyes began tearing up and he tried to fight them but they came anyway. Uninvited, unplanned for, a surprise to him and a shame and humiliation and he wasn't going to try and stop them or keep them quiet, just let them come because after five weeks away, five weeks pretending he didn't mind having all that weight fall off his shoulders, didn't mind being a single man again who didn't have to worry how unhappy she was and what she didn't do all day, who could stay out late running up bills at the Puma for a lying whore, who worked harder than ever all day and lied to himself that he wasn't going broke living this way, who lied to himself that he only missed his boy and not that woman standing on the other side of this door set in its frame in this cinder-block house they'd made into a home, then goddamnit let them come if they had to because they were real and it wasn't just a show.

Still, she wasn't opening that door. A door he could kick in with one shot because he never did put that dead bolt in—meant to—it was on his list—he just hadn't. And now this moaning and whining was coming out of him, and his wrist hurt so much he raised it up to get the blood out of it, and he was tired. Just so goddamned tired. It was like the weight had never left and now it was stacked on him high and heavy and he just had to lie down somewhere, but he was goddamned if he was going to let her hear any more of this, and he held his wrist and left his wet face unwiped and stepped off his stoop and missed the lip of the brick tread and stumbled forward, a sound still coming out of him as he got his balance, the hood of her Corolla glossy-looking.

"AJ?"

He turned. There she was in the doorway, the kitchen bright behind her. Her hair was curly now, a curly halo around her head. He wiped his eyes on the back of his good arm.

"You promise you won't start anything?"

He nodded, his throat a closed pipe in his sorry neck. She stood there looking at him, at his wet pants and swollen wrist he held up in the air. His eyes. She was barefoot and wore jeans and a big, loose T-shirt, her breasts hanging free underneath.

"Thank you." His voice broke on him. He was ashamed of himself and climbed back up on the stoop, was going to kiss her cheek or something but she backed into the house, holding the door like she didn't know if she'd shut it in his face or let him all the way in. Then he was inside, and he'd stopped his crying and just stood there in the kitchen's fluorescent light sniffling, taking in how clean everything looked, cleaner than when he'd been here—the dishes washed and stacked in the drainer, the countertops cleared and wiped down, the floor swept.

Deena looked closely at his wrist he'd forgotten he still held up. She touched it lightly with her fingertips, a soft burn. Her face was clean and free of makeup, her hair blond and fake at the ends of her curls. He could smell her; beneath all those new hair products that always smelled the same—was *her* smell, some woman-sweat center of her he'd never stopped loving. Never did.

"Place looks good."

She said something as she turned for the freezer door and pulled out an ice cube tray. He didn't know what she'd said, but it didn't matter. He'd forgotten the smell of his own home and now here it was like a gift somebody might jerk away any second—her good, greasy cooking, the fruity scent of the bubble bath she always gave Cole before bed, and something like cotton from who knows where: the pillows on the sofa, the clean sheets of their bed. The hallway was dark. He could see Cole's open doorway, the night-light stuck in the outlet there, a green and yellow palm tree.

Deena started dropping one cube at a time into a plastic Glad bag, the same kind she used to seal his sandwiches in. Behind her T-shirt her breasts swayed heavily and he felt that old desire for her, felt the dark hallway behind him, and he wanted to see his boy too, to kiss his forehead and kneel by his bed, to say a prayer for him, the kind he said every night from his mama's in Bradenton: *Dear Lord, forget about me if you have to, just take care of Cole, would you? Just please watch over him.*

"I'm not supposed to be doing this, you know." She zipped the bag shut and handed it to him. There was that tightening again. He was going to ask her, Why? 'Cause that order said he couldn't? *She's* the one took it out on him, didn't she? But he said nothing, took the ice bag and pressed it to his wrist, pressed all the words inside him back into their dark corners, too.

The ice felt good on his skin. He watched her turn on the faucet and run water over the half-empty tray. Her ass and hips were even bigger than before, and he felt sorry for her. Felt, too, as if he'd abandoned her, not just his wife but a friend, a friend in need.

"I *am* sorry for what I did, Deena. You gotta know that."

She turned off the faucet. "What?" She balanced the tray on her way to the freezer, glanced over at him, her round, sometimes pretty face studying him, her eyes narrowed.

"I said—"

"You said that the first time, AJ. I'm scared of you now." She opened the freezer door, pushed the tray in, said behind it: "I am." She shut the door and looked at him. "I'm scared of my own husband."

She looked like she might cry then but shook it off and moved by him to the small living room whose walls he'd framed and Sheet-rocked, had mudded, sanded, and painted. Did it all so they wouldn't have to look at painted concrete block, so it'd be more like a home. She sat herself down on the couch they'd bought new with the credit card he wouldn't be able to pay off for a long, long time, her eyes glancing back at the TV he hadn't paid off yet either, everything here from him and only him and she was scared? How about grateful?

How about goddamned *grateful*? There was a sudden tightening in his gut and across his sternum, the back of his neck. A tension only a deep holler could unwind, but he wasn't here for that; nope, there'd been enough of that.

He turned and walked down the hall to Cole's room.

"AJ?" Her voice high and nagging like it always was and she better not get up off her ass and try to stop him from looking in on his own son. The TV went silent, his hand cold against the pack on his wrist, just the drip and hum of Cole's air conditioner as AJ stepped through the doorway past the tiny lighted palm, Cole's bed right there in the shadows. A junior sleigh bed that had been Deena's when she was a girl, and they'd both painted it together on a tarp in the sun, listening to the radio, and now his son lay there on his back under a sheet and a bedspread covered with dinosaurs, his small chest rising and falling beneath the T. rexes.

His face was turned toward him, his eyes closed, his mouth half-open. It was like seeing the inside of himself somehow, the deepest center of who he, AJ, really was. He knelt on the floor. His knee pressed one of Cole's sandals. He dropped the ice pack and leaned forward and ran a finger along his son's forehead. Cole's eyes squeezed more tightly shut. He turned his face away. Cold fingers. AJ wedged them under his armpit, waited for them to warm up. Didn't want to wait. With his hurt hand, he reached out and ran a finger down his cheek.

A shadow fell over him, Deena's voice a whisper: "Please don't wake him up."

Why not wake him up? He doesn't want to see his own daddy? Doesn't miss him?

But she was right—he knew she was right. Wasn't worth much of a shit for a wife but she was a good mother, and maybe if he stood right now and did like she said, they'd get somewhere together. Somewhere better than this.

He stood. Couldn't see Cole's face too well now because of her shadow. But it was good standing here in this room. Just the two of them. Him and his boy. A man does everything he's supposed to-times ten—and fucks up once, maybe twice, and he loses it all.

All.

"Don't forget your ice." Not a nagging voice this time, not warm either but helpful. He squatted for it, took one last look at his son—his trusting profile as he slept—and backed out. She was just getting to the living room, her ass big and white under her T-shirt and shorts. He remembered how it felt in his hands, the warm womanly mass of it. He wanted her, hoped she might want him a little, too. She turned and crossed her arms and stood there on the linoleum he'd laid between the kitchen and TV room. Like she was stuck there and didn't know what to do or where to go next.

The Wild Turkey was starting to wear off. He pressed the ice to his wrist, wanted a cold beer but didn't want to ask for one in his own house.

"Your pants are wet."

"Yeah."

She gave him that look. Like he wasn't the man he tried to be and on good days felt he was. "I spilled something, Deen. That's all." He could hear the hardness in his voice and she looked a little skittish in the face of it, her shoulders hunching slightly. Like he'd done her a lot worse than he ever had. It wasn't fair she was scared of him. It hurt that she was.

"Do you mind if I sit, Deen? I just want to sit and talk, 'kay?"

Her eyes were on him as he walked over the blue rug he'd bought on sale at Home Depot, that he'd unrolled and tacked down and pinned with baseboards. The coffee table was covered with maga-zines, most of them the trashy kind full of movie stars. She had the stand-up fan going in the corner, its phony breeze rippling some of the pages, and next to the remote was a bowl of half-eaten ice cream, the spoon sitting in it.

"Go 'head, finish your ice cream."

"You want some?"

"I guess not." He wanted to ask her for a beer but she was already making her way to the couch and he didn't want to push it, so sat down where he always used to up against the arm under the lamp near the window. From here he could always see everything: the TV; what was going on in the kitchen; Cole playing on the floor; whoever might turn off the road into their driveway. The wind from the fan cooled him. The ice had killed the pain in his wrist. She took the ice cream and sat on the opposite end of the sofa, her eyes on the muted TV, a movie or one of the shows she liked, a bunch of good-looking doctors and nurses in an emergency room saving people and sometimes failing at saving people. He'd watched it with her a few times but didn't like seeing all the hurt everybody went through—car wreck and gunshot victims; cancer-ridden men and women and those with bad hearts; the drunk and insane, the stabbed, burned, and fallen. It was like watching your worst fears reeled out in front of you and he'd get up before it was over, check in on Cole, wash up, and check in on him again.

"You watching this, Deen? You can turn it back up if you want."

She looked over at him. Her mouth was set in a straight line, and again, he didn't mean to sound the way he did, as if he was giving her permission to do what she was already doing. She picked up the remote, clicked off the TV, sat there with her ice cream in her lap.

"You smell like a barroom, AJ. Is that where you've been going these days?"

Strip club, maybe. Not a barroom. "No. I haven't. Just spilled some on me." Her eyes were blue, a duller blue than Marianne's but blue all the same.

She raised a spoonful of ice cream, then lowered it back down, put the bowl on the table.

"You're behind in your payments, you know."

"Yes. I do know."

"My family's helping, but I hate going to them, AJ."

"You'll get it."

They were both quiet now. The fan whirred softly.

"Why don't you go to those anger meetings, AJ? You could see Cole then."

She was talking sweet, but that old bad feeling was rising up in him. He hated her right now sitting there with her hands in her wide lap, her ice cream melting in front of her. He rested the bag of ice on the back of a *TV Guide*. "Have I ever hit Cole, Deen? Or yelled at him? Or even raised my *voice*?"

She stared at the floor. Her back was straight and she looked scared, but he didn't really give a good goddamn except he wouldn't get anywhere with her like that, would he? He took a breath, let it out. "I'm just asking, Deena. Have I?"

"No. You're a good dad; everybody knows that."

"Do *you*?"

"Yeah." She glanced over at him, then away again. Shy, maybe. Maybe not. He could see her nipples behind her shirt. The wind from the fan was warm, and he scooted over, put his good hand on her bare knee. It was smooth and clammy and fleshier than Marianne's, but it was as familiar as anything he'd ever owned and worn or drove a long time and for a moment it was hard to remember how he'd ever been pushed away from its constant use. He touched her arm, let his fingers rest there lightly. "Except for what I did, I'm not a bad husband, am I?"

"No."

"Was I a good husband?"

A magazine cover flapped lightly in the breeze. He knew he'd pushed it too far with that one and wished he'd kept his mouth shut. She looked at him directly and it was like seeing her for the first time all over again, her eyes—for just a second—all round and blue and respectful. *Mr. Carey*. It was funny she'd called him that. But now an older, wiser light came into them and she looked away again.

"When you weren't mad all the time."

The magazine kept rippling. There was the whir of the fan blades, the far-off dampened hum of Cole's air conditioner. AJ's mouth was dry for a cold beer but he was thinking hard about what she said. Tried to remember being like that. Couldn't really.

"I wasn't mad *all* the time."

"Enough, though."

'Cause you went off to Fantasyland and never talked to me much any-more and looked at me like I was a nothing and spent my money on your stupid hair and never wanted to fuck—there was so much to say and more, but her arm was warm and she hadn't moved it and all he wanted to do was go lie in their bed together and talk later; talk, talk, talk it all away later.

From down the hall came a moan, Cole's small voice. Deena jerked her arm away and leaned forward. Cole said *Mama* and *truck*, a few more words AJ couldn't make out. But the sound of his son's voice cut through him and it seemed impossible that he'd been able to bear those endless days and nights he'd not heard it.

Deena sat back. "Talking in his sleep."

"How long's he been doing that?"

"Not long."

It was the kind of answer that pissed him off; how long was not long? Five days? Five weeks? Since he'd been gone, at least—he knew that.

This close he could smell her, Deena's smell, no one else's. It did something to him, had ever since they'd parked under a live oak tree off Myakka City Road and tore at each other in the cab of his truck. His wrist was throbbing again, resting there limp and thick on the cushion between them. He should put some more ice on it, he knew, but not now. Now there was his wife, unafraid and not bitching at him, not watching the TV or getting up to do something else. Just sitting there, stuck between two worlds. He reached up and touched her cheek. Warm and plenty of it. "I miss you, hon."

She blinked. Was she about to cry? He kissed her on the cheek-bone, the same one he'd blackened and blued. How could he have done that? How did he ever get to *that*? He breathed in her woman-smell, felt himself getting hard. His wrist pinched a bit but so what, and with his good hand he put his fingers to her chin, turned her face toward his. She closed her eyes. He leaned in, his lips parted.

"No, AJ. *No.*" She pulled away. Opened her eyes. Shook her head. She thrust her hands to her sides to push herself off the couch but one of them hit his wrist, then her weight was on it, flames raging up his arm bones into his shoulder and neck. His eyes began to water, and she was up, looking down at him, her hands on her hips, an angry female blur. "You think you can just drive up here drunk and every- thing's *okay?* You never *hit* me?" Her voice broke. She started crying, moving backward, one hand on her mouth, the other pointing at the door. "Get out. Please get out or I'll call the cops on you, AJ. I will, I'll call them right now."

It had to be broken. He could barely put his fingers around it. That big Chinese had started it and his beautiful wife had finished it and that's just how tonight was going to go, wasn't it? No sweet home- coming. No lying in your own bed with your own wife.

No Cole.

And it felt like a rabid dog was gnawing at his wrist. "You hurt my arm, Deen." She was still a blur he blinked at. He fumbled for the ice pack but couldn't even think of pressing it to his wrist, dropped it, got himself to stand.

"I didn't mean to, AJ, but maybe you should think about that. How's it feel when someone does that to you?" She kept crying, a low, mournful sound that made him feel sad and wrong and useless. He held his wrist up and walked around the coffee table past the blowing fan into the still air of the linoleum where she cried.

"You act like I'm a bad man, Deena. But I'm not. I'm not a bad man."

She shook her head, then sniffled and ran her finger under her nose, looked him in the face, hers puffy and plain but beautiful if you didn't think about it; hurt wrist or not, he still wanted her. He put his good fingers on her hip. She stepped back like she'd been burned.

"Just go to those classes, AJ."

Her face was tilted up at him, her chin exposed, her blue eyes rimmed with tears; he could see she loved him. She *did.* It confused him to see that and he could no longer look straight at her, lowered his eyes, saw her pudgy feet and toes, the nails newly painted a dark womanly red.

"You're supposed to go to thirty of them. Go to the first one is all I ask. Please."

"I'll go if you're asking me to, Deena, but not if you're telling me."

"I am asking, AJ. I am."

He looked back into her face. Saw a woman there. A woman who was probably stronger than he was. How did that happen? The thought left him feeling lonely. His arm buzzed and throbbed. "I need you, Deena. I really do."

She nodded at his wrist, red and swollen, fractured for sure. "You should go to the hospital for that."

"You hear what I said?"

"Yeah." She pushed open the screen door, held it for him. Her cheeks were damp, but she was done crying for now; he could see that. He stepped out onto his stoop and she let the screen door close behind him. Over her shoulder and down the hall, Cole's doorway was lit dimly from the night-light. He saw just the corner of his bed and wanted to go back there one more time. "It's not right I don't get to see my son."

She spoke quietly, steadily, carefully: "They said you could have those supervised visits when you start the classes."

Having to meet somewhere public while her folks watched everything he did with his own boy, sat there just to make sure he didn't touch Deena. He'd seen it in his head for weeks and that picture alone was enough to keep him from going to any damn classes. There was a sharp pounding in his wrist. He had to hold it up again.

"Call me after your first one." She wiped her nose on the back of her finger. "I'll let you talk to Cole. We'll set up a visit."

"Without your folks?"

"We'll see." She closed the door slowly, politely, the lock on the knob clicking into place. He stood there a moment. Felt like a man pushed out of his own boat into the black sea. The TV sound came back on but not loud enough for her to really hear it. Just a smoke-screen so he wouldn't think she was waiting for him to leave. He touched his wrist to his chest and walked directly to his truck, not looking back, squeezing between the bumpers of his F-150 and her Corolla. He couldn't get her face out of his head, all that hurt that could only come from loving somebody. All this time he was sure she'd kicked him out not because he'd hit her but because she didn't want him anymore—that was the real reason, and she even got the court to make it official. But climbing carefully into his truck, pulling the door shut with his right hand, the light from the TV room casting itself out toward him, it was as if he'd just gone to the big bad bank and gotten the promise of a whole new line of credit. And Deena was good for her word: one class; that's all he had to do. Just one.

He started her up and backed out of the driveway he'd lined with pavers. Out on the road, he shifted into drive and took one last look at his home, Deena standing in the window watching him, the blowing fan at her back, Cole sleeping safely and coolly in his concrete room. AJ flicked the lights in farewell, then the road was rolling out ahead of him and he knew he should go to the hospital, but first he needed cold beer and a handful of aspirin. And he thought of Marianne. It was wrong to think of her, but he did anyway.

T HE LOVE SEAT was crowded, Retro sitting between them, her bare leg pressing against April's.

The little foreigner had tossed the seven hundred dollars on the table so Retro could sit and now he seemed to forget about it. He sat against the arm, smoking, talking so low to Retro April heard only his murmur and the club music out on the floor. Except for her garters and high heels, she was naked. He had offered Retro a cigarette and she smoked it beside him, nodding her head at whatever he was saying, her hoops swinging slightly under her ears. April finished her champagne, reached into the ice bucket, and poured herself some more. She checked her customer's and Retro's, but they were still full, so she sat back and sipped, Retro's back to her, her warm brown thigh against hers.

At first she didn't like that he'd bought her for an hour too, but this one was odd and getting drunker and now it was nice just to sit back and let somebody else work him for a while. Retro was wearing her floor costume, a candy red miniskirt, red tube top, red garters, and red spikes. Four or five days a week at the beach with Franny had made April tanner than she'd ever been, but next to Retro's skin, hers looked pale. There was something deeply attractive about such dark skin. She'd always thought so.

Franny.

April wished she were back home with Jean and not sleeping in Tina's office, though the Moët had made her feel better, had slowed and blended all the sharp stops and starts of the night. She and Glenn used to drink together, before Franny. She never liked getting completely drunk, but this feeling, this gentle drift away from the shore of all the shit that always had to get done, felt sweet and she was even mildly disappointed her strange little customer hadn't asked her again why she did this. Because she had an answer for him. An honest answer, if he still wanted to know.

Did he want to know? She leaned forward and looked past Retro's smoothly muscled shoulder, the foreigner's eyes darting to hers. He nodded his head at something Retro said, then waved his hand and stood just long enough to clear off half the cocktail table, pushing aside the ashtray and cash, the empty snifters still sticky with Rémy. He sat there, then crossed his legs, the smoking cigarette between his lips and his eyes squinting out at them. He was drunker than she'd thought he was. Retro lay her hand on April's leg and squeezed.

"What do you want us to do, honey? Huh? What do you want to see?"

"Nothing. I want to see nothing."

"Really?" Retro sounded skeptical, her hand still on April, a warm weight she could feel all the way to her belly. The foreigner was studying her now, his eyes on her face, her nipples. He looked at them for what seemed a long time. The hundred-dollar bills were spread out beside him, one of them on its side against the ice bucket. It was hard not to look at them. She hoped he wasn't so drunk he'd forgotten their deal.

"Nothing, huh, baby?" Retro lifted her left thigh and rested her spiked heel on the table next to his leg. She let her right fall open, but he didn't look down at her brown belly or her crotch. He blew out smoke, stubbed the butt on the table, burning the corner off one of the bills.

"What is your real name?"

"We can't tell, honey, it's against the rules." Retro forced a laugh. Her hand lifted away from April and moved to him. She began to run her fingers in a circle over his knee.

"Do not touch me, please."

"C'mon, baby."

With his thumb and forefinger he gripped her wrist, picked her hand off him as if it were something poisonous, and dropped it over her spread legs.

"Tell him your name, Retro. He'll pay you for it."

"Only if she does not lie."

"How're you going to know, honey?"

"He'll know."

"No, I do not need this one's name."

"But you just asked me." There was a smile in Retro's voice, but the sassiness that'd been there a second ago was gone. Her hand lay on the cushion where he'd dropped it.

He shook out another Marlboro. "Remove this clothing, please."

Retro stood and began swaying her hips in time to the club music out on the floor.

"No, do not dance."

Retro stopped, her massive hoops catching the light in the smoke above April.

"Look, honey, I dance. If you don't want the *dance*, then you gotta *pay*."

He looked at April, his eyes dropping to her crotch. They lingered on the scar from Franny. He picked up a single bill and held it up to Retro. "Answer my question and you receive this."

She reached out for it, her fingers on it, his fingers still on it.

"Ask away, little man."

"What will happen for you after you die?"

"That's a little creepy, honey, but, you know—worm food, baby. I'll just be worm food." She pulled on the bill. He didn't let go.

"What does this mean?"

"It means we're just food for the worms, honey. You know, those little snakes with no eyes? Worms."

He held on to the hundred and he began to laugh. It was a tired, drunk, cruel laugh, and he shook his head and let go of the bill and Retro folded it lengthwise and snapped it under her garter.

He stopped and nodded, his eyes on her chest. "Clothing, please."

"Sure thing." Retro glanced down at April sitting there with her champagne, watching her, and April felt like an accomplice to some hostile action against her. Retro stepped over their legs and undressed quickly against the wall, leaving on her G-string, garters, and spikes, her hoops swinging back and forth. April had seen her breasts dozens of times, but here, in this tiny room under the smoky light on this cheap black love seat, drinking Moët, it was as if she'd never seen them before, small and beautiful, her nipples the color of tree bark. April looked away from them.

"Everything, please." He picked up another hundred-dollar bill, pointed it like a pistol at Retro's G-string.

"That's my sweet spot, honey. You want the sweet spot, you got to give me more than that."

"I have already paid for that, yes? I do not have to give anything more to see that."

"Only if we dance, honey, but you don't want the dance."

He sat straight at the edge of the table. He looked directly at April's face, and in his eyes was a hard, accusatory light. He picked up his lighter, flicked open a flame, and held it to the hundred-dollar bill.

"Mike," April said. "Don't do that."

"You see, I do not care for money as you do. I do not."

The bill flamed up immediately. Retro jerked it from his fingers

and blew it out, smacking and rubbing it against her hip, holding it up
to the light, a quarter of it gone. He picked another hundred off the
table and held it over the flame.

"Shit." Retro dropped the burned bill, hooked her thumbs under
the straps of her G-string, pushing it down her long legs, stepping out
of it, kicking it behind her onto her mound of red clothes. Her crotch
was only inches from April's face and she could smell it, the scent of
swamps, of fertile, wet, dark places where life comes from, and like
most of the girls, Retro was shaved, just a narrow strip of hair riding
up from her clit over her pubic bone. April didn't turn her head and
knew she was a little drunk: she let herself look at it as long as she
wanted.

Mike the foreigner handed Retro the bill, then gave her a second
one, too. "Thank you." She folded and wedged them under her right
garter and sat back down between them. One of the bills lightly poked
April's thigh.

She sipped her Moët. Retro's hip was warm against her. He held
the bottle by the neck and poured more champagne into both their
glasses, his eyes flitting from April's crotch to Retro's and back.

"They cut a baby from you, yes?"

The question made her feel more naked than being naked, and she
couldn't answer. Tried to nightsmile at him. Nodded.

"And you," he said to Retro. "You are mother?"

"Why do you want to know, little man?"

He put another cigarette between his lips. "Open your legs."

"Ask nice, honey."

He looked over at April, his eyes softer now, as if she were an old
friend he expected to help him. He gathered up the remaining bills
and wadded them into a tight crinkled ball and pushed them into
Retro's palm. She said nothing, just opened her legs and flashed him
some pink, her thigh across both of April's, her other hooked over the
opposite arm of the love seat. The club's music was country again,
Sadie already back on. One man whooped and there was a lot of roll-

ing drums and fast-picking guitar, and Retro was trying to look like she was excited, tilting her head back, rubbing herself lightly with two fingers, Mike staring hard at what she'd parted for him.

He didn't look quite as drunk now. His eyes were softer and he looked years younger. Like a kid, really. And Retro's skin against hers had felt nice, but now her leg was heavy and made April feel hemmed in. She just kept looking at the table, empty of the one-hundred-dollar bills she'd hoped would be hers.

▾ ▾ ▾

A TINY LIGHT UNDER the stairs. She gets on her hands and her knees like Jean's cat and there's a place there. Far away a door opens and closes and a grown-up's legs walk from the dark into the light. She can crawl under there. She just has to make herself small and she's not scared. She's not. She crawls into the wide low place and the floor is hard and dusty and the music isn't loud anymore but above her the wood squeaks under somebody walking or running. Her hand touches something, a long piece of wood that doesn't move. But it's not big and she crawls over it. Dusty dusty. Makes her want to cough. The music stops and she can hear only voices, feet squeaking over her head. How will Mama find her here? Loud music comes again and more feet squeaking over her head. So close. She sits on the piece of wood and reaches her hand up into the darkness and her fingers touch more wood.

She crawls.

More long wood pieces, but she's only a little afraid. *Do your best, sweetie. Just do your best.* And it's not far away. She's so close now so soon. She smells food like she ate for supper like she and Mama buy sometimes at the window the man gives them French fries through to their car. Boys smiling at Mama. And this hole is a square. A small square. The door opening and closing and opening. The light and smells on the other side. Another curtain too. The party over there she wasn't going to. And she sits like an Indian by the square in the wall by the stairs. A lady pushes through the curtain and she's carrying glasses on a big round plate and she pushes open the door to the light. A shiny metal oven, and a man takes the glasses and Franny doesn't want to go in there now. But she can't go back into the dark place. Her face is hot, her eyes burning wet, and she shouldn't make noise. She just shouldn't.

⌄   ⌄   ⌄

IN THE COOL darkness of his truck cab AJ's wrist was a swollen hurt he rested palm-up on his leg. The beer was cold, the can beaded with condensation, and every time he sipped off his Miller he pressed his knee to the wheel to stay on Washington Boulevard, Bob Seeger singing about being all alone again up on the stage. But AJ still had that good new feeling about Deena, that maybe she *did* love him and would wait there for him after all, that he'd get Cole back in his arms again and probably Deena, too; he was glad he'd disobeyed that damn order and gone home but now he couldn't stop thinking of Marianne, seeing her the way he first had under blue light, smiling shyly and shaking her tits at him. Nothing but a girl. It was her hand he kept seeing, her outstretched palm waiting to get paid even after that big sonofabitch bent and twisted his wrist till it'd surely cracked.

He drained his beer and tossed the empty over his shoulder where it landed on two others in Cole's car seat. A mile up ahead, for the fifth time in half an hour, were the yellow lights of the Puma sign rising up over the shell lot of cars and pickups and vans. AJ pushed on the gas, his F-150 responding like a gun. Under the canopy were three or four men yukking it up over some lying whore, and at the entrance was one of the hired T-bones smoking a cigarette, Sledge or Skeggs or something, nothing but whiskers and muscle and bad breath, the one who'd held open the door when the big chink tossed AJ out like trash.

AJ shot by the lighted club back into the darkness of Washington Boulevard. The big man had looked out at him like he was a problem he didn't need, but goddamnit, AJ didn't need for his wrist to be broken either, and unless he went into work tomorrow and made like he hurt it there, he wouldn't get a decent paycheck for as long as it was going to take to get better. He tried to picture it, how he was going to hide this swelled up useless limb. The CAT was at the job site, a municipal drainage ditch out on Lido Key. He'd get there before Caporelli's piece-of-shit son did; he'd toss the short-handled spade into the ditch, then lower the bucket and climb down in there and wedge his wrist under it. When Caporelli drove up AJ would yell to him that he was pinned, that he'd gone down to clean the teeth when the bucket dropped on him. He'd yell at Junior to get in the cab and free him.

That'd work. Especially with Caporelli Jr., just another lucky sonofabitch born into a cozy situation he never earned. He was five or six years younger than AJ and drove a V-10 he didn't need, not a chain or single tool in it, and he kept it shiny and spent most of the day in his air-conditoned cab talking on his cell phone to his girlfriend or his sports bookie. AJ'd have him drive to the hospital in Sarasota, let the Caporellis pay for everything, including the time he'd have off, a few weeks anyway.

He wanted another cold beer, but the pain had flattened out enough, and again, there was the feeling his luck was changing; with that kind of paid time off he could go to that one damn class and let them say what they were going to say and then Deena would call off the wolves and he could see Cole again. He could still hear his son's voice as it'd sounded in his sleep, that high, pure, ever-hopeful voice of the child he'd be happy to die for. *Happy* to. And tonight, after five long weeks, there was the feel of his smooth cheek, the way his hair had smelled so clean, these thoughts spilling outside into the headlight path of his truck, the long wire grass on both sides of the road, the empty beer cans, a flattened cigarette carton, the matted fur husk of a long-dead animal.

Up ahead were the hazy security lights of the industrial park buildings on the north and southbound sides. When he was Cole's age there was nothing out there but stands of slash pine and clusters of cabbage palm and saw palmettos, him and Mama driving home after her shift as a chambermaid at the big resort on Longboat Key. She'd be in her white blouse and black skirt, fifty already, smoking one Tareyton after another, looking old and dried up to him even then. And he didn't remember much now, but she'd said they let her take him in the rooms and clean with her, said he liked to toss the damp towels into the hamper, that he took pride in changing the toilet paper rolls on the pins set into the wall. And there were the later years working with his stepdaddy in Myakka City. Home repairs for old people mostly, replacing rotted sills under their houses, laying porcelain or ceramic tiles in their moldy bathrooms, building new porches and decks, patching their roofs, stringing a line and digging postholes and erecting steel or cedar fences, and all the while Eddie'd go out to the van every half hour or so for a nip of vodka or gin whose smell he'd mask with Wrigley's and cigarettes. By the end of the day he'd be red-faced and more tired than he should but laughing and telling loud lies to the old people while AJ cleaned up and put away their tools and, at fourteen, fifteen, sixteen, drove the van home.

And then one Friday morning, Eddie was just a stiff lump under the covers of Mama's bed and AJ got a night job after school down at Walgreen's pharmacy and was even better at numbers and inventory than he was with his hands and they were going to send him to school for more training, put him in charge of an entire store one day, maybe a chain, but there was Deena and her smell and the two of them claw-ing to get inside one another and now AJ's left hand felt like sausages about to burst over a fire.

He'd always worked. His whole goddamned life he had worked and worked and goddamned worked. He couldn't remember ever having time off. Ever. And he just wanted a rest, a place to rest that wasn't the foldout bed in Mama's condo. Marianne's skin and hair, her big, soft eyes. The way she'd look right at him when he talked about Cole, how she'd hold his hand with her small fingers, how, before tonight, she'd seem to look at him with admiration. Respect.

Had he scared her that much? Did he squeeze her hand that hard?

He slowed and checked his rearview mirror, turned into the median strip. He had to apologize. It was wrong of her to take his money when he was hurt like that, but still, he should apologize. Maybe she would too.

AJ felt like the one at the poker table who all night long gets noth-ing but shit cards he still has to play. But there was the new promise of Deena and Cole back home, some paid time off from Caporelli, and he felt the sparking hope not of the lucky but of the one who works at it, the one who watches and keeps track of the numbers and knows there're at least two jacks and one king left in the dealer's deck.

His truck rocked in and out of a rut, then leveled out onto flat asphalt, and he gave it the gas, the engine under his hood roaring like a loyal ally.

Y Y Y

THE JAZZ CALMED Jean quite a bit, and the station wasn't hard to find, the brushes on the high hat, the low, soothing clarinet. Still, she'd broken out into a clammy sweat and had already driven twice by the yellow neon sign of the Puma Club. Its parking lot was full of men and cars, the actual business just a low, single-story structure with no windows. Driving north, it was to her left on the other side of the median. Heading back south now, it was at her right, much closer, and as she approached it she could see the long covered walkway to the pink doors of the entrance, a pink that opened and shut obscenely.

Some riffraff smoked cigarettes against a pickup truck and watched her drive by in her locked Cadillac. There was still time to turn into the parking lot but she accelerated instead, feeling queasy and cowardly. There was a steady weight on her chest now. She turned up the soft jazz and breathed deeply through her nose. *It's just nerves, that's all. It's not your heart, you fat old goat. Just your nerves.*

On either side of the boulevard were the black reaches of the countryside. All weed and trees that in a few years would be transformed into subdivisions. She knew that was April's dream, to buy a place for her and her daughter. She'd never talked about it with Jean, but Franny did; rolling red and yellow Play-Doh in a ball she poked window holes and a door into, she said, "You'll visit us when me and Mama buy our house, right?" Or early one morning when she was helping Jean water the plants and flowers, upending a small pitcher Jean had bought her, "Will you make us a garden like this in our new house?"

Of course I will, sweetie. Of course.

Up in the distance the security lights of the industrial park glowed brightly over low concrete buildings, businesses that probably made microchips and Styrofoam padding, plastic brooms and office chairs, the kind of objects one eventually needed but rarely thought about. The compound was devoid of any beauty whatsoever and put Jean in mind of prisons and punishment and bad behavior. She felt afraid for Franny all over again and ready or not, panicked or not, she was going to drive back to that place and walk through that obscene pink door and take her.

⌄ ⌄ ⌄

LONNIE LOOKED OUT over the crowded floor, past the smoky blue lights of the VIP half wall where Zeke was leaning with Paco, pretending not to watch any of the girls. Andy sat on his stool, just a black shape with a big, pale head. What could Spring have done for two hours in there with her little customer? Her daughter. She'd asked him to check in on her and he hadn't had time to. But Tina had. She'd come down from Louis's office and gone back there. Then she was in the VIP bar for a while talking to the new girl in the shadows. Then she went back up to Louis's office. Maybe Lonnie should go take a look. How old could Spring's daughter be anyway? And did that mean she was married? Did Spring live with someone?

Lonnie pushed himself away from the bar, but down at the apron of the stage one of the Portofino boys was raising his voice at another, his eyes dark and narrowed, and Lonnie waited to see if it was a pocket or just drunk bullshit he could ignore.

How tired he was becoming of all this. Used to be he only thought about moving on during his off days, when he was alone and a great yawning emptiness would blow in on him and with every breath it'd be deeper inside him, this wide-open question as to just what he was doing here? Not in the club or even the Gulf Coast, not in all the places he'd drifted to and from—three universities, one in Austin where his old man worked, the others in New Jersey and here in Florida, all the class discussions where he held his own, questioning everything from Weber's "Theory of Bureaucracy" to the interlocking directorates of corporate boardrooms to the rise of postmodernism, whatever the hell that was, because he hardly knew. Whatever he knew, or thought he knew, came not from books but from class lectures he dutifully recorded in all the misspelled words only he could decipher. Such an irony, the son of the bookish man not being able to read books; but words were beautiful to Lonnie, as sounds, as airy vowels and iron consonants, as things to memorize and chew on later because he couldn't read like the others, never could. A word another's eyes passed over easily—*thorough* or *skate*—became math problems he had to solve before he could move on. Instead of seeing a graceful row of letters symbolic of specific sounds, he saw the broken arms and legs of insects, a pile of them that had to be put back together before their message could move and shine.

He loved music, though, and listened to it all the time. Tall and flunking at nearly everything but algebra and geometry, he walked the halls of his youth wearing Walkman headphones, his world suffused with Springsteen, Berlin, Mozart, 'Til Tuesday, Albinoni, the Clash. And Lonnie attracted women. Not those who shined so prettily at the top of the heap but the castoffs at the bottom like him, smart girls who smoked too much and didn't mind a warm beer on a cool afternoon out in the sage grass, who liked music as much as he did and liked even better how he moved to it, gently pulling them in one at a time, one or two seasons at a time, rocking to it, pushing himself inside till they were just one thumping note reaching a crescendo and he'd let go.

Some loved him, and over the years, as high school gave way to colleges which gave way to work, he came close to loving them back. In their presence, sitting in a booth over eggs and coffee or driving down the highway together or just lying in bed right before sleep, most times he felt a great tenderness for whomever he was with, for each hair, each blink of her eye, each tiny blemish or line in her skin. He'd be drawn to her voice and the smell of her breath, the sound of her car pulling up in front of the house, her dirty underwear balled up on the floor, her dusty bureau cluttered with whatever filled it: with one it was useless receipts, a hairbrush and coated rubber bands, an overflowing ashtray; with another it was tip money, a cell phone and pack of cigarettes; with one other, no clutter at all, just a cotton doily spread across it ready to receive nothing. And still, he loved them, or thought he did till they needed gold proof, and in days or weeks he'd be gone.

He planted trees in shopping malls in New Jersey. Drove a vending machine truck in Austin. Flipped rugs for prospective buyers in a carpet boutique in Houston. He'd rent one- or two-room places in neighborhoods people seemed to avoid, and at night he'd listen to music or books on tape.

Early on he discovered he had a high tolerance for being alone, preferred it really. Though come Saturday night that always changed. He'd want good live music, bourbon and cold beer, and when he found all three, he needed a woman to dance with, maybe take home if she wanted; sometimes he'd want it too, but that was hardly ever his first intention when he went out at night. He saw men like that all the time, though. At the bar or lounging around the pool tables or sitting near the band, they wore too much jewelry around their neck and wrists, their work watches left at home for a shinier mall model. Their shirts were ironed and their hair was cut just right, a lot of them carefully gelled and spiked. You could smell their aftershave above the cigarette smoke and they had the furtive, calculated look in the eye of young hunters.

And maybe because he did not look like them, maybe because he'd go out in a T-shirt, loose jeans and work boots, sometimes needing a shave, always needing a haircut, because he was so intent on the lead singer singing and the bass guitarist and drummer keeping time, he attracted women he wasn't even looking for; alone or taken, pretty and otherwise, they'd dance and drink and dance some more. He'd buy drinks and light cigarettes and they'd lean toward each other and talk. One of the lone dogs might come near right about then, another of them once again not seeing much when they looked at tall, rangy Lonnie who'd gone and snared their prey without the license they'd dressed and preened for.

And let them come sniffing. If she wanted one of them instead, if she went out on the floor and didn't come back, that was fine, too. He'd return to his music and Maker's Mark and let the night go where it went.

But if she didn't want the LD, Lonnie didn't mind asking him to move on. Some of them did. Quite a few didn't. He'd wait, say it again, and so often there'd be no more waiting and what he said got lost in all the movement after, the lone dog falling backward into a parting crowd in the joyful noise of a Saturday night band in a dark barroom, his arms spread all loose-jointed and useless, his mouth an oval hole of shock and surprise, the last thing Lonnie usually saw before he'd be asked to leave or leave on his own. Sometimes the woman would follow him out, more interested in him than before. Other times she'd move away as if *he* were the dog, one you thought you wanted to pet until it bared its fangs.

One, a short, muscular beauty up in New Jersey, followed him out and took him home. She lived in a condominium complex called Jersey Shores, and on her walls were framed photographs of her two grown children. In the fluorescent light of the kitchen where she poured them wine, he could see her face fully for the first time. She was ten years older than he'd thought, fifty-three or -four, her curly hair touched with gray. She washed his cut knuckles in the kitchen sink, his blood running over a plate and glass, and she dried his hand with a clean dish towel, squeezed his fingers, and led him down a hallway to her room where she undressed him as if he were a boy.

Later, lying in bed, their sweat drying, his arms and legs spent and tired, she said, "Where's all that anger come from?"

"Anger?"

"When you hit that poor slob."

"I wasn't angry." He noticed how the light from the hallway cast itself across the bed, how it cut them each in two.

"You weren't? You hit him really hard."

"Just to take the fight out of him."

"You fight a lot?"

"I wouldn't call it that." And he wouldn't. Just punching. Throwing punches at a live target because it had presented itself that way: a man's face reduced to two moist eyes, a beckoning nose, and inviting teeth; so you set your weight on your back foot and drop your shoulder and let it fly, for once nothing complicated or interrupted or pent up in you, just the sweet thrust of forward momentum that could make your point like nothing else.

Mornings after, he'd have a dry mouth and heavy head and feel badly about hurting another human being, though the clarity of his remorse was always clouded by some degree of athletic pride, knowing he'd hit his mark with the exact right force at the exact right time. Still, he'd tell himself to avoid doing it in the future and he'd go weeks, sometimes a couple of months, without any trouble. But there were so many men out there looking for it, he was like a dieter stepping each Saturday night into a full-course buffet of steaming entrées and desserts spread out before him on pressed linen.

Louis saw him then, in Houston on one of those nights. It was in a hotel bar near the Galleria mall in the theater district, one of the last places Lonnie hadn't been 86ed, and there was no band, just a mediocre piano player who flowed without shame from Neil Sedaka to Brubeck to Billy Joel. The bar was half-full with men and women passing through on business, the men's ties loosened, the women in skirts and heels, some of them on cell phones or answering pagers, an empty glass in their free hand.

Most of these people weren't much older than Lonnie but they looked thousands and thousands of dollars richer, and while he didn't want to be like them, throwing their lives away pursuing money and all they believed they could buy with it, he'd sip his bourbon and chase it with cold beer and watch them chat and laugh, and he'd feel the way he often did as a kid, as if he had shown up at a party that was already in full-swing and to which he hadn't been invited and never would. Not simply because he was not like them but because they had the easy confidence of master players in a game whose rules they knew by heart when Lonnie had never fully understood the point: there was hard work you did to survive; there was the occasional test of what you can do that not many men can; there was good music, good books and bourbon, every few weeks a woman. But that night, just as his mood was lifting from self-pity to a semi-bitter superiority over them all, a woman to his right jerked away from the man beside her, her face pale and drawn.

"Let *go* of me." Her shoulders were hunched slightly. A tiny silver earring swayed above the silk collar of her blouse. The man was a low-voiced presence Lonnie stepped away from the bar to better see, a handsome alpha dog, his black hair coiffed, his jaw straight and clean-shaven. He wore a dark blue suit that fell over his physique like an advertisement, and he was leaning close to the woman, squeezing her upper arm, his mouth an inch from her ear. Lonnie tapped him on a knuckle. "She said to let go."

The man took him in as if he were somebody's unruly child he shouldn't even have to talk to. "She's my *wife*, so go fuck yourself."

Later, his heart still beating in his chest like a one-winged bird, standing on the sidewalk in the moist belly of a Houston Saturday night, the bar manager watching him from the door, Lonnie was again surprised at how fast it always went—Words, Action, Reaction, then his ass once more out on the street. He'd laugh if his superior mood hadn't dissipated so completely. He'd smile and shake it off and go someplace new. But where was that? He'd outstayed his welcome in just about all of downtown. Would he have to drive out to the honky-tonks where his habit would surely get him killed? Because he could only go so long doing what he did before he got himself shot or stabbed. Maybe tossed in a cell somewhere.

And he'd miscalculated a bit this time too; the first right had caught Alpha in the side of the head, snapping it sideways, his shoulders slumping, his knees going, but the second caught only half his nose, and when Lonnie pulled back for a third, his knuckles grazed the ear of the shrieking woman he was standing up for, her earring flying. And now it was clear the bar manager, who had smelled like spearmint gum and body odor, was waiting for the Houston Police, and Lonnie wedged his hands into his pockets and started walking, his fingers swelling up.

"Hey." A man leaned against one of the hotel's columns smoking a cigar. He was decked out in pleated silk pants, an open-collared print shirt, and woven leather sandals. Around his neck and wrists were flashes of gold, his red hair slicked back. He held a business card out to Lonnie. "Take it."

And for nearly two years now Lonnie had been his main closer just because Louis had been west for a family wedding and a fucking inboard motor boat show and he'd seen Alpha Dog drop between the barstools like a pile of wet rags and Lonnie had moved to Florida because why not? But Lonnie was tired of barstools, tired of dropping men like Dolphins Cap and others like him. He'd never been superstitious but more and more over the months, this deep, wide emptiness inside him had darkened with hints of danger ahead; how long could he go before the pocket he tried to close didn't close, before the man he tried to drop wouldn't drop, or if he did drop, who's to say he wouldn't come gunning for him? Last winter a closer at a club in Venice got himself shot in the face. He lived, but half his jaw was gone and wasn't ever coming back.

And this time of night was the worst, an hour to go before lights-up when pockets were opening and closing all over the main floor, so much cigarette and cigar smoke in the air it burned your eyes, the dancers working hard to get men to the VIP for a private. At the end of the night a few would actually hand him a ten spot, that's it, when it was supposed to be five percent.

Only Spring passed out the right money on a regular basis. The second thing Lonnie had noticed about her, that she was honest and looked him in the eye when she tipped him and thanked him like she meant it. The way she held her chin up like she had nothing to be ashamed of ever, and that dark light in her eyes—warm, smart, and a little wounded. That's the first thing he'd noticed about her. That was the first thing, and now it was the last, and he took it with him most nights to sleep.

✓ ✓ ✓

"ENOUGH." THE FOREIGNER looked bored with Retro and what she showed him. He stood and pulled out all those hundreds, handing her three. "More drinks, please." Retro closed her legs. She stood slowly, giving him a long, cool look April could only see in profile. She watched Retro step into her red mini and shimmy into her tube top. On her way out Retro nodded at April like she'd better not let this little shit get the best of her.

"She will do anything for money, yes?"

April was a little drunk. She didn't plan to drink anymore, no matter how many times he tried to fill her glass. She shrugged and didn't answer him, but she had a good thirty minutes to go before she could check on Franny and that money in his hand was all she could think of. He was looking at her breasts, her crossed legs. Her face.

"Do you believe in nothing?"

"I believe in some things."

"What please?"

"Like keeping your word, Mike. I believe in that."

"What does this mean?" He was squinting at her, though the smoke in the room had cleared.

"You asked me why I danced." She nodded at the wad still in his hand. "You put eight of those down and asked me."

"But I know why it is for you doing this, April."

"Spring."

"April." He stood and sat back down on the love seat, the cash in his hand. So much of it. "Stand, please."

She didn't feel like standing. He pulled a hundred from the fold and dropped it in front of her.

Such easy, easy money. That's how she had to keep looking at it. She folded the bill into her garter, then set her glass on the table and stood, her crotch level with his face. He was looking up into her eyes. She could see how his hair was thinning prematurely at the top, his scalp smooth and brown in the recessed light. Again, he seemed like a boy, one who'd been curious about things and was now filled with a sadness that had turned hard. She wasn't afraid of him anymore. She almost felt like reaching down to run her fingers back through his hair, comfort him the way she would her own child. Then his fingertips pressed against her scar through her pubic hair and she stepped back, a band of heat prickling along the skin of her throat.

"No touching, Mike. You know that." She smiled. It was a stiff, half nightsmile and she was suddenly cold again, her nipples bunching up. She wanted to cross her arms.

"For enough money, you will allow me for touching you anywhere, yes?"

"No, not me. Go get one of the other girls for that. I don't do that."

He smiled, letting his bad teeth show. For the first time all night he looked genuinely pleased about something. He kept his eyes on hers and separated three more hundreds from the fold. Two drifted down onto the black cushion, the other bent over itself and fell to the floor.

"What's that for, Mike?"

"For that." He nodded at her crotch.

"What?"

"Where they cut you."

"It's just a scar. You don't want to touch a scar."

Two more hundreds floated and spun like playing cards onto the other two. Six hundred. He was crazy in some way, and unless he came back and did this again, she would never have another night like this ever.

"Why do you want to touch it?"

"I do, that is all."

"I need to know first. Or I can't do it."

"Know. Why do you need to know? You know nothing."

"About you?"

"About nothing."

"Why do you want to touch it, Mike?"

"I will touch it if I want to touch it, you know this, yes?"

"I'd have to call Andy. That wouldn't be good."

"Good? I can kill that man in many different ways, April. Do you want to know how many?"

The door opened, Retro swaying in with fresh Moët and Rémy, Celine Dion belting out her tune behind her.

"It's hopping out there, y'all. It is *hoppin'*." She squatted and set the Rémy down. There were three or four twenties in her fist, and she filled each of their flutes with Moët, April's bubbling over the rim. She watched it pool around her glass while Retro pushed the bottle deep into the bucket.

"Thank you, you may please leave now."

"'Scuse me, honey?" Retro cocked her head to the side, her earrings swinging.

He put a Marlboro between his lips. He nodded at the change she still held. "You may keep that."

"What's the matter, little man? You don't like black girls?"

"I like them, yes. Only I don't like you."

"That makes two of us, honey." Retro shot April a cold glance. She picked up her champagne glass and walked out, leaving the door open, April's face flushed as if she'd just betrayed her somehow. She could hear men hollering out there for Wendy's act and she felt a twist inside her to leave too, go back to the dressing room and check on Franny. She was probably still asleep, but with all the noise maybe she wasn't.

"Secure the door." He lit his cigarette, sat back, crossed his legs. She moved around the table under the light and closed it.

"Why don't you like her, Mike?"

He was studying her again, his elbow on the arm rest, the cigarette's smoke rising up past his face. "Because she shows me nothing."

"I thought she showed you a lot."

"No, I do not want that."

"Then why do you come here?"

He blew out a long, thin stream of smoke. "Because it is allowed."

"Allowed?"

"Yes, it is allowed for me, so I come."

"Allowed by who?"

"You would not understand."

"Your wife?"

"No, I have no wife. I will never have a wife."

"Never?"

"Do you not want this?" He left his cigarette between his lips and gathered the bills up off the cushion beside him and tossed them onto the table.

She glanced down at the one on the floor at his feet. "Yes."

"Please, come."

Her heart began beating faster. She uncrossed her arms away from her breasts and walked around the table, standing where she'd been before Retro came back. She'd never let any customer touch her before, not since the Empire where she'd had to do lap dances in the VIP, grinding herself against hard-ons under zipped pants, telling herself she wasn't a whore as long as she didn't touch them with her hands and they didn't touch her with theirs, she wasn't. Under her bare feet was one of the hundreds. Mike seemed to have forgotten about it.

"You will let me touch that and you will tell me why you think you do this and I will give you your dirty money."

"My scar?"

"Yes."

"No one's ever touched that but me, Mike." It was true, not even Glenn. Her mouth was dry. She could feel her heart beating in her head. She nodded at the cash. "That's not enough."

A hard knocking at the door. "Fifteen minutes. Everything cool?"

"Yep."

"Spring? Everything cool?"

"Yes, Andy!" The club noise thrummed on the other side of the walls, Andy's massive weight squeaking on the floorboards as he lumbered back to the VIP.

"You think he is here for protecting you, but he is not."

"You've never seen him throw anybody out."

"He only has power if I care what happens to me; he is not here to stop me from hurting you. I could have done that one thousand times. He is here only to punish me *after* for hurting you."

"That stops most people, Mike."

"Only you kufar." He stubbed out his cigarette in the full ashtray, exhaled out his nostrils twin trails of smoke. "You are in love with living, and you have no God."

"Some of us have a God."

"Then why do you worship your prophet? He was not the son. There is only one Allah and He had no son. These are your gods." He picked up his cash, handed all of it to her. "Here, take your gods. As much as you wish. I do not care."

"I don't believe you don't care." She took the stack of hundreds, her fingers trembling slightly.

"You see how you shake? You are in the presence of your gods. But I can burn your gods. You have seen me burn your gods."

"Why?" She didn't want to take time to count it out; he could change his mind any second, the way he had about Retro. She separated a half or three-quarters of an inch from the rest, handing it back to him, folding the money and dropping it onto her skirt and blouse on the floor behind her. Two or three thousand for sure. It was hard not to smile at him. "That's why you don't care about money, Mike. You have enough of it."

"My name is not Mike."

"I know."

"My name is Bassam."

"That's a nice name."

"Come here."

She stepped closer, a flutter inside her.

"Sit, please."

"Just the scar, okay?"

"Yes."

She sat beside him. He put two fingers to her shoulder and gently pushed her back. Both her feet were on the floor, her knees together, and this was an uncomfortable position to be in but she didn't want to lift her leg and give him a look at what he hadn't paid for.

He was staring at her pubic hair, the short horizontal scar beneath it. She thought of Franny yesterday at Siesta Key, letting the white sand sift through her fingers over and over again. Now his fingers passed over the knotted line of skin they'd pulled her from three and half years ago, how they botched the sewing job, Glenn sitting beside her, useless.

"It is very small."

She didn't speak. She hoped he'd forgotten the rest of their deal, that she didn't have to tell him anything. His face looked years younger now, and he was touching her so gently she was close to crying and didn't know why and she wished he'd just wanted her to flash him some pink, but not this. How could she let him?

"Tell me, please."

"What?" Her throat felt thick and doughy. If she kept talking she'd cry.

"Tell me why you do these things."

He was barely touching her, running his fingertip back and forth over her healed skin, a dull itch snaking its way into her belly. Her eyes began to fill up. She wanted to slap his hand away and stand, but in a few more minutes Andy would come knocking on the door and even if this one wanted to buy her again she'd leave. She'd take all the money he'd given her and leave.

"I am waiting." Now he pressed two fingers along the scar like a doctor trying to rule something out.

She took a breath. "For my kid, okay? I do it for her."

He glanced up at her, shook his head. "No."

"Yes." She was angry and she didn't care if he got angry back or not. She had his money and Andy would be here soon and this rich little foreigner could go fuck with somebody else.

He was smiling at her, his eyes bright. "You do it for this." He tapped her scar, scratched lightly the hair over it.

"What?"

"You do it for skin—what is this way you say?—for flesh."

"Flesh?"

"Yes, for your love of it. Even if you had no children you would sell your flesh."

"I don't sell my flesh. I dance."

"Are you dancing now?"

"That's enough." She sat up and scooted away from him, his hand grazing her thigh.

"I have paid you. *I* say when it is enough."

"You think so?" She knew she sounded as angry as she felt but this one was small and drunk and she still had her heels on, could lean back and kick one right into him if she had to.

He sat up, took the bottle of Rémy, poured some into his snifter. "You do it because you think it is allowed." He picked up his glass and swirled the cognac.

He stared into it like there was something in there only he could see. "But it is not. Not for you. Not for any of you."

᷉ ᷉ ᷉

I N BACK OF the club, a single bulb shone brightly over a screen door and through it was a pale fluorescent light lost in steam. Outside a couple of oak pallets leaned against an oil drum next to a Dumpster, the air smelling like hot Frialator oil and detergent. He pulled right up to the bumper of a Sable, then backed over broken shells past all the employees' cars into the wire grass under some black mangroves. He flicked off his lights and cut the engine down.

His wrist was throbbing again, a thick pulsing that gave him an ache as high as his shoulder and neck. He tore the seal off the Tylenol bottle, got it open, and shook four or five into his hand, chasing them down with beer. It'd be better if he still had that pint of Turkey but the rest of this twelve-pack would have to do, and damnit, had he left the empty bottle in the driveway? Deena shouldn't see that. It made him look bad.

He thought of Deena and Cole, how since he'd been gone he didn't think of them as separate, how in his mind he saw them together, mother and son, son and mother, her holding him in her arms, feeding him, changing him, bouncing him on her lap. Woman and boy, his family. That's what he wanted back, though he wasn't sure about Deena by herself, was he? If she weren't his son's mother, if she didn't go with that picture, did he really want her? And if he did, why was he sitting here waiting for Marianne?

He sipped his beer. The club music got louder, the front door probably open around the corner. He could hear one or two men laughing. Car or truck doors slamming, engines starting up. In the kitchen an old man pulled from the machine a dripping and steaming rack of glasses. Another man stepped into view. He was dressed in a fry cook uniform, a bottle of beer in one hand, an apron in the other. He stopped the dishwasher and started pointing here and there, giving some kind of instruction. Then he turned and dropped his apron in a bucket and stepped outside. He rested his beer on the lid of the Dumpster and lit up. He had a wide body and hardly any hair left. Probably AJ's old man's age, wherever he was. Whoever he was. Even now, when he'd sit with Mama out on her small concrete patio overlooking the walled lawn of bahia grass and her Virgin Mary statue and the goldfish pond nobody sat around, she still never told him.

"That old question again?" she'd say. "Just a ten-day mistake, honey. I've told you that. Eddie raised you. Think of him."

Eddie. Skinny, drunk, no-'count Eddie.

The cook finished off his beer and tossed the empty into the Dumpster. They stopped serving food at midnight. Wouldn't be long now.

The first thing that pulled him to Marianne was not her hips and hair, that sweet trusting face, but the music she'd moved to: "I'm Not in Love." It was big on the oldies radio when he was a kid working for Eddie, and seeing her dance to it made him think of the younger AJ, sad all the time. Hungry for girls who never seemed to see he was there. This half-naked woman smiling at him the whole damn song long. And it was like watching what he'd wished for back then come for him now, and he felt sure he loved her even before she'd finished her act and changed her clothes and made her way to his table.

The fry cook said something through the screen to the old man, then turned and walked into the row of parked cars, climbing into a new Chevy sedan. AJ watched him back up, his headlights sweeping the other cars and AJ's truck and the mangroves before he disappeared around the corner of the club. Maybe he saw him for a second. Maybe he didn't. AJ didn't care; he wanted to be seen. By his old man he'd never met. By Marianne in some honest light. Would she still look at him like he was a good man? Would his daddy? What would he see if he ever saw him anyway?

∀ ∀ ∀

JEAN'S FOOT PRESSED hard onto the brake pedal, her car jerking to a stop at the entrance to a parking lot full of men. Her headlights shone on them all. Young ones, older ones. Some leaning against the hoods of their cars or trucks, others milling about in twos or threes in the center of the crushed-shell lot, a few turning to squint into the glare of her headlights. Two men on motorcycles rumbled up to her left, one of them—his face a mask of whiskers and drunkenness—peered in at her like she might be an item for sale. A large invisible hand was pushing against her chest and she had to take short breaths. Sweat broke out across her forehead and the back of her neck, the palms of her hands gripping the wheel, and she couldn't, she just couldn't.

She put the Caddy in reverse and backed away into the blare of a horn, the swerve of bright lights, angry shouting from a young man in a convertible already speeding south, the motorcycles too. She was gulping air, her eyes burned with tears, and she despised herself for driving away but still she couldn't breathe. She pressed both window buttons to let in more air but what came rushing in was a warm blast of humidity smelling of engine exhaust and street dirt and it whipped her hair.

She drove faster. She tried breathing through her nose. The windows rolled shut and she didn't remember making them do that. She turned up the radio but now there was no jazz, just the voice of the disc jockey, low and melodious, and she made herself listen to it, not the words, just their sound—sonorous, rooted in great knowledge and articulation, a voice of reason in an unreasonable world.

The weight against her chest began to lighten and she was able to get a noseful of air all the way down into her lungs. The man's voice said *contralto* and *Hampton*. It said many more things, but it was the sound she heard, not the words. *Everything is as it should be*, it seemed to say. *This is how it was and this is how it will be. You simply need to listen, dear listener. Sit and do nothing.*

Y Y Y

A J STOOD PISSING against the trees. He was drunk and tired and when he shook himself off with his good hand he dripped onto his pants and couldn't get the zipper up. One girl had left already. A short Chinese he never did like. She had stubby legs, flat breasts, and dull eyes. He'd sat behind the wheel and watched her drive away in her Camry. So many new cars. All the lying whores driving nice rides because of sorry sonsabitches like him. Now he stood in the black shadows of the mangroves. He could hear the music coming from inside, some country song, and he knew that girl in the white cowboy hat and boots was up there now. And who was Marianne dancing for?

Inside the Puma's kitchen the old man was gone, but before he'd left he mopped up, his back narrow and humped-looking. Made AJ think of Mama's back, how hunched over she'd become and he knew it and it wouldn't be long till he lost her and then the only family he had, the only blood, as far as he knew, would be Cole.

That's something Marianne should know. That's the kind of thing that'd make her sweet eyes well up for him, for sure, though it wasn't right to think of cashing in on his own loss like that. It felt like bad luck even thinking that way. He and Deena, sitting out back of their house, sometimes holding hands, looking up at the constellations neither of them could name. And those tears she'd cried tonight. Cole's sleeping face. What was his daddy doing out here waiting for the woman who'd scorned him? Get your ass into your truck and back to Mama's 'cause you're gonna have to get into your work clothes before morning, aren't you? Caporelli going to believe your tale in your club clothes?

He'd have to slice the compressor hose to drop the bucket. Be careful and cut the rubber near the fittings where it was already worn, make it look like a natural rip because Caporelli Sr. was such a cheap sonofabitch, putting all his profit into his golf course house on Longboat Key instead of back into the business, letting his equipment go to shit. But now it occurred to AJ that maybe he was thinking too low. Not just worker's comp and a few weeks off. Instead he should *sue* him. Sue him for faulty equipment and unsafe work conditions. Really set himself up. Fifty, a hundred grand, maybe more.

He wanted another beer. He could hear muted hoots and hollers inside, the bass and drums thumping like some old and world-weary heartbeat.

$\mathbf{v}$ $\mathbf{v}$ $\mathbf{v}$

S HE SMELLS SOAP bubbles and old food and she's standing on a wet floor. It's warm and a little slippery and she remembers when the sun was still in the sky and she was sleepy on Mama's shoulder and her neck was sweaty and Mama carried her away from the green door she sees now on the other end of the kitchen. She wants her backpack and her books and flip-flops but she doesn't want to go where the big man is 'cause Mama can come back and get them later. *We'll get it later. We'll do that later. Let's do that later.* Mama and Jean always saying that.

She walks over the wet floor, touches her fingers to the big silver machine. It's smooth and hot and she pulls her fingers back. She sees a light over the door out there, so many bugs flying around it. Like the lights on over their porch when Mama used to wake her up on Jean's couch and carry her upstairs to their house. The bugs flying. All their wings flapping. Like Stellaluna's who fell into the dark woods anyway because she was a baby. And she's okay. Nice birds found her.

She stands at the screen, presses her fingers against the tiny metal holes and pushes the door open. But it smells bad outside and she can hear all the bugs against the light, flying away then against it like they want to get inside but they can't get inside. She stays in, lets the door fall shut and stays in the kitchen, thinks she's going to cry again, forgets when she stopped crying. Cars are outside past all the bugs and the bad smell. Their car. With her car seat in it and her two old sippy cups on the floor. A picture of her and Mama hanging from the mirror and she liked when they took that picture. At the store with the dark box they could sit in and Mama put a dollar bill in the wall. Before Jean's house when they lived in the motel with the big TV you could see from their bed and Mama's warm skin next to hers.

v v v

COLE WAS CRYING.

AJ could hear him clearly through all the nightnoise: the bass-heavy music thumping through the club walls, cars pulling fast in and out of the lot, the ornery hollering of drunks from inside—through it all came the high wail of his boy. And there, under a lit swarm of mosquitoes and moths and gnats, a crying little girl stood on the other side of the kitchen's screen to the Puma Club for Whores. It was such the last damn thing he ever expected to see it took him a second or two to believe it. The club music thumped louder, men roaring. Around front a car or truck spun shells back out onto the boulevard, some drunk sonofabitch laughing.

Who would bring their child into a night like this?

He walked quickly, stepping over crushed shells, lowering his hurt hand so he wouldn't scare her.

"Hey there, little one. Hey."

She stepped back.

"It's okay, honey. Where's your mama? Where's your mama at?" He squatted on the concrete stoop, the air rank with the smells from the Dumpster—rotted meat and greased fish. He could see just under the door's center rail that she was tiny—three years old tops, standing there barefoot on the mop-streaked floor, steam still seeping from the industrial dishwasher next to her.

"Where's your mama, honey?"

She nodded and began to cry again, softer this time. He stood, his wrist and lower arm feeling shredded. He squeezed the handle and pulled the door open just enough to lean in. "Where's your mama, hon?"

"Mama?" Her eyes all round now, rimmed with tears, looking up at him like *he* knew her mama and could take her to her. What if he was some sick sonofabitch about kids? What in *hell* was she doing a wall away from a nest of lying whores and a gang of drunks shouting out for pussy in the dark?

"Mama?" The young thing was pointing through the screen at the night behind him. Was she *out* here? One of the waitresses who'd already gone?

No. He slipped all the way inside. She stayed where she was, looking straight up at him, her cheeks wet and streaked. Her hair was the color of Cole's. She had on pink pajamas and her lower lip started quivering.

His arm ached. He squatted and rested it across his knee. The music was loud even back here, electric guitar chords slicing through his head.

She was saying something to him, her eyes scared but trusting him a little bit. He couldn't hear her, cupped his good hand behind his ear. "What, sweetie?"

She pointed. "Our car. Our red car."

"Is your mama in the car?"

She nodded again, her lips parted, her hair brushing her pink-covered shoulder.

"You want to show me?" He had to say it louder than the music. His mouth was dry and a headache was coming on. He should get his ass out of here back to Bradenton, get ready for tomorrow's ditch on Lido Key, but how in hell could he leave this one here alone? How could anyone?

And to see her step toward him and hold out her hand was terror itself. Was Cole this dumb about strangers, too? Her hand was warm and disappeared completely inside his. Something caught between his chest and throat, something thick and shot through with grief, the flesh-memory of Cole's little fingers. How long since he'd held them? He should stop and explain to her she shouldn't be talking to him at all, she should turn and run away. But to where? The fucking *club*? *Jesus.*

He pushed open the screen door with his boot toe, thought of her bare feet, how he was going to have to carry her.

"Bugs." She was pointing up at them all, flapping and buzzing and dodging at the light. She pulled back on his hand, looked scared again.

"Want me to carry you?"

She nodded slow, like she wasn't sure she did or not. He squatted and scooped her up, her small bottom resting on his forearm, her arm around his neck, though she was leaning away from him like he smelled bad.

"Just show me where she's at, okay?"

"Huh-huh."

Her mother wasn't in any car, he knew that. But he might be able to find out who she was.

"There. There it is!"

The little one's hair was partly in his face. It itched but he didn't want her to move. It smelled like watermelon and he followed her outstretched and pointing arm, could hear the relief and excitement in her voice, and he hadn't felt this needed in a long time. Even since before Deena kicked him out. Even before then.

"That's mama's car. *My* car."

"What's your name, sweetie?"

"Franny."

"We'll take a look, Franny."

It was a maroon Sable. In the kitchen's light he could see there was no one in the front or back, though.

"Your mama's not there, hon."

"Mama still in*side*?"

Her voice broke a bit and he didn't know if she meant the car or the Puma. He rested her on the hood. His arm was pounding again. In the shadowed light the little girl's eyes filled and if her mama was here right now it'd be hard not to slap her across her slutty face. "What's your mama's name, Franny?"

"*I'm* Franny."

"That's right. What's your *mama's* name?"

"Um, do you know where Mama *is*?"

AJ cupped his hands over the glass of the driver's window. An empty Styrofoam coffee cup lay in the passenger seat. Hanging from the rearview mirror was a picture in a seashell frame. "Stay right there, hon. I don't want you falling off."

A car seat was strapped in the back. A flattened cardboard Slush Puppie cup lay next to it but there wasn't anything on the floors or seat, and Deena's Corolla was a shithouse compared to this, Cole's books and broken McDonald's toys and old Popsicle sticks everywhere. This one, a neat whore.

From here he could just barely see who was in the picture up front, two people. One big, one small. He glanced over at the tiny girl sitting on the hood. She rubbed one eye and yawned. Now with each heartbeat his lower arm and hand pulsed out an ache that rippled up to his head. He wanted more whiskey, a handful of pain pills, a few hours' sleep before putting it to Caporelli. For a second he saw himself carrying the child back to the kitchen and leaving her there before he drove off to do what he had to. But he couldn't. The one and only thing that had kept him sleeping away from Cole all these months wasn't his wife's paper from the court but knowing his boy was in a concrete house way out where nobody went, that he was safe for a little while even without him.

"Do you know my mama?"

"Don't think so." He pressed his wrist to his shoulder and with his good hand tried the driver's door. It opened.

Shit.

Behind him, back through two skimpy walls, the crowd was louder than it would get all night, the final parade of bodies up onstage selling T-shirts. He leaned in, caught that smell that somebody else's car has, the one that's not yours, this one smelling like suntan lotion and vinyl. He plucked the picture off its string, straightened back up, studied it.

"That's mine."

"I know it, hon. I'll put it back." He held it over the roof of the Sable till the bug-drawing light behind him shone on it. It was one of those photo booth pictures and at first he didn't quite recognize her sitting there in a sleeveless sundress, her daughter on her lap, smiling openly into the camera. Then he did: Spring. One of the coldest bitches at the Puma. She had a fine body she knew how to make you hungry for, showing you just enough in her stage act you'd pay to get her alone in the VIP, which he'd done early on. She'd sat him down and danced and stripped for him, hardly ever looking away from his eyes, though it'd been like staring at somebody on the TV and getting nothing back. She'd show you her tits and her bush and her ass, but that's it. Nothing like Marianne, who hadn't learned how to do that yet, close some kind of steel shutters behind her eyelids that kept you from seeing *her*. But this Spring, she was a *pro*. Moving between the tables with her chin up like he and all the rest were beneath her. When he'd given her the money she took it and smiled like she meant it, but he'd felt like a fool.

"That's me and my mama."

"Yep." He dropped the photo on the driver's seat and shut the door. He looked over at this Franny, a strand of her curly hair hanging over one eye, her narrow shoulders slumped, staring back at him the way dogs sometimes do, like they think you've got a plan and whatever it is they'll follow you. But she looked scared too, her shadowed face all still, waiting.

He rested his arm on the roof. He felt woozy, needed something for it quick. "Your mama's in there. You better go on back inside."

She kept her eyes on him and shook her head. First slow, then fast, her hair swinging, her lower lip protruding.

"Don't you want to see her? I know your mama. I know she's in there."

Behind him, around the corner of the club, came men's voices, some drunk and loud, others quieter, more controlled, off to go do something. A few engines started up. A radio blared a metal tune he'd always hated and somebody was talking about shaved cunt, how he was sick to death of shaved cunt. The little girl was crying. AJ could only shake his head and with his good arm lift her up once more. She squeezed his neck tight and wasn't letting go. He could feel her small heart jumping in her rib cage. What was he going to do? Go back in there and say he found her when he wasn't even s'posed to be anywhere near here?

Then again it was late and it wouldn't be too long before her piece-of-shit mother came back out. He could put the girl in her car and wait with her. And what? Be sitting with a child in a car that wasn't even his when the hired beef finally came out to drive home? Do all this for a bitch queen who didn't even goddamn deserve his help in this way? Meantime his arm needed some serious painkilling right now, painkilling that wouldn't hurt his chances for getting up early.

Nope, he was just going to have to put her where he found her. He turned and carried her back, the noise from inside at its peak: hoarse-voiced losers calling out the fake names of the whores they'd gone broke over, the speakers blasting music so loud they were about to burst.

The air smelled like congealed grease and something dead.

"Let go, honey. You got to go back to your mama now. Let go."

She was squeezing his neck tighter than ever. He tried to grip her arm with his hurt hand but it was too much. He lowered her to the stoop, could hear her cries through the last-call Puma noise he'd like to toss a grenade into just to shut them all up.

"It's scary. I don't want to, it's *scary*."

God*damn*it. He straightened up, the little one sitting on his forearm. She was lighter than a bag of groceries and he walked hard and fast over the crushed shells for the dark shadows of the mangroves where his truck was and more Tylenol and cool beer to wash it all down. Did he still have some of Cole's car toys in his glove compartment?

"Here, we'll wait for your mama right here, 'kay?"

She sniffled, didn't say anything, though she lifted her head now to see where they were going.

"Okay?"

"Mama's coming *soon*?"

"I sure as hell hope so, Francie."

"My name is *Franny*."

"Hold on to my neck again." He fumbled for the handle, pulled the door open, and sat her down in the front seat. He could smell the Turkey he'd spilled earlier, the diesel grime and ditch grit that were the smells of his truck. She was so small she could stand in the seat and her head still didn't touch the cab's ceiling. She put both hands on the steering wheel to balance herself and he remembered that family parked outside a Walgreen's down in Miami, a young mama letting her two-year-old sit up front while she strapped the baby in the back. Only an old man parking his car bumped her front fender and set off the air bag and killed the two-year-old.

"Get in the back a minute, 'kay?" He scooped her up, his arm a bit too low, and she started falling backward but reached out and grabbed his bad wrist, a crackle of fire through his arm bones into his shoulder. "Ah, *shit*."

She started crying again, standing on his backseat barefoot in her pink pajamas next to Cole's car seat full of empty beer cans. He wanted to tell her it wasn't her fault, that he wasn't mad at her, but man he had to get some relief. He opened the Tylenol bottle and upended it into his mouth, swallowing five or six more, though half felt stuck in his throat. He reached by her, opened a Miller, and drank it down. Her crying faded to a whimper. He pressed the cool can to his wrist, thought about putting some ice on it, but that was wrong because it had to look bad under the bucket in the morning. The worse the better.

"Shh, shh, I'm not mad or nothin'. I just have a hurt hand. I'm not mad at you." *Not mad at you.* Sometimes he'd scream that at Deena, I'm not mad at *you*, goddamnit! Though he was. She could've made things easier anytime she wanted and she never did.

Up against the steering column, his work bandanna hung from the gearshift. A little crisp with dried sweat. He put the beer on the runner board, grabbed the kerchief, and gently wiped the girl's snot away. She cried harder, then slowed up, sniffling and wiping her eyes, her chest sputtering in and out with her sobbing.

"You're just real tired, aren't you?"

She was looking out his windshield to the back of the club and the bright kitchen door where he'd found her. No one was there.

"Hey lookit." He opened the glove box, fingered around the Ford manual and his registration, the Burger King straws and drill bits and tire gauge till he felt the hard bumpy plastic of a purple frog that would jump once you wound it up. He stepped down and handed it to her. She took it like she might get in trouble if she didn't.

"It's a froggie, see?" He pointed to it, wanted to wind it up, but he needed two hands for that and anyway that little jump might scare her all over again.

"Here." He leaned past her. He swatted the empty cans onto the floor. "Sit down, hon. There's a little table you can play on."

She looked up at him, her eyes dark and lost-looking, then sat down and seemed better right away. "This is like my seat. Is this my seat?"

"No, this is my boy's seat."

Above her head was the seat belt clasp hanging from the plastic tray AJ had left up and open since the last time Cole had sat in it. For weeks it had blocked his view out the rear window, still, he never put it down, couldn't even think of seeing that car seat buckled shut like Cole was locked out of it. Now he lowered the tray over the girl's head till plastic touched plastic and she had a smooth surface in front of her to put her frog on.

"It's like *my* seat." She ran her fingers over it, dragged the frog over it. She was calm now. But what was he going to do with her? He was tired, his legs heavy, his arm something he was just going to have to get used to for a while. He drained the Miller, tossed it in the trees behind him, then grabbed another and shut the back access door. He climbed up into his seat and had to reach across himself to pull his own door closed.

He just needed to sit and think a minute. Sip some cool relief. He adjusted the rearview mirror so he could see her without turning around. She was looking at the frog in her hand real hard, trying not to cry. His window was open, the lot getting louder with men leaving the Puma, some of them talking trash the little girl shouldn't have to hear. He wedged the can between his legs and started the truck, pressed the window buttons and flicked on the AC. She began to whimper again.

"Hey, we're not going anywhere. I just had to start the engine to get the cool air going, that's all."

He saw her peeking through her fingers, her eyes wide and shiny, staring out the windshield at one of the hired beefs, a big dim-witted sonofabitch named Deke or some shit, a man who looked like all he did was lift weights, eat, sleep, and lift more weights. Only now he looked upset, walking fast away from the kitchen door and Dumpster, stopping to look left and right, his hand on his hips, his arms two thick shadows silhouetted against the fluorescent light behind him.

The girl was crying quietly now. What, he *do* something to her? AJ's blood seemed to spread out through him, his heart revving up like a long-quiet engine. The man looked hard to his right at the loud parking lot, stepped once in that direction but then turned around and headed straight for the little girl's Sable. He cupped two hands to his face as he looked inside. First the back, then the front. He jerked his head up and looked around the car. The child was still covering her face with both hands, her crying muffled.

"Hey, it's okay. I'll take care of you." And as he said it he knew he meant it, though he had no idea how. The beef stopped and scanned the employee lot, then looked behind him out at the dark stretch of wire grass, turned, and ran back toward the club.

In the fluorescent-lit kitchen were a few dancers and the man who'd broken AJ's wrist. In that light AJ could see how flat and wide his face was, how much bigger he was than the other one as he stood there in a tight Puma Club T-shirt. With his foot, he propped open the door, glanced quickly outside, then let the door slam behind him.

The kitchen was empty. A fuzzy insect in AJ's brain clicked that this was the time to get out of his truck, take the little girl, and run her back inside. But to who? To people who might think he was a different kind of man than he was? They'd hold him and call the law in, and even though he had nothing to be ashamed of—he'd only tried to give the girl some comfort—he couldn't risk getting even the *thought* of that into the court. They'd never let him see Cole again.

But soon as they didn't find her they'd be out here again, and the county might get here even before that. He could put the little thing in her mama's car, drive off in his truck, and call the club on his cell phone to tell them where she was, but how could he leave her in a parking lot with all the men wandering and stumbling their way out of the Puma, fifteen or twenty of them in twos and threes, smoking and laughing and talking trash—a few of them off on their own, hands in empty pockets, heading for their rides to go off and do who knew what?

He looked at her in the rearview mirror. She was staring out the windshield behind her fingers, the frog upside down on Cole's tray, and his good hand gripped the gearshift and slid her into drive, his boot toe tapping the gas, his truck rolling over the crushed shells past the club's stinking Dumpster and bright back door. And now the air of his cab was ripped through with the high terrified cries of this child only he could save. Just under the canopy two or three business boys glanced over at him in their loosened ties, jangling their keys, and he flicked on the radio and turned it all the way up, a DJ talking weather, more heat tomorrow, and he disciplined himself to keep his eyes looking straight ahead, to not look back up in his mirror at the crying girl, to just wait for the Econoline in front of him to pull out of the lot, this fallen shithole of a place this scared, wailing child was lucky to get out of, lucky A.J. Carey had come along and found her just when he did.

H E WAS OFF somewhere now, smoking deeply, nodding to himself. In just minutes she'd be free of him. In these two hours she'd made six, seven, eight weeks' pay, and to think she almost didn't come, that for a few minutes she actually considered calling in sick.

She sipped the last of her Rémy, smiled over at him. He was drunk and back inside himself, and even though he scared her and pissed her off and made her feel like a liar, she couldn't help but feel a little grateful to him—crazy as he was. Strange as he was. All that money he could've given to anyone but he'd chosen her. And he never even tried to move his fingers away from her scar and down. Or to unzip himself and ask for something Wendy or Retro or Marianne would've sold him.

Part of her wanted to keep him busy in some way, to keep him talking, to even let him touch her scar again, to distract him the fact and that she was sitting here doing nothing while his wad was so much smaller than before.

Because she didn't believe him: how can anybody not care about money at all? And his talk about dying and fate, about none of this being allowed. Once she got some Christian telling her the same thing, tears in his eyes, staring at her nakedness he'd paid to see.

On the other side of the wall the customers were all hollering at once, so loud the music was just vibrations of sound; another reason to thank this one, that she got to miss selling T-shirts for Louis. There was the way he looked at her earlier in the shift, the feel of her arm brushing his. She could only hope he forgot it though she doubted he did. She knew she'd have to see him later. But she had Franny for an excuse. Just as soon as she changed and paid out she'd have to get her home. Maybe that'd be enough to scare Louis off for good—Franny.

"We raced Grand Am, do you know this?"

He was looking at her. He'd slipped off his shoes. His socks were thin and cheap-looking. There was a small hole in one heel and his feet smelled like sweat and leather.

"The car?"

"Yes, Grand Am. American. Like you."

"You raced it?"

"Yes, we were racers."

"Who?"

"Khalid."

"Who?"

"I and my brother."

"What's his name?"

He stared at her.

"That's all right, you don't have to tell me."

"Khalid."

"Halid?"

"No, *kha*lid. You cannot say this."

Earlier she might've tried to prove him wrong, but not now; her time with him was short. It was good to finish when things were calm like this. They could be a couple unwinding on the sofa after a long day and night.

"He was a fast boy. I was fast as well but Khalid, he was fastest. He was never afraid. He goes two hundred, two hundred twenty kilometers per hour. He was strong." He gazes at the black wall. "He would have become shahid. The best shahid."

"What's that?"

He glanced at her face, then away. "He hated the kufar, he hated all of you, but he wears a hat for baseball, he drinks Pepsi and Coca-Cola, he smoked only cowboy cigarettes."

"Why's he hate *us*?"

He looked at her for what seemed a long time. She was tempted to smile but didn't. "Yes, many of you are blind."

"Many of who?"

"You kufar."

"What's that?"

"I have said enough."

"No you haven't, I'm curious."

"What does this mean?"

"Curious?"

"Yes."

"It means you want to know something."

"Yes, there are many things you should know." He shook his head, looked like he wanted to say something but stayed quiet, his eyes on his cell phone on the table. The club noise was muffled and Andy would be here soon and she didn't want to take the money when nothing was being said.

"Do you guys still race?"

"No."

"Is your brother back home?"

"He is in Jannah."

"Where's that?"

"You will never know."

"Why not?"

"People like you go to hell, April."

People like her. She tried to smile but she was angry again and anyway their time was up. All that money, this was the price. Like lingering at your door with a Jehovah's Witness. Out in the club the noise had died down. Even the music was lower, the place slowly emptying one or two customers at a time. Andy was late, had to be.

"Time's up, Mike." She reached over the arm of the love seat, nudged the money off her clothes—still folded so neatly by him. She found her G-string and stood, straightening and pulling it up around her hips.

"You will not see me even once more, April."

"I'm sorry to hear that, Mike."

"Bassam."

She picked up her T-back, looked at him. Now he was young again, a kid at your doorstep holding a flower. "That's nice."

"It means for smiling. Something like this."

"You don't smile much, though." It was a joke, but he looked down and away as if she'd just offended him. She cinched her skirt and pulled on her blouse, her eyes on the door, the money on the carpet in the shadow of the love seat.

"I should not like you, April."

"Why shouldn't you?"

He lit another cigarette, inhaled deeply. "Because then I would be like you. And I am not like you. Someday, Insha'Allah, you will know me."

"I know you now, don't I?"

"No, but you will. Everyone will."

"I thought I wasn't going to see you anymore."

"Yes."

"Then how will I know you better, Bassam?" She laughed, but he was not smiling.

"You will see, Insha'Allah." He stubbed out his cigarette, though it was only a quarter smoked. "When will you stop doing this?"

"What?"

"This." He held out his arms and looked around the room as if it were much larger and more important than it was.

"Is that any of your business really?" She smiled at him, and it was *her* smiling, April, and she knew immediately it was a mistake, his face hardening as he took the snifter, stared at the Rémy inside like it was the ocean or a fire. "Yes, yes, laugh, and then wait until Youm al-Qiyama."

The knock echoed into the room. Andy's voice came muffled through the door like the guardian he was. "Time's up, Spring. And Tina wants to see you."

She kept her eyes on the foreigner's, squatted and grabbed her cash, such an unbelievably thick stack. He stood there like a spurned lover, the tail of his polo shirt hanging from his pants. She'd gotten sickos before and now it was easy being Spring again. Whatever he felt about her wasn't personal, she could see that. He was talking like it was but he hated all of them, didn't he?

Andy knocked louder. "Spring? You need me?"

Bassam lit up the last of his Marlboros, his eyes on hers. If she said yes to Andy, they'd throw him out and not let him back in for a long time, if at all. The door handle turned and there was Andy's shaved square head, his pink face and high cheekbones, his raised eyebrows that glistened slightly with sweat. He looked disappointed, like he was hoping to catch them fucking or to see the little foreigner strangling her so he could do something about it.

"You hear me, Spring? Tina wants to see you."

"Yeah." She gripped the money tightly in her hand, looked one last time into this Bassam's face. Now he looked drunk and tired and mean, just another high roller at the end of the night who'd spent too much and drunk too much and now had to watch her walk away and not look back.

"Everything's fine, Andy. Couldn't be better, really. Could not be better."

⋎ ⋎ ⋎

IT WAS ALMOST soothing being back in the dim glow of the VIP
toom. Nearly every chair was occupied by a man clutching a white
Puma Club T-shirt, watching his girl dance for it. April moved
quickly through them all, her fingers gripping the cash. The new girl
danced badly against the half wall and she looked right at the money,
her overly made-up eyes lighting up, and April knew she'd be hustling
hard for any available Champagne customer and April wasn't about to
tell her this never happens, nobody ever walks out with this.

She could hardly believe it herself and couldn't get back to the
dressing room fast enough, not so much because Tina wanted her
to—Franny probably awake again, missing her and wanting to go
home—but because she had to get that money into her purple bag
in her padlocked locker before anybody else noticed it. But was her
skimpy metal locker safe enough? She began to think where else she
could stash it till lights-up.

She squeezed the money tighter and made her way past the blue light of the VIP bar and into the white shadows of the main floor. A third of the customers were gone, though the ones left, the last-call lonelies, the drunk and horny assholes, were yelling it up, standing to watch Renée be a naked ice queen or sitting back with their arms crossed, their feet on an empty chair, their chins low. One or two eyed her buttoned blouse, her breasts, her face. One reached for her, his fingertips grazing her arm, and Lonnie Pike was already moving toward him from the Amazon Bar, his eyes on hers just a second before he picked up his speed. She felt like she'd been gone a long while. Her mouth was dry, and she had to pee again. Her head felt heavy then light. Louis was up at the bar and had a drink in his hand—always a Captain Morgan's and Coke with two lime wedges, the lights from the show reflecting off his glasses. He could be looking at anyone, though it was probably her. She *was* going to have to deal with him, wasn't she? Find a way to shut him down without getting fired. She was anxious to see Franny. She almost wanted to show her all this money, show her how good fortune had finally come their way, that somehow by putting one foot in front of the other and doing what she had to, her number was really coming up. Not the big one, but still, a little luck like this felt like bait for bigger luck.

She moved around the stage. The music blasted so loud from the speakers she could feel it in her temples. The cigar smoke was thick here and somebody had thrown up, that sour-gut smell, and April hoped Tina wouldn't put her back into rotation right away, that she'd give her a chance to check on Franny and store her money and go to the bathroom, then the makeup mirror to freshen up.

She tried to step carefully over the new rubber mats with the holes in them, but still, her heels slipped into each one, then another, and she wanted to unstrap them and go barefoot, but Louis was up at the Amazon and he'd see her and she wouldn't hear the end of it.

Fucking Louis. She yanked her heels one at a time from the holes till she was through the first black curtain, then the second. Through glass windows in the doors was the pale fluorescent light of the kitchen that made her squint. It was strange to see Tina and Zeke standing near the screen door, Zeke's arms crossed, looking down at Tina and shaking his head at whatever she was saying. In this light she looked old, her bleached hair dry and frizzy, her boobs ridiculously large. April pushed open the doors and let them swing shut behind her, Tina jerking her head toward her. Her lips were set in a straight line, like when she was pissed off, but her eyes were soft-looking. Afraid.

"What's the matter, Tina?"

And from Tina's red lips came the words April already knew and the floor seemed to drop away and she was falling, falling into a dark and empty sky.

H IS TRUCK'S AC had always been too strong. He turned it down so she wouldn't get cold in those thin pajamas. Poor little thing had cried only fifteen or twenty minutes before she whimpered herself asleep in Cole's car seat, her head at a bad angle against her shoulder, her hair lying across one eye and her parted lips. He finished his beer, dropped the empty onto the passenger seat, and disciplined himself not to have another.

Once again he was driving north into the darkness up Washington Boulevard. Just the hum of his V-8, the muffled whine of rubber on asphalt, the low rattle and purr of his AC, the child's breathing behind him he couldn't hear. He glanced back at her in the rearview, felt in the way he tilted his face up to do it just how many times he'd checked on Cole like that. It was good doing it again, to be watching over a little one like this. His wrist and arm were one massive ache, no more throbbing of sharp peaks with less painful valleys, just one long mountaintop of hurt. Still, he didn't care. He couldn't remember the last time he got to do something so pure for somebody else, to do something this good. *Shaved cunt.* He kept hearing one of them say it, and the memory of that and her crying there alone in the Puma's kitchen, the drunken noise behind her, then the driving away with her buckled behind him, felt like a calling of some kind. He'd *rescued* this child.

It was eleven past one on his truck's digital, three minutes slow. Almost a quarter after. The club closed in forty-five minutes but after seeing the T-bones—so high-strung—looking for the girl, they'd surely been looking for a while and would've called the law by now. There were those key-jangling corporate boys under the canopy, how they'd looked over at him when the girl started screaming. His back windows were tinted so they didn't see anything, but who knows what they could've said to who by now?

Way off to the west in the wire grass were the twinkling lights of a trailer park. Mostly old people. This whole damn state full of them. Like God picked up the country and shook it and all those who weren't nailed down with jobs and commitments slipped right out of their houses, their card games and visits with grandkids, their nine holes of golf and double dates with other old people who'd lived long enough to make it to dinner one more Saturday night—every year more and more of them just slipped out of their lives and fell to Florida.

And now Mama was one of them, though she'd lived her life here doing what only the Cuban women and the Asians and the blacks did now—cleaning up after other people who came down here just to flash money he never saw any of, her either. All those years cleaning motels on Longboat Key, St. Armand's, the Lido. Pushing her cart loaded with scrub brushes and cleanser, sealed bars of soap and tiny bottles of shampoo, fresh folded towels, sheets and pillowcases, wrapped rolls of toilet paper. His mama in her white sneakers, black nylons and skirt and white apron. The chain of keys she carried in the front pocket. Her hairnet and red lipstick and how she was always smoking and would unlock one of the motel's doors and leave her cigarette burning outside in a coffee can of sugar sand from the beach. She'd balance her cigarette across the tin lip and let it burn.

And how many no-count sonsabitches had played possum when she knocked on the door and let herself in only to see a man with his johnson hanging out or sticking straight up? Acting surprised to see her or not surprised at all—and really, what's a son ever to know for sure? When he had to come along, when he played on the floor under a window with his plastic Transformers, he'd never seen her do anything but work quick and efficient, sometimes humming a tune from before his own birth, just aiming to get done and back out to the hallway with the ash can and her smoking cigarette—but who knew later, when he was off to school or working with Eddie, if she didn't let a high roller pay her? There'd been those late-fights with Eddie, AJ lying in bed in the dark, the window open, the smell of their orange tree blossoming in the air, the smell of escape.

"Don't you lie to me, Virginia. Don't you goddamn *lie* to me. I heard some talk, damnit. I heard some goddamn *talk*."

A hundred yards up ahead the dented sign for Myakka City called to him, his headlights glinting off it like a turn east was possible. The look on Deena's face when he'd knock on the door holding this baby girl. He'd stand out there tired and hurt and tell her he had no choice but to help, but how could he do that without tipping his hand about the Puma? About his expensive habit there? About Marianne? And even if she took the girl in for the night—he knew her—she'd worry about the girl's mother and call the law. No matter how bad it might make him look, she'd call the police and wash her hands of it. But it was too late now. He couldn't turn around and drive back to the Puma, try and convince some county sonofabitch he'd probably saved this kid from the kind of man they'd take him for. And he still hadn't forgotten the two who'd come when Deena called, the way they took her words like they were straight from the Bible and pinned his face to his own wall, handcuffing him in front of Cole, standing there so damn quiet. It almost would've been better to hear him cry than hear that quiet coming from where he'd stood in front of the TV in his shorts and T-shirt stained with peach juice.

"It's okay, Cole. Daddy's comin' right back."

"You shouldn't lie to him like that." The big one had jerked his cuffed wrists behind him and shoved him out of his home, Deena just as quiet, standing off in the bright kitchen with her bruised cheek he didn't mean to color at all and you could almost call it an accident, his arm flying out from his side just to stifle her bad attitude, just to get her to back away from him one damn minute, that's all—and it was like watching somebody else's arm fly out and catch her across her cheek and nose as she seemed to lift up and fall from some force that couldn't be just him.

Like Deena was some perfect mother. How many times he catch her locking Cole in the car when she ran into the drugstore or 7-Eleven to get something? Cole said: *I wanted to go with Mama, Daddy. But Mama said she's coming right back. She always comes right back, Daddy.* How many times she check on him at night before they went to bed? Never. AJ's the one always walked in all soft on his feet, Cole's covers kicked off, his pillow half off the bed, his neck bent in a bad way. So he'd gently lift him and set him in the middle of the mattress, raise his head and adjust the pillow, pull the covers up over his chest and shoulders, bend down and kiss his forehead. Leave him, his son, to his dreams.

Close to one-thirty now. In five hours he had to be in that ditch on Lido Key. His stomach burned from the Tylenols and his mouth was dry and he fought the urge for just one more cool beer. He'd already had way over his personal limit for driving a child. With Cole, he never drove him after more than two beers. If they went out to eat and he had three or four, Deena drove. If she didn't feel like it, she knew to tell him before his third and he'd switch to water or Coke. These little things that never came up before a judge who'd write an order on you locking your ass out.

His eyes burned slightly. He could feel himself hunching over the wheel. He was just so damned tired. When he got that Caporelli money, he was going to rent a cabana out on Longboat Key, open the windows and sleep in a Gulf breeze for days or weeks. Then he'd wake up, shower and shave, go take that anger class he promised Deena he would. She'd let him move back home and they'd both work hard not to fall back to how it used to be. He'd pay off all those credit cards and layaway accounts, maybe sell their place off Myakka City Road for one closer to the water. Not the lake and Deena's folks, but the Gulf. One of those creamy-looking condos on sugar sand, a place where Cole could play and swim. He and Deena watching. A place with a view of the sun sinking into the sea every night.

But then he saw him and Marianne there. The two of them making love on a moonlit blanket.

He'd never been one for lying or cheating or stealing. Never. Even running Walgreen's late at night. How easy it would've been to skim here and there. Mess with the merchandise inventory figures. Pocket the difference. But they trusted him and he wasn't about to make them regret it, and what he was planning to do now was hardly even a bad thing. Caporelli had the insurance. He wouldn't lose anything from his own wallet and anyway he needed a good kick in the ass for neglecting his equipment. Leaving that and too many other damn details to his piece-of-shit son. And it wasn't like he'd be stealing from an insurance company either.

Well maybe he would be. But a hundred grand was a quarter down a street drain to those fuckers and, man, anyway it was *his* turn, damnit, A.J. Carey's turn to cash in on nothing but hard work nobody ever really seemed to appreciate.

Why hadn't he thought about it like this right away? Because you have always thought *small*, that's why. You have never thought *big*. Always happy just to have twenty or thirty bucks in your pocket and the bills for the month paid and something good to eat and cold Millers in the fridge. A woman to love him. A boy to hold. Maybe Deena tossing your ass out was the best thing could've happened, AJ. Shock your sorry ass out of the small and into the big. Time to god-damn think BIG.

With his new money he'd encourage her to go get some hobbies, maybe join that World Gym in Samoset, take a night class somewhere. He'd build onto the house, add a second floor with a master bedroom and a deck overlooking the pines. They'd make love again, have another baby, a little brother or sister for Cole to play with. At night, after the kids were asleep, they'd sit out on the new deck under the constellations, get a book and learn their names. Deena'd be happy and forget she was ever disappointed in him and that he'd done to her what he did; maybe he'd be happy, too. Whatever that was. Maybe happiness was just not being hungry or thirsty for anything much anymore. Satisfied to pull your boat into the slip and tie it off for good.

A boat. How many years had he wanted a *boat*? His whole life on the Gulf Coast and he'd been as locked on the land as a man in Iowa. How many hours of his life had he dreamed of owning something sleek and white and fast he could live on? That's one thing Eddie did. He did do that. Took him out four or five times on a charter boat down the Intracoastal Waterway between Sarasota and Venice. A lot of fathers and sons, a few women, fishing for snook and sheepshead, mangrove snapper, pompano, and amberjack. Eddie, lean and red-faced and unshaven, would crack his first Miller about thirty feet out, laughing it up with some other rummy drinking before 8:00 a.m. too. But it was good being out in the green-blue water, the early sun and salt wind in AJ's face, speeding by all the big homes on the beaches with their clipped bahia lawns and royal palm trees, like he could just reach out and pick one for himself. Then later, round noon, the sun high overhead, everybody chatty and relaxed, catching something or happy just to sit there in the gentle rock of the waves and wait. Off to the west and south, where the green haze of the water met the pale blue sky, there'd be boats, all kinds, some with tall sails filling and snapping in the breeze. There'd be speedy outboards hauling water-skiers. Big inboards with a fly bridge and a sunning deck on the bow, a kitchen and sleeping cabin below. Even then that's what he liked the most. The fast ones you could live on. Where all you needed was gas and maintenance money, a slip to dock it. If you lived on it, that couldn't be much money, could it? *Maybe Deena would go for that.* But the thought died in his head before it could take root. She didn't even like going out on the lake in her old man's outboard. She said it was boring and made her feel sick. And she wouldn't let Cole live on a boat. Be near all that water all the time. He saw his son falling overboard, him abandoning the wheel to dive into the white wake of his own motors, blinded by the salt water, swimming hard for what he could only pray was his boy's bobbing blond head.

He passed the sign for Oneca. The road was dark and empty, the occasional flash and glitter of broken glass in the gravel on either side. No, if he was real careful and made that bucket-drop look as bad as he could, made Caporelli look even more negligent than he was, he might get enough for his house *and* a boat. Daddy's boat. Something for at night and the weekends, a small cruiser. What was wrong with that? A little something to lighten his load. A place to go clear his head.

It's how the Puma felt at first. The first half hour of the first night before the first dancer came over and tried to hustle him for a twenty. Before that, there was just his drink and the soft, blue light, the good music, a naked woman with black hair and blue eyes dancing up there just for him. He knew she wasn't but that's what it felt like. How she'd let him look at whatever he wanted. The way she turned and arched her back to give him a better view. That little smile. Marianne.

In the rearview the child's cheek was touching her shoulder. He should pull over and adjust her head so she won't get a crick in her neck. But he might wake her up and then she'd get all confused and scared and start crying again. And how about when he got to Mama's? He couldn't leave the girl with her while he was gone for—what?— maybe half the day? He tried to calculate it: thirty minutes to the job. Another thirty or forty to put a tear in the bucket line and then crawl down and wedge his hand under it. That's an hour and ten minutes. Another twenty or thirty for Caporelli Jr. to drive up and get the bucket off him and take him to the emergency room. Two hours already. Add another two or three for X-rays and a cast and a call to a lawyer. A good half day before he could get back.

By then something might be on the TV Mama kept on all day long. Maybe they'd flash a picture of the girl. And even if that didn't happen just yet, even if the little girl wasn't so scared waking up to his old mama that she cried till neighbors called the law, even if Mama and the girl somehow got along for the morning, what was he going to do when he got back? Drive the child back to the Puma in the midday sun? Bring her back to the same damn place he'd rescued her from?

No, he shook his head and accelerated toward the dim lights of Bradenton miles ahead: he was going to have to drop her off somewhere tonight, a place she'd be safe and he could keep an eye on her till the law came, a place he'd be close enough to her he could jump in if some sonofabitch approached her but far enough away the law wouldn't notice him as he pulled away. But what was to keep her from taking off? Or stepping into the road? Or coming back to his truck or pointing him out to some county badge happy to do him harm?

Deena one morning last year. She'd taken that liquid Benadryl and squirted a stopperful into Cole's juice for their long ride to her cousin's wedding in Jacksonville. Four and half hours and he slept through the entire drive. But even after AJ got some into this little one, where could he leave her? It couldn't be just anywhere. And why didn't he search through Spring's glove box for her registration and address? He could lay the girl down on her own front stoop, ring the bell, then gun it out of there. But what if nobody was there?

A cool sweat had broken out across his forehead and upper lip. He reached over and turned the AC up just a bit. Getting close to two now. 301 curved off to the west, the neon lights of sleeping Bradenton coming closer. This was a good dry stretch and he wanted to push a wave of gas through his engine, not because he wanted to get there faster but because he wanted to feel the force and power under his foot and fingertips, this steel cage of his flying through this Gulf Coast September night like it was any other and he was in control and knew just what he was doing and what he should do next.

He shouldn't even try to sleep. Not with everything he had to do. There was an all-night Walgreen's on Manatee Avenue not far from Mama's. He'd stop there, lock his truck up, and keep an eye on it through the plate glass of the store. The same way Deena confessed she watched Cole, though he never liked hearing about that. Never did.

He glanced back up in the rearview at the sleeping child. Her head was so tilted to the side her hair covered most of her face. It was just as blond as Cole's. She could be his sister. Really. She could.

ᵛ ᵛ ᵛ

TWO DOORS NO windows.

Two doors no windows.

Those first stark seconds or minutes when she couldn't have breathed and couldn't remember now what she'd said or who she'd said it to, that's all April could think of—that there were no windows in Tina's office or the dressing room or bathroom, that Zeke had guarded the door and Franny couldn't've gone the other way or she'd be onstage so *where* was she?

Tina was saying something and Louis had appeared and Zeke and now Retro, but April was trying to be Franny, trying to be as small as she was, and whatever everyone was saying was just a zip of chatter in her way as she yanked Tina's couch from the wall and saw darkness, a coat hanger, a condom wrapper, a plastic lighter. She pushed past Tina, her hand pressing into her silicone flesh, and every locker with no padlock she jerked open calling her daughter's name, though she couldn't hear that either, just felt it in her throat and face and air in front of her, the metal doors clanging one against the other, all of them empty; her ankles kept buckling in her stilettos and she bent over and uncinched them, kicking them away. She looked under the makeup counter, saw dozens of sneakers and sandals and pumps, there were tote bags and duffel bags and bare linoleum in between and now things began to blur and she wiped at her eyes and yanked open the bathroom door again—pink toilet and sink, round mirror in a pink frame, Tina's rotation tacked to the pink wall, and her daughter's name was in the air, her throat straining behind it; she turned and rushed past Louis on his cell phone, Tina and Retro gone, Zeke standing there like a useless piece of garbage, and she headed for the blue-lit corridor to the stage. She stopped and rifled through the dusty curtain, she looked to the right into the black corner, squatted and waved her hand, felt air, the painted plywood wall. She felt now how empty her hands were, the money—where was it? Where did she put it? But it was like worrying about your coffee spilling as your car rolls over and over down the highway, and she peered into the blue darkness to her left, she saw two holes on either side of the stairs to the backstage. Then she was there, sticking her head in—

"*Franny! Franny!*"

She knew she'd shouted that but could only hear the thump, rattle, and cry of the club music above, the shouts and whistles and whoops of the men. On the other side of the low darkness was some light from the kitchen door, just enough, but it was too dark to see anything more and she was up and back in the brightness of the dressing room. The other door was open now, Zeke back at his post, Tina and Louis in her office—*cops*; Tina said *cops, call them*, and hearing this only made things blur again, Zeke looking down at her, his eyes flat and dull.

"Tina's got your money. You dropped it."

"Just give me your *fucking flash*light!"

Back into the blue dark, squatting at the hole beside the stairs, shining her light into her own terror because there was nothing to see but the wood frame of the stage, a few fluffs of dust, a flattened Coke can. Her eyes burned and she was crying. It was as if she were standing in a rock-strewn stream and the water was rising fast, the current getting stronger, pushing hard against her but she couldn't let it. She couldn't.

She ran back through the dressing room. Another girl there now, Sadie primping in front of the mirror for her act. April wanted to push her face into the glass for even acting like this was still a normal night in this normal dressing room of this normal club for normal fucking men.

"*Zeke. Did you ever leave the door alone? Did you?*"

"Yeah, for two seconds." Like she was a cop. Like she could screw him for this.

"*When?*"

"For Louis. Right after T-shirts."

She moved past him, the current pulling her through the kitchen that was well-lit and had no corners or places to hide. She pushed open the screen door and stepped under the light onto the crushed shells. A few stuck into the soles of her feet. A flurry of insects flew above her. There was the last-call noise of men out in the parking lot, rotten smells from the Dumpster, the cooling air. She shined her light onto the parked cars and found her Sable, the current sweeping her toward it. Her feet hurt, but she didn't care and even before she got there she knew her car was empty, that Franny was nowhere near.

v v v

A J PULLED HIS truck up into the fire lane and shut off the engine. She was still out, her small mouth open. Under the lights of the Walgreen's lot a half dozen cars were parked and in one of them a boy and girl sat in the front seat talking and smoking. At the store where he used to work the law cruised by twice an hour and he hoped the one around here had just come and gone; he could get cited for parking in the fire lane, but he wasn't about to leave the girl farther back where he couldn't see her too well from inside. He reached around with his good hand and flicked the ceiling switch so the overhead light wouldn't shine in her face when he opened his door. He took his keys, reached across himself to pull the latch, then slid out and down, pushing the door slowly closed until it clicked shut, locking it.

His legs were stiff and heavy, his arm a steady screaming pain he'd just about grown used to. But it felt good to be out in the air. The two kids were laughing about something and he thought how they were probably stoned and if they weren't careful would be off somewhere fucking and then—like that—your free years are gone and you're stepping into the fluorescent slap of a Walgreen's with a broken bone you have to ignore till morning looking for drugs to keep the little ones safe and asleep.

An old one behind the register. Somebody's grandmother. She was reading one of those Danielle Steel books Deena had a stack of. She eyed him over her glasses. AJ smiled, but he didn't care for her expression. Like he was up to nothing good. Like he'd never managed one of these stores himself and could've hired and fired her anytime he wanted to.

The allergy aisle was way in the back near the pharmacy. He turned and looked past a sunglasses display out the window, his truck sitting there, the girl safe within. He walked quickly and knew just where to find it. Nobody would see her behind his tinted windows anyway, and as he passed shelves full of wrapped candies, magazines and romance books, household cleaning supplies and notebooks, pens and Scotch tape, he knew if she were Cole he wouldn't've left him like that. His blood wouldn't let him.

The liquid Benadryl was right where he knew it'd be. There was grape and there was bubblegum. He picked the grape. Something low caught his attention. It was his wrist. Two, three times its normal width—all pink and puffy-looking. His hand swollen, too. Maybe he should try to get the swelling down. Maybe Caporelli wouldn't buy it if he looked like this right after the bucket was s'posed to've dropped on it. He headed down the aisle toward the pharmacy counter. Behind it stood a skinny pharmacist in thick glasses studying something AJ couldn't see. AJ held his wrist up to his shoulder and moved by him to the analgesics. Found some Extra Strength Motrin, an ice pack he'd have to get ice for. He squeezed the pack under his arm, the Benadryl and Motrin in his hand, and walked fast now past woman's hair coloring, combs and brushes and rolled umbrellas, past VHS tapes and rows and rows of batteries, more candy, then there was the lady at the register and he lay down his purchase. That's what they called them when he used to work in a store just like this—purchases. She closed her book slowly, saving her place with one of those bookmarks with scripture written across Jesus's outturned palms.

AJ's mouth was dry. He looked out the window, saw his truck and nothing else.

"What happened to *you*?" She scanned in the Benadryl. She had a voice like Mama's, scraped raw from smoking, and she didn't sound unfriendly.

"Accident."

"What'd you do?"

"Backhoe bucket dropped on it."

"You go to the doctor's?"

"Not yet."

"It looks broken to me."

"Yeah, I'll go in the morning."

"Honey, it *is* the morning." She laughed but not in a way to make him look stupid. He'd been wrong about her, hadn't he? Made him wonder what else he'd been wrong about.

"Seventeen forty-three, please."

He reached into his pocket, pulled out his last twenty. Thought of the thousands and thousands he'd get off Caporelli's insurance, the cheap half-assed sonofabitch. He watched her bag his things. She put in the Benadryl last and he pictured himself trying to squirt some into the little one's mouth without waking her up or making her choke.

"Here you go, sir. I do hope your hand gets better soon."

He thanked her, held the bag close. At the door, he turned. "I used to manage one of these. I'm with the district now. What's your name?"

"Gladys Evans."

"You just got your store a good report, Gladys. I'll tell your manager."

"Well, thank you." She smiled though she looked confused, glancing at his injured arm, supposedly by a damn backhoe.

"We're building a new store up in Tampa."

"Oh. Well you take care of yourself, sir. Thank you again."

He nodded and smiled back, pushing the door open with his shoulder. Outside in the humid air more voices rang out from the lot behind his truck. More kids. Too old for high school, too lazy or unlucky for more schooling, so they sit in their rides half the night doing nothing. And the lie he'd just told didn't feel like a lie. If he hadn't gone into heavy equipment he *would* be a district manager and he *would've* given that woman a good report for her efficiency and politeness.

He squeezed the bag between his knees, unlocked the truck, and peeked in. She was still deep asleep, Cole like that too: once he was down you could drive all over with the radio on, haul him out to go here and there, put him back into his seat and buckle him up and still he'd stay asleep. The hard part was getting him to go to sleep. But maybe this one was like that too, and he wouldn't have to give her anything after all.

L ONNIE HAD NEVER even heard of something like this happening before, a club owner closing up a few minutes early to clear the place out, bring up the lights, and look for a child. Spring's child. And why hadn't he checked in on her like she asked? He'd seen Tina coming and going all night. He should've gone and looked. Man, he should have left his station for two seconds and fucking *looked*.

Now Spring hurried barefoot through the lighted club, her usual poise and confidence gone. Her blouse was partly buttoned and her hair swung wildly in front of her face every time she bent down to look under a table, then straightened up and rushed past the last men, ignoring them.

Under the bright lights of closing time the club always looked dirty but tonight it was worse than usual: the Portofino boys had left layer upon layer of drifting smoke which hung in the air like remnants of some disaster. The tables were covered with half-empty cocktail glasses and beer bottles and overflowing ashtrays, the chairs scattered all over. The red carpet—worn to a bloody gray in most places—was gritty and soiled with boot and shoe filth, spilled drinks, stray coins and streaks of ash.

Paco and Little Andy were herding some of the men along, nodding their heads and shooing them to the entrance like little kids they'd be more than happy to spank. Most of the girls from the VIP were still naked or half-naked and they stood in the bright smoky light dressing and talking with one another, looking a bit startled. They reminded Lonnie of fire drills back in middle school, that same look on the faces of girls having to leave the gym in just their tank tops and shorts. Tina was clapping to get their attention, and Spring moved right through them. She was crying, her glistening cheeks smeared with eyeliner, and she looked to him as if she were breaking in two. He felt left out of something big and natural he should know more about than he did. She rushed through the curtains of the Champagne, all the empty rooms in there she could've hidden in while April was in one of them, though how could her child ever get through the VIP or the club without being seen first? *He* would have seen her. *Should* have seen her.

Lonnie moved between the empty chairs and tables of the main floor.

A little girl, Tina said in the VIP. *A three-year-old in pink pajamas.*

❤ ❤ ❤

H E WAS IN Bradenton now, heading west along Manatee Avenue. He passed one-story stucco houses with poured-concrete driveways, cars locked behind chain link. Some had low floodlights that lit up their pitiful houses and lawns hardly big enough for a barbecue, but this was a good town Mama had landed in; soon he was driving through the historic district on the Manatee River and there were old buildings—a stone courthouse wedged between wood-framed bungalows that went back to the time of the Seminoles and Spaniards. There was a clapboard boat hut used for rum-running back in Prohibition, and along the sidewalks and in the grassy median were live oaks older than the state, their long and gnarled limbs hung with Spanish moss. Between the old structures new ones were getting framed and closed in, big COMING SOON signs nailed to stakes out front. Every twenty or thirty yards, there'd be the mile-wide Manatee

River beyond, dark now, a few lights from Palmetto City trembling on its surface.

At Mama's he'd leave the girl sleeping in the truck, then go inside to change into his work clothes and make coffee and get some ice for his pack. He hoped smelling the coffee wouldn't wake Mama. It'd be good to go sit on her balcony and sip a cup, put ice on his wrist, and think. A church is what he was seeing now. Someplace holy to leave this girl. Someplace close to the ditch out on Lido Key.

His eyes burned and he slowed for the turn into the old folks' village where Mama was lucky to buy what she did. They never had much but Mama had always been good with her money, squirreling it away whenever she could, hoarding a little pile over the years that got a lot bigger once Eddie died. He'd had more insurance than AJ would've thought, Mama as the sole beneficiary, and he had two grown kids up north somewhere who didn't come to the funeral. The daughter, Nancy something, sent flowers.

He drove slowly down the paved road. On both sides of it was a four-foot lane of mulch lit up by ground sconces two or three inches above the grass. Late nights after the Puma, driving back to his mama's place when he only wanted to be going home instead, the lights always made him feel welcome, beacons to guide him. And right now it was good to have them there and he slowed to under ten miles an hour, pressed the window button with the elbow of his hurt arm. Warm air filled the cab. He could smell the river through the mangroves. The lane curved south and his headlights swept past the ruins of the castle owned by the man Bradenton was named after, the good Dr. Braden and his dream to live on this place, the poor sonofabitch, this whole spread—nine hundred acres—his sugar mill, his castle he'd built himself from poured tabby—sand, lime, crushed shells, and water—only to be overrun by the Seminoles and then, years later, burned half to the ground in a fire. Tourists came to see it, these great crumbling walls overgrown with flowers and shaded by cabbage palms, spattered with gull and pelican shit. But these long weeks living with Mama, AJ never did go take a close look, even when driving by; it was too much of a monument to tripping over your own feet and landing in a load of shit. It reminded him of his own stone house out in the slash pine off Myakka City Road where his son and angry wife lived, his only consolation being that he'd done his job by them and hoped to be back there in that solid little castle again one day.

But tonight, when his truck lights lit up the ruins, it was Caporelli Sr. AJ thought of, *his* castle falling, AJ the wily Seminole about to take a piece of it from his rich, lazy ass.

Now he was into the clearing, a wide lawn sloping down to where the Manatee River met the Braden. Up ahead was the dimly lit and sleeping complex of condos and mobile homes. It was just after 2:00 a.m. and he flicked off his headlights and drove in the yellow glow of the lamps along the ground. Nearly every condo had an exterior light shining over their front doors, old people, he noticed, more worried about break-ins than anybody. In front of every other building was a carport, its latticed roof laced with thick and flowering bougainvillea. Each one could hold two cars and he pulled into the third one down on the right alongside Mama's Buick.

In the quiet of the complex his engine sounded loud and wrong and he shut it off quickly, turned to see the top of the sleeping girl's head, her hair parted straight down the middle. Did her mother part it for her and brush it just right? Did she feel like a good mama then?

His eyes ached. He needed cold water on his face, a cup of hot coffee in his hand. The child's shoulders couldn't be more than ten inches from one to the other, and they rose and fell with her breathing. It'd be real bad if she woke right now and started bawling but he couldn't leave her head like this, her chin touching her chest. He got his door open and slid outside, then opened the access door and with three fingers of his good hand lifted her head up and leaned it into the padded corner of the car seat. Damp strands of hair covered her face, but he didn't dare move them away. The night had cooled a bit. Her feet were bare. Balled on the floor behind the passenger seat was a Caporelli's Excavators T-shirt Cap Sr. had proudly handed out from his F-350 like he was giving him a cash bonus. AJ grabbed it now, shook it off and smelled it—cotton and dried sweat and old diesel. He leaned in and draped it over the car seat tray, tucking it in lightly around her shoulders, draping it down over her feet. And again there was that sweet feeling rising up in him that he was doing something good for a stranger, though since Cole had made him a dad he didn't see other people's kids as strangers anymore anyway; true, before Cole, he'd never really noticed them; they were like the barking of a dog you hear but don't listen to so don't think about. But now, every little kid he saw—the loud ones in the Publix trailing their mamas' shopping carts, the quiet ones strapped into minivans he passed on the highway, the ones in front and back yards in neighborhoods he drove through, the ones he worried would chase each other into the busy street—especially them—they were all his; he loved and worried about them all, every single one.

Y Y Y

FOR MANY MOMENTS, when the lights became bright and the music ended and the protectors began motioning for all the kufar to stand and leave, Bassam assumed the time for closing had come and he was relieved, for after leaving the small black room he could not summon the discipline to go, to walk from this den of Shaytan and drive east for Tariq and Imad.

No, again he was too weak.

He sat at a table in the far shadows against the wall so that he might watch more dancing for the mushrikoon, so that he may see again what the black whore showed to him and what he did not have the courage to ask April to see. He had never seen one so closely before and still he trembled from it, his hatred for these kufar rising with the knowledge of his own weakness.

He leans against the Neon leased by Amir. He smokes a cigarette and he must calm himself for the red truck keeping him in this place is only temporary.

He had watched the young ones dress, watched them step into undergarments which still showed their backsides. He watched them pull on their black or red or silver brassieres, pushing their nuhood into them without feeling. The lights were bright upon them, and he could see on one a red rash behind her knee, on another the flesh of her rear area was dimpled when in the darker light it was not, on another—the one from China or Cambodia who had touched his shoulders—there was a raised scar on her arm as if she'd been burned or removed an inked symbol from her skin.

They were so plainly of this earth and they were not what waited for *him*. No, do not forget this, weak Bassam, do not forget for you and your brothers there wait women more beautiful than could ever be made here, women picked by the Creator, the Merciful, the All-Knowing Sustainer and Provider, do not forget He has chosen for you women who have never lain with a man.

And is it not better to go to them pure himself?

At the bar two whores smoke cigarettes. He makes himself think of cutting their throats, how the short blade must be forced into the skin below the jaw. The artery there. He does not care if they feel pain, for anyway it will be brief, and he does not worry of their souls burning for they have brought it upon themselves.

But to kill bodies he has never lain with—this is what weakens him.

MAMA KEPT HER condo cold as a crypt. Said it helped her breathe better. Sleep better. AJ usually didn't like it, but standing in the dark hallway, his keys in his good hand, the door closed behind him, it was like cool water in his face waking him up and clearing his head. He listened for Mama's breathing in her bedroom. She'd never snored till her lungs started to go and now she had to wear that oxygen tube which day and night gave off a slight whistle that got louder when she slept. Or maybe it didn't get louder, just seemed it when there were no other noises in the air. He heard her now, a rising whistle and falling wheeze that was the sound he'd almost grown used to these last few weeks.

He had to hurry. Couldn't chance the child waking up only to get scared and start crying and he wished Mama's place wasn't in the rear with no windows facing the carport. There wasn't an all-night coffee place anywhere near here. If he didn't get some soon he wouldn't make it till morning and goddamn if he was going to nod off and get in a wreck with that little kid in his truck.

He was just going to have to make it here. Get some ice for the pack too. He stepped into the darkened TV room where each night he slept on the foldout couch. If he went to the Puma she always set it up and made it for him. It was there now, and Mama had dragged the coffee table to the foot of it. He just wanted to stretch out and rest awhile. He dropped his keys on the mattress and sat on the low oak table Eddie'd built her not long before he died. It wasn't her birthday or their anniversary or anything but he used to do that sometimes, build her some shelves or a birdhouse or planter and he'd sand it, urethane or paint it, then present it to her as shy and proud as a boy, his face red, his glazed eyes darting from her to what he'd made, then back to her.

AJ sat on it, his hand and arm pulsing fire through his bones. He kept it pressed across his chest and with one hand got his boots untied and off pretty easy. He put them up against the TV and stood, heard a cry. He held his breath and listened. The cry came again and he moved quickly down the hallway for the door, heard it spaced evenly from the last—too evenly. He stopped. It was coming from Mama's room, just a variation of the whistle, that's all. Still, he had to go check on the girl.

He opened the door and hurried over the carpeted hallway in his socks down the short stairwell to the window in the entry. Cotton curtains of stitched golf clubs hung over it and he parted them and looked out at the carport. From here he could just make out through his windshield her bare feet sticking out from under his T-shirt. They were so small and unmoving. He opened the front door and stuck his head out. There were the running fans in the AC units, the ringing night quiet. But no sweet little girl stirring.

Hurrying back into the cool darkness, he thought how she *was* sweet, and he pictured being able to keep her. A playmate for Cole. A living doll for Deena to love and raise. And at that age—what was she? two? three at the most?—you could take a kid to a new family and after a couple years they wouldn't even remember the old one.

In the kitchenette AJ fumbled for the button on the stove's hood and pressed it, dim fluorescent light spreading over the burners. He dropped a filter into the Mr. Coffee, flipped off the lid of Mama's Eight O'Clock Colombian, and dumped in enough for a whole pot. He held his hot wrist to his chest and could see he'd have to put the glass pot in the sink because he couldn't hold it *and* turn on the tap; just a few hours with one working hand and his mind was already adjusting to the new order. That's what worried him about leaving Cole: kids got used to things faster than anyone, the cells of their brains and bodies multiplying and dividing all day and night, taking in new information and new food and growing up and over and through things like the wildflowers overrunning Dr. Braden's ruins. When he saw Cole again, would he come running? Or would he be shy and not remember how much fun the two of them had always had, would he forget how sometimes after work AJ would carry him out to the tall wire grass and throw him up toward the sunset, his boy's small face alight with fear and joy as AJ caught him under the armpits and let himself fall back into the high grass, the two of them laughing and wanting to get up and do it again? Would he have forgotten that?

AJ poured water into the coffeemaker, slid the glass pot under the filter and flicked the switch. It might take a while to sue Caporelli and then collect. Months probably. But he'd be on workers' comp and unemployment. He'd go to that anger class for Deena, then move back home. He wondered how she'd take the news of the windfall heading their way. Would she like the idea of adding that second-floor master bedroom and deck? Or would she just want to sell and go buy some place bigger and better? Maybe a house closer to the water, a stuccoed one-story out on one of the keys. He might get enough for that. Wasn't going to get much done on his place till his bones healed anyway and it'd be just the three of them all day long together. They could get in the truck and drive up and down the coast looking at places. They could go out for lunches at waterfront restaurants. They could play with Cole on the beach, watch the sun slide into the Gulf. It'd be a whole new beginning for them. How could Deena not be happy then?

AJ began unbuttoning his shirt with two fingers, a task he was glad to see he didn't need two hands for. He went back into the dark hallway and as quietly as he could slid open the bifold door to the closet Mama'd emptied for his clothes. He tried to slip out of his shirt without lowering his hurt arm, but the collar got held up at his shoulders so he had to drop both hands and clench his teeth and let the shirt fall behind him.

But the pants were the hardest yet. They were his cotton Dockers Deena'd bought for him, a silver clasp holding them closed above the zipper. If it was a simple button or snap, he could get it loose with a couple of fingers, which he tried, but it was no good; the left side had to be held still for the right to be pushed to the left, then out. That would put pressure on his wrist just where that big prick had broken it.

For a half second he thought of leaving them on, put on a work shirt and his steel-toed boots and hope Cap Jr. didn't notice. But no. This one had nice pleats in it, which is why he saved them for the Puma. If he left those pants on, he may as well shitcan his plan. Could he ask Mama? Get her to help him? No, it wasn't quite three and she needed her sleep.

He was alone. It's what he was used to anyway, wasn't he? He gripped his pants between his pulsing thumb and forefinger, squeezed his eyes shut, took a breath, clenched his teeth, and pushed what felt like a molten sword up his arm into his brain and the air around his head. He let out a cry, he must have, because the room seemed to be in echo and his head felt too light. The smell of fresh coffee filled his nose like a reprieve from God himself.

"Alan? That you?" Her voice was muffled, then clear, like she'd talked into her pillow, then lifted her head.

He waited. Maybe she'd think she dreamt the sound he had to've made. But he was sure she could see the stove light now, and smell the coffee too.

"Alan?"

He heard the squeeze and release of her bedsprings. With his good hand he held his pants up and hurried over to the open doorway. "It's me, Mama. Go back to sleep." Her room smelled like cigarette smoke—old, new, and future.

"What's wrong, honey? Were you hollering?"

"No." His arm hurt more now than it had all night. He pictured the fracture in the bone opened wider by what he'd just done. "You must've dreamed it."

A pale light from one of the security lights outside shone through the curtains. In it Mama looked small and old. Her head was bent low, and the oxygen tube ran from her face down into the darkness of the floor and the air-on-wheels tank.

"Why you making coffee? It's three in the morning, hon."

"Pipeline broke over in Sarasota. I got called in for overtime."

"Oh." She reached for her cigarettes, shook one out, and lit up with her lighter. It was a motion he'd seen her perform ten thousand times, as much a part of her as her voice and hair, her eyes and smell. Still, he never liked seeing that open flame around the oxygen.

"I didn't hear the phone ring."

"My cell phone, Mama." He reached for her doorknob. "Want me to shut this so you can sleep?"

She exhaled a blue stream in the dark air in front of her. She shook her head and stubbed out her cigarette. "No, I'll make you something to eat."

"No time, Mama. I'll get something later. Go back to sleep." He walked into her room over the vacuumed wall-to-wall, holding his pants up and letting his hurt arm down like there was nothing wrong with it. He kissed the top of her head, her once-black hair gray and white now, thin and dry. "Go on back to sleep."

"You be careful."

"G'night, Mama."

"That wife of yours know how hard you work?"

"She does."

She slid back under the covers, her oxygen tube slapping the bedside table. "I hope so, son. I hope so."

⌄ ⌄ ⌄

JEAN SAT IN the dark under the mango sipping Shiraz. She'd gulped the first glass and half of the second, and this and the high walls around her garden and the garden itself—its night-blooming fragrances, its dim tangle of beauty laid out before her, calmed her enough that she could breathe more easily now, the weight momentarily lifted from her chest. But she kept seeing the face of the man on the motorcycle, his whiskers and vacant eyes, and she shuddered at the thought of being naked on a stage in front of such men. How did April do it?

Of course it might be easier if you weren't ashamed of your body—as Jean was, as she'd always been—then it wouldn't be so hard to flaunt. But still, they had to show everything, didn't they? Their breasts and bottom, their *crotch*? She'd never done that even for Harry, and it had pained her whenever they made love in daylight and he would peek down there as he positioned himself between her legs. The shame she'd always felt. Why? But she shoved the question away as if it were an errant fly: she didn't deserve the right to this kind of introspection; she'd set out to bring Franny home and failed. Jean knew April liked her money, that she had nice outfits and plans for a home, but she couldn't have called in sick just this *once*?

Jean's heart was beating dull and quick in her chest. She made herself lean back and breathe deeply through her nose. She tried to relax her shoulders and upper back. Her arm was sore from where the IV had gone, and while she knew she hadn't had a heart attack today she did have two of the other kind and how many more could her old heart take?

Though for all her fears, the ease with which she slipped into a panic, death itself did not frighten her so much; when she was ten or eleven years old in Kansas City, Papa would let her ride out with him to the plains where he went to deliver the babies of farm women. All those fields of wheat, the big barns and farm machinery, some of it horse-drawn, the unpainted clapboard houses under the trees, the smells of pig manure and the chicken houses, her father's sweet pipe tobacco smoke as she followed him in her pride and happiness up porch steps to wait while he climbed to the room where the women were.

And sometimes the babies were born dead. On the way home he drove quietly, reaching over now and then to squeeze her knee or pat her shoulder; he'd speak about nature, and Jean could feel his failure inside the car like thick air and she'd be grateful *she* hadn't died coming into this world. He'd tell her how pioneer women used to have many children, partly because they knew some would die and so it was a constant cycle of hope and loss, hope and loss, though these were not the words he used.

For days or weeks after each stillborn, Jean would move through her afternoons in a state of wonder and gratitude. She'd look across her sliced pork roast and snap peas at her two brothers, both older, both heavy and obnoxious, and she'd be thankful that the worst for her was simply having to put up with them, their calling her Jean the Jelly Bean, the way they both treated her as if she were some kind of mistake, nearly worthless. But she knew better: she had survived being born when so many did not. *She* had lived and, therefore, if for no other reason, she was special in a way, was meant for something in this world.

Now, decades later, pouring herself the last of the Shiraz under her own mango tree, the invisible bully's weight temporarily off her, she had no idea what her purpose had been—raising money for parks and museums? being Harry Hanson's companion and lover all those years? tending this garden and looking after Franny Connors? These were not silly pursuits really, especially the last—if it weren't for that child, Jean believed she'd be almost ready to go. Before Franny there were really only objects to leave behind—her house and car, her investment portfolio, her lovely garden.

Even now, in the darkness, what she could see and smell was a feast for her; all along the wall were dozens of white flowers of her frangipani; at her feet, in cedar boxes, were the yellow hibiscus and trumpet-shaped allamanda, and beyond them, hanging from the palm trunk, were the dim orange flowers of the bougainvillea vine, the jacaranda. Before Franny Connors this was all she worried about leaving behind: Who would care for them? Would the new owners keep them or tear them up to put in a pool or lawn, toss them—roots and all—into a Dumpster somewhere? Just thinking this could bring on the fears, and for the past few months, as they got worse, she assumed it was partly because her garden had gotten more lush and breathtaking, that witnessing its zenith was already triggering in her the expectation of its demise.

The night was quiet now. Jean squinted at her watch, a useless exercise in the dark. Still, it had to be very late, close to two probably. Within an hour April would be home, lifting Franny from the car and carrying her up the back steps. Jean's mornings with her—it was as if her body at this late stage had just discovered an organ it didn't know it had, one that made her feel more alive and necessary than before. It was a feeling she'd never completely had for anyone else: her father, her husband—love wasn't a big enough word.

Far off on the Gulf came the low echoed blast of a freighter's horn. Jean sipped her wine, its warmth spreading out in her chest, and she knew that if Franny's life would be long and joyous if she, Jean, were to die in her dark aromatic garden right now, then let it come. Let Death come and find her happy to go. Happy to.

✓ ✓ ✓

AJ HAD PICKED out a pair of Wranglers he could snap with one hand. Untying his work boots had been one thing, but tying them back up would be another. Maybe after he'd iced his wrist awhile he'd be able to use it, though he doubted it. It hurt worse now than it had since Deena put her considerable weight on it. As soon as he got to the hospital he'd insist on some pain pills, the kind the pharmacist at Walgreen's kept locked up.

He poured himself some coffee into one of Mama's mugs. She had a collection from all the hotels and inns she'd ever worked. This one had an etching on it of an alligator, sailboat, and two crossed tennis rackets. He blew on the coffee and sipped it, strong and bitter the way he liked. The T-shirt he wore was clean and he decided to just leave it on and wear that with his jeans and boots he wasn't going to bother trying to lace up just yet. He opened Mama's front door, made sure it was unlocked, then carried his coffee down the hallway and front stairs and outside to check on the girl, his bootlaces slapping along.

He walked around to the front of his truck. She was still out, her face pointing up at the ceiling, her mouth half-open. He could see the tiny soles of her feet, his T-shirt covering her legs. He shook his head and sipped his coffee. Fucking Spring. That chilly smile of hers and the way she walked through the club like everybody was beneath her. The way the child was crying when he found her, standing there all alone in the kitchen, lost and afraid of the bugs outside and the man inside. And that sonofabitch better not've done anything to her.

It was getting closer to three now. Three and a half hours till he could start up the CAT and climb down into the ditch. For all the fuck-off that Cap Jr. was, he was punctual about showing up when AJ's shift started at six-thirty. Maybe he should get there fifteen or twenty minutes early in case Junior showed up first. There was no way to hide his hand otherwise. He *had* to get there first. And who knew how long it would take to get this girl someplace safe.

Safe. Where the hell was that? Maybe a church wasn't the place. There were all those stories in the news about priests fucking kids. Maybe a Jewish temple would be better. He'd seen one out on Lido Key. Some kind of synagogue. It had an arched entryway and if she stayed asleep he could lay her down in the dark inside corner where nobody'd see her from the road. Across it was the lot of the marina and that's where he'd park till a cruiser pulled up to the temple and he'd drive slowly away and out to Lido Key. But even if it all went like that, even if she did stay asleep and he could drive off without getting stopped, where would the little girl go? Back to her fucking mother who loved her so well? Back to the Puma?

He drank the last of the coffee and went inside. He wanted his driving cup Deena had given him, a Nissan Stainless she always made him go back out to his truck for so she could wash and dry it for him. That's where it was now. Back at his house clean and upside down in the cabinet over the sink. So much of what he wanted and needed at home. He never should've gone back to the Puma tonight.

He should've come here and tried to get some sleep. Now he had a whore's child in his truck and if he got caught with her they'd arrest him for sure.

Why not lie, though? Why not drive to the county sheriff's and tell them he found this little girl walking alone on 301? That'd get Spring into even deeper shit and he'd be a good Samaritan. It might even help his situation with Deena and Cole. The judge would see what kind of man he really was. That was the only way to go, wasn't it?

Except the girl could talk.

She could talk just fine and she'd tell them how and where she really got in his truck, wouldn't she? In fact, what was to keep her from talking about him and his truck once they picked her up at the synagogue?

His heart was knocking inside his chest. He picked up the ice bag and squeezed it between his hurt arm and his ribs and twisted off the cap. He reached into the freezer, the cold air hitting his face. He couldn't hear Mama anymore so she was probably still awake, lying there listening to him out here in the kitchen as he dropped in nine or ten cubes, shut the freezer, and screwed the cap back on the bag. No, he was scaring himself for no reason. The girl couldn't talk *that* well. She wouldn't be able to describe him much and there were only four million pickups on the Gulf Coast. Still, it'd be better if he could leave the girl inside somewhere. When he was a kid, the Nazarene church on Briar Road was never locked. Sometimes he'd walk in late at night and just sit on one of those empty pews. It'd be dark except for a night-light up near the altar the minister always left on. AJ never did pray or anything but it was nice just sitting on the smooth wood in the quiet building made for people to come to. This was before Mama'd met Eddie, when she had a string of boyfriends, two or three a year it seemed like, and their fucking was hard to hear, the way Mama moaned like she was hurt. AJ'd slide out of bed and let himself out the front door and walk to the church or else just go walking. Maybe the synagogue was unlocked too. It'd be better if it were.

TWO PATROL CARS swung swiftly and quietly into the lot, their blue lights spinning, their antennae swaying. April had checked every truck, car, and van there, her eyes burning, her throat sore, the bottoms of her feet cut and scratched, her heart somewhere above her head as she ran over to the first cruiser and put both hands to the glass, though she knew this was a crazy desperate stupid hope because Franny never would've walked off in the dark by herself to be found by them anyway. But she looked, saw yet another empty seat, the interior light coming on above the cage between the front and back.

The first cop was saying something to Lonnie and Louis. Some men called out they wanted to press charges for being held up. April ran to the second car, its blue lights whipping across her eyes, the driver's door opening. She tried to go around it. A hand stopped her. "Whoa, whoa, where you going?"

The policeman's grip was firm, his voice neutral—how could he be neutral? How could anything be the same old nothing right now? *"Did you find her? Do you have her?"*

"We've got nobody. Are you the boy's mother?"

"Boy? I can't find my *daughter.* She's three and somebody's—" She was crying again. The cop walked her around his cruiser, some of the men watching from their cars and trucks, standing around, smoking, talking low to each other, looking right at her like it was her fault they had to stand here and deal with the police and not go on their way. The foreigner from the Champagne was apart from them all, leaning against the trunk of a new white car. He was lighting a cigarette, his eyes on hers.

The cop opened the front passenger door for her. Through a wet blur she saw a clipboard on the seat, a computer monitor and radio set in the dash. In the cup holder was a black mug with gold letters: *#1 Granddad.* April couldn't stop crying. She wiped at her eyes and watched him standing in the shifting blue light talking to the other cop and Louis. Lonnie had walked over to where Paco and Little Andy stood near some men in a truck cab. More men were spread out in the darkness, one of them calling out something to the police, and April's eyes burned and Franny was out there somewhere and it was so wrong for her to be sitting inside this car doing nothing.

The granddad cop lifted a long flashlight and swept it over the customers. He yelled something. Truck and car doors began to open and men climbed out and other men just standing around started walking back to the club. Lonnie and some of the floor hosts stood and watched them go. She'd asked him to check in on Franny, hadn't she? And did he? Did he even once? The older cop climbed in behind the wheel, reached for the radio, and called in to the dispatcher. He waited a second. He glanced over at her like she was a problem he had to solve quickly. The dispatcher's voice came over the radio. A woman's. He talked to it, said he needed another patrol car if there was one and be on standby for a possible Amber.

April knew what that was. Every mother knew what that was. April cried harder now, her whole body shaking with it. She tried to stay quiet so he could hear and do his job and she covered her nose and mouth and there was Tina coming around the corner from the back lot, the headlights on her, the blue lights on her, her face set all scared and worried and April was out of the cruiser yelling over her open door. "You fucking *bitch*! What have you done to my *baby*? *Where is she?!* Where's my *baby*!?!"

Then April was on top of Tina, who was somehow on her back on the ground, the cop lifting April, threatening to handcuff her, saying he'd arrest her if she wanted that. She was breathing hard, a clump of Tina's hair in her fist. She felt better and worse and now he made her sit in the backseat, the door slammed behind her. No handles to get back out when she wanted to. In front of her was wire mesh, and she watched the #1 Granddad get back behind the wheel and reach for his clipboard and it was through this cage he told her to calm down and he asked her to describe her daughter, it was through this she had to tell him all about Franny.

I T WAS HARD not to be even more curious about her now. More cops had pulled up and she was out back with them, answering their questions. The house lights were flat and bright. Under them sat twenty-three customers at tables that needed clearing and wiping down. A few talked quietly with each other, a couple others laughed over a joke or told story, but most were quiet, looking down, then around, then down again like any kid ever held in detention in a room he thought he'd have left far behind by now.

At the Amazon Bar Lonnie waited his turn with the rest of the floor hosts. They were each getting interviewed by a young cop in the pink light of the entrance hall. He'd already let the DJ go home and now it looked like Big Skaggs and Larry T were heading out too. Skaggs stuck his head through the front curtain and called to Louis he'd call him later, but Louis, Retro, and Wendy were busy serving coffee to any customer who cared for some. Most declined but they seemed to like seeing Louis go around with a pot of coffee and a bowl of sugar packets, creamers, and plastic stirrers. By now in the shift he'd have bought the boys a round before locking up, and Lonnie missed his Maker's on the rocks, his Heineken chaser, the way they smoothed out the adrenaline barbs lodged in his muscles and brain. Little Andy sat on the stool beside him. He kept turning his college ring over and over round his finger. It was hard to believe he'd ever gone to school at all. On the other side of him Paco chewed gum and checked the messages on his cell phone, looked out at the detainees on the floor like they were furniture somebody should've put away by now. One of them touched Retro's hip as she leaned over the table with a cup and saucer, but it didn't open up any pocket for Lonnie: it was just a sunburned tourist asking her a simple question, his eyes respectful, and anyway Lonnie's shift was done and he couldn't give a shit—let Louis take care of it or one of the sadists sitting beside him. What he really wanted to do was go out back, get Spring, and help her find her daughter. He still felt as if he'd let her down, and he kept hearing her scream for him to stop the traffic from leaving the lot, how he pulled his Tacoma across the entry, her lovely face contorted in dark-eyed desperation and panic. She could've asked any of them to do it, but again, she'd turned to him.

But why did she have to bring her kid here in the first place? She might be married, but he doubted it. Sadie was the only one here with a husband, a bodybuilder who stripped at a gay club up in Tampa. He'd come in once to see his wife's act. He sat at one of the front tables in his designer's tank top, his tanned and shaved muscles on display for free as he smiled at his naked wife and whistled and clapped as she bent over and flashed him and others her ass. It was like seeing a boxer ringside at another's fight, appraising his style and skill and choice of combinations. It was, Lonnie guessed, the only way to be married in this business.

But most of these girls weren't married and half didn't even have boyfriends; how could they? You work till two, hang around and have a drink till three, then go home and try to sleep but you're too wired and on edge so you flick on the TV and drink. You've got cable and two hundred stations but there's never anything that holds your interest: a lion eating the cubs of the lioness he intends to mount; a set of kitchen knives that'll cut through Sheetrock before slicing your tomatoes with one stroke; music videos of black kids up in the cities with their goofy loose clothes and gaudy chains, their shiny cars and sun-washed mansions; a nun smiling serenely into the camera, quoting from the Bible—a book Lonnie meant to get on tape but kept forgetting to order; there was a cop show from when he was a kid that his old man watched because he liked the big-muscled wisecracking lead; there were shows dedicated to reducing the size of your waist and ass; shows on how to become rich without ever putting down one of your own dollars; there were cable news stations of executions in the Mideast somewhere, bearded men shooting people where they knelt in the soft ground of stadiums where on another day athletes would kick a soccer ball over the blood; there were sports channels, dozens of them, all those bright uniforms and flying balls and over-excited fans; and there was history: world history, United States history, even the history of torture devices—an Egyptian designed a hollow brass lion under which would be prepared a raging fire and it was built so that the condemned inside the lion, the one who screamed his last screams, would sound like the lion, its brass mouth open, and into this device the Egyptian torturer was confined by his king, eager to see how it worked.

It was all enough to make Lonnie drink more than he probably would have, flick off the TV and walk out to his small, coarse lawn. He'd watch the sun rise over the marine supply store across the street. Go back inside and cook eggs and sleep till two or three, then wake to drink coffee and watch more TV till it was time to get back to the club at five.

But this was just his claustrophobic routine; he knew the girls had it far worse. After a night of hustling for cash, moving all the time, pulling off the same clothes over and over, shaking their tits and spreading their legs over and over, acting like they wanted to be nowhere but here over and over, after all that they drank too much at the VIP bar, Louis giving them only one round, then happy to take their money on top of what he already charged them to work here. Soon they'd leave in twos and threes and go find a place to party, but a lot of them had been high most of the night on lines or Oxy anyway and a few smoked dope out back just before their act. Some would take the business cards pushed into their garters and call the cell phones of the men back at their hotels in Sarasota or Tampa Bay, the ones who promised a lucrative time in a suite overlooking the Gulf. And that's where a handful always went and later woke and sobered up or got high again just in time to come back to the club by sundown. And after months or years of this their judgment worsened and the rich men didn't spend so freely anymore and they didn't bring them to suites but inland to motels where they promised free drinks and free drugs if the girls would just let them take a few pictures, just a few shots of what you show all night anyway and c'mon, why not a little video? Just one blow job for my private collection? Or maybe two. And why not do it for me the way I like? It's all for fun and I'll keep you high for weeks, honey. Weeks.

Tina stepped through the curtains from the kitchen. She stood on those new rubber mats, squinting at the houselights, her hair all messed up on one side. Lonnie liked her. Her years of turning men's needs into cash for herself were over and she seemed content taking care of girls who could be her daughters now. It was why she looked close to tears, standing there waving her arm at Louis to come out back; she'd failed at the one thing she was here to do: take care of the girls.

Y Y Y

THESE KUFAR, LOOK at them. They sit at the dirty tables in this dirty hole wearing the short pants that show themselves. They smoke and laugh and some of them seem frightened of their own police as they are asked one at a time into the front area to be questioned. Soon Bassam will be as well. Twice he has checked his pockets and three times he has inspected his license to make certain it is the one from Florida. Not Virginia. Though his part will be activated in Massachusetts, a word he cannot say. Only Boston. This he can say.

Most of these policemen are young like him. They believe they are strong but it would be easy to kill them. He has learned so many ways to do it—hand to hand, knife to gun, gun to bomb. At the camp for training he was best with small weapons and there is the feeling he has been given a gift he will never use. Beside his table two men laugh. On their fingers are the rings of wives. One of them wears a tie and shirt, his sleeves folded back to reveal a gold watch, and he smiles briefly at Bassam, who does not return it. But he nods so as not to incite an argument, so as not to draw attention.

A young policeman curls his finger to the businessman, who jokes with the other and rises. Bassam must be permitted to leave soon. There is the drive back to the east. He should be there before sunrise for the first prayer. Amir is in the north now but each dawn for days the Egyptian has kicked his mattress and Tariq's mattress and the mattress of Imad. "The time of living like the kufar is over. Get up and perform your ablutions, my brothers. We must pray for strength. As-salaatu khayrun min'n-nawm. Prayer is better than sleep. Rise!"

The Jew owner moves among the tables grasping his pot of coffee. He sees to the comfort of these people he wishes to come back again and again. One of the whores, the white one with the red hair, follows with cream and sugar, and Bassam allows the Jew to pour his coffee though he will no longer touch the cup touched by the Jew.

This hatred gives him strength.

The hatred that was so pure and clear in the disciplined months in camp, the hatred that began to weaken in Dubai and has weakened further here in this Florida with its heat and all the women who each day show so much of themselves.

Amir has moved them to many places. Del Ray Beach, Boynton Beach, Hollywood, Deerfield, the small rooms smelling of men and incense and the pizza they often eat, the empty boxes stacked upon the floor near the kitchen sink where they would perform their ablutions.

But moving so much has kept them united. Bassam and Imad and Tariq like one man now, a shahid with three heads but one heart.

One heart.

With Amir they had enrolled at gymnasiums in each town, places where the kufar go to keep their bodies as well maintained as the Grand Am and Le Mans and Duster Bassam and his brothers had driven in their old nothingness. At the first one in Venice, because they knew nothing of lifting weights, the gym manager assigned them a trainer Amir ignored. He did not change into exercise clothing as the others did but remained dressed in a collared shirt and pressed pants and leather shoes from Germany. He moved from machine to machine, pushing or pulling on whatever handles or bars there were to hold, sweating lightly, not speaking to or even looking at the woman trainer named Kelly who tried to correct him.

She was young. The age of Bassam, Tariq, and Imad. Tariq, that habit of never closing his lips fully which makes him look stupid though he is not, he stared at her body you could see so easily in its tight gym clothing, her uncovered arms and legs, centimeters of her flat belly too. And Imad, tall, heavy Imad who back home had told jokes and laughed which made everyone else laugh, since the camps he has grown quiet, his laughter turned to stone, and he listened to the young trainer talk as if deciding the most efficient way to kill her.

But Bassam liked her brown eyes, her brown hair, how she had it tucked up into pins revealing her neck. How she smiled at him and touched his shoulder or arms or back as she instructed him. She was kind. He could see it and feel it. She was kind.

As were so many others. Gloria, the real estate woman who found them their first apartment in Del Ray Beach. She was short and wore very much jewelry and lipstick, but she laughed at whatever she said and looked into Bassam's eyes with hers, blue and smiling, and he felt liked by her even though she did not know him. It made him want to sit with her, a kafir and a woman, and sip tea and tell her things he had never told to anyone. She asked them their names and tried to pronounce them correctly though she could not and she laughed at herself, squeezed his arm, and he could not bear being in her presence any longer.

There was Cliff, the man at the fuel station store three blocks south. Taller than Bassam, he was as old as his father, his hair colored blond, his whiskers gray. Upon his arms were inked figures of naked women, and when Bassam came in for more milk or bread or Cokes, he asked how his studies were coming, was he having any goddamned *fun?* There were the women who served them food in restaurants, the young ones or older ones, the pretty or the ugly, they were polite and smiled while looking them in their eyes. Except Amir's. Their smiles changed then. They could see and feel his hatred for them, and Bassam had felt soft and weak and not worthy of the title shahid; these people should fear him, too. He was prepared to do what he was chosen for. They must not doubt this. No one should question this.

It had been months since their training and now he and Tariq and Imad were back home. After the purity of camp, where daily they had fought hand to hand, where they fired the AK-47 while running, where they wired plastic explosives while reciting from Al-Anfal and Al-Tawbah, where they fasted and cleansed themselves and where their softness fell away like fat from a lamb, it was difficult being once again in the dusty and idle streets of Khamis Mushayt; Karim and the others wanted to race, to smoke, to gossip, to stay baboons. Imad and Tariq had grown beards and tried to teach their old friends to stay away from these evils. But Karim, standing before them in his Nike cap and T-shirt and jeans, his shiny cell phone in his hand, he was already lost; for two years he had studied in London, something he was always boasting, and he showed them the photograph of the Zionist girl from Jerusalem who had loved him, his mind soiled, his heart falling to the West. Karim told them they should not believe everything the Imams say. "Read the Qur'an, my friends. It says Ahl al-Kitab, the People of the Book, *Christians and Jews*, deserve respect because they are fellow monotheists. Have you read all the suras? Because I have. Read 3:113–115: 'They believe in Allah and the Last Day; they enjoin what is right and forbid what is wrong; and they hasten in the emulation of all good works. They are in the ranks of the righteous.'"

"And that is why they enslave the Palestinians?" Tariq said. "That is why they occupy our land and kill our brothers in Iraq? You have fucked a Jew, what can you tell us about anything? Go play with your cell phone. You are not going where we are going."

"Yes," Karim laughed. "Have a nice trip." And he turned and walked away, the sun on his back, dust on the soles of his Nike shoes; soon he would be an unbeliever and after his death he would walk the bridge over hell as all souls do, and Bassam could only leave it to the Most Merciful to spare him from the fall to Jahannam. For Karim and the rest did not know who they were talking to: shuhada', martyrs who would sit in the highest rooms with Allah, men whose names would never be forgotten.

The moon was high. It shone blue on the dome of the mosque across the street. It was after Isha, the final prayer, and Bassam sat in the outer building of their home before his father. Many of Bassam's brothers wanted to sit down as well, but Ahmed al-Jizani told them to leave until the meal was served, he wanted to talk alone with Bassam. They sipped hot tea. Inside the main house Bassam's mother and sisters were preparing lamb kufta. He could smell it and knew they would squeeze lemons over it and serve it with tahina sauce and there would be laban bi khiyar and he was very hungry from the fasting in camp. His father sat against the wall dressed in a new thawb the color of linen. It was too loose upon him and he appeared tired.

"So you have taken up jihad?"

"Yes, Father."

"Do you understand what this means?"

"Yes."

His father looked at him as he had always looked at him, as if all the sons before Bassam had been the best. "Tell me then, what does this mean?"

"It means I am prepared to die for Allah."

"No, that is not jihad. That is a lower meaning of it." His father sipped his tea, his eyes on him. "What did they teach you at this place?"

"The Truth, Father. They taught me the Truth."

"And what is the truth, Bassam? Who can know the truth but Allah?"

Bassam nodded. He would not receive his father's blessings. Why sit here any longer? Why sit before this man who had built a mosque, yes, but also buildings on the air base of the kufar. His father was an important man, an al-Jizani, but his mind and heart had become weakened by the ahl al-shirk, the polytheists and the unbelievers.

"Father?"

"Yes, speak."

"They want to occupy our land. They want to separate us from Islam. Khalid—"

"What of Khalid?"

"Nothing."

"Do not say this. What of Khalid?"

"He was lost. He died because he was lost."

"Your brother drove too fast. Do you understand this? He was no more lost than am I."

Bassam looked down at his hands. They were clean, his feet as well, his body strong and pure and prepared, yet he was ashamed. He sat there before his own father ashamed. Of *him*. Of Ahmed al-Jizani.

His father sat forward. He lowered his tea quickly, some of it spilling onto his hand. "You have never been a bright boy, Bassam, so you must listen to me carefully. Jihad is this: it is a struggle within yourself, that is all. It is the struggle to live as Allah wishes us to live. As good people. Do you understand? As good people. Now go call your brothers please."

Soon they were all eating kufta, and it was clear to Bassam, the dull boy, the slow one, that his father had favored not Rashad the officer or Adil the engineer, not the businessmen so many of his brothers had become, three of them moving their families to Riyadh, not even the one who had worked so hard as a stock boy for Ali al-Fahd, no, their father had favored the one who had done nothing but dream of the West and smoke and drive too fast listening to an American Jew.

And Allah took him from Ahmed al-Jizani.

Allah took the son whose death would hurt him most.

Because Ahmed al-Jizani, builder of air bases for the kufar, he has forgotten the Creator, the Mighty, the Sustainer and Provider. As have so many others across the kingdom. They have allowed television into their homes. They have installed satellite dishes onto their roofs and now their families gather between Maghrib and Isha and watch programs from the West. Censored yes, but the women are uncovered and the men carry weapons and drive shining cars in their fallen cities. On Fridays, the Day of Gathering, entire families used to picnic in the desert between the evening prayers; now they stay inside to be drawn into the television of the kufar while thousands of young men like Karim lounge in the streets in kufar clothing, secretly listening to their music and dreaming of lying again with Jews.

Meanwhile the Zionist/Crusader alliance slaughter their Muslim brothers and sisters in Chechnya and Kashmir, Afghanistan, Bosnia, and Palestine.

It was two hours before the final prayer. The mosque was empty. Bassam, Tariq, and Imad were dressed in clean thawbs and they had performed their ablutions slowly and with care. Tariq's beard was thick while Imad's was light and bushy and in it was a crumb of bread his ablutions had not found and Bassam reached out and picked it free.

Imad's eyes grew light, as if he were about to joke, but then he nodded and they knelt facing Makkah. They held hands, Tariq's small and worn, Imad's large, still damp from his ablutions. At camp, many times during the day they were told to recite the Shahaada, and so they did it now, their heads bowed. "La ilaha illa Allah wa Muhammad ar-rasulullah. There is no god worthy to be worshipped except Allah, and Muhammad is the messenger of Allah."

Imad looked down at Bassam as if he were unsure what to do next. Bassam closed his eyes and breathed in the air still sweet from the incense burned for Maghrib. Inside his head and heart were the words he had recited again and again while cleaning his weapon at camp, pulling free the loaded magazine, blowing dust from the breech, ramming the oiled rod into the barrel.

"And from His Book: 'O Lord, pour Your patience upon us and make our feet steadfast and give us victory over the unbelievers. Lord, forgive our sins and excesses. You move the clouds. You gave us victory over the enemy, conquer them and give us victory over them.'

"Allahu Akbar, Allahu Akbar, Allahu Akbar. There is no god worthy to be worshipped except Allah."

And yes, Bassam, say again the oath you made in camp. "The pledge of Allah and His covenant is upon me, to energetically listen and obey the superiors who are doing this work, rising early in times of difficulty and ease.

"Bismillah. In the name of Allah."

And once more, the Shahaada: "La ilaha illa Allah wa Muhammad ar-rasulullah."

Bassam stood first, Imad and Tariq following. Imad's eyes were shining. He smiled down at them and put his arms around their shoulders. "Brothers, we have bound ourselves to the Holy One as shuhada'. This bayat has sealed this. Insha'Allah, we will live together forever in Jannah." And he hugged Bassam and Tariq to him, his thawb smelling of fresh linen, his throat of soap and water.

Before leaving for Dubai, Bassam embraced his mother at the door. When he was young she only wore kaftans under the jamah, but now she was in a dress made by the kufar, a modest purple dress with long sleeves that covered her arms, yes, but still a dress made by our enemy, and she smiled at him, his short, round mother with her graying hair and deep brown eyes she'd passed to him. She appeared as if she might weep, for he was traveling to a place he could not name to her. She held him and kissed both his cheeks, calling him Bassam when he was now Mansoor, the Victorious, the name he decided to take with his oath.

Since he'd become a jihadi, living among his family was like living in a dream except in the dream everyone else is sleeping while you are awake. They sleep and do not know they sleep. His mother did not even know she was no longer awake with the Creator as she should be. She smelled of perfume and the amber incense she preferred to burn. He could not hold back any longer. "Soon, Allah willing, everyone will know my name, O Mother. You will be very proud that I am your son."

"Bassam, darling, I *am* proud. Please, don't do anything foolish. You are a good boy. Please, where are you going? Please, tell me." She rubbed her thumbs along his cheeks, the stubble there.

He nodded to his sleeping mother. He took her wrists and pressed her hands gently together. "I will call you. I will call you soon."

Though he never had. Months now, and he never had.

The black whore blows out smoke from her cigarette and she looks at him from the bar. She stands near the Jew owner and they drink coffee from white cups like his he has not touched. She smiles at Bassam, and he looks away. He knows when they are let go by these police she will try to get more of the money he should not have spent. She will offer him her qus, and not just to view, he knows this, and it is like bleeding in the Red Sea, sharks smelling his blood from kilometers away, his weakness, Shaytan trying to pull him from the highest rooms of Jannah to the lowest and hottest of Jahannam. How deceptive he is, and yes, Bassam is afraid he will like it too much to leave this earth; he will lose his resolve, his bayat with his brothers and with the All-Knowing will be broken and is there any fire more hot than that reserved for a failed shahid? For one who loses his way?

But what is worse is what he never would have known as he hardened and purified himself in training, as he prayed steadfastly in tents and motel rooms and autos, that he would *like* these kufar, that he would like Kelly and Gloria and Cliff, and yes, this April who calls herself Spring, her brown eyes that could belong to a good girl from Khamis Mushayt, whose skin is soft and warm and whose hair is shining, and who smells not of lust but of companionship, he likes her as well. And there is a sting in his heart for what he told her last, not because it is not true—because she will burn, they will all burn—but because he was using the truth to push himself away from her and his own weakness. Her scar from delivering her child, so dry and raised, the color of old goatskin, not as if it had been cut and healed but burned, like the skin of the burned. He made himself see her entire body that way, bare belly and hips and legs, her round shoulders and throat and face, her nuhood he so weakly and strongly wanted to touch. He forced himself to see it as it will be.

All the money he gave to her. How could he justify it? How would he explain it to Amir, who would know precisely how much.

"Sir?" A young policeman points at him, curling his finger rudely for him to come be questioned.

There are four kufar remaining. As Bassam stands, one of them nods and smiles at him as if they are all brothers in this misunderstanding, as if this is a small price to pay for their pleasure here, the only price.

Bassam ignores him and walks away from the empty tables and chairs, damp with spilled alcohol and scattered with ash. His shirt sticks to the sweat of his back and he is thirsty. He keeps his eyes on the young policeman but Bassam can feel the eyes of the black whore upon him, her smile, her long dark legs and arms, her white teeth, Shaytan reaching from inside her to pull him down with these mushrikoon.

Bassam does not look at her. And he will not look at her. The time for looking is over. The time of living so haram is through. He lifts his chin and follows the policeman. The curtain is parted by one of the men paid to protect these whores, this one tall and without muscle, looking down at Bassam as if he were a dog, a dog someone should have caged such a very long time ago.

✌ ✌ ✌

DEENA COULDN'T SLEEP. She had for a while, but now she was awake, lying on her back in the dark, the constant wind from the fan blowing across her face. She kept thinking how bad AJ had looked. His hand was broken somehow, his eyes red from drinking and crying, and even though he'd hurt her and she did the right thing calling the police, it seemed her fault he was turning into such a mess. She kicked off the sheet.

The first few nights he was gone felt like when hurricane season is finally over. She and Cole had sweet, quiet suppers together, and whenever he asked about Daddy, she told him his mama was sick and he had to go take care of her. But then she got scared. She thought of all the news stories she'd heard of husbands ignoring restraining orders and coming back madder than they were before. There was that woman with three kids down in Venice. Her husband had been beating her for years and she finally called the police and had the order on him less than a day when he came back with a shotgun, kicked in the front door, and chased her past the kids into the bathroom and killed her. She couldn't picture AJ doing anything like that, but then she never guessed he'd ever hit her either. And how could he not be getting madder and madder having to live with his old, wheezy mother and stay away from his son?

One night at the end of that first week, after Cole was asleep, Deena had taken AJ's .22 rifle out of the closet. It was a good-looking gun with a shiny stock and a long straight barrel. AJ's stepdaddy had left it to him, and AJ wanted to teach her how to shoot it but she already knew how; her father owned all kinds of guns and when she was eight or nine he carried their picnic bench down to the beach and lined up Budweiser and soup cans and it wasn't long before she could hit each one with a rifle just like this. She was good with a pistol too, but Daddy's semiautomatics scared her with their kick in her hand and how easy it was to fire off three or four bullets just like that.

I'll kill him. Daddy in their kitchen at home, his lined face and big belly, the way he glanced over at Mom like he was expecting her to say something though she didn't. *He lays so much as a fingernail on you, I swear to Christ I'll shoot him where he stands.*

That didn't help anything. Four nights in a row after AJ got driven away, her father had come over and played with Cole and watched some TV with her, his .380 strapped in a holster on his belt.

"Daddy, you can't keep coming over here."

"Yes I can."

"What if he comes and you shoot him? Then I lose you, too."

"What do you mean *too*? You *miss* him?"

"He's my husband."

"You can get another. A better one."

Could she? Really. Could she? Daddy had always ignored how dumpy-looking she was. How in high school she'd only had Reilly, who was skinny and hated people and animals and with his mustache and pointy nose looked like some kind of rodent. He called her a fat whore, and that was after they'd done it on the moldy couch on his parents' sunporch.

"Please go, Dad. If he comes, I'll call the police like I'm supposed to."

He did go but not before he unstrapped his .380 and laid it on the kitchen counter. "Keep it."

"I don't want that in the house with Cole. If you leave it here I swear I'll throw it away."

He smiled sadly, took it back, hugged her. "You call me."

"I will." Though she knew she wouldn't, knew if she ever had to because of AJ that her daddy would drive up with another loaded gun. It's why people owned guns in the first place, wasn't it? Because they were just itching for a good reason to use them, a better one than picking off cans and shooting squirrels? But Daddy showing up like that had scared her even more than she'd been and for a week or more she slept with AJ's rifle on the floor by his side of the bed. Each morning before Cole woke, she'd put the loaded clip in her bedside drawer, then lean the rifle back in the corner of the closet behind AJ's button-down shirts.

Seeing those shirts made her sad. He wore them only to church or a dinner at her family's house on the lake, and she knew if they ever fixed things between them that Mom and Dad would have to welcome him back, though it would never be the way it was before he'd slapped her not once, but twice, and the last time had sent her flying across the kitchen in front of Cole and she had to call 911, she just had to.

Still, by the end of the second week the fear was gone and all she felt was sad and guilty and alone. She'd read and sing Cole to sleep, then watch TV and skim magazines and eat a snack. When she finally went to bed she left the rifle in the closet and tried to rest but she couldn't. She kept thinking about him, remembering him really, from before, when she worked at the Walgreen's and he was her boss. She wasn't so big then and she was good at her job, her drawer hardly ever over or under. What she liked about him was how shy he was, how he might be telling her and another cashier about a new special or an updated store policy from the district manager and his eyes would pass over her breasts and he'd look away fast, his face reddening up. He was polite and looked handsome in his white shirt and tie and khakis with the crease up the leg. She wondered if he ironed them himself. He wasn't much older than she was but he had to be pretty smart to be a shift manager already.

Then that cool night in January when her battery died. She was the last cashier to leave. She was still sitting in her car when the overnight manager relieved AJ and he came out and saw her there. He stood on the sidewalk, the fluorescent light of the store behind him, looking at her behind the wheel of her mother's Geo like she might be sick or hurt. For a second it didn't look like he was going to do anything but stand there. Then he walked over and she opened the door and told him about the dead battery, that she was about to call her folks but didn't want to wake them.

"I'll drive you."

His truck had smelled new, and sitting in it, buckled up beside him, driving out of the parking lot riding so high, she felt as if she'd just won something. He said he was thirsty, that it was a Friday night and did she want to get a beer somewhere?

"I'm only nineteen."

"That's okay, I'll pick up a six."

It was cold and went down real smooth after seven hours on her feet. She was surprised he drank his Miller so openly driving down the road. He seemed so careful at work. He asked where she lived and she told him.

"You do?" Like he was surprised, like he hadn't expected she'd live in a house on the water. But then he glanced over at her and smiled. "You got to stop calling me Mr. Carey."

"Well what's your name?"

"AJ."

"What's that stand for?"

"Ask Jesus."

"You're teasing me."

He looked over at her. He switched on the radio, got a good station from Tampa. They were on Myakka City Road driving in the dark. He finished his beer and opened another. She did too. They drove quietly a while, just listening to the music, REM singing about a man on the moon. He turned it down low. "Where'd you go to high school?" His voice was soft and he sounded interested and like he wasn't just making conversation.

"Bradenton."

"You have any brothers or sisters?"

"My brother Reggie. He's in the army."

"So what do you like to do?"

"What do *you* like to do?"

"I don't know—work, I guess."

"For fun?"

"Yeah, I like work. You?"

"What?"

"You like to work?"

"It's all right. I like to read, watch some TV. I play cards with my mother a lot."

He looked at her a little longer than was safe. "I play cards with my mama, too." Her cheeks had heated up and her mouth went dry but it made her feel good, that look he gave her. Then he pulled off the main road and parked under a tree. He cut off the engine, left the radio on. "You got a boyfriend?"

"No."

His hand on her knee and how she had to lean forward to get that first long kiss that so quickly turned into something she hadn't seen coming, but it wasn't at all like with Reilly; it was gentle and got her excited and she knew she should've made herself a little harder to get than that, but how could she know if he'd ever drive her home again, if she'd ever be with him like this again? And after, the way he dropped his forehead to her breast, lay his cheek against it.

Then that one-room studio of his in that loud, smelly complex behind the mall. It seemed all they did was make love, watch TV, and eat, then make love some more. Her breasts got tender fast and she felt a little off.

She'd been alone at his place when she peed on the stick over the toilet. She hadn't known how to tell him. Didn't know if she ever wanted to tell him. But she wasn't the kind to go and get rid of it so he'd have to know and they'd have to figure out what to do next. He'd never even told her he loved her, though, so what was he going to say to this? And how was she going to tell him? She decided to just leave the stick on a napkin on his counter near the coffee machine. She tore off the corner of a grocery bag and wrote: *Call me. Deena.*

It was after one and she was falling asleep in front of Jay Leno, waiting for the phone to go off in her hand. Her eyes were closed and there were the TV voices, then another one, a tapping. A tapping that became a knocking that opened her eyes. She looked behind her through the dark living room and kitchen and could see under the outdoor light his face framed in the door's window.

She didn't know if she'd dozed off or not. She was a little worried about her breath but didn't want him to keep knocking and wake her folks. She got up and let him in. He followed her to the living room lit only by the light of the TV, and she found the remote and pressed the mute button. He was still in his Walgreen's outfit, his tie loosened. He kept looking at her, then away, just like he used to whenever he couldn't help but glance at her breasts.

He said, "I guess we shoulda been more careful, huh?"

"Yeah."

He looked at the screen. A new truck was climbing a mountain road, then it was carrying a load of lumber, then a load of kids and dogs pulling into a green field to play ball. "We gonna keep it?"

She liked that he'd said we. She knew he was going to do the right thing, whether he liked it or not, and she felt like crying though it bothered her to see him sitting straight as a soldier getting orders. "Yes."

His eyes were back on the TV. "Get married too?"

"If you want."

"Do you?"

"It'd be better for the baby, wouldn't it?"

He nodded, looked at her. "Yeah." He smiled then, though he didn't look happy.

"C'mere." She patted her leg and he lay his head in her lap. She lightly scratched her fingernails through his short hair and she wanted to say something to make him feel better, though she didn't know what that was. Now the room was too quiet. She pressed the mute button and Jay Leno's teasing voice was in the air again. AJ seemed to be watching it and she was watching him: Who *was* he anyway? Out of all the millions and millions of men in the world, how did this one get to be the father of her baby? Did she even know him? Love him? Did she *love* him?

She didn't think so. Not yet. And she tried not to study too much his physical qualities, how his ears stuck out a bit too far from his head, how his trunk was short and his legs kind of long; his eyes were a handsome blue, but they were set too deep under a forehead that wasn't high enough. It made him look less intelligent than she knew he was. Would their baby look like that? A little dim-witted?

Her face grew hot and she stopped scratching his head. On the TV Jay was interviewing an actress she recognized though she couldn't remember her name. She was probably Deena's age exactly and had millions of dollars and long black hair and a body no man anywhere would ever say no to and how could Deena have forgotten how AJ could hardly keep his hands off her? How could she forget so soon that he treated her as if she looked like *that* girl on the TV right now?

"AJ?"

"Yeah?"

"You okay?"

He raised his head. "Can you turn this off?"

She did. He sat away from her at the end of the couch. The living room was dark and she could only see his face in the pale light across the floor.

"I feel pretty stupid, Deena."

"It's not all your fault."

"I know, but—" He shrugged, sat there.

"What?"

"I should've pulled out."

"No, I don't like that." Reilly coming on her belly, no tenderness at all.

"It could get rough. I don't make much, and wouldn't you have to be home with the kid?"

"Yeah." She wanted to ask him then if he loved her. She could feel the question right there in her throat, but he might ask her back and what would she say?

"Your folks know?"

"Not yet."

He looked away again. She was aware she was sitting there in just her baggy T-shirt and loose pajama pants, her hair messed up, no makeup on, yet she felt a way she never had before, like she held all the power that could be held, that she was completely and utterly in charge and was beautiful because of it, no matter how lost he seemed to be right now, her toes pressing against his knee. She lifted her T-shirt and began to pull off her bottoms.

"Your folks."

"We'll be quiet."

When he came, his pants around his knees, he whimpered and she held him close. "Do we love each other, AJ?"

"We will."

There was the justice of the peace and AJ training in heavy equipment, then working with Daddy. They bought this abandoned house

AJ fixed up himself. The baby grew and grew and she came to love this new direction her life had taken. She loved how much attention her mother and father gave her, how her mom would take her shopping for baby things and at night and on weekends Daddy would smile over at her the way he did when she was a little kid, as if she were the only girl ever invented. Before falling asleep beside her, AJ would say those three words to her and she'd say them back and she didn't feel like a liar saying them but she didn't feel them much either. Then they were in this house and she didn't want to be ungrateful, but it was a tiny house. They painted it in whites and yellows, but still, she couldn't breathe in it. During the long long days when AJ was at work and she was here alone with Cole, his toys scattered over the floor so she couldn't walk anywhere without stepping on one, she'd take him outside to play in the grass and she'd sit in a lawn chair and try to get some sun on her legs and face and arms. She'd skim her magazines and try not to eat anything. That's all she wanted to do—eat. She didn't want to admit it and felt like an awful mother even thinking it, but she was *bored* just taking care of Cole. She loved him more than she loved the pumping of her own heart; she loved seeing the faces he made—curious, angry, confused, even sad and full of joy; she loved the way he would turn his blue eyes up at her as if she were the only other human being who ever lived; she loved that he came from her body yet had his own; she loved his hair and skin, his ears, and nose, and knees, the way they turned in like hers; she loved his sweet-milk smell, she loved his high voice and how he couldn't say his *r*'s; she loved how he climbed into her lap to watch a video, how he fell asleep against her breasts.

Still, she needed to go out and *do* something. Even working at Walgreen's had felt like something; she was serving people who needed things when they needed them and she got paid to make sure they got them. She liked that part the most. Getting that check with her name on it and cashing it and having that money in her pocket she'd earned. She saved over two thousand dollars but had to give every cent of it to AJ to go toward this place. That gave her some sense of pride, though—it did. But now she felt her time out in the world was already over. They couldn't afford day care, but wouldn't her mother watch Cole now? At least a few days or nights a week? Was Deena really going to spend the rest of her life just taking care of others? Her son and maybe more children, and AJ, who, these past three years had become a tired, short-tempered tangle of wants and needs she alone had to see to: she washed, dried, folded, and put away his clothes. She made the bed after he left it, wiped down the sink after he'd shaved there, all those dark whisker nubs pooling at the faucet she had to wipe off too; she made sure he had his lunch packed— almost always the same thing, smooth peanut butter with strawberry jelly, two bananas, a bag of Ruffles chips, and a thermos of lemonade. If she made him tuna instead, or substituted apples for bananas, she'd hear about it that night when she heard about everything else she wasn't doing right: *Why can't you pick up the goddamn toys off the floor, D? Why do you cook with so much grease all the time? Didn't Cole wear that shirt yesterday too? Why can't you keep a couple cans of beer cold in the fridge, Deena? You have any idea how goddamn hot it gets running heavy machinery in this fuckin' heat?*

It always came down to that: his anger at her, his resentment that he had to do something all day he hated while she got to stay home with Cole and play house. That's what he called what she did—"playing house." Then, the once every four or five weeks she actually spent a little money on just *herself*, to color her hair a bit or put a wave in it or something small like that she did so she didn't feel completely invisible, he'd yell at her, tell her she'd looked better before and how much did that cost anyway? She'd lie and tell him thirty dollars when it was really twice that and still he'd cuss and shake his head, grab another beer from the fridge and sit down in front of the TV, Cole playing on the floor at his feet.

And later, when they were in bed, lying stiff and quiet beside each other, hardly breathing it seemed, she wanted to ask him why he was so damn mad and miserable all the time. Was it just the job? Because if it was, why not quit and go back to work at the store? How many times had he pushed that in her face? *I could've been district manager by now, you know. I'd be making just about as* much. She wanted to ask him these things but part of her was so hurt by him and mad at him for how he treated her, for how little he valued what she did, that she just couldn't open her mouth to start. Then he'd turn to her and she always got fooled. She didn't know why she did but she did; she thought he might speak for once, to talk to her even a little the way he used to, but she'd feel his fingers running up her leg, feel his palm push against a soft thigh to part them. It was the last thing she wanted to do, not because she didn't like it, but because she didn't like it when she didn't like *him*.

There were those hot afternoons when she sat in the sun in shorts and a T-shirt, barefoot, Cole pushing his truck over the grass, and she'd close her eyes and sometimes get that warm thick throb between her legs, picture them opening for the man kissing his way up to what she offered. Sometimes it was AJ's face she saw, that low forehead and big ears, those soft blue eyes she tried to concentrate on, but other times it'd be other men. Most of them were faceless or nameless but some were actors she liked and read about a lot: Pierce Brosnan and that sneaky smile, like he had a surprise for you and still wouldn't tell; Billy Baldwin, Brad Pitt, and strange to say, Morgan Freeman, not because he was black—though she was curious what the difference would be—but because he was older and seemed so kind and caring with that sad, knowing smile of his like he'd know just what to do if she ever gave herself to him.

But it wasn't other men she wanted, or even sex; it was that feeling she'd had early on with AJ, that not only was she desirable but likable. That she was *liked*. And those tears on AJ's cheeks tonight. Was he just feeling lonely and sorry for himself or did he really miss her? And if he did, was it just the sex. Or was it *her*? And if it was her, was that a good thing? Did she really want him back? Or was he just better than nothing? Better than nobody?

Deena swung her legs out of bed and walked down the darkened hall past Cole's room into the kitchen. She opened the freezer and reached for the last of the ice cream, got a spoon from the dish drainer, stood at the counter, and ate slowly. She thought of AJ's broken wrist. She had a vague curiosity about how he'd done it, but not much. She just kept thinking how hard it would be for him to hit her with it now, how much it would hurt.

Y   Y   Y

D RIVING DOWN MANATEE in the predawn, it was no use even trying to sip his coffee *and* ice his wrist *and* drive *and* listen to the young girl whine for food and her mama. Maybe he shouldn't've woke her up just to get some Benadryl down her, but he knew how things went—you don't look out for one thing and then the other comes up and hits you on the back of the head: What if she woke up when he planned to lift her out of Cole's seat at the temple on Lido Key? How could he lay her down somewhere then? But now she was as up as Cole used to get after a good nap, sitting straight, pushing her hair back from her eyes, looking out at dark, sleeping Bradenton.

"I'm hungry."

"It's late, Francie. You go back to sleep till we get to your mama's house."

He glanced up at her in the rearview. She seemed to take in what he'd said: Sleeping, then her mama.

"My name is *Franny.*"

"Franny." He smiled at her in the mirror. He liked her spunk, but what would come of it? Spunk turns to sassy turns to bitch turns to whore. Just like her mama. Who's to say this runt wouldn't grow up into another Spring? Another Marianne? Just smiling and shaking her tits and leading you on till you're broke and your Visa's full and you're holding your dick in your hand?

"I'm hungry."

His numbed wrist rested against the door handle. Every time he slowed or sped up or made a turn, the ice pack slid off onto his leg and he had to press his knees to the wheel to hold it steady and readjust the pack with his good hand. He wasn't even going to try to sip the coffee from the holder. He never did find a cup worth a shit for driving and had settled on a red plastic one from Busch Gardens with no lid and already a third of it had sloshed out all over his truck carpet. He needed to stop and get a proper cup. He needed to stop and get this girl a snack so she'd get quiet again and the Benadryl could kick in.

"Please, I'm hungry. And I'm thirsty."

"I heard you, hon."

In the darkness he drove under live oaks, Spanish moss hanging down like nagging reminders of something he'd forgotten to do. He passed by scrappy yards and small houses, everybody in them asleep, probably curled up to someone they loved. He'd never gotten tired of that with Deena. Even after she'd gained all that weight. Even after nights of bitching and screaming, it'd all be over by one or two in the morning and they'd just be echoes in his head and she was a soft, warm body he'd curl up against, his nose in her hair, his hand and arm on her soft hip. Whenever he dreamed of Marianne, he never did get that far with her—the way he saw Deena, like she wasn't just a woman but home itself.

"I'm thirsty."

At the turnoff to 301 the lights of the Mobil station shone whitely and there was a convenience store section and he bet they had coffee brewed in there. He checked his gas gauge. Quarter tank left. He'd get coffee and gas and buy this girl a snack. But did he want that? Wouldn't that absorb some of the Benadryl he'd given her? Wouldn't that make it harder for her to go back to sleep? He didn't know, but he couldn't have her hungry and going on and goddamned on.

He pulled up to the pumps and cut the engine, the ice bag slipping off his wrist onto his leg. He tossed it onto the leftover twelve-pack on the passenger's seat.

"I want a Shush Puppie."

"A hush puppy?" Mama used to make them when he and Eddie would come home with fish, wonderful cornmeal and eggs and green onions rolled up in a ball and fried in hot oil in an iron skillet. He smiled and opened his truck door. "They won't have hush puppies in there. Does your mama make those?" His respect for Spring maybe rising just a bit, picturing her frying a meal for her girl.

"No, *Slush* Puppie. Can I have a Slush Puppie, please?"

A fucking slush. Well Cole liked them too.

"Yeah, you can have one."

He swung the plastic tray up over her head. She was a cute little thing, looking up at him with her tiny face, some of her fine hair sticking to her cheek.

"I want grape."

"Okay." He was about to lift her out of the cab, then remembered the gas. "Hold on, honey. I've got to buy gas first, 'kay?"

He started to close the access door but then left it open, pulled the nozzle free, uncapped his tank, and began pumping. He could see her through the hinge-crack standing there, her head not even reaching the tops of his bucket seats. She yawned and rubbed her eyes with her fists. She stepped closer to the door's opening and looked at him through the tinted glass. "I want Mama." But she didn't cry. Just looked at him like she was almost mad at him, that it was his fault she wasn't with her mama right now. And she had a point there, didn't she?

"You want a grape Slush Puppie, right?"

She nodded.

"Just a minute then."

How bad could Spring be if her daughter missed her this much? Maybe other than being a lying whore and taking her baby to a place no kid should even know about, she was all right. You did what you had to—no, bull*shit*; there was that woman in Oneca a few years ago who beat her eleven-month-old with a stick and even then, the baby would come crawling back to her, to his mama, to the only hope he had, the same place that gave him nine broken bones. And Spring should fucking *thank* him for taking the time to drive this girl away. She should get down on her knees to him. But she won't. The best he could hope for was to scare the living piss out of her.

The pump clicked off. Almost thirty-four dollars and that wasn't for a full tank either.

"I want a Shush Puppie, please."

His arm pain had moved permanently to his neck and head. His eyes ached and the swelling in his hand had gone down but not much. He'd have to ice it again, longer this time. Stop somewhere so the pack would quit slipping off his wrist. He should just drive right to the marina across from the temple. Park his truck near the palm trees and protected mangroves and ice it for a good hour. He'd have that much time before he had to carry her over. And as he carried her now, careful to hold her at his side away from his bad arm, he enjoyed smelling her hair and feeling the slight weight of her. She wasn't afraid of him and that made him feel good. Like he was the kind of man he knew he really was, the kind who'd never have papers on him from a judge keeping him away, but a good man who'd been wronged.

Taped to the door of the Mobil Mart was a poster for a boat show in Tampa. After the hospital and calling a lawyer, after a day and night's rest, that's the first place he'd go. And wouldn't it be fun to take Cole with him? Wouldn't Deena maybe want to come too? To the coast city to look at big gleaming boats?

His name was Sergeant Doonan. He'd told April to sit up front and buckle herself in, and now she sat there on the other side of his computer screen and radio while he drove her without her child, without her Franny. April's nose was stopped up, her throat sore from screaming and crying, and it was as if each white line passing under the patrol car was taking with it her intestines and stringing them out along the road in the dark, leaving her a shell of muscle and bones with a heart that wouldn't stop pounding for what she'd done and for what she hadn't done and for what she couldn't do now—hold her and keep her safe, and God, Oh God, please God, just *find* her.

"We will."

Did she speak? Was she talking? She looked over at him, his glasses halfway down his nose, this grandfather taking her home to wait for a call because there was nothing to do now but get out of their way and let them do their work. And her car was evidence, the picture of her and Franny ripped from the yarn it'd been hanging from, lying on her seat like she and Franny had been the target of somebody who knew them both when she'd been alone here; there was just Jean. And there were people back home.

"Here you go." The cop's hand held out a tissue. His watch was gold. The hairs on his wrist grew around it, his voice deep and strong, not like an old man's at all. She hadn't known she was crying again. She took the tissue and pressed it to her closed eyes, but in the darkness was Franny's face when she slept, her eyes closed, her eyelashes impossibly long, her hair pulled back from her cheek, then a man's hands under her chin, a knife, a belt, duct tape, an old blanket and weeds, a muddy ditch, gasoline and flames, Franny underwater, her open mouth—Oh God, Oh God, this moan rising up from deep beneath the scar April had let the foreigner touch, as if selling her child's place of origin had violated her beginning and so fated her end, dissolving her, cursing her, making her disappear.

ʏ ʏ ʏ

T HE KAFIR OFFICER holds Bassam's license. He looks from
it to Bassam, then at the license once more. He turns it over.
Bassam's heart beats too forcefully inside him for the cash still
strains the seams of his pockets. Will the policeman ask to see what he
carries? And what will he tell him? In the kingdom they would have
stripped off his clothing by now, taken all that is his. They would torture him until he told everything. Until he gave up everyone. Bassam's
mouth is dry as smoke, and he is afraid when he speaks his tongue will
stick slightly, revealing him, and he makes a silent du'a to the Mighty
to protect him.

"What're you doing on the Gulf Coast?"

"Visiting a friend."

"Where?"

"Venice."

"What do you do in Deerfield Beach?"

"I am student."

"Where?"

"Gainesville."

"So why're you in Deerfield Beach?"

"I have a job for summer only. Pizza."

"You make pizza?"

"Transport it."

"Pizza?"

"Yes."

"You deliver it?"

"Yes, I deliver."

"Did you see a small girl tonight?"

"No, only women. Many women."

The officer smiles weakly. He hands to Bassam his license. "You're freetogo."

"Excuse, please?"

"You're free to go."

Bassam looks at the kafir, at the rash on his throat from shaving, at the dark hair upon his arm like his own. *Freetogo.* What does this mean?

"Go ahead." The policeman motions forward with his hand, the same motion Ali al-Fahd would make when in Bassam's earlier life he wanted him to hurry, and now he understands and turns and leaves this den of Shaytan, brightly lighted now and dirty.

In the parking area there are more police vehicles than before, their flashing blue lights, the air cooler and smelling of the exhaust of their running engines, but there is a lightness in the air around him, and Bassam starts the Neon and closes his eyes. *All praise is for Allah by whose favor good works are accomplished.* He shifts the auto into reverse gear and backs slowly over shells from the sea, his eyes upon all the policemen behind him, some standing beside their autos, others seated inside, none of them watching as he pushes the shifter and disappears.

———————

He drives south, the yellow light of the tall sign in his mirror growing smaller. The screams of April. So very like the screams of his own
mother, how they came much later, after his father washed Khalid's
body, cut and broken and bruised, in the required order of ablutions.
For the final washing he added camphor to the water, dried his body
with a towel, covered it in white. At the mosque his mother recited
with the others the salaat-l-janazah and she did not weep for she
knows the soul of her son is with the Sustainer. Khalid's grave lies not
far from a grove of fig trees and there was comfort in knowing they
had buried him before one full day had passed.

But later, after the three days of mourning, she could not hide her
cries. They came always behind the doors she closed. Her face was
pressed to pillows but her sounds could not be softened. They were
of a woman being stabbed by a hot sword. Bassam's sisters or even
Ahmed al-Jizani, his face gray, his eyes dark and full, they would go to
her but she could not be stopped. Her suffering could not be stopped,
and Bassam would leave the home in search of Karim or Tariq or Imad
or even a cigarette he could smoke as the bad Muslim he had been.

Earlier, as he leaned against the Neon and smoked and watched
all these kufar, these men whose nothingness will never be over, he
watched April run from one vehicle to the next and the sound she
made confused him for it was nearly the same as his own mother for
Khalid and how can this kafir love and fear losing in the same way as a
good wife and mother under the Creator in the birthplace of Muhammad? How can this be?

Again, the confusion and weakness. How could it be possible her
cries were difficult for him to bear? How could it be possible he
wanted to help this April who calls herself Spring? In his fingertips
he feels still the hair above her qus, but it is the long hair of her head
he wishes to touch. He wishes to hold her face and kiss her lips. He

wishes to look into her proud eyes. For this is as close as he will ever be to a woman from this earth, and was it close enough?

On the cell phone, in the small black room when he sent her for champagne and cognac, he told Imad not to worry, he would return later than planned but he would return.

But Bassam, where are you?

The den of Shaytan.

Where?

This club for men.

Why, Bassam? We must be prepared.

I may have been followed, Imad. I came here to appear normal.

Bassam, you've been drinking. You must stop and be very careful on your return.

Yes, Insha'Allah.

Please hurry, Bassam. Hurry, and do not waste time.

But he *has* wasted time. And money. So much of it. It is this alcohol. He has become too fond of it. The feeling of freedom it gives to him, of floating above all that is here he cannot control. And it makes him more brave to talk to an uncovered kafir woman in a place of evil that holds him. When he approached her in the shadows, her body so close to his own, his heart was speeding and it was difficult to look at her face and into her eyes and request time with her alone. It was something he could not have done if he had not been drunk. Again the wisdom of the Provider and the Sustainer as taught by the imams he had ignored. They know these vodkas and beer and cognacs and champagnes, they are the colors of water and earth but they have been made in the fires of Jahannam. They only cloud men's minds and weaken their discipline and turn their hearts to caring only for the flesh that does not last.

That first time in Fort Lauderdale. The Egyptian feared they were being monitored, the same white minivan parked across the street of their motel for days, and he instructed them to leave the apartment laughing and smoking cigarettes, to walk directly to the outdoor beer café on the beach. They took a table near the street. They ordered glasses of beer from a thin waiter, a piercing in his ear. The first sip with Imad and Tariq, their first as well, it was sweet and bitter and the Egyptian said: "You look like girls. You call too much attention to yourselves. Here," and he drank down the entire glass and raised it for more. Imad followed first, the foam of the beer clinging to his whiskers. Then Tariq and Bassam, and it tasted better going down quickly, his stomach full but his thirst remaining, and as he lowered his glass only to see the waiter returning with four new ones on his tray, the Egyptian scanning the cars in the street, there was the understanding that for him and his brothers this taste of the haram could only make them wiser, stronger, though Tariq was laughing and Imad looked at the Egyptian and would not touch his second until Amir swallowed his own.

Perhaps it *had* made them wiser, but what good is wisdom if your resolve to use it is weakened by the same liquid that leads you to it?

Bassam accelerates onto I-75 south. He glances at his gauges, calculates he has enough fuel for 160 or so kilometers. At the Everglades Parkway, there is only one station halfway across, and he will fill again the tank and he will buy cigarettes and Coca-Cola to keep him alert. But he has not relieved himself and needs to now. He drives into the sleeping city of Sarasota, its banks and boutiques closed and dark, its traffic lights pulsing yellow. In courtyards and rotundas there are thorn trees and palm trees and he would be hidden there, but no, he will look for a fuel station or an alleyway for there are only three days remaining and he will not relieve himself upon a tree like one from home. He will not desecrate any trees from home.

∨ ∨ ∨

I N HER KING-SIZE bed, her cat Matisse sleeping on a pillow not far from her face, Jean dreamed she and Harry were making love in a nightclub in front of a jazz band. He was still dead and she knew it, but he didn't look dead. He looked like the Harry he'd always been except every few seconds he would stop and withdraw himself and look down between her legs. A spotlight from the ceiling would shine on her there, though it was a light with sound, a motorcycle engine, and it was hard to hear the music over it and that bothered her more than anything. Not Harry stopping to have a light shine on her crotch, but the engine so loud she couldn't hear the piano and trumpet and brushing cymbals. Then Franny was on the stage, holding her mother's hand, both of them dressed for the beach.

Jean opened her eyes to the knocking, her dream already fading, Matisse leaping off her bed.

"*Ma'am?*" It was a man's voice, the knocking hard and insistent. Her first thought was the hospital, that they'd come for her whether she wanted to be there or not. But this was no way to wake her, her old heart jumping as she pulled her robe from its hook and stuffed one arm into its sleeve, then the other. On her bedside table, the time glowed green: 3:47.

"*Ma'am?*"

She moved quickly down the darkened hallway, tying the robe closed at her waist. The flood lamp above the kitchen door had come on and standing there in its harsh light was a policeman and April. Her hair needed brushing and her eyeliner was smeared, her cheeks damp. Clutched to her chest was Franny's backpack, and Jean couldn't get the door opened fast enough.

"What? Where's Franny? What is it?"

"What are you *doing* here? I thought you were sick. I thought you were *sick!*" April was crying, her shoulders heaving, the tall policeman's arm around her now as he walked her into Jean's house where she stood in her robe and heard the news—that her fears were not a neurotic condition after all but a prophecy that what you dread the most is precisely what comes for you in the dark in the form of a soft-spoken policeman and this young woman you've never really liked and now despise; her long hair hanging over her weeping face, her wrinkled blouse and short skirt, her bare legs and high heels and painted nails, and more despicable than anything was the way she hugged her daughter's backpack as some sort of evidence that she'd only done her best—Jean despised her, all of her, and how cruel that he nodded and told Jean he could leave her now that he knew she was not alone. How cruel.

Then he was gone, the floodlight switching off and the two women standing there in the dark kitchen, April sobbing. Saying nothing. Just sobbing. And to step forward and hold her would be the humane thing to do. The good and loving thing to do. But Jean didn't move.

She couldn't. She crossed her arms over her breasts and hugged herself as if she were cold, Franny's face mercilessly in her head now, the way she'd turned to wave at her yesterday before her trip to the beach. That almost secretive smile they shared. "Oh April, I'm so mad at you I can't even—"

—the back pack hit the floor and April's arms were around Jean's neck, her crying loud and piercing in her ear, her breasts against Jean's crossed arms she had no choice but to uncross and drop to her sides, April's hair smelling of cigar smoke and sweat and men's cologne: Jean wanted to push her away, but she was close to crying too, though she fought it, Franny's backpack pressing hard against her bare shins.

⋎ ⋎ ⋎

ALL THESE TYLENOLS had finally shucked their skins and dissolved into his bloodstream, his wrist and arm just dull memories of pain now. Things had calmed and steadied: the night, the girl, his plans for the morning. He drove south in the darkness down Gulf of Mexico Drive, sipping hot coffee, his knee pressed tight to the wheel. Off to his left were the homes of the rich. To his right, their private beaches of sugar sand, then the endless salt water they claimed too. Miles out there were the twinkling lights of an oil freighter or commercial fishing vessel, he wasn't sure which. There was a lot about the water he didn't know, except that in hurricane season it could rise up and whip into homes and sweep away whatever it is you thought you could never do without. He'd have to get a boat that wasn't too big, one he could haul and keep inland, him and Cole and Deena safe in their hurricaneproof house. He kept glancing at the little girl in his rearview, kids like dogs, how quiet they went when it was time to feed. At the gas station he'd bought her a cookie and it was gone before he even got to the Gulf and turned south for Lido Key. Now she sat there looking straight ahead, sucking hard on the straw sunk into her Slush Puppie.

"You want a spoon?"

She looked at the back of his head and nodded. He fitted his coffee cup in its holder, pressed his knee tighter to the wheel, and with his good hand lifted the console cover between his seat and the passenger's. He punched on the overhead light. There were credit applications and a flash of loose coins, ketchup packets, a torn work glove, three or four roofing nails, and a bottle opener, the truck swerving toward the beach. He grabbed the wheel and let the cover slam shut. His heart was thumping and that hurt his hand somehow and he pulled over onto the narrow shoulder and put the truck in park.

"I want a spoon."

"Hold on."

He checked his side mirror, saw the red glow of his brake lights, then the black air. If the county pulled up he'd say he and his daughter were on their way home from a family outing up north, Montgomery or Savannah, and they'd been driving all night.

Daughter. It'd be sweet if she were his, wouldn't it?

He lifted the console lid and kept it up with his elbow while his fingers pushed aside the glove for the white plastic spoon that'd been there at least a year, probably from Deena's hand, the ketchup packets too. Always hording shit like that. Sometimes he admired that about her, how she hated to waste anything. But other times, seeing her stash condiments and plastic utensils, it made him feel like she doubted his ability to provide, that there'd come a hard time when they actually *needed* this shit.

Like now.

He let the lid drop, wiped the spoon on his shoulder. He reached back with it and watched her in the mirror pull the straw out and wedge the spoon in. She lifted too much blended ice and put it in her mouth all at once, her eyes widening before she spit it out onto Cole's tray top.

"Too much, huh?"

She looked from it, then back to the melting puddle in front of her, her eyes welling up.

"It's okay, that ain't nothing. Don't worry about that." He grabbed his bandanna and dropped it onto the tray. But she began to whimper and he reached across himself for the door handle and slid out of the truck into the moist air and the Gulf-smell of dried seaweed and old oil, the road dark and empty to the south and north. He pulled open the access door, the cab lamp lighting up this crying little girl, her blond hair hanging over one eye and wet cheek, cookie crumbs in the corners of her mouth and on the front of her pink pajamas, her lips purple. "I want Mama. I want *Ma*ma."

"I know. I know you do. We're going home right now. We sure are, honey. We sure are." He put the Slush Puppie and spoon on the console, dropped the sticky bandanna on the empty beer cans on the floor and unbuckled and lifted the tray over her head, careful not to snag any of her hair, something he never had to think of with Cole. She cried now with no words and already there was less conviction in it, not because she didn't miss her whore of a mother but because she was dog-assed tired and the Benadryl had surely begun to kick in. Right now she needed to be held, didn't she?

He slid his good hand under her armpit. His palm was against her ribs, and he could feel her heartbeat. He pulled her gently off the seat till she was standing and crying louder, looking over his shoulder and outside like she was searching for something. He scooped her under his arm and lifted her out.

"Shh, shh, it's okay. It's okay."

He carried her to the shoulder covered with the same crushed shells as the Puma. She gripped his shirt. She went quiet. He'd done the right thing avoiding 301. He could hear the surf up in the distance rolling in and pulling back, rolling in and pulling back, and the sound or maybe it was him—maybe it was *him*—seemed to calm the girl because now she rested her forehead against his shoulder, her fingers clutching his shirt. Her hair was against his cheek, her thin legs around his ribs, and he turned from side to side and could hold her with one arm like this all night long if he had to. And couldn't she feel that? Couldn't she feel his power he'd use only to keep her safe? Couldn't Deena still? If he never touched her like that again? That wouldn't be so hard, would it? All she had to do was love him, that's all. Just love him and quit her bitching and bad habits, maybe lose some weight. Or maybe they just needed another baby. Like this one. Born of a cold whore and she couldn't get much sweeter, could she?

And so sing her a song, AJ. Or at least hum something. But he'd never hummed anything in his life, ever, and knew no songs. How about her real daddy? *Was* there one? Maybe he had it all wrong and there was. Maybe he was a sorry, kicked-out sonofabitch like him.

He spoke into her hair. "Fran? Franzie?"

"I want to go *home*." Her voice was muffled against his shoulder, her breath warm.

"We will, hon." AJ kept turning from side to side, his eyes on those tiny lights so far out on the Gulf. "How 'bout your daddy, though? Is he home, too? Or he live someplace else?"

She said something he could feel against his shoulder, but it got lost in the hiss of the surf.

"What'd you say, honey?"

"Heaven."

"Heaven?"

She nodded against him. AJ stood there a long while. He could feel her breathing grow more steady and he wanted to ask her how long her daddy'd been up there and how'd he die and did she ever know him? But she was almost asleep again, this child with no father, and he began to hum a tune he didn't know he knew; it started in his throat, then sunk into his chest. And it was good the little one could feel or hear it there, this song of grace, how sweet the sound, of a man once lost but now—found.

⌄ ⌄ ⌄

LONNIE DROVE SOUTH for Sarasota. His right headlight
seemed dimmer than his left and both windows were open, the
road wind whipping around in his cab—how in hell does one
even *try* to find a child? And he wasn't impressed with the questions
either.

Did you see the toddler tonight?

No.

Do you know her father?

No.

Does the mother have a husband or boyfriend?

I don't know.

Any suspicious customers?

Just every damn night. *The lone dogs. The sulking drinkers. The
brooders.*

Lonnie told the young cop about Dolphins Cap, about his disrespect and having to shut him down and throw him out. The cop sat on a stool in the vaginal pink light of the entryway and wrote down the man's description, the cap and the beard and the clothes Lonnie could remember him wearing. He thanked Lonnie and handed him his card and told him he could go. Then he called in the next man, the foreigner Spring had spent so much time with in the Champagne. Lonnie held the curtain for him, this little runt with bad teeth and narrow shoulders smelling like cigarettes and body odor and after-shave, brushing past him without a thank-you.

Louis was at the Amazon Bar drinking coffee, smoking a cigarette. Lonnie still wanted those three fingers of Maker's over ice, but Louis looked over at him with such a pained expression he knew this wasn't the time to pour himself anything on the house. He was about to keep walking toward the kitchen, the back door, and his Tacoma, but Louis waved him over.

"They clear you to leave?"

"Yep." Lonnie leaned back against the bar and scanned the room. The men were louder now, talking in regular voices. They seemed more relaxed, like they knew this was a procedure they'd have to wait out like a line at the bank or the DMV. Just the cost of doing what you had to, or chose to; one of them, a big man in a loosened tie, was talking about the Devil Rays. Baseball. Just another thing Lonnie had never bothered with.

"Tina really fucked me this time, Lonnie. I mean *fucked* me."

Lonnie nodded, thought of that word and how we used it for one of the best things that could happen to us and the worst.

"I'm not shitting you. They could close me over this. You watch, they'll fuckin' lock the doors and take the key."

"They tell you that?"

Louis shook his head, looked over his shoulder toward the entry-way. He lowered his voice and Lonnie leaned in, could smell the cof-fee over the rum over the fear.

"That one who took Spring home, he says no one under twenty-one means no one under fucking twenty-one. And what if something happens to that kid? What fucking then, Lonnie? I'm telling you, you can start looking for work." He shook his head again and took a deep drag off his cigarette. He blew smoke out his nose. "Fucking cunts."

Who? Lonnie wondered. Every single woman who'd come here and rented herself out and made him rich? Or just Tina and Spring, who some cop was driving home now without her daughter? Lonnie kept hearing her screams as she ran barefoot from car to car in the shell lot of this joint he didn't give two shits about closing. And there'd never been anyone in his life it'd hurt him that much to lose.

Nobody.

Not his mother and father back in Austin. Not any of the women he'd tried loving over the years. Maybe Troy, his golden retriever run over by a masonry truck out on Martin Luther King Boulevard when Lonnie was ten. Maybe him.

Louis was bitching about how this place was never a fucking day care, and Lonnie kept nodding. Sleep wasn't even a possibility tonight; he was thinking of Spring, how she'd asked him to check in on her girl and he hadn't. He had to go see her, offer himself up in some way.

"Am I too nice, Lonnie? Is that my fuckin' problem? 'Cause Tina's been coasting for I don't know how long and I never punched her ticket like I should, you know why? 'Cause I felt sorry for her. She is used up and so over the hill you can't even see her, but I kept her, I kept her 'cause I know she don't have shit, and now look, Lonnie. Now look."

Lonnie rested his hand on Louis's shoulder, felt flesh and bone under silk. "I hope everything works out, Lou. I'll call in later."

"I just hope I'm here to answer. You hear what I'm telling you?"

"Yeah, I do."

Louis nodded, his eyes on his reflection in the bar mirror behind the liquor he sold at a thousand percent markup. Lonnie headed straight out back. The makeup room was empty but the lights were still on over the mirror. In its bright light on the countertop were a few hairbrushes and combs, a zipped cosmetics bag, five or six empty cocktail glasses and two full ashtrays, the butts brushed with lipstick that made him think of his mother.

Tina stood in her small office folding a linen tablecloth, her massive breasts straining against her shirt. They put him in mind of clowns and balloons and a party gone terribly wrong.

He was somewhere north of St. Armand's Circle now, driving up and down streets of houses only a few blocks from the beach. Most of them were behind stucco walls roofed with terra-cotta tiles and he flicked on the overhead light of his Tacoma and read again the address Tina had written for him: *April—44 Orchid Avenue*. Up ahead was a Mobil station, its pumps shining under fluorescent light, and he pulled up beside a white compact and went inside.

The place was too bright and smelled like disinfectant. An Indian or Pakistani sat at the register. Behind him, just beneath the cigarette shelf, was a boom box turned down low, the cry of a woman singing a love song in his language.

"Evenin', I'm looking for Orchid Avenue."

"Yes, Orchid Avenue."

"Can you tell me where it is?"

"Yes, there." The man pointed out the window past the pumps to the street.

"This is it?"

"No, one street more, sir. West."

A toilet flushed somewhere and Lonnie thanked the man, but he was thirsty and headed for the lighted cooler and grabbed a spring water. A door opened in the rear wall. A man Lonnie knew but didn't know glanced at his face, then walked quickly past him, his tropical shirt tucked into his pants, the little foreigner who'd bought April all night long.

Lonnie watched him leave and climb into his car and pull away.

Again the cool cave opening up inside him. *Did* she just dance for him? For *that* long? Just that?

Now he drove down a softly lit boulevard of royal palms, which didn't feel right, this neighborhood of affluent retirees. Why not, though? Did he expect her to live like he did? On a loud main road across from a marine supply strip? And her name—April; he'd known it wasn't Spring, but the truth was, it disappointed him; the only April he'd ever known had been in middle school, a slow girl with an underbite. He'd had to sit with her in a room for kids who needed extra help with their reading. And just recently there was that poem he'd listened to from a book on tape. T. S. Eliot, right? *April is the cruellest month*. And so the word itself came to mean cruel and slow and not too good to look at, nothing like Spring, who'd always been warm to him and was the brightest girl in the place and better-looking than all of them because she looked more real somehow, real because of her pride, the knowledge you got she was there for her, not you.

He turned right onto Orchid. Number 44. There it was, both numbers glinting under a lighted sconce set into the wall of a closed garage. He slowed to a stop in the middle of the street. The house was Spanish colonial, its sides a turquoise stucco that matched the high walls surrounding the courtyard. It had to be close to three in the morning but lights were on in the upper windows and beneath each one were flower boxes overflowing with blooming vines. Maybe he should just keep going. Maybe she needed to be alone right now or had someone looking after her already. But there was the way she ran screaming barefoot from car to car in the lot, her blouse unbuttoned, her long brown hair flapping wildly against her. *Don't let them leave, Lonnie! Don't let them leave!*

He turned into the driveway. The high walls on each side made him feel embraced and slightly claustrophobic. He killed the lights and engine. He sat there feeling foolish. What could *he* do? Sit with her and hold her hand till she got some kind of call? Why was he really here? Wasn't he just trying to keep up the momentum of her need for him? Apologize for letting her down though it was never really his job in the first place?

A light came on to his left. There was a wooden arch and under it a short mahogany gate, half-open, its latch the same brass as the numbers on the wall. In the electric-lit shadows on the other side was a garden, dense with flowers and vines and through which a woman now came into view. She was older than Spring and much larger, her graying hair cut above the shoulders. She wore a robe she held partly closed with one hand, and as she pushed the gate open and stepped into the brighter light of the driveway, Lonnie thought this must be her mother. Spring lives with her mother.

He opened the door and climbed out of the truck.

She said: "Have they found her? Have they found her?" She was looking him up and down, taking in the club's logo across the front of his T-shirt. She had a midwestern accent.

"No, ma'am, they're still looking." He stepped forward and extended his hand. "I'm Lonnie Pike, ma'am. Are you April's mother?"

She shook her head quickly. Her palm was small and sweaty. "Do you work with her?"

"Yes, ma'am." He glanced up at one of the lit windows. "How's she doing?"

"She took my car." She was looking past him into the empty street, one hand pressed to her chest, her mouth open.

"You okay?"

She shook her head again, her double chin moving with it. "I need to go back inside. I should get back inside." The woman took a deep breath, her round shoulders rising. "Please, she doesn't have a cell phone, we can talk inside."

He followed her wide body. She was wearing cloth slippers open in the back, her heels pink. He pulled the gate closed behind him and she was already around the corner of the house, the entire courtyard a profusion of plants, flowers, and trees. He could smell some kind of night-blooming blossom—skunk and honey. She left the door open and he stepped past an outside staircase and walked in just as a fat calico leapt onto the kitchen counter and the woman took a wineglass from a cabinet above the sink.

"I'm sorry, I get these attacks. Would you like wine?"

"No thank you."

She pulled a rubber vacuum stopper from a half bottle of red and poured into her glass. "I was at the hospital. That's why she had to take Franny. Because I couldn't babysit." She drank deeply from the wine, her eyes on the darkened living room behind. Above the sofa hung a mirror, its frame covered with crayon drawings; a lot of them were figures of people standing around houses under a shining sun. He was tired and his feet were sore and he needed coffee.

"I tried to go get her. I left the hospital but I couldn't do it. Oh God, I just couldn't do it." The woman began crying silently, three fingers covering her mouth. The cat walked across the counter and rubbed up against her arm. Lonnie wanted to leave; he wanted to get back in his truck and go find Spring.

The woman sniffled, shook her head, drank more wine. She swallowed and looked down. "I couldn't even drive into the parking area; I had an attack and I—I just couldn't. Oh God, do they think she was *taken*? How in the world did this *house* mother *lose* her? How does that happen? Please, tell me!"

"I don't know the details."

The cat stepped over her hand. Her fingers were stubby, her nails clipped. Her eyes passed over the lettering across his chest and he felt guilty of something he may have done without knowing it.

"What do you do there? If you don't mind." She poured more wine into her glass.

"I'm a floor host."

"A host?"

"Bouncer."

She nodded. "You're there to protect the women."

"Yes." He felt like a liar. "What kind of car's she driving?"

"My Cadillac."

"I should go look for her."

"Please don't go just yet. I haven't been well."

She didn't look well; her wide, wrinkled face was pasty and there were dull splotches under her chin, her fingers trembling against the stem of her glass. The calico jumped to the floor and walked indifferently down the hallway.

"I'm worried. I don't know, I—"

"Maybe you should lie down."

"No, I—not until—no, I can't. Would you like coffee? Are you hungry?" She breathed deeply through her nose, patted her unbrushed hair. "Can I fix you something to eat?"

"I really should get going."

"Please, not yet. Please."

"Coffee'd be fine. Thank you." And he sat on the counter stool and watched Spring's landlady, sick and worried in her robe and slippers, drop a filter into her coffee machine and ask in a slightly wavering voice if he liked eggs. She'd be happy to fry him some eggs.

∨ ∨ ∨

A PRIL WAS DRIVING too fast up Washington Boulevard in Jean's Cadillac.

I'll go with you, April. I'll drive you.

No, *somebody has to be here so please just give them to me.*

Jean's round face as she handed over the keys, no more judgment in her eyes, just fear and distrust.

The car felt stolen, its brights on, bits of broken glass glittering on both shoulders, then the high weeds of Florida, but no Franny, no Franny, and that picture of the two of them they'd taken together in the Walgreen's photo booth—why had it been faceup in her seat, the hole for the yarn ripped through like it was left behind by somebody who knew her? Somebody angry. In the kitchen's fluorescent light at three in the morning, her mother in her T.J. Maxx nightgown, smoking a cigarette, April telling her where she really worked and what she did there, that she made more in one shift than a week at Subway's, that this was just temporary, just till she could save enough for a down payment on a house for her and Franny.

"Temporary." Her mother took a deep drag and shook her head and blew smoke out her nose. "You won't quit. Not after such easy money." She stubbed her cigarette out in the ashtray. "I want you gone."

Then McGuiness's Christmas party. Her waking naked under a wool blanket. Everything sore. Everything hurting.

Calling in sick and that one night at Stephanie's, April and Franny sleeping on her foldout couch, the walls covered with framed prints from the mall: airbrushed mountains, forests, rivers. The one above the TV was of a sunset over water, the Gulf of Mexico, and waking up to it the morning after she'd left her mother's, Franny sleeping half off the pillow beside her, April stared at it a long time, heard her mother's voice over and over: *You won't quit. You won't quit. I want you gone.*

She had four thousand dollars in the bank, would've had a lot more if it weren't for McGuiness raising the house fees so girls who didn't do as well as she did had to have a Saturday night every night they worked, which they wouldn't so their house debt would rise and rise and some of those poor bitches had to make a video for him to break even. But she was paid up and she wasn't going back. She had money and two credit cards and nothing here to hold her.

Except Glenn.

But that wasn't even real; that was just a memory kept alive now by a weakening hope that he'd change, that one day he'd just show up a man instead of a handsome stoned boy, still in love with her, holding a toy for the daughter he never claimed and never helped pay for. She could go after him for that. If she hadn't started working at the Empire, she would have. But something had changed. Something in her. She thought it was her body or how she regarded it—from being hers to being theirs. How easy it is to get used to that; how easy it is to get used to being naked and go deep inside yourself and shut the door and stay there till your body, face, and eyes are done for the night.

How easy it is on the drive home to simply leave it behind by looking ahead, always by looking ahead: to a hot shower or bath, to kissing her fingers and touching them to her sleeping daughter's forehead, to curling up in the clean sheets of the bed of her childhood knowing this is just till she's set: and Stephanie said in Florida you could buy a house not far from the water for cheap; the club fees were reasonable and business was always good, every night a Saturday night if you worked the floor for the VIP. She said the customers were classier, the only thing she'd been wrong about. But April was making ten thousand dollars a month every month and had grown to love, need, and depend on that. Not for the money itself but for the feeling it gave her, that with each deposit into her account she was gathering more strength and independence and respect. She had over fifty thousand dollars, already a down payment on any two-bedroom house for sale up and down the coast. But why stop at one house? She could work another six months and buy two, then rent it out for enough to pay both mortgages. She could work another year and buy a third or a fourth. And then she'd just be Franny's mom. She'd be like Jean, collecting rent, her days and nights her own. She'd be rich then and wouldn't need anything from anybody ever.

"You lie." His fingers on her scar, that look of total certainty in his face. "Even if you had no children, you would sell this."

"Oh Franny, *Franny!*" She was talking now, talking out loud in Jean's Cadillac, and she told herself to slow down. The club was only a mile away. Franny could've gotten this far. She could. April fumbled for the window buttons, pressing whatever her fingertips touched.

There was an electric moan in the doors, the windows sliding down, warm air skimming across the side of her face, and now her throat and arms prickled with anger because she'd always been disciplined and careful and in complete control and this shouldn't've *happened.* Over a year at the Empire and six months here and she hadn't met anyone as disciplined as she was. Nobody. None of them looked ahead the way she did, not one, not even Stephanie, who spent all her money on clothes and jewelry, on facials and manicures and pedicures, on a new convertible, on her tits, lips, and ass. But April was better than all those weak bitches who drank every night and would give blow jobs in hundred-dollar VIP booths for a week's worth of Oxy, those rude, shiftless women who were so ignorant they couldn't even see the hole they were falling into.

She peered out the driver's window past the swath of the headlights into the trees. At the side of the road was the curved spine of a small body, her heart plummeting into a black nowhere, but the body was covered with fur, one ear sticking up, the rib cage collapsed. "It's a dog. It's just a dog."

And she rolled up the window and drove faster up Washington Boulevard.

$$\scriptstyle \vee \quad \vee \quad \vee$$

I T WASN'T EASY getting her back into the truck. She was deep asleep against the shoulder of his good arm, the other stiff and useless at his side. Once he got the door open with the hand that held her, he leaned back so she'd stay against him, then fumbled for the lever under his driver's seat till he gripped and pulled it and the seat slid up to the wheel. There was a pinch in his lower back that wasn't even close to the dulled but still jagged heat in his wrist. He was breathing harder, his heart pounding against the girl's. He raised his knee up to the cab floor, rested his elbow on the cushion, then pulled his other knee up and leaned over and set the child into Cole's car seat. Her head fell back against the padded upholstery. He stayed there on his knees a second or two and stared at her. Her head was tilted back, her mouth open, her hair away from her face. Tiny cookie crumbs still clung to the corners of her lips and he took the chance and lightly flicked them off. He held his breath and put two fingers behind her neck, running them along the back of her head till her face wasn't pointing up so much. He lowered the plastic tray into place, but with one damn hand he couldn't get the male end of the belt into the female buckle, which kept dropping away from the web of his thumb, and twice the male end missed and his knuckles were pressing against her and he was afraid he might wake her up, and finally the male end slid and clicked into place—*shit*.

Her hair was so fine. So fine. He covered her again with his work T-shirt, tucking it first over one shoulder, then the other. Little thing was out deep now. Could he really just leave her someplace all alone? What if that temple was locked shut? Was he going to lay her down on the concrete landing in front of locked doors, then wait across the street in the marina's parking lot for the county to show? Hope no dog came sniffing around first? No bats or bugs? No creep out for a dawn's walk on Lido Key? How was he going to do this really? If they even responded fast to his call, could he just drive off in his truck without being noticed? And he pictured some patrol car chasing him down, maybe the same sonsabitches who shoved him out of his own house in front of Cole.

How good it would be to lay this girl down in Cole's bed. Plenty of room. And he'd just tell Deena the truth: this was a neglected child. We have an obligation to her. But he knew she'd never allow it. She'd think they'd stolen her. He knew this, so why keep thinking about it? Nope, he was just going to have to put aside how much he was growing to like this young girl and get her safe inside a building and he'd be gone before he made the call.

He started his truck. He reached over his lap to pull the door shut and he was fifteen again, standing on the chum-smeared deck of the boat, the green Gulf out there, the sun in his eyes as he dropped an underweight snapper back over the side, the flick of its tail fin as it righted itself and dived deep, this fading hope in his chest it would live till he caught it again, Eddie drunk and red-faced and winking at him like he knew the end of that story already and AJ didn't and never would.

❧ ❧ ❧

I T WAS FOUR in the morning, her son gone an hour, and Virginia poured herself some cold coffee, put the mug in the microwave, and pressed the button. She leaned one hand against the counter and smoked. Alan always made too much. In the mornings he'd drip a whole pot and drink only a third while she drank another and had to dump the rest down the drain. The oxygen flow in her nose tube was getting weak. She was going to have to switch to the backup tank soon. Later this morning, when the sun rose and businesses opened, she'd call the air people for a refill.

The microwave beeped. She pulled out the hot mug, poured the steaming coffee into a cooler cup, then spooned in three sugars and laid her cigarette in the ashtray and carried it and her coffee out to the dark living room, her air hose dragging lightly behind her.

Alan's bed was untouched, the blanket and sheet pulled back from the pillow the way she did for him. Called into work early and he was still out doing Lord knows what, though two or three times she'd seen on the end table among his change and crumpled bills a wadded cocktail napkin, the black shape of a naked woman under the name of the place. She knew where it was. Years ago it'd been a pool hall she and Eddie would go to till they started fighting about his drinking.

She shook her head and made her way around the foldout to her chair by the sliding glass door. She set her ashtray and coffee down on the end table and was about to sit, but the air tube pulled against her upper lip and she turned to see it snagged under the bed leg. *Your own damn fault, Virginia. Don't even start.* It was a running conversation she had with herself. This ball and chain she had to wear so she could breathe because she never was able to quit. Even now.

She nudged the tube free with her toe, pulled the slack behind her, sat in her easy chair. She took a deep drag of her cigarette and held the hot coffee under her nose. It was night still though the sky had lightened to a dark blue and soon she'd be able to see her patio and tiny lawn, the statue of the Virgin Mary that Alan had set for her against the fence. He'd done it on a Sunday, hadn't he? Because she remembered sitting with his wife at the patio table while she breast-fed the baby and the two of them had talked about God.

"You going to christen him?"

"We don't think so." The girl looked down at Baby Cole suckling her. She ran her fingers over his scant hair, blond as Alan's had been. "God's everywhere, isn't he?"

"So's the devil, Deena. Have you thought about that?" Virginia's voice had sounded more ornery than she'd intended, but who was this plump and plain girl with no fire in her eyes and never a smile on her face? What did Alan see in her anyway? And him over by the fence sinking a shovel into a wheelbarrow of crushed stone, lifting it out and dumping it into the box he'd set into the ground so carefully. Always a worker. Always working.

"Do you really believe in the devil, Virginia?" Her daughter-in-law was looking down at the baby.

"Yes. How can I believe in God and the angels if I don't believe in the dark one too?"

"I just don't believe in all that. Hell or a devil."

"Then what about heaven and God?"

The girl glanced back up at her, the flash of a challenge in her eyes. "Sometimes I do. Sometimes I don't. I don't know." She looked back down at Virginia's grandson, pushed two fingers into her breast to give him more room to breathe, but it was Virginia who needed room to breathe; what kind of house was this child going to be raised in? Alan didn't even like her to quote the Bible and it was her fault because she'd been in darkness till only recently; she'd done her best but she'd raised him with no guidance from above and now he was drinking and wasting his hard-earned money, locked out of his house away from his son, and she blamed that Godless fat ass he'd married for that. She did.

Virginia stubbed her cigarette and tried not to light another for at least five minutes. She could see the clock radio on the kitchen counter on the other side of the room: 4:24 a.m.; everything else was going—her lungs, her leg strength, her bladder and bowels and hearing, but she could still see as well as she ever could. At least across a room. She needed her reading glasses, but who didn't?

She sipped more coffee. Every day she wanted to call her daughter-in-law and say just what she thought of her, and every day she prayed for the strength not to because she knew how that could hurt Alan's case. But God forgive her, she never did like the woman, especially now that she'd sent her son into darkness. And the way that girl always looked at him, her dulled eyes narrowed, sizing him up, forever looking like he fell far short of her expectations. She didn't even know how blessed she was to have a man like Alan James. A man who worked enough for three men. A man who didn't lie or steal or cheat. A man who was kinder and sweeter to his son than any man had ever been to him.

She could still see him sitting beside her in the front seat as she drove from one cleaning job to another, his feet not touching the floorboards, his blond hair and little face as he held his chin up so he could see over the dash and out the windshield. How many nights when he was young—when she was alone and not taking in the first man to give her a wink and a smile—had she lain in bed and tried to wish a father into her boy's life? And how many nights—*Admit it, Virginia; there were one or two*—did she lie there and wonder why she'd kept that baby?

She was already forty-one years old, cleaning rooms for the leisurely and the wealthy, content for the time being to put in her hours and live alone, knowing love always comes again somehow. Was she thinking that when it happened? Was she thinking at all?

It was a Sunday afternoon at the resort on Longboat Key. She was more than halfway through cleaning the weekend checkouts, the beach white under the sun, the Gulf a lovely deep green that stretched out blue to the horizon where there were no clouds. She was standing at the window, looking forward to a cigarette and admiring the view. She heard the door close behind her. She thought it was the other girl from housekeeping, but it was a man, standing there in a V-neck T-shirt and white tennis shorts, his thick forearms and legs covered with curly blond hair, his eyes a brighter blue than she'd yet seen, but he wasn't handsome; his features were all scrunched down from forehead to chin, and she apologized, said she thought the room had been vacated, and she dropped her duster into her cleaning cart, something she remembered because he moved toward her just as the duster landed on dirty towels, and even before he got close to her she could see how drunk he was, could smell the liquor and his aftershave, one of those men from the tropical bar on the beach under the thatched roof drinking his morning away dressed for tennis.

Her heart was beating so fast she felt sick and there was a flat light in his eyes that scared her more than his hands on her shoulders, more than the air she was now falling through, more than the bounce of the mattress against her back. She turned and tried to swing her legs off the bed but his hand squeezed her throat and she could feel all the strength he was withholding and she only looked at his face once more and had to look away because it was clear he'd made up his mind about this long ago, his hand reaching up her skirt and jerking down her underwear, her apron now raised up over her belly and breasts, and then he let go of her and she heard his zipper and *you could've kicked him and run;* for thirty years these words bled themselves into hundreds of quiet moments like this one, now ruined, as she herself had been ruined; dry and beginning to chafe, it took him such a long, long time, and when he was done she was bleeding, knew her blood was mixing with his seed, the early-afternoon sun beginning to slant itself into the room.

It was hard to breathe under his weight. There was a deep burn between her legs. Would he kill her now the way thousands of women over thousands of years had been killed? And in a shuddering breath, as if from her own memory, she felt joined to them on all the dusty floorboards and alleyways of ancient cities, the damp blankets of ships at sea; in horse-drawn wagons and roadside ditches and empty box cars; in the backs of trucks and buses; in hay-strewn barns, dark basements, and dank tool sheds; on barroom tables and the cooling asphalt of a parking lot; in the mud of river bottoms, cornfields, and woods, and in beds in sunlit rooms like this one on a Thursday when she was alone and thinking about love—she was part of them all now, yet one more in this sisterhood none of them had sought.

It seemed odd that he was being so quiet, so still. He'd softened and she could hardly feel him inside her and she wanted his weight off her chest and knew she was a fool for wanting that much. But his breathing had steadied. She could hear the breath through his nose and half-opened mouth, could feel the slow rise and fall of his chest against her. How familiar this all was now, to slide out from under a drunk who'd be out till he came to and would he even remember? And if only she remembered, did it really happen?

She was afraid to try and push him off her. She grabbed the edge of the mattress and pulled till she was halfway free. His head was on the pillow now, his face turned toward hers, his breath bad, and she hated him, this passed-out piece of trash who took her for himself as if she went with the suite and clay courts and beach. She pulled harder and wiggled her legs and hips till he was off her, belly down, his tennis shorts around his sunburned ankles. She avoided looking at the rest of him. She slid off the bed and stood, his seed running out of her and down the inside of her thigh, and she yanked a towel from her cleaning cart and wiped it off her as if it were gasoline near a flame. She pushed the towel between her legs, wiped hard, and dropped it back into the cart.

The sun was in her eyes. She shielded them with her hand and found her underwear under the window. He was snoring, his rear big and pale. She stepped into her torn panties one shoe at a time, then let her skirt fall back over her knees. His arm hung off the bed, his gold watch glinting in the sunlight. Her underwear was loose on her. She still burned and knew she would for days and what if he came to right now?

The kitchenette drawer slid out too loudly as she reached in and gripped one of the pearl-handled steak knives. It was heavy and cool. She was thirsty but afraid to turn on the faucet. An inch of leather was sticking out the back pocket of his shorts and her heart had slowed and she almost felt calm as she stepped over and with two fingers pulled out his wallet. It was thick and worn. She opened it. Under her blade was a picture of him smiling into the DMV camera. Her fingers were trembling. Ward Dunn Jr. He was ten years younger than she was and lived in Louisville, Kentucky.

Ward Dunn Jr.

She reached in and took out all the bills—hundreds, twenties, fifties. She pushed the money into her apron and fought the feeling rising up in her throat that this now made her a whore who'd asked for it.

Ward Dunn Jr. was still snoring. She'd like to stab him in the neck. The head. The face. But what would happen now? Just go to the manager and tell him? Would he believe her? Would the police? But even if they did, she'd lose her job, and how could she stay here anyway? How could she ever come back to this place where Ward Dunn Jr. might be?

There were business cards with his name on them, two telephone numbers under the etching of a horse. Ward Dunn Jr. was a horse breeder. A racer of horses. The Kentucky Derby and money in the bluegrass hills. She'd heard of these things and now hated him even more. She felt sick again, but her fear had lifted and she pulled out the photos behind his driver's license. Black-and-white baby pictures, four of them, then one of a younger, fitter Ward Dunn Jr. in a tuxedo, his arm around a short blonde in an ivory wedding dress.

Virginia dropped the photo into her apron pocket. She pulled out Ward Dunn Jr.'s license and one of his business cards, took them too. She looked back at him once more, the knife handle pulsing in her hand, and that's when she saw the mole on his rear, the one she described much later.

She'd been smoking and driving for hours: south, east, north, then south again; She stopped and bought a Coke and a carton of Tareytons, and later, when her Chevrolet ran out of gas outside Myakka City, she pulled into a Texaco station and asked a skinny boy with grease under his chin to fill it up. She handed him one of Ward Dunn Jr.'s twenties. She was still in her cleaning uniform, the black skirt and white blouse and white shoes, though she'd untied her apron full of money and carried it rolled under her arm, and even though she burned where he'd been, she couldn't get out from under this feeling that she was fleeing a terrible crime she'd committed.

In the ladies' room, she washed her hands. She ran the water hot, wet a paper towel, raised her skirt, and scrubbed the inside of both thighs. She folded it into a small dripping square, then pressed it between her legs. Dabbing and wiping, she wanted to push it all the way inside her and scrape off the walls of her own flesh.

She washed her hands again. She dried them. She reached into her purse, found her lipstick, and put some color into her lips: burgundy red. Her fingers trembled. Her eyes looked tired and old to her, the whites flecked with too many capillaries.

She left the bathroom with her purse and apron full of Ward Dunn Jr.'s money. The boy was cleaning her windshield and maybe he'd even checked the oil. She felt momentarily cared for, and she sat behind the wheel and smoked a cigarette and waited for him to finish. She watched him work the squeegee, watched him wipe off the rubber blade onto his jeans after each stroke; it made her think of swords, blood dripping from the blades before they were wiped clean. And penises. Were they wiped clean, too? Would Ward Dunn Jr. come to, remember, then clean her dried blood off himself?

The boy dropped the squeegee into the pail. He buffed the glass with a dry rag, working his hand in quick circles. It was hard to watch and she blew smoke out her open window and looked past the pumps to a dense stand of mangroves, the sky above a fading tangerine. Near the road was a phone booth. It leaned to the left.

The boy finished his work. He walked around to her window and handed her change. Bills and some coins. His fingertips grazed her palm, and she jerked her hand away, a quarter falling to her lap.

"Sorry, ma'am."

She said nothing. Started the car and put it in gear and drove across the lot to the telephone booth. She stubbed out her cigarette in the ashtray, unrolled her apron on the seat, and pulled out Ward Dunn Jr.'s driver's license, his wedding photo, and his business card. She reached into her purse for her reading glasses. The quarter was still in her lap.

The booth's door wouldn't slide all the way closed. Sweetheart initials and dates were carved into the side of the telephone, and a phone book hung from a cord against the glass. She laid the wedding picture on the metal shelf and stared at Ward Dunn Jr.'s wife, her face and eyes and hair, and she read her telephone number to the long-distance operator and told her it was a collect call from Ward. It was urgent.

"Honey, is that you?"

Honey. Ward Dunn Jr.'s wife had a high voice and a heavy Kentucky accent. Virginia could hear children in the background. Fighting or playing, she couldn't tell which. And there was music. A radio or record player. They sounded happy. They sounded like a happy family. Still, she should know. She *must* know.

"Ward?"

"No." Virginia tried to swallow. "No. No, I'm the woman your husband raped today in his room in Florida, and don't hang up, Mrs. Dunn, because I'm telling you God's honest truth and I can tell you he has a mole on the right cheek of his rear end and I'm sorry, but—"

There was a click and a dial tone. Cars passed by on the road. Virginia hung the phone into its cradle and wiped her eyes; she hadn't meant to hurt his wife like that, just him. But it would have to start with her, wouldn't it?

What now? She couldn't imagine driving north back to Samoset to her quiet apartment in the new complex. Some nights she'd walk out to the lighted pool and swim. Go back inside, heat up some soup. Smoke a cigarette and read a magazine. But that had all changed—even if she drove home right now she wouldn't be the same Virginia in that pool or on her couch or in her kitchen. She was a new Virginia, a dirtier, weaker, stronger but less able Virginia who was already trying to put a bad afternoon behind her; that's all it was, wasn't it? A bad afternoon she was going to have to forget?

So leave Ward Dunn Jr.'s wedding photo in that booth. Leave his business card, too. But keep his money. Buy yourself dinner somewhere you could never afford before. No, there'll be people there. Men and women she might have to talk to and smile at, so go home. Put your dirty money in the dirty bank and try to put this day at your back and never think of it again.

Virginia lit up. Six and a half minutes had passed. She was getting better, though she needed to get to ten minutes, then twenty. Why not shoot for one hour? Only fifteen or sixteen a day? That should give her a few more years. Surely, the sweet Lord would allow her that. Was it too much to want her grandson to know her enough to remember her? She already loved him so, and even though she wasn't fond of baby Cole's mother, she was relieved he'd gotten more of his looks from her side of the family and not Ward Dunn Jr.'s.

Her poor son. She placed her smoking cigarette in the ashtray, closed her eyes, and offered her first prayer of the day for Alan, may he find strength and the light to guide him back to his family, even with that Deena, may he get Cole back real soon, and may You watch over him, dear Lord, as he works into the rising sun this morning, operating that heavy equipment, and repairing that pipeline out there on Lido Key.

⋎ ⋎ ⋎

THE COFFEE WAS weak but hot and Lonnie sipped it and finished his eggs. She'd fried him three in butter, laying them down with two slices of toast on a flower-bordered plate. She rinsed her pan in the sink, then set it in the dishwasher and wiped down the counter, and he scraped the yoke with his fork and ate quietly but quickly; he didn't want Spring coming back to find him so comfortable when she was suffering. And her landlady, whose name he still didn't know, kept asking him questions he couldn't answer: Where *was* Franny? How could someone have left her *alone*? Where could April have gone looking anyway?

"She should be here in case they call. Damnit, she should be *here*." She finished her wine, then pushed the rubber stopper back into the bottle. "Are you seeing one another?"

He shook his head, swallowed the last of his toast. "No, ma'am."

She ran the water in the faucet, caught some on her fingers, and dabbed at her neck and throat. "She could be hiding, couldn't she? Couldn't she have become frightened and hidden someplace?"

He nodded, though he knew the girls had searched the club as well as anyone could. Then the deputies. "Thank you for the eggs."

"You get enough?" She took his plate and fork.

"Yes, ma'am."

"I'm sorry, I've been rude; my name is Jean."

He watched her rinse his plate and fork and put them into the dishwasher. The sky outside her kitchen window had some gray in it. The sun would be following soon and he had a vision of the little girl's body lying bloody in the weeds out back of the Puma. He shook his head and drained his coffee and wanted to get back out there and do what he could, whatever that was, he didn't know.

"Do you have a picture of her girl? I'm 'fraid I don't even know what she looks like."

She studied him a moment. She seemed relieved, like he'd just passed some sort of test. "Please."

He followed her down the hall to a room made for a child. She turned on the bedside lamp, and the shade gave off a pale blue light through the swimming figure of a mermaid, her red hair flowing past her tail. The bed was small and covered with a quilt. There were three or four pillows in the shapes of the moon and stars. On the walls were posters of characters from a kids' TV show he didn't know, and one of a child's hand and outstretched arm against the blue sky.

She handed him a framed photograph. He stepped over to the lamp and held it low under the light. The woman began to weep behind him. There she was in the picture smiling into the sun with the girl sitting on her lap. She had sun-streaked curly hair and a round face and didn't look much like Spring except in how her chin was raised proud.

"She's a cute kid."

Jean took a breath and sniffled and held out her hand for the picture he gave her. She placed it on the bureau and turned it toward the door.

Lonnie stepped into the hallway; the photograph and the room felt like a shrine and he had a bad feeling, like he was suddenly some-place deeply private and he had no business being here at all. None whatsoever.

But the eggs and coffee had revived him and he couldn't go home without seeing April at least once. *Can you keep an eye on her?* Her breath against his ear, her warm shoulder under his hand. And again he told himself there'd been no time to do it, that it was Tina's job after all, but where else to go now but back to the club? The inside was bright and the smoke had cleared and Louis sat at the Amazon with Tina. Most of the cops seemed to be standing around doing noth-ing. The one who'd interviewed Lonnie let him in, and he walked up behind the bar.

Louis raised his head. "Get a drink."

Lonnie thanked him and reached into the beer chest for a Hei-neken, though he no longer wanted one.

"Your little friend Spring came back too. Even after they told her to fuckin' stay home."

"C'mon, Lou." Tina's hand was on his forearm, and she squeezed it softly. "Did you go to her house, Lonnie?" Her voice was tired and contrite. Under the house lights her blond hair was too blond.

"Is she here?"

"They sent her packing, Lonnie Boy."

"Lou, that's enough." Tina reached for her cigarettes. Lonnie sipped his beer and looked past the empty stage into the kitchen. Somebody had pinned the curtains back and propped open the doors. Outside, bright lights on tripods shined onto April's car, and a woman in gloves kneeled in the front seat dusting powder over the steering wheel and dash. She held up a square of cardboard, a piece of string hanging off it. She aimed a blue light at it and stared.

"Spring see them doing this?"

"No," Tina said, "but the sergeant thinks they'll find this person if he's in the system. He did say that." Tina lit a cigarette and drew in deeply, her eyes on something straight ahead but far away.

"Somebody should tell her," Lonnie said. "She should know that."

Louis raised his rum and Coke. Then he looked at Lonnie over the rim of his glass as if he'd just said something for the first time, something he didn't quite catch.

T HERE WAS THE darkened industrial park, high weeds along
both sides of the road, bits of broken glass glittering, but nothing. There was nothing, and it was hard to breathe and she'd
driven back to the club where the tall one stopped her at the door and
told her to go home and wait. *Wait.*

The deputy who followed her was younger than the others. She
didn't like how he stood in her doorway now and kept glancing at her
half-buttoned blouse, her bare legs and feet.

"You're gonna stay put, right?"

His tone was half-reprimanding, half-gentle. She didn't like either.
She nodded, watched him leave, thought of Franny's backpack still
downstairs with Jean. She wanted it here with her, Franny's things.
And she felt the money there just outside her thoughts of Franny, a
sickening heat flashing across her face.

Again the images came.

Franny's legs spread open. A man's hands. Her terrified face. Oh God, God no. No, think of anything else. Anything else. Couldn't it be a woman? That crime in Nebraska, wasn't it? Nebraska? And this young pregnant woman dead in her own laundry room, a bullet in her brain, her baby cut out of her womb and it only took a day for them to find her a town over, brought home by a lady who told her husband she'd had her baby, an obese woman who could've been pregnant or not, and her husband believed her, the woman who'd killed a mother and stolen her child.

All those childless bitches at the club, the way they tried to fawn over Franny when she'd carried her in tonight. How April had kept moving, giving them her back because she didn't trust any of them, didn't even like them, because she wasn't really one of them. Could it be one of *them*? Not for money but just to hurt her?

Well please let it be that then. Let it be China, who everybody knew gave blow jobs in cars in the lot and pocketed every penny, or let it be Cowgirl Sadie and the Oxy shine in her eyes, or even VIP Wendy, who'd sell her own family for a shot at the Champagne. Please let it be one of those bitches because none of them would hurt Franny—April knew this; none of them were that cold or hated her that much.

Footsteps on the outside stairs. She heard it through the screen door and could see the night lifting, the sky breaking open to a band of coral above Jean's walled garden and the rooftops of the houses on the next street, the tall palms and acacia trees.

She rushed to the door. Lonnie stood under her porch light, squinting at her. His shoulders were hunched slightly in his Puma Club T-shirt, and there were two Dunkin' Donuts coffees in his hands.

She let him in. Her arms were shaking.

"I just missed you at the club."

She nodded. Her hand wiped at a tear, pressing it into her skin. He handed her a coffee. The Styrofoam cup was hot against her palm. She thanked him and invited him in and reached by him and turned on the overhead light of the kitchen. There were the dishes in the sink from yesterday's lunch, the bowl she'd made the tuna fish in for their sandwiches for the beach, the plastic pitcher she'd emptied into a thermos.

"I can't stay in here." She pulled the cordless phone from its cradle and stepped to Lonnie's side and out onto the landing. The mango branches were inches away. Down below was the light from Jean's kitchen on the worn stairs, always damp, and she hoped Lonnie would follow her. But hurrying down the steps was like escaping a burning house and leaving everyone you love inside, and how terrible it was to carry coffee down the stairs she carried coffee down every morning, the sun hot and bright, Franny running out of Jean's.

April ignored Jean's lighted windows and walked over to the Adirondack chairs under the darkened mango tree. The soles of her cut feet burned. She waited for Lonnie before she sat down.

"It's all right I'm here?"

"Yeah." She rested the hot cup on her knee, remembered burning herself with the Mobil station coffee yesterday afternoon driving Franny, the hurried walk into Tina's office. "I could kill Tina, Lonnie. I swear to God I want to kill her."

"She feels pretty bad."

"She should. She fucking *should*."

"But I should've checked in on her like you asked. I just didn't—"

"No, Lonnie, it was *Tina*. I paid her for that." She meant it; she wasn't mad at him. She raised the cup to her lips but her throat closed and her eyes began to fill and she was ashamed. "I should've called in sick, Lonnie. But fucking *Louis*."

"They're lifting prints in your car. They think they'll find something."

She watched him sip his coffee, his Adam's apple rising and falling in his throat. "You mean find some*one*."

He nodded. The garden beyond him was shadowed in the blue-gray light, and Jean's door opened, her slippers slapping against the soles of her feet. She stood in front of them both. Her robe was cinched tightly and Franny's backpack dangled from her hand. April's stilettos stuck out of the half-zipped flap.

"Any news? Is there news?"

"No, ma'am." Lonnie sat forward. "Would you like to sit?"

"Thank you, no." Jean was looking down at April. "Where did you go?"

"Everywhere. Nowhere." April couldn't look at her. She shook her head.

Jean held out Franny's pack. "That's an awful lot of money."

April took it and lowered it to the ground at her feet. She could feel her heart beating behind her eyes and she wanted to tell Jean she never made that much, that she got a drunk foreigner in the Champagne, that every single bill in there meant nothing to her now, nothing.

"She works hard," Lonnie said.

"Yes, I'm sure."

"Are you judging me, Jean?"

Jean folded her arms.

"Who are you to fucking judge *me*?" April pushed herself out of the chair, her cup falling and spilling onto the bricks. "You've never worked a fucking day in your life. You don't even know what work *is*. This wouldn't've happened if you weren't such a hypochondriac and had to go to the *hospital*. I had to take her 'cause of *you*, Jean! *You!*"

"*April.*"

The phone was in a spreading puddle of hot coffee and April snatched it up and grabbed the backpack and moved around Jean standing there, the stairs ahead of her April wouldn't climb, Jean's apartment she couldn't stand with more of Franny in it than upstairs where she really lived, in her real home, and she yanked the backpack strap over her shoulder and walked toward the growing light of the driveway, Jean calling her name.

∨ ∨ ∨

A J DROVE SLOWLY along the southern tip of Longboat, his eyelids swollen with fatigue. Past the pale beach was the Gulf he could just begin to see in the dark and it'd be daybreak soon and he didn't want to drink a beer while driving the child but what else could he do? The coffee was long gone and hadn't done anything but give him heartburn and a dry mouth. He needed some kind of fuel for just two more hours. That's all, just two.

He pressed his knees up against the wheel and reached into the passenger's seat for one of the Millers. The can was cool and he wedged it down between his legs, popped the tab, kept his eyes on the road, and took a long drink. Up ahead were the dim lights of the drawbridge over to Lido Key. His heart picked up a bit. He glanced in the rearview, could see in the darkness her hair over his T-shirt covering her.

YOU ARE NOW LEAVING LONGBOAT KEY

The sign was streaked with pelican shit, and he passed the empty expanse of the aquarium's parking lot, then the thick mangroves where they'd built boardwalks snaking through the trees. He'd wanted to take Cole there when he got bigger, go look for bobcat and manatee and osprey. And he would. He would.

He drank and accelerated up over the drawbridge onto Lido Key. He finished his Miller and dropped the empty onto the passenger seat. Soon enough he pulled into dark and quiet St. Armand's Circle, a few streetlamps shining dimly among the palm trees and hibiscus in the center, and he guided his truck around the circle John Ringling designed before he died. He built the causeway over to Sarasota too, used his circus elephants to haul the bridge timbers. AJ had always like reading about Ringling, a man with vision and balls, a head for numbers and no fear of hard work, a man AJ frankly believed he had much in common with; he just needed some help getting started. He just needed to get pointed in the right direction.

AJ drove the full circle. At his constant right were locked tourist shops and bookstores, ice cream parlors and cafés. No light came through their windows and some were covered with steel shutters padlocked to the sidewalk. Most of the buildings were painted white as oyster shells, even Mario's-on-the-Gulf he'd planned to bring Marianne to, his headlights sweeping over it now—the red canopy and diamond-shaped windows, the outdoor tables and their collapsed umbrellas as tall and still as sleeping vultures; there was the feeling he was a dog-assed fool who'd never be allowed in such a fine place with such a fine-looking woman on his arm and he reached for another Miller, but the lights of a car shone out at him from twelve o'clock, and he eased up on the gas and cut the wheel to the right and shot his truck away from the circle.

He gunned along a palm-lined street of fine homes behind stucco walls. Coming up on his left was an opening between two of them and he turned into it, a route for the trashmen and deliverers of food and ice, a place in the shadows for men and women who kept things running smoothly. It was dark and narrow and he was about to stop when a corner revealed itself to the right and he turned again and parked in a shortened driveway leading to a garage, its security lights coming on bright in his face, but keep cool, keep cool. They're on motion detectors, that's all. Just like the ones he almost bought for him and Deena. So sit still and they'll go dark soon enough. Switch off your engine and sit tight.

All was quiet. He opened the Miller and turned to look at her. Her chin was touching her chest, the part in her hair straight from front to back. Again he pictured Spring doing that with a comb before she brushed it—*somebody* had to've done it—and there was the feeling he'd done something wrong, that maybe there was more to all this than he knew. And if the cruiser—'cause what else could it be? poor neighborhoods don't get looked after all night like rich ones do—if it pulled up on him now, sitting in this service entrance waiting for the light to go off, they'd bust his ass for sure and there'd be no chance to cash in against Caporelli. No chance for anything but trouble.

He hated to see her sleeping like that, though; she'd wake up with a sore neck. He leaned past the seat and with two fingers pushed her head up till he could see her face, but then the cab went dark, the air outside too. He let go of her and hoped her chin didn't loll back to where it'd been.

                              ⌄ ⌄ ⌄

S HE IS OLD. She is the old of his dear mother. Her skin is dark
      as his own, her face round, and her hair is gray and black and
      her eyes are black as well. Before her is a small television and
her hearing must be bad for it is so loud Bassam can hear all of it on
the other side of the shop, the sound of shooting, of shouting, of autos
racing, and more shooting. And it is here under this white light before
the cooler of bottles of water and Gatorade and Pepsi and Coke that
he knows he is still not yet himself, that he is still damaged from the
drinking.

    The blackness out there, kilometers and kilometers of it. Over one
hour driving and only one auto coming at him from the east, its lights
blinding. Then more blackness, the Neon's headlamps cutting into it
dully, weakly. The whores' protector at the fuel station. Bassam had
felt followed and bought no fuel or drink or cigarettes. He disciplined
himself not to drive too fast and once in the countryside he turned on

the radio, but it was meaningless talk in this language he hated, the language of the far enemy his father insisted all his children learn. And so Bassam had learned and it had made him more valuable than Ahmed al-Jizani could have ever known, and his son opens the glass door and removes three plastic bottles of Coke and at the counter for paying she smiles at him, and perhaps she says to him words, he does not know, her television so very loud.

Behind her are magazines of whores. Above them stacks of cigarette packages. He asks the woman for Marlboros. She shakes her head, turns down her television. "What, honey?"

"Please, Marlboros."

She turns for them. On the back of her clothing is written: Miccosukee Indian Resort. *Indian.* He does not know this word, or the one before it. He pulls from his pocket too much money, the surprise in her old eyes. Too much surprise.

Outside once more, the air is warm yet beginning to cool, and the cigarette package and three bottles difficult to hold at once. He shakes his head at his own foolishness, at his own continued recklessness. The white Neon is parked beside the fuel pumps, and he rests upon the roof two of the plastic bottles and opens his door, but one of the bottles rolls down over the windscreen to the ground at his feet. He lowers himself to it, and grasps it and as he rises he tells himself to be careful with this one, Bassam. Be careful with the one that may explode.

ʏ　ʏ　ʏ

ONNIE LEANED AGAINST his driver's door and looked at April. In the peach-blue light, she sat low in the passenger seat, her daughter's backpack on the floor between her bare calves, the cordless phone in her hand. She still wore her makeup from last night but her cheeks were drawn and he wanted to kiss her.

She was looking out the windshield at the empty street. "Say something, Lonnie. I can't have any quiet right now. I can't." She began tapping her bare foot on the floor.

He reached past her and pulled open the glove compartment, five rows of cassettes wedged on top of his registration and manual. "Books on tape. I listen to them 'cause I can't read." He shut the hatch, his wrist skimming her bare knee.

"Really?" She was looking at him now. He felt about fourteen years old and wished he'd kept his mouth shut.

"I'm not illiterate. I can read signs and shit. It's just sentences. They get all fucked up in my head. Unless I hear them. Then the words don't crash into each other."

"What do you listen to?"

"Novels. Some poetry."

April kept looking at him. Her lips were parted. She opened the glove compartment. "Can we listen to one? Can we just sit here and listen to one?"

She pulled out a tape. T. S. Eliot.

"Poetry. You want that?"

"Anything."

Lonnie didn't like the voice of the reader; he sounded like one of those little shits he'd seen in clubs over the years who'd gone to prep schools on the East Coast and somehow ended up with a British accent.

But Eliot was Eliot and April wanted to hear him. Lonnie turned his ignition quarter way and pushed in the tape. "Want me to rewind it?"

"No."

"This is from *The Waste Land*."

"'On Margate Sands.
I can connect
Nothing with nothing.
The broken fingernails of dirty hands.

My people humble people who expect
Nothing.'
       la la

To Carthage then I came

Burning burning burning burning
O Lord Thou pluckest me out
O Lord Thou Pluckest

Burning

          IV. Death by Water"

April jabbed at the buttons. "Stop it. Turn it off."

He did. She was breathing hard, shaking her head. Lonnie put his hand on her shoulder. "It's all right." He could feel her lungs filling and emptying down there inside her. "It's okay." He began rubbing her back but her muscles tensed and he pulled his hand away. She was squinting out at the road like there was something coming from a long way off. Lonnie looked but there was just the purple asphalt and the palm trees and hibiscus along rose-colored walls.

"Lonnie? You know that foreigner I had in the Champagne?"

"Yeah?" Nicotine- and cologne-smelling little fucker, the way he walked right past him at the filling station.

"He kept saying something bad's going to happen to us all. He kept saying we're all gonna burn."

"In hell?"

"I don't know. He just kept predicting something bad."

"You believe that?"

April sniffled, dabbed at her nose. "He looked at me like one of those born-agains. Like I'm dead and don't even know it."

"They blame you for their own weakness, April. I can't stand those people."

"Maybe they should."

"What?"

"Blame me."

"For what? Showing them what they came to see?"

"But I've made money dancing, Lonnie."

"Good."

She stared down at the phone in her hand. "A lot."

"Not as much as Louis." Lonnie's eyes felt dry and his arms were heavy and there was still a swelling in his finger from where he'd caught Dolphins Cap in the mouth. He wanted more coffee.

"I always kept it separate, Lonnie. I swore I'd never be one of those bitches dragging her kids to the club and I didn't, Lonnie, I never did." She shook her head and lowered her chin. "I was only going to do it till I didn't have to anymore."

"Nothing wrong with that."

She nodded. She looked again at the phone in her hand. "Keep talking, Lonnie. Please, just keep talking." She shook her head and started to cry and he leaned forward and wrapped his arms around her. He began to rock her. Then he smelled her hair, and felt like a real lowlife for doing that.

∨ ∨ ∨

H E TURNED SIDEWAYS in his seat and watched her sleep. Her hair was in her face, and she had a slight snore on her inhale. The beer had cleared his head: forget the temple or any other public building out on the circle or just off it. He couldn't chance the county cruising by again. Outside his truck window and over the stucco wall, the stars had faded. She was a sweet child and he didn't want to let her go just yet but dawn was twenty or thirty minutes away and now was the time to move.

He upended his Miller, laid the bottle on the seat beside him, reached across himself with his good hand, and was out of the truck three or four seconds before the light switched on bright all over him again. *Just don't wake the girl. Just don't wake her up.* His hand and wrist pounded hot at his hip and he could see the flecked paint above the garage door handle he squatted for now, gripping it, standing and pulling, a hollow shriek of spring and wheel in an iron track that needed oil.

His heart was kicking again. He held on to the handle above his head, stood there looking at a new Honda Civic sitting in front of him like a gift.

He let go. The door slid up another foot or so, bobbing once against its spring, then all was quiet but that goddamn door had been loud—*he* wouldn't've slept through it—and if he was going to do what he had to do, this was the one and only moment he had to do it in. He moved quickly over the concrete floor and hooked his fingers under the handle of the rear door and pulled. The door didn't budge and what'd he expect? He began to look around for a place he could put her where somebody'd see her right away, where she wouldn't be run over, his fingers hooking under the front door handle now, the metallic click in his hand as the door swung open, the interior light coming on.

There was a leather briefcase on the passenger's side, stacks of papers on the backseat. He jabbed the unlock button and opened the rear door and knocked all those papers onto the carpet, the air smelling like a new car, like just-molded plastic and spotless upholstery, rustless steel and dustless electronics, clear oil and smooth glass—it was the smell of First Place, a just reward for one's hard-earned dues, and AJ took it as a good omen, his own prize coming just as soon as he did the right thing by this child.

He walked fast back to his truck, the floodlight on him too damn bright, as if it had its own sound, and he had to focus his mind and ignore his broken bone and move her as quickly as he could.

He got the access door open and leaned in. He smelled Wild Turkey and diesel, coffee and grape Slush Puppie and dirt. He was breathing hard and closed his mouth, felt his heart bucking in his head. He'd doubled her dose but maybe he should've tripled it—man, what if she woke up? What if she woke and began to howl?

He'd leave her anyway.

He lifted his shirt off her, reached between her legs for the buckle, but he couldn't get at it unless he pushed his palm against her leg. He began to raise his left hand but it was swollen useless. The air at his back felt crowded and he put his fingers around her bare ankle and pulled it over just a bit, then he pressed on the button and the buckle let loose and he swung the plastic tray up over her sleeping head. He wanted to part the hair from her face, he wanted to do so much more than he was, but this was it, and he leaned close and snaked his hand behind her back and let her cheek rest against his shoulder, his fingers scooping her up beneath her butt, in his head Marianne's shaking at him from the stage under blue light, how it wasn't right that a little girl could grow to end up doing that—so many things weren't right and he pressed his face to her head and backed out of the cab on one knee. He was breathing hard and the concrete under him tilted a second, like the whole town was a boat out on the Gulf, a boat of revelers, and surely there was somebody who'd look after Spring's girl better than she had.

The Honda was low. He had to bend down, her head resting against his palm, her warm back against his arm, and his knee slipped on papers but he laid her down on the new seat in the new car in the clean garage. Now her hair encircled her face like flowering ivy. One hand was under her, the other across her belly. He wanted to pull that arm free but she'd stopped snoring and she could come out of it and he straightened up and half ran back to his truck for his shirt to cover her again. But—shit—Caporelli written all over it. They'd trace him in no time. In a couple hours the air would be plenty warm, but now it had a chill to it and there was nothing else to cover her with.

Except what he had on; he grabbed his back collar with his good hand and yanked it over his head, gathered it up in his fingers, held his breath as he raised his bad hand, and yanked again, dropping it through the sleeve.

Too much time had passed since he'd opened those doors. The sky was a lighter blue, and he could see the black rise of a gabled roof over the wall, the dark shuttered windows.

He leaned into the Honda and lay his T-shirt over the girl, tucking it in lightly around her hips and legs. She had such a pretty little face;

he didn't see Spring in it anywhere. He kissed his finger and held it over her, then he backed out and pushed the door closed. He pressed the lock button on the driver's door, all four of them thumping down, and he pushed that door closed too—*quiet, quiet*—and pulled on the handle but could no longer get in and neither could any other sonofa-bitch except the owner and he was going to chance that the driver of this new car, the handler of all those papers on the floor, was a decent man like he was, a man who'd do the right thing.

Still, he should call the law soon as he could, tell them where she is. But can't they trace a cell phone call? Pull up your cell bill faster than you can press the End button? These thoughts running through him as he reached up and grabbed the handle and with too much noise pulled the door clacketing back down. He wanted to leave it halfway open, let some fresh air in, but when he let go, the door began to rise back up. He pushed down till it was a foot off the concrete but it rose up again and goddamnit he had to close it all the way, run back to his truck, start her up, the engine tearing a hole through the quiet of the alleyway. He got his door shut and, bare-chested, backed away.

He switched on his parking lights and moved slowly down the alley the way he'd come. He looked up over the walls and the dark rise of roofs to the sky, a hint of peach in it from the east. The digital on his radio told him he had just over thirty minutes to set himself in the ditch under the CAT, and it was going to be hard to make a cut in the hose look like a tear. Maybe he should loosen the nuts on the clamp instead. Shitty maintenance could shake those loose too. His ratchet set was in the toolbox, wasn't it? He wasn't sure, but why wouldn't it be? His heart began to slow down now but his head felt heavy on his neck, his eyes and shoulders ached, and he wished his wrist and hand weren't so damn swollen. Not that Cap Jr. had a brain in his fucking head about anything like this. But would the doctor at the hospital say anything? They might. And that could change everything.

At the alley's end he pulled to a stop. Across the street, in the deep blue light of dawn, an armadillo crept over the bahia lawn of a rich man's home. AJ's lights were on him but the creature took his time, the bony plates of his hide shifting as he went. It was the right thing to lay the girl down away from bugs and reptiles, but there was a cool emptiness inside that pulled on him the way not seeing Cole had pulled on him, and as he turned left away from St. Armand's Circle, he knew there wasn't much time but he couldn't just leave her back there without a call to the county. There had to be a pay phone somewhere. He looked behind him at the street sign. A palm tree was in front of it and he had to stop and back up and read the words in the white glow of his reverse lights—*Fruitville Road*.

He looked down the alley once more, couldn't even make out the building, and he put his truck in drive and accelerated, the V-8 pulling him ahead under a cobalt sky, getting lighter and lighter to the east.

ASSAM TURNS OFF the engine and sits. It is dawn in the parking lot of the Acacia Inn and across the street are two hotels, their many balconies lighted from beneath. He can see the ocean between the buildings. The sky above it is now nearly visible, a blackish blue that makes the water appear gray, its waves breaking on the sand. His chest aches. Beside him is the half package of cigarettes he smoked on his drive west, the three empty bottles of Coke. Khalid.

Bassam pushes the cigarette package into his pocket and leaves the small rental car. At the fuel station halfway across the state, before driving away, he counted his remaining money: nine thousand five hundred sixty-five dollars. But from the bank he had withdrawn over sixteen thousand he was to wire directly to Dubai. He does not wish to do the subtraction, and he steps onto the concrete walkway, the keys in his hand.

The room is dark and smells of cheap incense and his sleeping brothers. Soon it will be time for the first prayer but today they travel north so he will let them sleep a few extra moments. Softly he closes the door. He is pulled backward, an arm squeezing his chest, metal pressed to his throat.

"Bassam?"

"Yes, what is wrong with you?"

Imad drops his arm and Bassam steps away, his heart beating too quickly. His legs feel weak and he breathes deeply and the shadow of Tariq moves around the corner of the kitchenette.

"Bassam?"

"Yes, what is wrong with you both? Who is going to have a key but me?"

The bedside lamps illuminate, Imad standing there at the wall switch fully dressed in shirt and pants, his feet bare. Weeks ago he shaved his beard and mustache and looks to Bassam like a big boy, his eyes shining.

"Why didn't you answer my calls? You were supposed to be back by Isha."

"I couldn't."

"But where were you?" Tariq too is dressed. He is younger than them both, but his trimmed mustache makes him look older, almost handsome. "We thought you were caught."

"No, excuse me, I again should have called."

"But Bassam," Imad tosses the retractable razor onto the bed, "where were you?"

He can lie. Bassam can stand here and lie to his brothers, but to do so would be as if he'd lain with the black whore. His face warms with shame, a baboon crying in a thorn tree while they sit around Shaytan's fire.

"One of the whores lost her child and the police held us searching for her."

"Bassam," Imad says, "what if they held you longer? You could have ruined everything."

"Did you wire the money?" Tariq's button-down shirt is tucked neatly into his pants. Seeing it, Bassam feels dirty, unprepared. "We will wire it before our flight, Insha'Allah. Brothers, don't worry. I went there to strengthen myself. Now hurry, the sun is rising and I must perform my ablutions and after Fajr we need to pack and go."

Bassam moves past tall Imad and looks no longer at Tariq and steps inside the bathroom. *O Allah, I take refuge with You from all evil and all evildoers.* He pulls closed the door, but it is dark and he must open it again and fumble for the switch and turn on the light. Imad stands by the bed. Bassam ignores him and closes the door. Around the sink is a puddle of water, black whiskers floating there. Two disposable razors. A bottle of cologne Amir prefers. Three toothbrushes lay on their sides, and Bassam closes his eyes to prepare himself for ablutions but in the darkness there is the lie he told to his brothers, that he went to the whores for strength when it was the opposite—he went there because he could not stop himself. And the money he gave so freely, yes, it will be used for the future, Insha'Allah, and he should not have given it to the kafir, but sitting there drunk amid the whores, burning one bill, then the next, he could feel his resolve strengthening once again, for of all the treasures of this earth found again in Jannah, he knew money would not be one of them, dirty money and every sin committed for more and more of it.

The man in Dubai may be angry, as will Amir in the north, but Allah is pleased. And Bassam al-Jizani opens his eyes and begins to wash this body he is so nearly free of.

⌄ ⌄ ⌄

T HE ICE CREAM had helped, had calmed Deena's stomach and made her sleepy. But sleep never came and she lay in bed another hour and maybe she dozed off because she couldn't be sure her thoughts were dreams or her dreams were thoughts: there was AJ crying tonight, smelling like liquor; there was his face after he'd hit her months ago, like he was just warming up but wanted somebody to stop him too, his blue eyes sorry but not sorry; there was Cole eating the breakfast she knew she'd make for him sooner than she'd be ready to, French toast covered with melted butter in a pool of syrup—she could see herself cutting it up before she served it to him and her heart started beating faster in preparation for this task and she kept telling herself to stop thinking and sleep, fool. *Sleep.*

Then she opened her eyes to the darkness. Maybe she did sleep because she couldn't remember what had just been in her head and there was a sour taste in her mouth and she gave up and climbed out of bed to go brush her teeth. The bathroom was the nicest-looking room in the house. It was bigger than most, and AJ had laid blue tiles that made it feel cool and she'd hung lime curtains and it was always here she felt his best intentions and would regret how things were between them.

She wiped her lips on the towel, avoided looking at the plain woman in the mirror. She turned out the light and crossed the hall to check on Cole. He was curled on his side, his small back to her. He'd be up soon and she knew this lack of sleep would hit her hard after lunch, that she'd need a nap then. Sometimes she put him in front of a Disney movie and slept on the couch, but one afternoon she woke and the TV screen was blank and Cole was in the front yard piling pebbles onto the plastic yellow seat of his John Deere. Less than an hour later AJ got home, and if he'd seen that she'd never stop hearing about it. Just more proof that she wasn't good enough. She'd never be good enough.

She was still surprised by how he'd looked tonight, so lonesome and sorry. And again came the feeling she'd been too hard on him; honestly, part of her believed she deserved what he'd done, that it was her punishment for not loving him more than she did.

It was after five. She should just give up and make coffee and start the day early. The sun came up around seven. She could read her magazines and watch some TV, then go outside while the sky lightened above the pines across the road. She'd sit with some fresh coffee and think a bit, reflect on things. Virginia called it prayer. Deena envied her really, having faith there's someone or something out there who loves you and cares about what happens to you and maybe even watches over you. She wished she believed that herself, but she just didn't. It made no sense, some eternal being who knows each one of us. And what about the other people from other religions with their other gods? Did they really believe theirs was the true one?

In the kitchen Deena put some water on for her instant hazelnut she was already looking forward to. This tiny house was so quiet it unnerved her but she didn't want to go turn on the TV just yet; more and more she noticed she was always craving something or moving toward something else or someplace she thought of as better or more comfortable. How many times, even when she was full, did she want to be eating more ice cream or another grilled cheese sandwich or handfuls of salty potato chips? How often was she reaching for the remote control and roaming from one channel to the next and never satisfied? How many magazines did she look through a week? Six? Seven? And she rarely read an entire article, just skimmed all those glossy pictures and advertisements of a sexy, rich life she'd never live.

It was clear Virginia didn't think much of her, but there was a kind of stillness to her old mother-in-law Deena admired. She smoked and she liked her coffee and always seemed to be drinking it, hot or cold, but the woman could sit out on her patio alone with no radio on, nothing to read and nobody to talk to all day long. She'd sit there with those oxygen tubes under her nostrils and look at her small lawn AJ kept trimmed. She'd look up at the sky or stare at her Virgin Mary statue. Maybe this was part of getting old, when you're too tired to move around much and you spend a lot of time looking back. But that wasn't it. Virginia just *knew* there was a God watching over her and it was like she was visiting with him somehow, talking to him.

Well, what a comfort that would be.

The water was roiling and began its low whistle. Before it could get high and shrieking Deena grabbed an oven mitt and lifted the kettle off the coil and poured the steaming water into her cup. God was for the weak, that's what she really thought. It was for people who can't face that we're born alone and we die alone and for great stretches of our lives we're just alone. Nobody looking out for you but you and maybe a handful of people who love you because you're family.

Until Cole, she hadn't understood that, the love her mother and father had for her. Or maybe, as she got older, she hadn't felt it all that much. But just as sure as she could feel this hot mug in her hands she knew there was a love in us we can't explain. It was hard to believe in a god, but she did believe in this warm, dark pull inside her that she would do anything, *anything* for that little boy sleeping down the hall.

Even kill. Even die.

Isn't that enough? To have just one human being love you like that? Can't the memory of that keep you going? Be like a living prayer inside you?

She poured cream into her coffee and dumped in three spoonfuls of sugar and suspected she was full of it; she'd been loved by her own all her life and it wasn't even close to enough. And then she had a healthy baby and a solid home built by the man who loved her and none of it had been enough; she wanted a bigger home and a more successful, better-looking man, and she wanted more children, four or five, but more than anything she wanted a different *her*: she wanted prettier eyes and a smaller face; she wanted a body she wasn't ashamed of, one that wouldn't crave food all day and night but instead would take in only what it needed; she wanted to go to college and read books she'd never even heard of and be an interesting person with interesting things to say. She wanted to tell AJ she was sorry for how much she wanted. But she also wanted him to stop scaring her with his temper, to stop scolding her all the time, to quit making her feel like everything that was going wrong right now was her fault.

Some of it was. But some of it was Virginia's, too. Late at night, sometimes after they'd made love, AJ would tell her about being a boy in her house, how until his stepfather Eddie came along, it was one boyfriend after another. Some would stay for a few weeks, others months. He said he spent a lot of nights alone in front of the TV while his mother and her boyfriend drank and played cards and laughed and smoked in the kitchen, or else went to her bedroom early and he'd hear them doing it, hear the bedsprings and the way his mama moaned and he'd turn up the TV or leave the house. There'd be fighting too.

"Anybody ever hit her?"

"I don't know. I'd go walking."

"What if one of them *hit* her?" This before he'd ever hit *her*.

"I was a boy, Deena. Jesus Christ, what do you want?"

He was right. She knew he was right. She'd lay her cheek to his chest and tell him so. It was wrong to judge a little kid like that, but she didn't like what that said about him even then, that when trouble came to someone he loved, he just got up and walked away from it.

But Virginia, she never loved him enough, never held him or played with him enough—at least he couldn't remember if she did. And now he had no real confidence in himself. Now he was a man who could hit his own wife, even if she had been hard on him in a way; was she asking for it? Did she really believe that?

Like a sudden answer to her question, the front room lit up from outside and two men climbed out of the lighted interior of a police car, its long antennae swaying in the red glow of its taillights, Deena thinking, AJ—drunk, crashed, gone. And her face felt on fire for what she felt, not fear or dread or worry, but hope, not that she was wrong about what had just happened to AJ, but that she was right.

She could hear the men's footsteps on the gravel and with trembling fingers she put her coffee down on the countertop and went to answer the door.

A J DROVE FASTER than he knew he should, passing all the sleeping homes, some with their lights coming on in their back bedrooms. It was a sight that made him miss Deena and Cole, and all night long he'd felt he'd done a good thing for this child and now he wasn't so sure. What if the owner of that Honda was away somewhere or planned to sleep late and take the day off? The windows were rolled up, and man, once the day got going it could get real hot in there. And how would she feel when she woke up in a strange car in a strange garage by herself?

Goddamnit, he should've taken her inside Mama's or back home to Deena. If he was going to do something good for this girl, then damnit he should've done it all the way.

He was driving north when he should be heading south to Lido Key, but there was the municipal fishing pier at the north end of

Ringling's Causeway. He might be able to find a phone booth there, though he doubted it; since cell phones, they just didn't seem to exist anywhere anymore.

His head ached. He was hungry now, and thirsty. But it was too late to reach for just one more Miller. He didn't want to smell like beer when Caporelli drove up to find him pinned under the bucket. He raised his bad hand and looked at it in the dim blue light of dawn. His wrist was wider than his forearm, and the fingers of his hand thick and curled. It'd been over six hours since that big motherfucker broke it and again AJ had no worries about Cap Jr. believing his tale, but wouldn't the doctors know the difference between what had been done to it and how long ago and what he was going to say? Or maybe they wouldn't. Maybe they'd be as busy as those poor sonsabitches in that show Deena liked, and they wouldn't have time to even think about it. A broken bone was a broken bone.

For a flashing moment AJ considered letting go of the plan entirely. Just go to work and carry on, but with a laugh that came from a knowledge he'd forgotten, he lowered his useless hand back to his lap. If he did *not* go ahead with this, then he'd be out of work with nothing for weeks, maybe months. He might be able to collect but how good would that look to the judge? Cole's daddy laid up because a bouncer at the Puma thought he was being too rough on one of the girls.

Too rough.

Goddamnit but his blood started to shoot through him all over again and he gunned his engine and shot his truck onto the concrete causeway, the rubber expansion joints clicking under his tires steadier than his own jagged heartbeat. Off to his right lay the purple waters of Sarasota Bay, then the early-morning lights, the streetlamps and traffic signals above empty intersections, the fluorescent glow of first-floor security desks of the office buildings downtown, the neon glow of what had to be at least one all-night coffee shop where he could get a cup and a muffin. But there wasn't time. Already the sky was visible over the buildings to the east, a band of blue lifting to gray to a rose that made him think of Marianne, her black hair, the rose he was going to give her on their night out. A flower for a flower. A man treating her like a lady. A *gentle*man with a *lady*.

What a sorry-ass sack of shit he really was.

He eased up on the gas and coasted down the causeway and turned left into the asphalt lot of the city pier. With his elbow he pressed his window button and could already smell the salt water and dried fish guts, the pelican shit and shell dust.

It was chilly without his shirt. He left his window open and rode down to the water's edge. The Gulf was dark gray under a steel sky and his headlights shone over the wide planks of the pier, its weathered two-by-six railings, the white masts and hulls of boats moored below. They swayed from side to side in the early-morning chop.

He left his engine running and slid out of the truck and ran down the pathway to the only building around, a one-story hut with new windows and a thatched roof like the old Seminoles'. In front leaned a couple vending machines, Pepsi and bottled water. And at the far right side, bolted into the trim, was an oval sign: PHONE. His arm pulsed and throbbed and he held it up and ran around the corner, saw the half booth attached to the hut, its metal shelf and plastic phone book cover hanging on a brass chain, but no phone. No damn phone.

He turned and walked fast back to the truck, thinking, Fruitville Road. She was in the first garage in the first alleyway to the left going east of St. Armand's Circle on Fruitville. Why not just open his cell phone, call the county, and say that? He could do it in less than a minute. But man, that's all it would take to get his number and him. Why didn't he leave her something to drink? He could've put her melting Slush Puppie right there on the floor for her to find. It'd be cold and sweet, familiar too.

A breeze kicked up from the east and blew across the lot. It felt good against his face and bare chest, but it was already warming up, the sky clear in its lighted strip on the horizon. It was going to be hot. He had to go back. It was in the same direction as Lido Key and just a few blocks north of his CAT. He'd get the garage door open, leave her the Slush Puppie, then catch the exact street number of where he'd left her. On his way to the ditch he'd call 411, try and get a number from an address, then call the Honda owner directly, tell him or her about the little girl in the garage. Hang up.

But shit, then his number would be on *that* phone and anyway it was getting too light now. Neighbors might identify his truck. And what if Francie woke up when he went back in? And goddamnit, he couldn't get back in anyway, he'd locked her in!

Shit. He opened the access door, reached in over the empty car seat for his T-shirt and pulled it over his head. He was careful with his hurt hand, nudging gently for the arm hole, the world darker now and smelling like diesel and dirt and his own sour sweat. It was a dead-end smell, the smell of a life that would know only work, work, and more work. But as he poked his head and good arm through the right holes, the Gulf breeze blew back in his face, something shifting inside him: the girl was no longer his problem; he'd done what he could and now it was somebody else's damn turn. It was that simple. He was just going to have to trust in Mama's God that this child would be taken care of because he had about twenty minutes before Cap Jr. drove up to make a show of getting the day's work started, and A.J. Carey still had to get that one-and-three-quarters yard bucket into the ditch where his wrist and hand were supposed to be, this poor good-luck arm he now had to reach by to pull his door shut. AJ put her in reverse and backed up too fast, swinging around to face south, the sky over Sarasota a pale coral, and just moments from the sun.

⌄ ⌄ ⌄

THEY CAME JUST as the sun began to light the yard, the Virgin Mary's alabaster face looking sadly accepting of all things, even the murder of her only son.

Virginia was still in her robe. She had the morning news on the TV and was in the kitchen making her toast when the buzzer sounded and she thought, Alan, but he has his key and anyway he's working, and she pressed the intercom button and asked who's there. And when he told her, the air itself seemed to be without air and she saw her son crushed under an overturned excavator or buried alive in a ditch, and she buzzed the men in and met them in the darkened hallway, her oxygen tube trailing behind her only so far, two policemen from Sarasota County and one from Bradenton, the uniforms different.

"What is it? Is it my son? Is it Alan?"

There was a tall one, older and wearing glasses, and he asked if they could come inside, and yes, yes, but you have to tell me. And now they were gone, their visit inside her small kitchen so brief it felt like a bad vision.

Except there was the tall one's card on the counter, his name and rank at the Sheriff's Department, the kitchen air smelling like after-shave and the spearmint gum the one from Bradenton had chewed quietly while the one with glasses had shown her a picture of her own boy holding Cole on his lap, both of them squinting into the sun.

"Is this a recent photo?"

"Yes, it is."

She'd let them walk through the three rooms of her apartment, and one of them ventured out into her enclosed yard. She didn't want to tell them anything, but what could she do? She gave them the name and number of the company Alan worked for, and she told them about Lido Key, that he'd been called in to work early out there, something about a broken pipeline.

Virginia left her toast in the toaster and, careful to keep her tube from snagging under the foldout bed, she walked quickly to her chair by the window. She sat down, muted the television, and picked up the phone. It was Deena she wanted to talk to, Deena she wanted a few answers from, but her finger was punching Alan's cell phone number instead. She was breathing with some difficulty. On the TV there was footage of a baseball player being hit in the back by a pitch, throw-ing down his bat and running after the pitcher, punching him in the face before the field was full of players from both sides, punching and kicking and screaming at one another.

"Yeah, this is AJ. The phone's off or I'm workin' so leave a message."

"Alan? It's Mama. Some policemen were just here looking for you. They think you know something about a missing little girl." Virginia checked the clock across the room. "It's 7:16 and they just left, honey. I had to give them your boss's number and they know you're out at Lido Key. Please call me, honey. Please tell me what's going on."

She pressed the Talk button. She'd forgotten to say she loved him and wished she had. She began pressing the numbers to his home, but they weren't coming right away. There was a four and seven in it, but was the three first or the five? Her eyes were on the TV, a jumble of sports news of big men in bright colors chasing little balls.

7435. Those were the last four digits to her son's home, and of course this had to be one big mistake: she knew her son; she knew he liked his beer and occasional whiskey; she knew he was brokenhearted and missed Cole, that he was spending money he didn't have on fallen women in that fallen place, that yes, he'd had enough and slapped that woman and shouldn't have, but he was no danger to children. Not Alan. Not her son.

She pressed the numbers of the home he was locked out of and his phone began to ring. On the screen came a photograph of a young girl. It was one of those photo booth pictures, and she was sitting on the lap of a pretty woman. The girl had curly sun-streaked hair and plump cheeks and she was looking into the camera with great purpose, as if she knew taking this picture was meant to be something special. At first Virginia thought the girl's name was Amber. Then she remembered seeing it quite a few times before for all children with names far different, boys and girls, but mainly girls. This little one was Franny Connors. There was a number to call. Then the image was gone, replaced by a beautiful young housewife loading happy children into a shiny new minivan.

v v v

Just seeing the job site under a brightening sky made him feel halfway normal: the yellow excavator and its tall boom folded in close to the cab, the bucket sitting beneath it like a loosely clenched fist; there were the clumps of clay and tree root he'd dumped yesterday along both sides of the ditch, the stands of cabbage palms and saw palmettos and jack pine between his work and the houses to the west. If it weren't for his bad wrist and hand, this could be any workday morning, but as he pulled his truck into the clearing behind the excavator, the word *reward* came to him and he felt all the weeks and months and years he'd worked since he was fourteen years old, his childhood a blur of claustrophobic classrooms and loud, hot construction sites and long fluorescent-lit hours at Walgreens in a tie, then Deena and remodeling their hurricaneproof house and training with her daddy on heavy equipment and being too tired to even play with Cole, then boiling over and having to live with Mama. Well today his reward was coming, and it was way past due.

He only had about fifteen minutes before Cap Jr. drove up. AJ was out of the truck, walking fast around the excavator. It was too late to put a realistic tear in the hydraulic line. The only thing left was to say the bucket rolled when he went to change it. But couldn't they say it was his fault then? And how was he going to change the bucket over with one hand anyway? *Shit*, he'd spent too damn much time and energy on that bitch's child when he should've been thinking more about *this*.

With his good hand he grabbed hold of the safety handle and stepped up onto the track and swung open the cab door. He held his hurt wrist to his chest, climbed in, and started her up. It was a comforting sound, the diesel engine rattling with all that power under him. The only thing left was to lower the bucket into the ditch and say the hydraulics failed, which would be highly fucking unlikely.

His mouth and throat were dry. His entire head ached nearly as bad as his hand he only hoped wasn't too swollen now to look freshly injured. He checked the side view mirror. The road behind him was an asphalt snake cutting back through sunlit trees, and maybe it was a good sign the right-hand joystick would do all he needed without him having to reach across himself for the other. He gave the Caterpillar some gas and raised the bucket over the ditch, the hydraulics whining. The CAT needed its morning lube and Cap Jr. would have the grease gun with him, though he only took it out half the time he should. AJ uncurled the bucket.

Something moved in the mirror and he shot a glance at the glass, his face a furnace. A Seminole Spring Water truck cruised by and was gone. He pushed open the cab door and was swinging his legs around when he saw, through the scratched Plexiglas of the windshield and just above the bucket, the bright factory yellow of the new coupler Cap Sr. had installed. He'd just put them in all his machines, not for safety but to change buckets over faster and save his ass some *money*. It was an upgrade AJ had forgotten about and he hopped out of the cab and ran to his truck for his tool chest and channel locks. With those he could release the coupler with one hand and drop the bucket and say he was down there with his shovel when the new coupler failed and almost *killed* his ass.

He just hoped the channel locks weren't in the middle of the chest or he'd have to climb up into the bed, which would take too damn many precious seconds. He held his hurt hand high and reached over the wall of his truck and pulled the tool chest handle and got the lid up. There was the sound of a far-off car or truck getting closer and he didn't even want to look out at the road; if it was Cap Jr., he'd stick with his first story about failed hydraulics, say he was lucky to get his hand unpinned.

He was leaning hard against the truck, pushing aside an old tarp, his tow rope, the broken handle of the weed whacker he'd never gotten fixed, a deflated beach ball of Cole's, two or three empty Miller bottles till there was the ash handle of his tool box, and he felt past the open-ended wrenches and odd ratchet heads and loose screws and nails till his fingers touched the rubber-coated handles of his channel locks he yanked up and out of the box, the car louder now, its engine like some force that can't be controlled, *won't* be controlled. It was coming from the north, Cap Jr.'s direction, and AJ had to look because what would he want channel locks for if he'd just crushed his goddamn wrist?

It was a pickup, a creaking piece of shit, the front bumper gone, the hood red, the body a dented sky blue. A shirtless old man was driving it. He was small and brown, his face mottled with gray whiskers, and he lifted a hand to AJ as he passed. A trail of light blue exhaust hung in the air. AJ walked through its carbon monoxide smell for the CAT, feeling vaguely blessed by a stranger. Something about the old man's eyes taking him in, then the wave of his hand, and AJ knew then that everything was going to be all right, everything would be fine.

He closed the channel locks around the coupler. He squeezed, jerked downward, and the spring load popped free and the bucket let go with a *whump*, driving itself into the ditch, its vibration rippling through the ground under AJ's boots.

He turned and whipped the channel locks into the trees. He grabbed the short spade shovel off the cab floor, tossed it in the ditch, and jumped down into it. The bucket had wedged itself into both sides and there was a good foot of air between the teeth and the clay bottom, too much to fool anyone; he took up the shovel with his good hand and began stabbing the sandy soil at the side of the bucket. He was sweating a sick sweat, his mouth gummy, his throat dry, a well of heartburn rising up. But he'd gotten lucky with no roots and in no time had carved a small dark hole and he knelt and eased his broken wrist into it. It was cool in there and AJ sat back against the wall of earth, stretched out his legs as far as he could.

And now he waited. He waited for help.

・ ・ ・

THE SUN BEGAN to rise over her garden wall outside, shining down the corridor and into her bedroom, and Jean had tried to rest but she couldn't. "*I had to take her 'cause of you, Jean! You!*" April's face, the hurt and rage in it, disgust even. *Disgust.* And did she really believe that? Was she taking *no* responsibility whatsoever? But what she'd said about Jean and work, well those words were now inside her like broken glass, and she'd been fighting it since the policeman and April had shattered her sleep, had held her breath to stop it, had drunk three glasses of wine to stop it, but now she couldn't hold it back any longer, this image of her dear dear Franny floating in shallow water, her eyes closed, her lovely hair writhing in the current, her throat purple and blue, her arms and legs naked and pale and stiff. A cry welled up from Jean's middle and she shook her head, but there it was and it wasn't going away. For seconds or minutes she tried to think of anything else, but she saw only Franny, her mornings with her, her nearly sacred mornings with her, and now the images of her dead were all the clearer and sharper, cutting into her, cleaving her. Then the bed shifted and the ceiling seemed to cant to the side and Jean told herself to inhale deeply through her nose and let the air slowly out her mouth—*breathe in, breathe out, breathe in, breathe out.* She did this for what felt a very long while. Then, like air rising from the deep, there came a black airless calm, Harry slumped in his chair, his narrow chest sunken and still beneath his shirt; she'd told herself it was the gray afternoon light that was fooling her. Through Chopin's rising and falling piano chords she called her husband's name and could hear the lie in her own voice for her heart already knew what the rest of her hadn't the strength to accept. It was disrespectful, this denial of his true state there in front of her: the least she could do was be a witness to him, or to what was once him, this cooling sculpture of all his years and his last moments too, this body she'd fed and loved and lain beside since she was a young woman; the least we can do for those we love is to look their fate in the eye squarely and with clarity, devoid of manufactured hopes and surface lies.

Matisse leapt onto the mattress and walked over Jean's belly. She picked him up and pulled him close, but he pushed his claws into her shoulder and moved to the pillow behind her. And there he settled himself against her head as if she should know better, as if she should know more than she ever did.

＊ ＊ ＊

In AJ's dream, his left arm was stretched out away from him and Deena was naked and sitting on his hand, which was all the way up inside her. It was cool and sandy there, and she wasn't moving. She kept turning around to smile at him. She looked like he'd never seen her before, like she was finally happy about everything and it had to do with his hand. Something about his hand.

Cole was sitting off to the right in a plastic lawn chair. He was dressed up in pants and a button-down shirt and clip-on tie. His feet were bare and didn't touch the ground and Marianne was sitting next to him in a black dress, her lips full and red. They were talking in low voices. There was the slam of a door, boot steps above.

"AJ?"

He opened his eyes, saw the ditch wall ahead of him, felt the big iron bucket at his side.

"Shit, you *hurt*?"

AJ looked up just as Cap Jr. jumped down, his gut covered by a clean Caporelli's T-shirt tucked into new jeans, his black hair still wet from his morning shower. AJ could smell his aftershave.

"*Fuck*, AJ."

"Bucket came down on me, man. The coupler popped."

"Shit, can you move? What'd it hit?"

"I don't know. I think just my hand." AJ glanced up at Junior. His eyes were fixed on AJ's lower arm wedged between the bucket and the earth. Sweat broke out on his forehead and AJ felt as if everything he'd just said was the absolute truth.

"Can you get it out?"

"I tried. I guess I blacked out."

"*Shit.*" Junior. picked up the shovel, held it a second, dropped it. "We shouldn't mess with this ourselves." He pulled his silver cell phone from its belt clip, and as he called 911, the sky clear and blue above him, AJ closed his eyes, wanted cold water but knew it was coming, knew everything he needed would be coming to him now.

Junior was telling the dispatcher where they were, naming the road and describing the excavator and two trucks they would see there. AJ looked forward to the cool clean sheets of a hospital bed, a long afternoon's rest, the call to Deena, the love and concern in her voice, and would he tell her about the money due them? Would he tell her then or would he wait?

And wasn't it strange to see a patrol car pull up just feet from the ditch, Junior not even off the phone yet? There must be an open line to the dispatcher or something. AJ hadn't expected the law, but having them here could only help, couldn't it? He could tell them about the coupler failing and it'd be on record.

The passenger door opened and a cop rose up out it. He was young and wore the same green uniform as those who'd cuffed AJ in front of his son. He looked down into the ditch at AJ, at his buried hand, the bucket and its dull teeth still crusted with yesterday's dirt, then at Cap Jr., who held his open cell phone in front of him like he still had calls to make.

"His hand's pinned. I just got here."

The cop nodded once and two more walked up, one on each side of him, both older, one in a blue uniform.

"You call an ambulance?" It was an older one in green. The morning sun glinted off his glasses, and he was tall and slim and seemed to have figured out the scene faster than the other two.

"Yes, sir, I did."

The tall one nodded at AJ. "How long you been down there, son?"

"Long enough to wish I wasn't."

"You Alan Carey?"

AJ nodded. Whatever moisture was left in his mouth went dry and his heart beat hard behind his eyes. How in the *hell* he know that?

The cop looked down at Junior. "And what's your name?"

"Mike Caporelli. I own the excavator." Cap Jr.'s voice was unsteady, the same tone whenever he just got news of a bad bet or when an inspector showed up wanting to see paperwork.

"This young man work for you?"

"Yessir. Listen, that was a new part. I don't know how it popped like that."

"We're not here for that. Come on out of there, we need to talk to Alan." The old cop offered his hand and Junior took it and kicked the toe of his boot into the clay and climbed out. Junior looked down at AJ, the cell phone still in his hand, his face wide and pale against the blue sky.

"Go have a seat in your vehicle till I call you, all right?"

AJ watched him go, his heart throwing itself against his sternum. He had a hard time looking up at the three men looking down at him and they could be here for only one thing and that just didn't make any *sense*.

The older one squatted, rested his elbows on his knees. His holster was black and worn. "You in pain?"

"Yes, I am. How'd you know my name, sir?"

"I believe I'll ask the questions if that's all right with you."

AJ stared at him. There was the sound of Cap Jr.'s truck door pulling shut.

"I know you're hurting down there, Alan, but help's on the way and listen, I need you to help *me* right now, okay?"

"You?"

"That's right. You were at the Puma Club over on 301 last evening, weren't you?"

AJ tried to swallow, couldn't.

"You know where I'm going with this, don't you?" His voice was calm and relaxed. AJ's heart had slowed but he felt like throwing up and maybe he should tell the truth; maybe if he didn't, he'd look like he'd done something bad when he hadn't. But they were already treating him like he did, and maybe he did, but damnit not like they think.

"No, sir, I don't."

"Alan, we've been to your home. We've spoken with your wife." The cop looked down at his clasped hands. "We know you violated your RO going over there but my concern's finding that little girl, Alan, and before you say anything, I want you to imagine it was your boy we're talking about here. Think about that. How bad it would be not knowing where he was or what had happened to him or if you'd ever see him again. Nobody should go through that, Alan. Nobody deserves that."

"You sure?" The words came out of him as unplanned as a belch and there was no taking them back and anyway it felt good to say them. There was a tingling in AJ's face. He saw again the girl crying by herself behind the screen door of the hot, bright kitchen of the club.

The old cop pushed his glasses up his nose. He turned in the direction of the one in blue. "Would you and my partner go take Mike's information, please? I'd like a minute with Alan here."

"It's AJ."

The other two walked off together, disappearing beyond the excavator.

"Your wife calls you that, doesn't she?"

"Used to."

"You've had some troubles lately, haven't you?"

AJ looked away. At his hand buried in the dirt.

"Your wife tells me you were pretty upset earlier."

Heat flashed through AJ's torso: Did she mention his hand? Did she mention his goddamn *hand*?

"You miss your family, don't you?"

A thickness gathered in AJ's throat. He didn't know this man and didn't like the uniform he wore, but he felt seen and listened to for the first time in a long while. So far back he didn't know when.

"You work hard too, don't you?"

AJ nodded.

"And it's no easy job, I can see that."

That's right. That's goddamned *right*.

"Your wife tells me you're a good daddy. That you and she have had your problems but you've always been there for your boy."

AJ's eyes burned and he wasn't ashamed of what fell from them now, first one, then the other, because this was a man who *knew*. A man who was doing his job, yes, but goddamnit, he *knew*.

"You saying, AJ, maybe the girl's mama shouldn't have that child?"

AJ wiped his eyes. He could see Spring peddling her ass on the floor, walking so proud from table to table, her long hair thick and shiny. "They don't let me see my son and she brings her baby to the fuckin' *Puma* Club?"

"Go on."

"She was all by herself. Man, she was terrified, crying her eyes out looking for her mama. I told her to go back inside, but she said it was scary and I didn't know what kind of sick shit was going on so I just got her the hell out of there, that's all."

"You were looking out for her."

"That's right."

There was the sound of tires rolling onto the dirt shoulder. This man looking down at him understood things, but the more AJ talked the more he felt himself slip into a bad place he didn't deserve and he heard car doors open and close and he hoped it was the ambulance because he was ready to go. The old cop swung around and held up his hand as if there was danger down here he had to protect them from. Whoever was walking over stopped in the dirt.

He turned back around, pushed his glasses up his nose. The morning sun was full in is face now and AJ could see he wasn't so old, maybe sixty, sixty-one. The age his own father would be.

"Is that the ambulance? 'Cause I'm hurting here."

"And you'll be getting help real quick. Just tell me where I can go get the child and I'll be on my way."

AJ shook his head, looked down at his boot up against the ditch wall. Above his toes was the sharp and rusted corner of something embedded in the soil—scrap iron? The broken tip of a de Soto sword? There was the girl's face as he lay her down in the backseat of the Honda, her curly hair around it like a nest.

"AJ?"

"I didn't know where to bring her. I thought about bringing her to you all, but I didn't want you to get the wrong idea. You know, it could look bad."

"Where is she, son?"

"I tried to put her someplace safe. I'm not proud of leaving her there."

"Just give me the location, AJ. I'll take care of the rest." The old cop's face had no expression; his lips held a thin straight line but in his eyes was the dark light of fear that something had happened, and AJ knew then he may never be able to convince him or anybody else otherwise even after they found her all in one piece in the Honda he told him about now, in the closed garage down the alley off Fruitville Road he told him about now.

Then the old cop was gone, and the EMTs were down in the hole, two big men wearing white latex gloves, one of them picking up the shovel to dig, the other taking AJ's pulse and talking to him like they were old friends, and if it weren't for the young deputy watching from above, his fleshy arms crossed over his badge, his eyes set on AJ in what felt like a hatred barely contained, this was the morning scene AJ had hoped for, this was the one he'd counted on all night long to bring about a change. A change for the better.

⌄ ⌄ ⌄

ONNIE WAS SITTING asleep on her couch, the back of his head against the wall, his mouth half-open. He was the first man to enter this place since she'd moved in and it was like being dropped into a life that would never be hers again and how would she ever continue if this was true?

Her mouth tasted like metal. Her heart felt weak in her chest. She'd changed out of her club clothes into the same shorts and T-shirt she'd worn to the beach yesterday, which made her feel less like Spring and more like April, which pulled her even deeper into the black jagged air she found herself in, her kitchen and living room filled with sunlight.

It was almost eight. They'd sat over an hour in his truck and she began to fear her phone may not be working that far from the house. On the way in, there was her empty cup lying in the spilled coffee on the bricks. And now, making coffee, taking that one small comfort, had felt like a betrayal, but she poured herself some in a mug the color of avocados, one she rarely used, and she held the mug with two hands and sipped the coffee carefully. The thing now was to be very careful and very quiet, not to speak too loud or move too fast or do anything but bear the waiting that had become a stillness that may as well be wired with explosives. She'd called the police department three times and each time the same man, young and no kids himself she was sure, told her to just sit tight and wait.

Sit tight.

Lonnie's mouth was open wider now, though he slept without a sound, and she walked on her toes into the living room and sat on the edge of the chair. It was a maroon plaid with a matching skirt, the couch too, what Jean had furnished the apartment with and only now, or maybe before too, when April had first walked in with Franny and their suitcases and two cardboard trunks from Staples, did April see it for what it was, somebody else's home entirely, hers only when Franny was in it. And now she was not.

It was not possible to sit any tighter than this. But she must. She must be very still, and drink her coffee and stay awake and sit very very tight.

At the Empire the waiting was bad. Waiting to go on that first time. No longer a waitress with her breasts swinging beneath the tray she tried to cover them with, but Spring, onstage. McGuiness watched her from under a neon Absolut sign on the back wall, his eyes a line of shadow, his bald head blue in the light and looking like cold bone, and her song began and she pranced with too much hip, one drunk hooting for her, the rest quiet, testing her, and it was before she even began unbuttoning her blouse she felt April slide back and down inside herself, slamming the door, locking it, pulling shutters behind her eyes that would only glitter now and not shine.

That cold stare he'd give you when you were dancing, appraising you, looking for weak spots. Mandy had come out of his office holding her face, crying. After closing, Lu sat at the bar with club soda because her ass was too fat and he'd told the bartenders *nothing for*

her with even one fucking calorie in it. Dee and Rhina worked off their
house debt to him on their knees in his office or in front of a camera
in one of his condos. Some of the men they fucked were floor hosts,
one was McGuiness, the camera never on the men's faces anyway, and
he played these movies on his widescreen at the annual Christmas
party, Dee and Rhina laughing together on the couch like schoolgirls
watching their taped talent show. April had gone with Stephanie, who
said they had to be there.

Summer and Spring walking in together, the two warmer, more
hopeful seasons though it was winter outside, plowed snow piled icy
and dirty at the edge of the parking lot of the condos. McGuiness
owned five of them.

Nobody was allowed to smoke but the place seemed smoky. Something with a lot of bass was playing. It was crowded with all the girls
from the club, some with a boyfriend standing here and there in a
Christmas sweater holding a light beer, gawking at all the fake tits and
made-up faces and flashing teeth and teased hair. The one with Jenna
kept looking from Rhina to the widescreen where she was riding a
man, his hands gripping her hips. Most of the floor hosts stood at
the bar to the kitchen looking big and slow though Alex had his wife
with him, a short, heavy girl in a black party dress that made her look
beached and ostracized, and there was McGuiness in the kitchen, his
bald head glistening under the overhead light, his shoulder and chest
muscles showing roundly under his blue satin shirt. He held a drink
and stood talking to a stubby man in a leather jacket.

Stephanie handed April a shot of Jägermeister. A small voice inside
her said, *No, don't drink. Stay a few minutes and go.* Then she was tossing it down with Stephanie, who was charming the floor hosts like
only she could, then raising her empty glass for another.

Beside the widescreen a gas fire burned in a stone fireplace and three
of the girls were one at a time kneeling over the hearth and snorting
lines off a mirror. Above them on-screen, a man, maybe McGuiness,
was coming onto Dee's fake tits, and somebody had turned up the
music louder, bass and drums and a man singing in German or Polish

or Russian, and April wanted to leave. She'd go up to McGuiness and be polite, then she'd give Stephanie's arm a tug and they'd go.

People kept pulling open the slider to the deck to walk out and smoke, the cold air coming in before the glass slid closed and then the room was too warm again, smelling of sweat and wool and a dozen perfumes and colognes. There was a hot tub out there, curls of steam rising off the glowing water.

McGuiness was staring at her. Her heart started beating faster though it wasn't a look she'd even seen from him before. He wasn't appraising, he was admiring, his features softened somehow, his eyes not so dead-looking. He raised his chin and almost smiled and she knew she was being beckoned and went. So many of the girls, even Stephanie, had dressed to show off leg and ass and cleavage but she'd worn a sleeveless emerald dress with a high neckline that accented only her waist and hips and went almost to her knees. The man with McGuiness gave her a twice-over and April smiled at him, then McGuiness.

"Merry Christmas, April." His face still, his bald head shining. "Where's your drink?"

"Gone."

"I'll get you something. Spring, this is one of my distributors, Angelo."

"You just called her April."

"For you it's Spring." McGuiness didn't smile. He moved past him to the sink, stepping between two of the girls and grabbing a glass. Angelo the distributor had a bad eye. Glassy blue with brown flecks when the other was just brown. His face was shaved too close, a rash on his throat, and she could see where he'd dyed his mustache, the roots gray under his nose.

Both his eyes, good and bad, passed over her face and torso, her bare arms. "You work for McGuiness?"

"No, I work for myself."

"Good answer. You should do film, though. You'd make a fuckin' mint."

"Watch the mouth." McGuiness handed April a crystal glass of eggnog, nutmeg sprinkled across the top. "This one's not like them. Go have a smoke or something, all right?"

The man left without a word. April imagined him out on the deck smoking a cigarette, staring into the empty hot tub with that bad eye. Above music and talk and laughter, she heard Stephanie's laugh and turned to look for her but only saw the broad backs of the floor hosts, two of the girls dancing badly on the stone hearth in front of the low-burning flames. Above them and the mantel, a massive Christmas wreath hung on the wall, gold and silver bells dangling from it.

"You decorate this place yourself?"

"I don't do anything myself. Taste your drink."

She did. Cool sweet eggnog with whiskey or brandy. She hadn't had one in a long time.

"You're not afraid I'll get fat?"

"I told you to lose some weight and you lost it. I don't have to worry about you, do I?"

"No."

"Then why bust my balls?"

"I'm not." She smiled, felt weak for smiling.

He smiled back. A real smile. The lines in his face got shallower and his eyes flickered with a light that wasn't all business. Another man came up to him, this one thin with sloped shoulders and a goatee. April excused herself and went and stood by Stephanie. Alex was telling a joke, a long one, and April drank deeply off the sweet drink and she avoided looking up at the widescreen. The music was too hard and too loud but at least she didn't have to hear the sounds of fucking. Stephanie and the others began laughing. She nudged April and handed her a shot. "I have one." And April raised her glass and toasted Christmas with the rest of them.

She finished her drink and was ready to go. She was about to lean in to Stephanie and say so. "Follow me." McGuiness took the empty glass from her and pushed a full one into her palm. He took her hand and led her through the crowded living room. Stephanie was laughing over the music, her eyes catching April's as she passed, her caps white and glistening, her tongue dark from the Jägermeister. Through piercing electric guitar a singer was shouting "White Christmas" and April felt half-drunk already, her hand in McGuiness's, big and dry and callused.

They were walking down a hallway, its walls white. Every foot or two was a framed black-and-white photograph of a shining car. Most of them were from long ago, black and boxy with spoked wheels. She could hear different music now, jazz playing, and the cars were still gleaming but now they had holes in them sprayed across the sides and front. Around each hole in the windshields was a white web radiating out and the white looked too white, and she was relieved when they stepped down into a billiards room.

There were people here she didn't know. The carpet was an inch thick. A huge fat man in a suit sat in a leather chair in front of another gas fireplace. On a sofa beside him two women her mother's age sipped brown drinks in glasses like the one she held. The light was dim here, even the green lamp over the walnut pool table where two men played. One was black and handsome as a movie actor, the other white, his long blond hair pulled back in a ponytail. He wore a turtleneck and his sleeves were rolled to his elbows and every bit of skin, even each finger, was green and blue and purple tattoo.

At the bar she let go of McGuiness's hand. One of the women glanced over at her. Her gold earrings were three or four inches long, angels, their gowns brushing her clavicle. She looked away, her angels swinging, and April sipped her eggnog and watched McGuiness walk behind the full bar. He pulled a chilled bottle of vodka from a minifridge, poured four fingers into a glass. The vodka was thick and syrupy and he raised his glass and touched hers with it. She felt the vibration but didn't hear it.

"What're we toasting, April?"

"Peace?"

"I'm serious."

"I am too."

"You've got a kid, right?"

"Yes."

"A boy?"

"Yep."

"Summer told me she's a girl."

A saxophone wailed in the air, brushes tapping cymbals, April's heart beating behind her eyes. "Yeah, that's what I said."

McGuiness seemed to nod his head without nodding, his eyes sizing her up again, measuring her, then his own hunger, as if she were raw meat butchered and laid out on a slab in front of him. "What's her name?"

She wanted to lie, but he already knew. He already knew. "Franny."

"To Franny then."

"Yes, thank you."

He tapped her glass and she swallowed more thick sweet eggnog, felt sleepy, didn't want any more. Wanted to go home. He'd poured himself so much but he sipped from the glass as if it were hot tea. "You want something else?"

The crack of the cue ball behind her. Like a slap. The sound in the room strange. Out of balance somehow.

"It's going right to my head." In the mini-fridge she'd seen cans of Coke. A row of cold red cans. Christmas cans. "You have any Coke?"

"I didn't think you did that?"

"Cola."

That smile again, his eyes distracted, looking ahead somehow. "Go see the ladies by the fire. I'll bring you one."

She didn't want to go but she went. Or, her legs and feet went. There was the soft carpet, her footsteps silent, the saxophone whining now, the pool balls colliding, and the fat man watched her. His lower lip was so much thicker than the upper and he reminded her of a dog of some kind and her legs were watery and she sat down in a leather chair by the sofa of two ladies talking. The angels swung toward her, the lady's earlobes stretched by their weight. The lady wore a blue-sequined dress and said something to her, smiling, and April said something back, wasn't sure what. But the vibration of what she'd said was still in her throat. *Merry Christmas*. Was that it? The angels swung back, and the lady was talking to her friend again, who kept looking past her at April, this woman prettier, but older, her nose small, her lips red and pursed as she listened. Now the drums were loud, the fat man studying his fingernails. He crossed a massive leg over his knee, his brown shoes shining, the bottom gritty and ringed with road salt. He bit off a nail and chewed it, looked into the gas fire. Bubbling Coke in a glass in front of her. McGuiness's hand around it. The blue veins in it.

Thank you. She felt the air move through her vocal cords, felt her tongue shape out the words behind her teeth, but the drums were rumbling low, then high, then low again and McGuiness stood there with his back to the fire like he hadn't heard her. The glass was heavy and cool and she drank deeply from it. Cold sweetness and carbonation, an ice cube nudging her lip. *Go home. Just get out of this chair and start walking.* But she *was* the chair now. She'd become the chair. She drank more Coke. Had she eaten? Yes, her mother's American chop suey. The canned tomato sauce and hamburger and macaroni noodles. The red stain of it on Franny's chin. Her mother smoking only three feet from her, giving April a look, the green dress she'd bought cheap at Marshall's. She'd eaten, hadn't she?

She drank more Coke. McGuiness and the fat man were talking. She could hear their voices. Could see their lips move. The drums were gone. It was just piano now. The keys getting plinked, the pool balls plinking too. The man in the ponytail kept staring at her, both hands cupped around the end of his pool stick, the other end in the carpet at his feet. Like he had his hands on a big lever and if he pulled it the floor would open and they'd all fall in. Now he smiled at her. He had an overbite. She made herself turn away. Everything thick and slow, so thick. Like trying to run in waist-deep water. The prettier woman sipped wine from a glass, still listening to the lady and her angels and blue sequins. April's arm lifted the Coke to her lips but the glass seemed far away even when it was touching her lips, some of it running cool down her chin as she swallowed once, twice. McGuiness and the fat man still taking. Equals, though. No fear in the fat dog's eyes looking up at him. Business partners. Biznis. Busyness. The Coke wasn't working. Her chin was dropping and she tried to lift her head but couldn't. Her mouth half-open now too.

The pretty woman stood and glided over in gold and stooped and picked up the glass at April's feet, her hand empty. When did she drop it? The ice cubes one at a time plinking in the glass. The piano and pool balls and now the ice. The pretty woman rising. Shaking her head at McGuiness. "Drunk girl." Angel ears and blue sequins frowning. Looking away. *Drunk girls. Drunkurls. Drurls.* The dark where her mouth opened till her chin touched her chest and the drool rolled ticklishly to her jaw. Then sleep, a rough sleep. Her cheek bobbing against satin muscle, a beating heart there. A wide cool bed. Bright lights beyond the dark she couldn't open her eyes to see. The pool stick being pulled back and the floor dropping, then the falling and falling, her body pulled and pushed to sitting, the unzipping of her dress, a hand at her back, but still falling, her dress shucked past her arms, then down her hips and off her legs and feet. The rip of her bra. Her panties unrolling, knuckles against her knees. Still falling. Falling. Cold now. Cold. A hot mouth on her nipple. Sucking. Biting. It hurt. She cried out but in sleep there's no sound and nobody listening and something pushed into her mouth and she couldn't breathe and began to gag and choke, her legs pushed apart, the nudging, then the ripping, all this falling landing her onto a fence post, was pulled off it, then dropped on it again. Pulled off it, then dropped. Coughing and gagging and gasping for air, her arms and legs as still and inert as if they were dead.

She watched Lonnie sleep. He took a long breath and let it out through his mouth. His flat belly rose and fell. His hands looked like accidents of nature on his knees, big eggs broken open into fingers.

His arms were long and she pictured him holding Franny in one and using the other to knock down men coming for her, Franny holding tightly to his neck, her eyes squeezed shut, the men falling one at a time at Lonnie's feet. But then they all got up and rushed at him and April was making a sound through tears she wiped away with two fingers, her breath coming in ragged gasps, the ring of the phone boring into her head and heart like a drill.

Y Y Y

How tired he is. How tired, his head aching as well from the champagne and the cognac and the bright sky they fly through. The sun reflects off the wing and he cannot bear it and pulls down the plastic window shade. Imad beside him eats. As does Tariq across the aisle. But he cannot. The thought sickens him and he closes his eyes and leans his head against the shade of the window and he sees her. Her soft questions about him. About Khalid. Now she is gone and it is the qus of the black whore he sees, such a color he would never have suspected. In the camp a Yemeni running the obstacles tripped and pulled the trigger of his weapon and shot another ahead of him, the wound in his upper leg a shredded hole, and Bassam thinks of that, how similar they nearly appeared, yet still he would push himself inside the black whore's.

He must stop this. He must cleanse himself of these thoughts. But how is it the Egyptian and his own brothers beside him could have visited these places and not been tempted so strongly to return? How could they see these uncovered kufar women and not—what? What, Mansoor Bassam? *Mansoor? Victorious?* It is a lie to have named himself this. How can one so weak and distracted become victorious? How could he have been chosen for the highest of honors when he is so clearly—what? What, Bassam?

He opens his eyes.

Afraid.

He has become *afraid.*

These last days he has heard often in his head his mother, her cries for Khalid, yet she had the comfort of knowing his body was washed, of watching his body lowered into the ground facing Makkah. For Bassam, there will be nothing for Ahmed al-Jizani to wash.

Please, don't do anything foolish. Would she consider this sacred mission foolish? In three days, Insha'Allah, the entire world will know her son's name. The entire world will know of the al-Jizani family, not as merchants and engineers and builders of buildings, but as a shahid, a shahid for the Judge and the Creator and the Ruler. A chosen *shahid.*

There was no moon and the Afghani sky was black, the air cool. Hassan al-Huda had sent a boy to their tent, Bassam's, Imad's and Tariq's and a quiet one from Yemen. "They want you three. You three from Asir. In the big tent."

There were two others. Both Saudis from Abha. In their black kaftans they looked young and thin, but Bassam had seen them in hand-to-hand fighting, how fast and fearless they were, the shorter of the two, his gray eyes. The tent was lighted with halogen lanterns made by the kufar, their white light shining. The air smelled of dust and canvas, myrrh and gun oil. Hassan al-Huda, who allowed weakness from no one and who had lost three fingers in Chechnya, whose left leg had been shattered in Bosnia, he instructed them to stand around the wooden table. There, in the hissing white light, was a map of the land of al-Adou al-Baeed, the far enemy, its large mass poised between two oceans.

"You have been chosen for a great, great honor."

And Abu Abdullah himself stepped forward and looked them each in the face, his eyes not unlike an old imam's—wise, clear, and unafraid because he is lifted and carried by his faith and there was love there for them, for each of them, as if they were his sons.

One at each time they were sworn to secrecy, they were told not to speak to even their fellow mujahedin, and they made the bayat, *The pledge of Allah and His covenant is upon me, to energetically listen and obey the superiors who are doing this work, rising early in times of difficulty and ease.* Bassam stood erect, his hands clasped before him. *It is happening. It is happening.* There was no longer time existing yet there was too much time and it moved so slowly he could not breathe, this moment he had been waiting for without knowing it, working toward without knowing it, fasting toward and denying himself in a way never before possible in the old nothingness he could only thank the Most Merciful he had escaped. Abu Abdullah took a red marker. His fingers were long and thin. He began to circle cities.

Outside, the mu'adhin called for the final prayer, his voice raspy but pure, and their emir bowed his head to them. "Tomorrow, Insha'Allah, you will leave here for the west and specialized training. You should be very happy and very proud; destiny has chosen you for the highest rooms of Jannah."

The young men looked at one another, Tariq blinking his eyes as if waking from a dream. These boys from Asir, who could have known what sort of blood had always been in their veins? But why such surprise? They were Qahtanis, tribesmen descended from Noah. Why should there be surprise? Other fighters began entering the tent for Isha barefoot, their beards dusty from performing tayamoom with clean sand, the dry ablutions of the hands and face Hassan al-Huda insisted upon as water in camp was scarce.

Outside the tent, in the cool night air, Bassam and the others removed their boots and knelt to the ground for handfuls of sand. "Bassam," Imad whispered, "Tariq." As if to make certain he was still Imad from Khamis Mushayt who only months before was a silly gossiper on Mount Souda. A racer of kufar cars on Highway 15. A man who may not ever see Jannah at all.

Soon they were purified and in the big tent, prostrating themselves toward Makkah, praying aloud behind their commander, and as Bassam performed the raka'ats, he had never pronounced each word so clearly or with such intention, had never loved the Holy One so deeply, had never understood the teachings of His Prophet—peace be upon him—so fully, and a warmth rose inside him from the soles of his bare feet through his legs and loins and chest, his eyes spilling for he had never felt so loved before by anyone, not merely accepted but exalted, and that thread of blood which tied him to his own father and mother, his two sisters and thirteen brothers, it was both severed and strengthened; he was an al-Jizani yet forever beyond being an al-Jizani, forever beyond his own family and clan and tribe—he was instead a child of the Creator who had fashioned each of them, the Creator who now called Bassam to fight and die for Him, to fight and die for them all.

Bassam opens the shade. The brightness of the clouds hurt his eyes but he does not look away. These kufar have done this to him. Their haram way of life, these women so happy to show themselves, this alcohol banned in his kingdom which has made him sick today when he should be strong.

"Sir? Would you care for coffee?" She takes Imad's tray yet she addresses Bassam. She is older than the others. Lines in her face she covers with cosmetics, her hair dry, blond when it is not blond. How easy to kill her, to slaughter her like a goat.

"No, Coke please. Two Cokes."

Imad's eyes are closed, his large hands folded one over the other upon his table, and Bassam looks past him and watches the woman bend forward for the cans, watches her pull one free and open it, her buttons unbuttoned so he can see far too much of the crease between her aging nuhood, and he can feel her face in his hand, her head against him as he draws the blade across her throat.

She gives to him his drink and the two red cans, cool and slippery.

His fingers tremble, his heart beating more forcefully now. She is smiling her smile at him and he returns it but it is as if he has pressed a button inside himself, and when she looks away, his smile diminishes at once.

Across the aisle Tariq sits beside no one. This morning he shaved his mustache too quickly and there is a small cut beneath his nose. He looks out the window. Above the white of the clouds, the sky is a deep blue that, seeing it, makes Bassam a boy: his mother and her sisters painting the family home in Abha. He had nine or ten years and couldn't wait for Ramadan to end, for the Festival of Fast-Breaking and all the good food to eat: kabsa and marquq and minnazzalah, the sweet fried turnovers of qatayif, and his favorite, asabi' al-sit, cinnamon and almond pastries soaked in sugar syrup, all things he had to wait for until the festival, so he squatted in the dirt playing with stones while the women repainted designs on the shale walls of their house built into the hill, the blue like the sky beyond Tariq—boiled from indigo plant, the green from alfalfa, the black from vegetable tar. But so often now the women of Abha use paint from a can, paint mixed by the kufar, Shaytan laughing at them as they prepare for the end of Ramadan by covering their homes with the colors of unbelievers.

In front of Tariq a man and woman laugh. It is early afternoon and they drink. The laughing woman chews celery, her woman's legs fat and wrinkled and tanned and completely available to him. She is like Gloria, the plump realtor, this friendly one, like her. How easy it was for Amir to ignore her, to hate her. And Bassam had tried but it was like willing himself to like the Egyptian; he was brash and arrogant and short-tempered, and he monitored them as if they were not the chosen few; he often spoke to them the way Ali al-Fahd had ordered Bassam to do this and to do that. The Egyptian was their commander, yes, but his place in Jannah would be no higher than theirs. He would be loved by the Protector no more than they. *Absolute obedience, eternal vigilance, endless patience.* How many times had Amir used those words with them? Bassam had been offended when he said them, for he was certain he did not need to hear them. How many floors and mattresses had he slept upon since leaving his home? How many kilometers had he driven to airfields and back? To banks and stores for food and Laundromats and telephone booths and cell phone stores? How many libraries had he visited to download flight information, airplane specifications, GPS systems?

But he had not obeyed absolutely, had he? When the Egyptian flew to Las Vegas, he and Imad and Tariq took operations money and rented mopeds and rode along the hard damp sand of the beach. They did this whenever he went away. Many times. Why not? They had worked hard in the gym. The trainer Kelly told him their muscles grow only when they rest, so why not rest on the seat of a speeding moped? The wind in their faces? The sun and the sky and the sea? And yes, all the exposed bodies of young women, Bassam and Tariq looked and looked as they drove along the beach, though Imad did not. More and more he did not look at any kufar woman at all. In his presence Bassam began to feel as he did with the Egyptian, not as pure or strong, and yes, not as chosen.

But how could he not look at them? Never had he seen so many uncovered women, their bare skin shiny with oil. And nothing happens by mistake. All is part of the plan of the Sustainer and the Judge. They were put on these beaches under the hot sun for a reason; perhaps it was to give him and his brothers a taste of what waited for them.

But this woman across the aisle, Bassam cannot look at her any longer, at her fat sunburned leg, the dimpled flesh of it—she does not even know how deeply she sins against the Creator. None of them do. This is what has troubled him. On the flight here from Dubai, he expected to see kufar like the American officers in the souq, tall disrespectful warriors laughing at them as they walked through the day fully aware of their actions. But not these stupid people living to please Shaytan and not even knowing it. They are like dogs except they are worse than dogs because they work hard to put you to sleep as well, to make you drunk, to take your money and your clothes and your dignity and your faith.

Their very way of living itself seeks to separate you from the Ruler.

Eternal vigilance: the Egyptian has been correct all along not to join himself to any of them—with a smile, a shake of the hand, a polite hello or goodbye. He has been right to turn them away with his eyes. He has protected himself and their mission and now it is what Bassam must do as well, that is all—separate himself from those who would separate him from his own faith.

The woman laughs once again and he feels a hot anger flare inside him and burn: how close he has come to truly losing his place in Jannah and it is their fault—Kelly's and Gloria's, Cliff's and April's and the black whore's and every waitress to whom he was polite, every librarian, every fuel attendant, and he only prays his judgment has not compromised what, Insh'Allah, will be done. He only hopes he left nothing behind in the Neon. He checks his pockets but there is no paper. Did he forget the receipt of his wire to Dubai? And why did he leave the tote bag in the trash? He should have put the contents into another bag within the container. But now a kafir maid may want the tote bag, a new black Nike, and she will have to empty its contents. And what will she find? Everything. The aeronautical maps and flight manuals, the Egyptian's protractor and German dictionary, the flight-school books and Imad's book on judo and the computer printout from the airline companies. What will she think then, Bassam al-Jizani?

‎ Y   Y   Y

THE DOCTOR WAS a woman. She had long gray hair streaked with black she kept pinned away from her ears, and she wore no lipstick or eye makeup, but when she held his broken wrist in her cupped hand, AJ felt cared for once again, first by the old cop and now this doctor, and he felt bad telling her the bucket came down on it. She just nodded and listened. It was hard not to look at the smooth pale skin of her throat.

"When did this happen?"

"Hour, hour and a half ago."

She kept her eyes on him, hers behind her glasses a blue-gray that wasn't cold, just neutral, like she would never judge him but needed the truth and knew he wasn't giving it to her.

He looked away. There was a color chart of the human body, intertwining strands of red sinew pulled from bone to bone. She laid his hand back down on his leg.

"It's fractured. A nurse will take you to X-ray and we'll go from there, all right?"

She smiled at him, but it was that deputy who took him, his hand squeezing AJ's good elbow all the way down the corridors.

"You can ease up, sir, I'm not going anywhere."

"That's for damn sure." The deputy said nothing more. AJ could smell his deodorant and dry-cleaned uniform, his judgment of him, this man maybe even younger than AJ, who was treating him like he'd done something sick and wrong but they would find out soon enough that the girl was fine and he'd taken good care of her just the way he said he had.

But now he sat in the backseat of a moving patrol car, one cuff loose around his cast, the other snug against his wrist. Outside was too bright to look at, the sun glinting off car chrome and concrete, a palm frond drooping as if he'd let it down somehow, and he shouldn't be surprised they were taking him to county but he was.

You can't just drive off with somebody's child, he knew that, and maybe he should be thinking more about it than what kept running through his head, the old cop's words: *Alan, we've been to your home. We've spoken with your wife.*

Man, she could say he was crying, she could say he was drunk and driving, she could even say she hated him and never wanted to see him again—just don't say anything about my bad hand, Deena. Please, honey, tell me you didn't say I was already hurt when you saw me last night.

⋎ ⋎ ⋎

J EAN LAY ON her sofa with a pillow over her eyes. She was trying to calm her erratic heart, trying to breathe, trying to fully accept whatever had to be accepted, the fear returning, swelling inside her as if it would swallow her, and April's words still tore through her head like a whip of barbed wire.

Then Jean heard her actual voice calling for Lonnie to hurry, please hurry. There was the slam of her door upstairs, the fall of her feet on the outside steps, then Lonnie's, heavier, and Jean was off her sofa and at the door so quickly she felt faint and grabbed at his arm.

"They found her. She's all right." Then he was gone.

She may have wept. She remembers kneeling on the floor of Franny's room, her forehead pressed to the pillow, her eyes squeezed shut. Now her body felt light and loose in the joints but it wasn't easy to breathe and her mouth was dry and briny. She told herself to rest, to try to get a few moments' sleep, but when she lay down on her bed it might as well have been electrified.

Franny, oh Franny.

She made herself eat a slice of buttered toast. She made herself drink coffee, though it only added to this feeling her body was somehow drifting away from her, something old and tired that had its own needs whether she liked it or not. And it needed rest. But not till Franny came home, not until Jean had held her and kissed her and started doing for her whatever could be done. But how much longer would this take? They'd been gone over two hours.

She watched the news. There was a police photo of the man from a previous arrest for beating his wife. He had a boyish face, though he wasn't handsome; he looked unintelligent and angry, something seething beneath the surface, and Jean was certain she would kill him if she could. But *she isn't dead she isn't dead she isn't dead.* This phrase ran itself over and over inside her steadier than her own pulse. It was there as she stepped out into the vapored heat that smelled of bougainvillea and mango leaf and damp roots in soil; it was there as she reached into the slatted shadow of the stairwell and turned the water faucet until the hose stiffened over the dried coffee April had spilled; it was there as she squeezed the nozzle's trigger and sprayed the ixora and allamanda, the bougainvillea and cabbage palm and jacaranda; and it was there inside her, a mirror to her own astonishing aliveness only two days after the suffocating knowing that, she, Jean Hanson, was going to die here in this garden Harold never got to see.

She was smiling. She turned the hose on her face, her mouth open to the warm mist that tasted like rubber and brass, and she swallowed and swallowed, the water beading up and running down her forehead, cheeks, and chin.

∨ ∨ ∨

IT WAS SERGEANT Toomey who stood in the sun beside the emergency room door. A pair of green aviator lenses were flipped down over his glasses, and as Lonnie pulled up the Tacoma, the old cop saw her and smiled and she got the door open and ran to him and hugged him hard, pressing her wet cheek to his chest, his big hand patting her back.

"We found her, hon. We sure did. We sure did."

He led her to a small yellow room and left her alone. It was cold with too much air-conditioning and April couldn't sit down at the table or one of the chairs against the wall. She crossed her arms over her chest, goose bumps rising across her skin. The only window looked out at a corner waiting area where Lonnie sat talking to Sergeant Toomey.

The last minutes now were almost a hallucination. Did he really say she couldn't see her daughter just yet? Did he look her in the face and say *that*? "Just yet?"

And now Lonnie on the other side of the glass, shaking his head and shrugging at whatever Toomey was asking him. This new friend of hers who knew nothing about her and that's what she was seeing, wasn't it? They were talking about *her*.

Franny asleep in her car seat, purple syrup on her chin and at the corners of her mouth, the hot coffee spilling on April's thigh like some scolding God she should've listened to, the drunk little foreigner and his money, again the images searing her—her daughter's small thighs, her smooth abdomen, Franny's eyes wide when she chokes, these things seen by someone else, in a different way, a sick way, and they find her in some *car* in a *garage*, and her mother is not staying in this room without her another fucking second!

The door opened just as April reached it. Sergeant Toomey held it for a short woman in a cardigan sweater who glanced at April and pulled out a chair and placed a notebook on the table. She looked over at April, the door closing behind her.

"Are you April Connors?"

"Yes."

"I'm Marina." She offered her hand.

April ignored it. "Are you a doctor? Where's my daughter? I want to see her right now."

"Please, have a seat, Ms. Connors."

"I don't want to sit. I want to see my daughter." Her voice broke. She took a deep breath that moved unevenly through her. Pinned to the woman's blouse was a laminated ID card, her photo there, some writing.

"I'm a child protective investigator, Ms. Connors. Please, do sit down."

Child. Protective.

April pulled out a chair. Her head throbbed. Her mouth was dry and tacky. There was the dead dog curled on its side on the shoulder of Washington Boulevard, its matted fur and sunken rib cage. "Is she okay? Just tell me—" She tried to swallow, looked at the woman's knees. "Is she all right?"

"She appears to be, yes."

April covered her face with her hands, her crying filling the room like the air itself had been waiting for it, Franny swaddled in a blanket in her arms, her pink face, her closed eyes, that thin patch of hair on her head. And it was as if a rope had been lifted away from April's throat.

"Here."

April lowered her hands. She wiped at her eyes and took the tissue from the box the woman slid over to her. "Thank you."

"You're welcome." The woman glanced at April's T-shirt and bare legs, her flip-flops. She looked down at her closed notepad, then back up. "This has been very difficult, I'm sure. But you should know that in situations like this, where a child is left unattended and is put in some kind of danger—"

"She wasn't una*tended*. I paid someone to take care of her! She was not unattended."

The woman raised her hand. "Please, let me finish." There were gray hairs at her temples, though her skin was smooth, her eyes warm but guarded. Like a nurse. "It's clear to me you love your child very much."

"Of course I do."

"But we have a set of guidelines we go by—we must go by—whenever a child has been placed, knowingly or unknowingly, in a potentially hazardous situation."

"But, she—"

"Please, Ms. Connors, let me finish." She took a breath, straightened her shoulders. "The medical exam indicates your daughter was not sexually abused."

The woman blurred. April looked down and shook her head, the quivering breath filling her lungs a gift, everything a gift.

The woman patted her hand. "Your daughter will have to be examined further, by me, to make sure of this. But the physical indications do look good. Would you like a glass of water?"

April nodded. She dabbed at her eyes, blew her nose. The woman was in the corner of the room, filling a paper cup from a spring water dispenser. April looked out the window. Lonnie was watching her from his seat. Two old women were sitting next to him, talking to each other.

The woman handed her the water. It was cold and April drank it all. "I just need to see her. Please, she needs me."

"Yes, she does. But—" The woman picked up her pen. "Because she was put in a situation where her abduction occurred, I'm afraid I'm required by law to assess her home life before she can be returned to you."

"*What?*"

"Is there a relative she can stay with?"

There was a jolting inside April's chest, a queasiness spreading through her belly. "What are you saying? For how *long*?"

"It could be a few days, it could be longer. We have ten days to complete the investigation."

"Ten *days.*"

"Yes. Is there someone I can call?"

April stared at her. She wasn't quite sure what she'd just said or meant. Did she just say what she'd said? Franny had never spent one night away from her. Not *one.*

"Ms. Connors? April?"

"What?"

"Where is the father? Does he live with you?"

"No."

"Can I contact him?"

"No, he's up north. He's nobody. He's nothing."

Marina DeFelipo, that was her name, April could read it clearly on her ID card, this child protective investigator, who opened her notepad now and was writing.

"Grandparents? Aunts or uncles?"

Her mother smoking at the kitchen table, waiting for Franny to hurry up and eat. "No, I have no family here, but my landlady takes care of my daughter. She has her own bedroom there and everything. Look, she watches her all the time, I only took Franny to work last night because Jean was in the hospital; she can stay with Jean, can't she?"

"It's possible. What's her address and telephone number?"

"It's the same as mine."

"What's the same?"

"Her address. We live above her."

Marina DeFelipo sat back in her chair. She shook her head. "I'm sorry, it can't be the same residence we're investigating."

"Why *not*?"

"That would defeat the purpose, wouldn't it?"

April said nothing. She could feel her heartbeat. The sick emptiness inside her. The cold air of the room. But it was all so unreal. This conversation could not possibly be real.

"Do you have any close friends I can call?"

Stephanie in her new condo in New Hampshire, her fake breasts and polished nails and sincere smile, Lonnie out there, alone now, skimming a magazine, his Puma club T-shirt under the fluorescent light.

"April?"

She shook her head.

The woman wrote something on the pad she quickly closed. "Your daughter will have to be placed into temporary guardianship."

The air in the room had knives in it, a whirring, an electric hum. "A *foster* home?"

"Yes, she'll be safe."

"She's already safe! I can't fucking believe what I'm hearing, I paid someone to take care of her and she didn't and it's not my *fault*. I want to see my daughter. I want to see her right *now*!"

The door opened, Sergeant Toomey there, one hand on the knob. "Everything all right?"

"Yes," the woman said. April was breathing hard. She didn't remember standing. Her knees were water and she was caught now between both of them, this investigator of families and this policeman who hadn't slept all night either, who'd found her daughter and brought her here safe. In his presence she felt ungrateful and very tired, a blood-deep tired she spoke through now: "I just want to see her. Please, she needs to know I'm here. Please. She needs to *know* that."

THEY HAVE TWO rooms attached one to the other. Two beds in each, a polished television cabinet, a clean bathroom with golden floors that shine, a kind of stone not found at home. The carpet is new and will not be an insult to pray upon, and the window has a view of a courtyard, small tables beneath the trees.

Imad takes one room for himself, though the Egyptian may stay here with them for one night, Bassam does not know for sure. From the minibar he takes a Perrier water and opens it and drinks half of it and lies upon the bed. The room is cool, comfortable. He is tired from the trip and from his night of no sleep. Tariq stands before the open television cabinet, the remote control in his hand. He presses the buttons until there is a picture. He presses more and then there is sound. A man swings a long steel rod and watches the ball fly into the air and land so far away on the short grass near the hole, a flag sticking out of it, hundreds of kufar watching silently behind ropes on both sides of the green. The low voices of the announcers. As if this were a holy place, as if what these people were doing was important.

Again he is a boy, standing behind rope in the crowd in Riyadh. He has six or seven years and he is here with his married brother Adil and their uncle Rashad. Bassam no longer remembers why he is in Riyadh, so far from Khamis Mushayt, but he is standing in a crowd of many people, his brother behind him, his hands on his shoulders. There is a wooden platform. Two men are upon it, one standing, one kneeling. It is after the midday prayer and the sun is high and it reflects sharply off the blade of the sword held by the man in the black kaftan. At his feet the kneeling man weeps from under a hood, his hands bound behind him, he weeps and recites the Al-Fatihah. This seems to confuse the other man for he pauses and holds the sword high and waits for the weeping man to finish.

Not of those who have incurred Your wrath.

Nor of those who have gone astray.

The sword falling in the sunlight, the soft cracking sound, the thump of the hooded head as it rolled along the platform, blood spraying from its base so redly. In the crowd there was the cry of a woman, prayers muttered by men. And Bassam could look at the hooded head but not the body that held it, not that.

In a teahouse later, his brother and uncle argued over the executioner's decision to wait. Uncle Rashad said it was right and just that he wait but Adil said no, no, Respected Uncle, and he cited the Al-Tawbah sura: "'For they denied Allah and His apostle and remained sinners to the last. . . . Through these Allah seeks to punish them in this life, so that their souls shall depart while still in unbelief.' He should have slain him in a pure state of unbelief, Uncle. Let him taste Jahannam."

"But Allah is merciful, Adil. The man should have his chance to repent."

"No, there is no repentance."

"I disagree, my nephew. I disagree. This also from Al-Tawbah: 'They knew there was no refuge from Allah except in Him. Therefore

He turned to them in mercy, so that they might repent. Allah is the Forgiving One, the Merciful.'"

"Yes, respected Uncle, for believers. Not for this killer and adulterer we saw today."

Uncle Rashad stroked his beard. He looked down at Bassam sitting at the table beside Adil, Bassam who loved asabi' al-sit, but he could not eat it. Each time he looked at it he saw the hooded head rolling along the platform, the blood spraying from it. And he both wished he could see the man's face and was glad he could not. Uncle Rashad smiled down at him and sipped his tea and looked out the window.

A knocking.

"Tariq? Bassam?"

Tariq opens the door for Imad. On the television now this country's map, a smiling kafir in his suit explaining the weather.

Imad stands beside Tariq. Again, with no beard and those smooth cheeks, he looks so much younger, the boy Bassam knew in school. The large one respected only because he was large.

"Which number is this? I could not find it on my TV."

"Look," Tariq says. The smiling kafir in his suit points to boxes, each named the week's day, each with a picture of the sun shining.

Tuesday it shines brightest, and Bassam supplicates: *All praise is for Allah by whose favor good works are accomplished.* The kafir in his suit, he smiles through the screen at them in this last hotel room. "Beautiful," he says. "The week will be beautiful."

T HE MEDICAL UNIT was one cell with six steel bunks, three lined up across from each other along concrete walls. The floor was concrete too, a slab painted gray though the walls were cream-colored and fluorescent light shone down from fifteen or sixteen feet up. When they brought him in, an old wino was sitting on the toilet grunting and making noises and the entire room smelled. There were four other men in the unit, two of them sitting on the edge of a bunk playing checkers. One was skinny and black with gray in his whiskers, the other bald and white, his right arm in a canvas sling, his gut pushing at the seams of his county-jail orange; there was a black-haired Asian stretched out on his mattress reading a paper-back, his hair long and straight against his pillow, and he glanced up as one of the deputies handed AJ a small plastic bin that held a plastic cup, a bar of soap, toothbrush, and tube of paste rattling around at the bottom. Before pulling the iron door closed, one of the deputies told AJ his first appearance before the judge would be at 0900 hours tomorrow.

He lay down on the bunk, his eyes aching with fatigue, but the fifth man in the unit was looking right at him. He had blond hair and pale freckled skin. His whiskers were brown and soft-looking but his eyes were a sad, wired blue and he got up from his bunk and hobbled over. He stood looking down at AJ like they knew each other.

"You see me on the news?"

"'Scuse me?"

"I was the one in the Benz, man. You didn't see it? Out on fuckin' Longboat Key? Man, you shoulda seen it. It was on Channel 5. They had the helicopter cam on me the whole time and you know those fuckin' nail strips they throw out on the road ahead a you?—well I didn't give a shit, I drove that fucker sparkin' flames like Robbie Kneivel, man, I drove that Mercedes on the *rims*. I seen that tennis place and I put it right through the fence onto the court and I run off for the water 'cause I don't give a shit, I'll swim with the fuckin' shark and jellyfish 'fore I let 'em bust my ass 'cause I wire rides every day and this is only the fourth time they got me and they wouldn'ta if I didn't break my ankle. But man, you—"

"You done?" AJ sat up. "'Cause I'm hurt here and I could use some rest so would you please just shut the fuck *up*?"

"Hear that, O'Brien?" It was the bald man in the sling. "The man said to zip it."

The kid swung around and squinted at the two men as if they were in a bright light. They ignored him completely and he turned back to AJ, his lips parted before he closed them, his face settling into something hard. "Fine, but only 'cause you said please. I just thought maybe you seen it 'cause there's no TV in the fuckin' med U." He limped back to his bunk, and AJ lay down. He felt a little badly about shutting the kid up like that but not enough to apologize. At the hospital they'd given him some pills for the pain and they'd worked for a while but now they were wearing off and his lower arm felt encased against blades cutting into bone.

After his pat-down he'd handed over his wallet and truck keys and wedding band and signed for them. A deputy asked him a bunch of health questions, and maybe he should've used his one free call to get hold of Deena instead of Mama. But what if the calls were recorded? What could he say to her anyway? And he didn't want Mama to worry and now he was glad he'd called her; her voice had sounded small on the phone, old and weak. She kept asking him, "What'd you do, Alan? I don't understand, honey. What exactly did you *do*?"

He told her the truth, that it was a misunderstanding, that he'd taken care of a neglected child, that's all. Soon they'd be thanking him for what he did. Then, in case the call *was* recorded, he told her the bucket had come loose and fell on him this morning. "It broke my wrist, Mama. When you call to come visit, you tell them I'm in the medical unit, okay?"

She had more questions: Was he hurt badly? How long would he be in there? Should she find him a lawyer? But his time was over and they led him up one floor where he was fingerprinted and photographed again, where he had to strip and step into a cool shower, holding his cast out of the spray while with one hand he washed with lice-killing soap that smelled like melted plastic and bleach. The whole time a deputy stood there, his arms crossed, watching AJ dry himself with a thin towel, then step clumsily into county jail cotton.

But the shower had revived him, and as two deputies led him to an elevator and the third floor, he began to feel hopeful Deena had said nothing about his hand. Why would she? They were just looking for the child. And they found her, hadn't they? They must've, right?

A cool sweat beaded out on his forehead. He closed his eyes and tried to ignore his arm. There were Marianne's naked breasts in the warm orange light of the VIP room, her hand in his. He was telling her where he would take them, to the best outdoor table at Mario's-on-the-Gulf, and her face changed and she went cold and distant on him; there was Deena and her ice pack, her wide crying face; there was Cole sleeping in the glow of the night-light, and the little girl crying in the kitchen of the Puma; there was holding her and singing to her on the dark beach, laying her down asleep in a new car. And now there was the breath-squeezing fear rising up in him that he may be here for quite a while, that he would get to know these men far better than he would like, and Marianne's breasts again, her small hand in his that for some reason he couldn't let go of, that for some damn reason he just had to *squeeze*.

SATURDAY

IKE THE FOREIGNER sat at her kitchen peninsula burning money. Between his lips was a glowing cigarette and he squinted at his own smoke as he kept reaching into Franny's backpack for bills and held one at a time over the flame. The hundred-dollar note flared up before he dropped it curling into black ash on the floor, and Retro was down there on her hands and knees scooping up the ashes and trying to stuff them into her garter, her brown thighs streaked gray. *Motherfucker, mother*fucker. Franny was curled on the living room floor watching a movie. She began sucking her thumb. The air was thick with smoke and Mike the foreigner and Retro were gone and the kitchen was on fire, flames licking the ceiling, and April yelled to Franny to get out. Get *out*!

April was curled on the couch under a sheet. The TV was on and muted, a cartoon of robots zapping one another. In the gray light that must be very early morning the remote control lay on a carton of fried rice, the coffee table covered with cartons because Lonnie had bought too much.

The apartment was too quiet. Empty. She put a picture in her head. *Franny sleeping now. Asleep in a room of stuffed animals and natural light and when she wakes up a kind woman will speak kindly to her and tell her kind lies about her mother wanting her to be where she is. She'll make her a big breakfast and treat her only kindly.*

Yesterday she would have murdered another human being just to see Franny for five minutes, just for Franny to see her. But they wouldn't let her, and it'd taken Sergeant Toomey and Lonnie to get her inside the car. That newswoman, pretty with small features, blocking April's way into the garden, sticking the microphone in her face. *Is it true you took your three-year-old daughter to the Puma Club for Men?* There were the aiming cameras and Lonnie stepping in front of them while April ran into Jean's yard. *Is it true your daughter's been placed in foster care?*

She held her breath and listened. There was the mechanical purr of the air-conditioning ducts somewhere in the walls or ceiling. No outside noise of any kind. They were gone, on to the next story of bad people doing bad things.

Alan James Carey. Had she dreamed his face? No, seen it. There on the TV on the late news she shouldn't have watched. She and Lonnie at the garden gate in the sun, her eyeliner smeared, her face cold and hard as her mother's. Then *his* face, Alan James Carey, a mug shot of a low forehead and deep eyes, his ears sticking out. Resentful-looking. Angry. One of Marianne's, and Oh God she'd danced for him. She'd danced for him before in the VIP. That resentment staring at her crotch, her belly, her breasts. And the newscaster said he "maintains" he'd taken Franny to protect her from men at the club. To *protect* her.

April turned off the cartoon and jerked the sheet away. In the bath-

room she peed and brushed her teeth and tried not to think of anything but Monday morning when the investigators would come. She
washed her hands and face with soap and hot water. Her ponytail had
come loose and she pulled it back tight again and walked down the
hall to her bedroom where she would start. It was just after seven.
Later she would ask Jean for a ride to get her car. But the terrible
things she said to her. She didn't even mean them. She needed to
apologize, right now, right after she made coffee.

The pot was still half-full from last night. She poured some into a
cup ringed with dried coffee. Lonnie's maybe. He'd been so sweet to
her, too sweet; it felt a little suffocating. She rinsed his cup and put
it in the microwave and pressed the button, the picture of her and
Franny staring at her from the fridge. She pulled it from its mag-
net. Their first week here. Living in the motel. This photo booth
at a drugstore in Bradenton. They were both laughing and looked
happy; there were a lot of places for rent and she knew she was close
to finding one. She had enough money for a few more weeks anyway.
Spending all that time with Franny had felt like a vacation. They'd
spend their mornings at the pool, then go back to their room and
she'd make them sandwiches from the cooler. They'd carry them back
outside and eat at one of the tables under an umbrella. On the other
side of the fence, cars sped by on the highway, the sunlight flashing off
their windshields, and she and Franny would count all the red ones,
then the blue, then the black.

After lunch they went looking at apartments, driving and driving
because even with a map April didn't know where she was. Franny
napped or listened to her Raffi tape on the stereo. She snacked on
crackers and a juice and looked out at the world going by. Some of
the places were on the water, all glass and steel and carpet and cost
way too much. Others were in neighborhoods of squat houses behind
chain-link fences, guard dogs snoozing in their shacks, car radios blaring. And April didn't even go inside to look. But she wasn't worried.
She bought three newspapers every morning, and there were so many
apartments listed. She'd find one.

Late in the afternoons they went shopping only for the things they needed. Just enough food for the next day so it wouldn't go bad or get soggy in the cooler. And she applied for jobs. Waitressing mainly. She'd walk into the air-conditioned restaurants holding Franny's hand. She'd smile at the hostess and ask for the manager, then fill out an application at a table where Franny drew in her coloring book. There were so many places, though, and only a few could be busy. One manager, young and tanned with gelled hair, held her application without reading it, then nodded in the direction of Franny. "You have someone to watch her? I need somebody I can count on."

She could see her life. Training on lunches for next to nothing. Working months before she was in line to get a Friday or Saturday night shift and probably not even both. How would she pay her bills? How would she pay someone to watch Franny? And Stephanie holding her, rocking her, crying herself because she hadn't warned her about taking drinks from McGuiness. *But you walk away, honey, and they win. You're out of work and broke and they win. You got to get back in the game, sweetie. You got to use them till you're set, then you walk. Then you walk and let them kiss your gorgeous ass on the way out. And Louis is nothing like McGuiness. Louis is a big stupid teddy bear with a boat. Use him, honey. Use him.*

In this picture she didn't look like a bad mother. Maybe that day they'd gone into the drugstore for toothpaste or more sunblock or tampons. She didn't know. But she looked confident and full of love for the girl on her lap whose face she couldn't look at now because she looked so trusting. So trusting of her.

The microwave beeped, and there was a knocking, Jean on the other side of the glass. April opened the door. She felt dirty, guilty of more than she was guilty of; Jean looked awful, her skin pale, a sheen of sweat along her forehead. She was breathing hard from the climb and her sundress was damp under the arms and dirty at the hem. "April, please, I didn't sleep, you have to tell me what's happening. I need to *know.*"

"I'm sorry, Jean. I'm sorry for what I said to you."

Jean shook her head, waved her hand in the air. "Forget it."

"No, you've only been good to us."

"And you've been good to me."

"No I haven't. I haven't." She couldn't look at her anymore. Her throat thickened and she opened the door all the way and stepped back. "Please," she said. "Please, Jean, come inside."

＞　＞　＞

L ONNIE STEERED ONTO the crushed shells of the lot. It was
just after noon, and not a car or pickup anywhere. He pulled up
to the canopy and left the engine and AC running and got out
with his driving cup of dark roast he'd brewed at home. It had taken
him a long time to sleep and then it didn't last and now he was drinking too much coffee but he felt strong and light on his feet; there was
the feeling that the big machine he was enslaved to had sputtered to a
stop and spit him out and now he was free.

He walked under the canopy to the front entrance and the X of yellow tape across the door. Tacked to it was a posting from the county
licensing commission. He skimmed it, wondered where Louis was.
He could be parked out back, he might be inside.

Lonnie walked around to the rear of the club. April keening from
car to truck to van to car, him running after her.

A legion of flies buzzed in the Dumpster and around the grease barrel. There wasn't any tape across the door casings but the screen and steel door were locked and a hot wind blew at his back. The smell of the place had ruined coffee for him. He uncapped his cup and poured it into the ground. The sky above the trees was graying to the west, thunderheads gathering over the Gulf. They were in hurricane season now, and once they were deep in it where would he be? What would he be doing?

He was glad she'd let him go get them some Chinese last night, but she wouldn't let him pay for it and had pushed two twenties into his hand. It was a gesture too familiar to them both and they ate quietly on the couch in her living room, though she was done after half an egg roll and a bite of rice.

"Want me to leave, April?"

She looked over at him. She'd pulled her hair back in a ponytail and it made her look younger, her eyes dark and distracted-looking. "Yeah."

At the door she'd let him hold her but pulled away before it could go anywhere. She looked up at him like she wanted to say thank you but said nothing and without her makeup she looked like someone he'd known a long time without knowing it.

"I'll call you tomorrow. See how you're doing."

She'd nodded at him, smiled faintly.

When he'd called this morning there'd been no answer and no machine. He wanted to drive by the house but didn't want to be a parasite either.

Grit blew in his eyes. He stepped off the stoop and walked blinking back to his Tacoma, the engine still running like it was poised to whisk him off somewhere in particular. He wished it would. He sure as hell didn't know what to do next. He had about twenty-five hundred in the bank. He might be able to collect but how much and for how long? Part of him wanted to go home, go back to Austin, maybe stay with his folks out in the bluebonnets and get back into the university.

Lonnie got into his cool cab and sat there awhile. Classrooms weren't made for people like him. He'd tried that and worked hard at it and failed at it. He was lying to himself anyway. He didn't want to go west; he wanted to go about six miles south to April's place. He wanted to hold her and kiss her and help her any way he could.

He put the truck in gear and headed south on 301. The clouds were blowing in from the water and soon there'd be a cleansing rain. He accelerated and pushed in the cassette April couldn't bear to hear:

> *"As he rose and fell*
> *He passed the stages of his age and youth*
> *Entering the whirlpool.*
> > *Gentile or Jew*
> *O you who turn the wheel and look to windward,*
> *Consider Phlebas, who was once handsome and tall as you."*

＊　＊　＊

J UST BEFORE NINE this morning two deputies secured plastic
cuffs loosely over his cast but tight on his wrist and escorted
him downstairs for his bond hearing.

His public defender's name was Harvey Wilson, a tall, scrawny
fucker with curly hair and an expensive tie who stood next to AJ while
the judge studied the papers in front of him, his silver hair combed
back straight, his eyes steady behind his bifocals. The judge glanced
at AJ's public defender, then he looked at him; he leaned forward on
his elbows and took off his glasses.

"It's written here that you say you were trying to protect the child,
is that true?"

"Yes, sir."

"From what, if I may ask?"

"She was wandering out back of a strip club crying and scared, your
honor. I couldn't just leave her there."

"Why didn't you go look for her mother?"

"I guess I didn't trust her, sir."

"You didn't trust her?"

"Yes, sir."

"About her own child?"

"Yes, sir. I mean she brought her there, your honor."

"Why didn't you call the police?"

"I don't know, sir."

"Then why not, at the very least, drive her to the police or sheriff's department?"

"I'm not sure, your honor. I was afraid somebody'd get the wrong idea. I don't know, sir."

"What wrong idea?"

"I don't know, sir. I guess I wasn't thinking clearly."

AJ watched the judge stare at him and AJ saw himself as the judge did, standing before him with a blue cast on his wrist in an orange jumpsuit talking like a fuckup. The judge glanced down at the paperwork, flipped a page over.

"I see you have a restraining order against you."

"Yes, sir."

"And last night you violated that restraining order."

"Yes, sir, but she let me in. We just talked."

"But you violated the order."

"Yes, sir."

"Not to mention you were evicted from this club you refer to for manhandling one of the dancers, isn't that true?"

"I wouldn't use that expression, your honor, sir."

"Which expression?"

"Manhandle, sir."

The judge looked down at his cast, nodded at it. "How did you hurt yourself?"

"An accident with my excavator, sir."

"The officer's report says otherwise, Mr. Carey. Your wife says you came to the house injured and intoxicated. So who am I to believe here?"

AJ shook his head, a million red ants crawling behind the skin of his face. *Deena. What'd you do? What'd you go and fucking* do? He tried to keep looking the judge in the eye but couldn't.

"And instead of calling law enforcement for this child, you take her, keep her all night, then dump her somewhere like so much trash."

"No, sir, your honor. I left her in a safe place, I—"

"You left her in a locked vehicle in a garage where she might well have died from the heat before noon today, Mr. Carey." He raised his hand. "Enough." He turned to the public defender. "The charges are as follows: interference with custody, felony of the third degree; false imprisonment of a child under age thirteen, felony of the third degree; and kidnapping of a child under age thirteen, felony of the first degree. Bail is denied." The judge raised his gavel and brought it down and the sound echoed through the room.

Wilson turned to AJ, whispered, "Bad luck, this one hates wife beaters." He was zipping up his leather briefcase like that was it, nothing more to talk about.

"How long before I get a hearing then?"

"Hard to say. Could be three months or six, even eighteen. You're in for a long haul now."

His escort deputies were on either side of him. Wilson said something else to him, pushing his card into the front pocket of AJ's jail top, but AJ only heard the words still sitting in his head like toxic waste—*eighteen months*. A year and a half before he even got a hearing, never mind a trial? And for *what*? For doing the right thing? For trying to do something *good*?

It was late afternoon and he lay on his bunk, his cast resting hard over his eyes. He tried to ignore the stench of the shit Daniels just took. He tried to ignore O'Brien tapping both feet against the floor while he played over and over some song in his head. He tried to ignore Edwards's throat-rattling snores or García's pages turning one at a time one bunk over. He tried to ignore the slow-healing bone ache in his wrist and how the NP had only given him Tylenol, which gave him gastritis, his gut a raw fire of acid eating away at him. *Eighteen months.* Even if the public defender was wrong and it was just a few weeks, what then? He needed a real lawyer now, didn't he? Those guys cost money. And Deena had taken care of that. She sure as hell did her best to take care of that.

His body felt like poured concrete, like it would never sit up or stand or walk again. But the girl. That little girl had to be okay because he'd've been charged with more if she wasn't, right?

There was the tap of O'Brien's feet on the floor, then his hands lightly slapping his legs. There was Edwards snoring and Daniels or Johnson sliding chess pieces over the board. Every few minutes García would turn a page. But there was something else too. Something rising and falling. Like applause far away, and AJ lowered his cast and opened his eyes. Fifteen feet up the wall, just beneath the iron joists, was a small square window. Tempered glass, unbreakable. Eddie. That one time they'd built a room for a man who didn't want windows. He was old and stooped over. He wore thick glasses and read a lot of books. He wanted the room to be a cool, dark cave. A place where he could disappear. That was the word he'd used too, smiling with his bad teeth—*disappear.* AJ cutting all the studs and plates under the sun, feeding them to Eddie, who framed the walls with no rough openings for windows, just one big enough for an air-conditioning unit. Eddie chewing his Wrigley's, his nips wearing off. *"This ain't to code, you know."*

"What?"

"This fuckin' cave. You can't legally call it a room."

"Why not?"

"No egress, numbnuts. You always gotta have more than one way out."

And this window, so high off the floor—the applause was rain, rain blowing hard against the glass.

AJ closed his eyes again, laid his cast over it. Saw his hurricaneproof house out in the wire grass, the tall slash pines jerking and bending in the wind. Far enough away he didn't have to worry about where they might fall. How was she going to keep up the payments without his monthly check? They could lose the house, and where would his son go? His grandparents' place out on the lake? Cole's daddy and his cinder-block house just fading images in his head? No, AJ could sell the truck. He could have Mama do it. He had enough paid off on it. That'd buy him a few months of mortgages at least. Goddamn this was *wrong*. He shouldn't have to be worrying about any of this. He'd taken care of that child, god*damn* them.

His heart was bucking in his chest. Daniels laughed and there was the tap-tap of him making a move on the board. O'Brien was humming now. Some metal song AJ had always hated. *This one hates wife beaters.* Fucking Deena. The words were there inside him but there was very little anger behind it. It wasn't her fault, was it? She didn't backhand herself across the kitchen. She didn't get her wrist broken for not letting go of some lying whore's hand. Marianne could be blamed. She certainly could. But what sang through AJ's blood right now aimed itself for him and him only, and it was like a gun going off inside him, the emptiness and ringing quiet.

Maybe a hurricane was coming, maybe just a storm. His family would be inside now. He saw them. Deena and Cole, Cole sitting on Deena's lap on the couch watching a cartoon movie. Deena sharing her ice cream with him. And was she thinking about her husband? Did she even know where he was? Did she care? Oh man, was she *relieved*? Please don't tell me she's sitting there feeling that, the ice cream sweet in her mouth.

❯ ❯ ❯

THE LAUNDROMAT SMELLED like lint and fabric softener and bubble gum. Jean had never stepped foot in one before. Now she sat in a hard plastic seat across from a bank of front-loading washers watching the clothes of strangers turn round and round. She could clearly see bras and underwear and blouses tossed one over the other. Jean had insisted to April that she use her washer and dryer in the laundry room back home, but April had stood in a light rain in the garden holding her bundle of dirty clothes to her breasts, her pocketbook dangling from her shoulder, her long hair pulled back tightly, and said no, "Thank you. I just need things to be familiar right now. I need to do what I usually do."

April pulled her wet clothes into a basket, then carried it over to the dryers. Two women sat beside each other over there thumbing through magazines. A young man with a goatee spoke on his cell phone, and he eyed April's rear as she leaned over the dryer for the settings. April was dressed in long khaki shorts and a blue top, nothing provocative. There was the feeling that Jean had somehow missed something all these years, had missed seeing something she should've seen, knowing something she should've known.

She had been feeling superior to April, smarter and more mature, but now, rain whipping onto the sidewalks and street outside, Jean felt pampered and naïve.

April dropped the empty clothes basket onto the stack of others just like it. "You think the car's there yet?"

"It's only been an hour. They said two, didn't they?"

April nodded. "You hungry?" She pulled her pocketbook up over her shoulder.

"Yes, would you like me to go get us something?"

"We can both go."

"What about your clothes?"

"I don't care about them, Jean. I need to get out of here." She looked away and started walking to the door.

The wind bent the palm trunks forward and back, the fronds snapping and rippling, the rain pricking dully against Jean's face and arms as she hurried beside April. They walked into the first place there was, a burrito bar where young people sat laughing at two tables side by side and above them hung a widescreen television of skateboarders performing impossible stunts between curved concrete walls. There was rap music playing, the relentless staccato of the singer's voice and words overwhelming whatever instruments there were. Jean hated it, but water dripped off her face, and her hair was ruined and her pantsuit would have to be cleaned and it was nice just to be indoors. She laughed. "Well this is better."

April looked distracted and pale. Her hair and shoulders were wet, her nipples erect.

They sat in a booth under a glassed display of skateboards. There were no menus. The man behind the counter waved them over, and he asked what they wanted and he'd make it for them. Under the glass were stainless steel containers of chopped tomatoes and lettuce, three kinds of shredded cheeses, four kinds of beans, and warmed pans of chicken, pork, and beef. They each ordered the same thing, a chicken burrito with lettuce, tomato, and pinto beans. Jean asked for bottled water and April iced tea. As he handed them their warm burritos wrapped in foil, the man's eyes passed over April's breasts and face, something she ignored completely as she unzipped her leather pocketbook.

Jean said, "I'll get this."

"No." April raised her hand as if to stop more than what she'd just offered.

"Thank you." Jean took her food. She glanced down at April's small leather pocketbook split open with tightly packed bills. It was all that money from that night, the money she'd come home with instead of Franny, and now she wanted to get away quickly and drive April back to the police department for her impounded car, then drive home alone.

April sat down across from her. Rain blew against the door and windows. She lifted her burrito and kept looking over Jean's shoulder at the buffeted glass. Her arms were brown from all her mornings in the sun but her face was blanched, her eyes shining under the electric light.

"Are you all right?"

"She's afraid of storms, Jean." April shook her head. She began to bounce her foot under the table. She held the wrapped burrito to her lips but didn't eat.

"I know she is. But she's with professionals. They'll know how to distract her."

"She's in a fucking *foster* home." A tear shot down her cheek.

Jean reached over, made herself touch her arm. "On Monday they'll see a good home and bring her back right away. Why wouldn't they?" *Franny's disgusting room, your job.*

"You think I deserve this, don't you?"

"Of course not. Why would you say that?"

"I don't know, I know you don't approve of me."

I think you don't know what you've got. "No. No, I think you're ambitious, April. And sometimes ambition's a train that speeds right by other things. Other people."

"You think I *like* what I do?"

"I have no idea. And it's absolutely none of my business."

"Because I *don't* like it. But I have goals. I'm not one of those stupid bitches snorting all the money up her nose, you know. I've saved every penny I've ever made."

"I believe you." Jean put her burrito down. She pulled a napkin from the steel dispenser against the wall and wiped her fingers. How strange to have known someone and not known her. Jean's friends, how after Harold's death they treated her differently and she saw them differently, as if she had always driven up to her own house from the south, then one afternoon came from the north, how much smaller it looked from here. The spruce obscured the elm and the clapboards were curling.

And now Franny gone, God help us, for only the weekend and perhaps Monday, but without her between Jean and April as a constant physical presence, the two women were different with each other; they could actually talk to one another now.

She looked past April to the table of laughing young people, teenagers, three of them sitting right beside each other talking on cell phones. She drank more water. The rap music was quieter now, though the reciter's voice still sounded angry, rain whipping against the glass like a spray of bullets.

❮ ❮ ❮

APRIL COULDN'T EAT anymore. She pushed her burrito to the side and sucked her iced tea through her straw. Wind gusts kept hurling sheets of rain unfolding against the window and it began to sound like part of the music, the drums of some angry, deaf drummer locked out of the show. She could feel Jean watching her and for the first time she wanted to tell her things. She wanted to tell her about McGuiness. She wanted to tell her it was a game and she'd learned how to play it so she came out ahead. She wanted to tell her about the real estate she would own, not just one house but two, three, more. She wanted to tell her how close she was to quitting, six more months through the high season of winter, maybe just a few more after that. But she kept seeing Franny outside, curled up on the sidewalk in just her pink pajamas, the rain pelting her narrow back, her bare feet and hair, her hands over her face, calling for her.

"It's okay, honey. It's okay." Jean put a napkin in her hand. April nodded and stood and wiped at her eyes. "I need to go."

The rain and wind had eased up as they pulled off Ringling Boulevard and into the lot behind the police station. There were five or six parked cruisers, a K-9 van, and a tow truck, its orange roof lights flashing as the driver lowered the front end of April's car to the puddled asphalt. A section of yellow police tape hung wetly from the driver's door and in this gray light her Sable was a dull maroon she'd never quite noticed before, a pitiful color really, the color you choose that you think is cheery when it's really more brooding and unlucky.

"Would you like me to go in with you?"

"No thank you. I'll see you at home." That last word rippled through her. April felt shy and glanced back at her laundry—clean, folded, and rain-damp on the backseat.

"Leave it, April. We'll bring it in later." Jean's hair was wet, her pantsuit wrinkled.

"Thank you for all your help."

"You're welcome. Let me know what I can do about tomorrow. Getting ready, I mean."

April closed the door of the Cadillac. She hooked the strap of her pocketbook over her shoulder and hurried through the light rain into the police station. If she saw the directory on the wall, she didn't take it in, that the upper floors of this building were cells and in one of them sat A.J. Carey, lying on his bunk and trying not to think of all the judge had denied him, all he'd taken away.

SUNDAY

BASSAM SITS AT the outdoor table beside Tariq. The morning is warming, the sky clear above the buildings of Harvard University across the street. The high brick walls and black iron gates of this place everyone in the world knows of, even him, even a boy from the province of Asir. This best school for the unbelievers. This best school.

It is the morning of their day of worship. Bells ring in the air for the polytheists, and the shops and cafés are open for business as usual. The square is crowded with students and tourists. There is traffic in the street beyond the full tables of this Au Bon Pain and its umbrellas and young trees shading the tables. At many of them men and women sit together in twos.

They have as many years as he does, and they smoke cigarettes and drink coffee and laugh or lean close to one another and speak quietly. One girl has hair the color of copper wires. It falls in long curls down her back, and she smiles at her boyfriend with her eyes only. She wears tight blue jeans and boots for cowboys, her legs crossed at the knee, her nuhood behind a white T-shirt so rounded and soft-looking. But it is her face Bassam watches. How happy and satisfied she looks sitting at the table of this thin boy with his books and his dark hair and his eyeglasses, a Jew—she looks like the animal who has eaten well and knows she will again. And she loves the boy for this, doesn't she? She loves this boy for giving that to her. And today they woke together in a warm bed in a room in a building on the other side of the wall of this best school.

She is beautiful, yes, but this is not why Bassam cannot stop watching her. It is her love for the boy. It is her love for her youth and her health and her freedom and her life in this world, and Bassam is stronger now than he was even one day before for he is not weakened witnessing this love; this *is* how Shaytan works among the kufar. He seduces you to love this life they love too well. The whore April, Bassam had felt alone with her, by himself while being with her. The same aloneness that had infected him back home before he'd been guided back to Allah. As if he were not loved. As if he were not protected. As if he would not continue to live after his own death. How could he have felt these things? Him, a *shahid*, Insha'Allah.

Again, it was the yielding, the yielding to the mushrikoon. And it was Khalid who, through the Creator, saved him. It was the body of his brother lowered into the grave that brought him back to the Judge and the Sustainer.

When Bassam left home Khalid's possessions were still in the room they shared. His Saudi clothes and the clothes of the kufar, Levi's blue jeans and shirts made by the Gap, his Nike shoes and hat like Karim's. Above both their beds, their mother had hung woven tapestries, and behind Khalid's, pinned to the back, was a carton of Marlboros.

Ahmed al-Jizani, how angry he would be to find those. How hurt. When Bassam was still asleep in this world, he believed his father to be a true believer. He never hurried his ablutions or skipped any of the daily prayers. He prayed inside the mosque—the mosque he built—not simply on the Day of Gathering but all the week long. He demanded his daughters be covered, even at home, that his sons never smoke or find music, that one day they make the pilgrimage to Makkah as he had.

But this is the same man who built housing for the kufar to live in while they attacked our brothers and sisters. This is the man who took so many dollars he converted to riyals, thinking the money was clean now, pure, as if he had not sinned against the Ruler and the Judge and his own people.

On the table beside Bassam's empty cup is the notebook he bought yesterday afternoon in the books and supplies store crowded with the kufar. The pen, he purchased from Cliff at the fuel station store in Boynton Beach, a black Bic he pulls the cap from now.

"Bassam?"

"Mansoor."

"Mansoor." Tariq has been watching the young women, his feet tapping beneath the table, and he has smoked two cigarettes quite fast. Last evening, before the final prayer, he lay on the bed and pressed the remote button until the movies appeared: Family, Comedy, Drama— Adult; he held the remote control in the air, the sound off, his hand slightly shaking. In this land of the far enemy, there have been so many opportunities to see these films—through any video store, for sale behind shop shelves not far from the eyes of kufar children, and in hotels like this one, an expensive one they have not stayed in until now, and so this, their first real opportunity. Bassam's heart had begun to beat more quickly.

"Tariq, don't. We must prepare ourselves. Soon we have to wash and pray."

"You went to that club, Bassam. You were there a long time."

Bassam remained quiet. He did not want Tariq to go any further and he did want him to go further.

Then Imad's knocking came and Tariq turned off the television and they prayed together in Imad's room upon the carpet. He had brought incense and it burned sweetly though the room was nonsmoking and

Bassam was distracted in his prayers and hoped there was no alarm, no way of their knowing.

There is the sounding of a horn, the laughter of one of the young women in the light of the sun. Tariq drops his shortened cigarette into his teacup. "Mansoor, we should go to the gym with Imad. Where is it?"

"The hotel. The exercise room."

"We should join him."

It had been more than two weeks and Tariq is right, but with such little time left, Bassam cannot justify it. "I am as strong as I will ever be, Tariq. You go. I must write to my mother."

Tariq looks at him. "Isn't your will enough? Let our actions speak for themselves, Bassam."

"Go see Imad, Tariq. I will try to join you later, Insha'Allah."

"When is Amir coming?"

"Tonight, Allah willing. Tonight."

A young black kafir walks by their table, her brown skin exposed between her shirt and jeans, a glittering jewel attached there. Tariq stands quickly and leaves and twice he looks back at the young woman as she enters the café. He is not troubled by his desires. Before sleep last night, he lay in bed reading the Book in the lamp's light. Bassam was nearly asleep in the bed beside his, entering a dream where he sat on the pebbled ground of Mount Souda in the firelight. The whore April stood on the other side of the fire. She was fully dressed and her hair was long and shining and she was smiling at him, the moon full and high over her shoulder.

"You see, Bassam." Tariq's voice, Tariq leaning on one elbow to read something from the Qu'ran. "This is from the Al-Imran sura, Bassam: 'Women are your fields: go, then, into your fields whence you please. Do good works and fear Allah.' Brother, Insha'Allah, we are shuhada'. Do you think the Creator cares if we turn on this television and watch what other men do in the fields?"

"It is haram, Tariq. I know you know this."

"The Holy One knows all. Why would He have this available in our room if He did not want us to see what awaits us?"

Bassam said nothing. Nor could he say anything, for he wished this to be true. And perhaps it was. They were not real women but only those on film far away who could not actually tempt them. But no, no. "We must rest, Tariq. Close the lamp. We will need our strength, Allah willing."

There was the closing of the Book and darkness, then quiet. Autos drove by in the streets below. Far down the corridor, the soft ring of the elevator bell.

Go, then, into your fields whence you please.

April who calls herself Spring, he can't stop thinking of her. The coarse hair above her qus, the baby's scar there. Her eyes as she sat beside him uncovered. Brown and warm. Her voice as she asked about Khalid. As if she truly wished to know.

Her screaming later in the parking area among the men. Her screams.

❧ ❧ ❧

Early Sunday morning, they sat on towels on the damp Adirondack chairs under the mango tree sipping hot coffee each of them had made in their own kitchens. Jean's garden was a glistening profusion of green and white, of flaming red and orange. It smelled earth-sweet and fertile. She'd slept badly, Franny in her dreams, though she could remember only her presence there, nothing else.

April crossed her legs. She was barefoot, her toenails still coated in the polish of her work. She'd brushed her hair but had put on no makeup, and her eyelids looked swollen.

"I can't stop thinking about tomorrow morning. What will they be inspecting anyway?"

"I don't know—drugs, alcohol, a gun in the house."

"I would never have a gun in my house."

"Nor would I allow it."

"Or drugs."

"I didn't say you do. Please, you're getting defensive again."

"I'm sorry." April said it automatically and Jean didn't believe her. She lowered her cup and rested it on the arm of her chair. "Why not tell them you're going to quit?"

"I plan to."

"Are you?"

"What?"

"Going to quit that job?"

"Yes. In about six more months."

"Why not now?"

"I don't have enough yet."

"Money?"

"Yes."

"For a house?"

"At least one."

"That's a lot of money."

April nodded. She sipped her coffee and squinted at the bougainvillea vine. A phone rang from inside, a muffled electronic ring coming down through the mango leaves. "It's yours, April." But she was already out of the Adirondack, running up the stairs in a way Jean never could.

It wasn't Franny, it wasn't the people watching her, it was Louis, his voice low and hoarse like he had drunk too much the night before and hadn't slept. April was breathing hard, could feel her heart beating in her hand around the phone, his first words a language she couldn't quite decipher.

"Really, Spring. How is she? She all right?"

"I don't know. Why are you calling me?"

"New policy, hon. Sorry, but no more mothers. Come clean out your locker, Spring. I'm here till noon."

April lowered the phone to its charger. She stood in her immaculate childless home. It smelled of Pine-Sol and coffee and a new start. She felt kissed and she felt slapped. Of course he was knocking her off rotation and out of the building. He'd have to get rid of Retro now too, and Sadie, and that Chinese girl who had two kids and lived with her sister. No time for mothers. Time to purge himself of mothers. And how fucked to get fired by a man she *paid*. And what about tomorrow? Would this be good? Or would they expect her to have a job? She had fifty-two thousand dollars in her account, and there were a few thousand more from the foreigner. Yesterday she'd driven in the blowing rain by her bank but couldn't deposit it. Not before Franny was back. It would feel like an exchange then.

But that much money would look good to them, wouldn't it? Then she'd say she was through dancing and was looking for something else even if she couldn't be, not yet. There was the Pink Pony in Venice. She could get in there, though it'd be harder. Wendy had talked about it. The porn playing on widescreens on the walls while you danced, and because of bitches like her the VIP rooms were full-contact and men expected hand jobs or blow jobs and got them for cheap.

She'd heard of a classier club up in Tampa, a national chain. Gold was in the name. Something Gold. The phone was ringing. April lifted it and pressed it carefully to her ear.

∨ ∨ ∨

THE HUMIDITY WAS back in the air. Yesterday's rain had evaporated from the asphalt but the sandy dirt at the shoulders was darker and so was the green in the wire grass all the way out to the industrial park, the chain-link fence around it glistening silver in the sun. Just beyond it people were leaving the Methodist church. The men were in short sleeves and ironed pants, the women in bright skirts and dresses. One of them stood on the top step wearing a straw sun hat decorated with flowers. She was talking to the minister in his flowing robe. Lonnie wanted to ask April how she was doing. He wanted to reach over and rest his hand reassuringly on her knee. But he was surprised to find he felt awkward.

When he'd called she told him Louis had just 86ed her and she didn't want to be alone with him in the club while she emptied her locker, would he go with her? He'd quickly showered and shaved, pulled on a T-shirt and cutoff jeans and his Tevas. She was waiting for

him in her driveway. Her hair was pulled back. She wore a maroon
sleeveless blouse and khaki shorts and the only makeup was something on her eyelashes. She smiled at him. It was Spring's smile, the
one she'd give him after every shift when she pushed money into his
hand, thankful. But this was the woman he'd driven to the hospital
and back home where he'd pushed past newspeople for her to run
inside, had sat with her and shared food with her—this was April. And
as she climbed into his truck, she seemed like someone entirely new.
He hoped he looked good to her sitting behind the wheel.

He pointed at the one-story church as they passed. "You ever go?"

"When I was little. You?"

"Never." He laughed. "We're a couple lost souls, aren't we?"

She didn't say anything.

His face heated up. "I'm quitting."

"The club?"

He nodded.

"Right now?"

"Looks like it." Rising up ahead on the other side of the boulevard
was the yellow Puma sign, its black silhouettes of two naked women
looking tawdry and pathetic under the sun.

The screen door was propped open by a cinder block but the exterior door was locked. Lonnie had to rap on the glass awhile. He and
April stood in the Dumpster stench together and finally Louis came
to the door and opened it. He stood under the fluorescent glare of
the kitchen in a graying T-shirt. It hugged his gut and was wet in the
center of his chest, his legs pink and freckled beneath baggy shorts.
He was breathing hard.

"You two come together?"

"Yeah, I gave her a ride."

"Good, you can help me clean this fucking dump." He glanced at
April. "I'll be out front when you're done."

Lonnie followed him into the cooled air of the club, his adrenaline kicking in low, like a pocket had opened and he was forced to rise and drift toward it and close it. The houselights were up. Louis had stacked all the tables and chairs against the stage and along the walls. In the middle of the worn carpet was a commercial rug cleaner, beside it a jug of something blue.

"This thing's costing me by the fucking minute. I'll get up on the stage and you hand me the tables first, then the chairs."

"I can't, Louis."

"Yeah you can. On the clock. We'll take the boat out after. Have some drinks."

"I quit, Louis." It was like throwing the punch they never saw coming, Louis's stunned look, his freckled hands at his sides, useless.

"You're shittin' me, right?"

"No. I appreciate everything you did for me, Lou, but I need a change."

"What? More money?"

"No, I just need to do something else." He turned and walked past the rented rug cleaner and the dusty stage.

"You better not be going to the Pony, Lonnie. Tell me you're not going to the fuckin' Pink Pony."

Lonnie stopped and looked back at him, this unhappy rich man in shorts and a T-shirt, his mouth half-open like he'd just been pulled from his bed to be given this news. And it wasn't unlike the remorse Lonnie'd begin to feel after laying somebody out, the questions he had about himself after. "No, Louis. I won't be going to the Pink Pony. Good luck."

And he meant it. The Pony part and the luck part, April walking out of the dressing room just as he entered the kitchen, a pair of jeans rolled under her arm, zipping up a purple bag in both hands as if it held a secret she may tell him once they were both far from here.

Y Y Y

S HE IS UGLY and what she does is ugly and Bassam feels poisoned watching her, but he cannot move or speak nor is he breathing fully and his face burns with shame for the hardness he can only hope is not visible under his clothes. Tariq lies silently on his own bed, still and quiet as well. The shades are drawn and the room is darkened to the afternoon, the television's screen so clear, the woman's sounds turned low but so clear, her cries of pleasure.

She is thin and pale. Her nuhood are small and her hair is dyed the white-blond so many of these kufar prefer. Along her belly, close to her qus, is inked a man's name: *Joseph*. On her ankle, a flower. On her shoulder one of the men grasps, is the cross of Mary's son these ahl al-shirk worship as if their prophet were the Holy One and not simply one of His messengers. Stupid. *Stupid.*

But Bassam does not look at these inked markings. It is the man thrusting himself into the woman, the wetness of her, how deeply he can go, how fast. Bassam cannot believe how deep and how fast.

How does this not harm her? How does she enjoy this? This ugly whore Bassam cannot turn away from. And Karim, the only one among them to leave their home. His studies in England. The Zionist he boasted about lying with. Did he do it to her like this? Did he turn her over and enter her as a dog? Grasp her hair and pull? Did she scream like this one? Did she?

Enough.

"Tariq, turn it off. We must turn this off."

"We pay for it. We should see all of it." Tariq's voice is high in his throat, like after racing or just before.

Bassam closes his eyes, his face a wash of heat, his shame softening him. His shame, and yes, his disappointment. This act as ugly as something animals do. How will it be any more beautiful done by him? Will he not be given back his human body in Jannah? Won't his companions have the bodies of women? How can he bring such ugliness to the highest rooms of the Creator?

The woman cries louder and she tells the man to push harder, harder.

"Tariq, please, turn it off. This is haram, brother. Please."

"It is *not* haram, Bassam. It would not be here if the Creator does not deem it. Please, let me watch this in peace."

Bassam stands. From the bedside table he takes his notebook and the pen from Florida. "Yes, Tariq. But we say 'Asr in less than one hour. Remember this."

Tariq says nothing and Bassam steps quickly past the television he disciplines himself not to view any longer. At the door he slips on his shoes. He looks once more into the room, sees only the television's light moving upon the carpet and beds. Tariq's feet, his long feet. From here, the woman's cries sound manufactured.

He pulls closed the door. Checks that it is locked. He walks past Imad's door; knows he is resting there. Resting after his long exercis-

ing. Perhaps giving supplications to the Holy One, the Protector and
Sustainer, and again, a hot shame moving through Bassam's blood and
skin; how can he even begin to question what waits for them in the
highest rooms? How can he even begin to think he knows the beauty
there? The women, chaste and chosen for him only, lying upon soft
couches in lush gardens watered by running streams.

On the street his legs are too light beneath him, the grip upon his
notebook weak. In his head only the pale whore. He passes an old
woman, her lips red with cosmetics, the wrinkles deep in her face. She
walks slowly with a wooden staff to aid her and she smiles at him and
he sees the man's hands on her, the thrusting so fast and so deep into
her old body. Bassam runs across the street. The blare of a horn, the
yelling of the taxi's driver. An Arab. His accent Egyptian. Living here
among the kufar, becoming one of them. Three women now pass
on the sidewalk. They are girls not yet in university and two reveal
their bellies, their legs behind tight jeans and their nuhood bouncing
to their walking and they laugh and do they know how they will be
penetrated? Have they already done this? And was there love? When
they sinned, did they think it was love?

Oh, these kufar! Look at them. In front of a shop, two men play
a guitar and drum. One's hair is long and dirty. The other has no
hair, and they play loudly and fast and the guitar player sings with
a voice that only shouts, and look at the kafir woman dance to it in
the sunlight. Her nose is pierced with silver, as are her ears and the
skin above her eyes. Her hair is red and black and blue. Her ugliness
is only surpassed by her lack of modesty, her nuhood beneath her
T-shirt bouncing and jerking with her movement.

He hurries past them and the happy kufar watching. There is the
guitar case of money, of loose change lying in blue fabric. All the
money he let the whore April take. She must think him a fool or crazy
from drinking. Or both. These people are only happy if you burn
with them, and he cannot stop seeing the thrusting. Each woman he

passes, he sees her on her hands and knees, the man's hands grasping her, the thrusting into her, a depth he did not know they had.

He is nearly hard again and he passes the newsstand. Gray stacks of newspapers, magazines in wooden racks and behind glass and inside the shadows of the shop. Is it possible that even one does not have upon its cover an immodest and beautiful woman?

How weak he was to lie there and do nothing as Tariq pressed the buttons. How *weak*.

There is more music, more dirty musicians in more doorways. Like the various radios playing on the bright beaches of Florida as he and his brothers rode their mopeds, the conflicting sounds then. Always such noise here. Three doorways. Three sorts of music. The young men and now an old one, his beard white, his hair tied backward like a woman, he plays an electric guitar, the sharp notes like needles puncturing the skin. And near the main square and the passing autos, in front of the bookstore and its stone columns and glass doors, a Japanese or Chinese kafir is playing the stringed instrument she holds at her shoulder beneath her chin, her music more beautiful than the others', but her hair is long and straight and black and he sees her penetrated, only now it is *his* hands grasping her, *his* thrusting.

Do you see the work of Shaytan? Can you feel his power? He is working hard now, is he not? Is he not working hard to confuse him, to weaken him and Tariq? Shaytan has not been able to influence Imad or the Egyptian or, please Allah, any of the others. But he is working hard now to corrupt two of the four who will travel first.

There are the autos and vans passing before him, the smell of exhaust pleasing to him, a scent from home, though the conflicting music behind him is too much, the stringed instrument of the girl, the electric piercings of the old kafir, the drumming farther away, the voices of all the young and old kufar passing him on the sidewalk. Again the horns blaring at him, and Bassam does not remember running into the traffic with his notebook away from the musics and the girl from the east he can see now uncovered.

There is yet another newsstand, this one larger. Many hundreds of magazines. So many. The shelves are the color of bare flesh. He wants to go inside. But it is Shaytan pulling him. And Bassam runs past the newsstand away from the square and its crowds and shops and warring musics, the Au Bon Pain where earlier he attempted to write to his mother but could not. There were too many young women. The air warm—not like Florida, not like home—but warm so they wore little, these waking, laughing jinn from the fires of Jahannam.

He would write the letter back in the hotel, Tariq exercising with Imad. But Imad was resting and Tariq lay there watching the life of this world as filmed by the kufar, then he pressed Movies. Then Shaytan pressed the rest.

Tariq, you must be strong, brother. You must help me find the river south. You have to be clear, brother. You have to be pure.

This time no horns. He is across the street upon the sidewalk. The sun shines on the red stone of the high wall of the best school. It shines in the hair of the mushrikoon girls and boys, and Bassam walks among them and through the arched gate into the shaded grounds of this Harvard. There are no guards to stop him. No policemen. Only the young students and the deep green grass beneath the trees. The paved walkways wide and clean. Already there is more quiet. The drums an echoing in the traffic behind him.

O Lord, I ask You for the best of this place and ask You to protect me from its evils.

He is walking beside a girl and boy holding hands. Her hair is long and blond and she is tall and her back is straight. They speak about someone, a friend, a Jules, lawskule. Bassam cannot place the word. She sees him. She smiles and turns back to her friend, continues her talk of Jules. But her smile is so warm and open and not paid for. Kelly, the trainer, her smile like that. Her bare neck, her hair pinned above it. And April, for just those moments in the end, when he spoke of Khalid, her face a face with no lies masking it. And because this blond girl's smile was warm, Bassam falls behind and follows them.

Along the high walls beyond the trees rise stone buildings, some of their sides covered with vines and green leaves. And now they are climbing many steps. They are long and each could hold twenty or thirty people. Some students sit on them and smoke or speak on cell phones or read books or write in notebooks such as the one he holds. He could be one of them. In appearance he could be one of these kufar. He is better dressed than many of them, his khaki pants ironed by himself this morning, his polo shirt clean from the hotel's laundry service, and before dressing he made the supplication for it. He looks over the students on the steps and enters through the glass doors, and he sees many faces from other parts of the world—Japan, Italy, perhaps Algeria and Bahrain, Cambodia or Vietnam. And of course all the healthy white faces like those of the two he follows into the largest of buildings.

A security officer sits upon a stool beside a desk. He laughs and nods his head with a woman there, the woman's eyes passing over Bassam for only a moment. The floor is polished stone and gives way to a deep carpet. Everywhere there are students sitting in chairs or at long tables, their books and papers open before them, yet this endless room is quiet. There are only the sounds of turning pages, a cough, whispers. Bassam sits. At this shining wooden table are many chairs but those near him are empty. At the end a black kafir woman writes. She is very dark, the color of a Sudanese. Her eyes move to his and he sees she does not see him but what is in her head to write and he looks downward, again the black whore sitting beside April, the brightly colored flesh she parted for him, just the beginning of a great depth he knows now. He forces the picture from his thoughts. He opens his notebook.

High shelves across from him rise meters in the air. They are filled with books. He can smell them, their dusty pages. Their thick covers. He has never been in a place such as this, but there is the feeling he has—many times. All the people, quiet, working together but separately on similar tasks, the rising ceiling, the carpet beneath him—a *mosque*.

Bassam feels at the farthest edge of falling into a new knowledge, but who are these people to give a building of books the same respect as the holy place for the Holy One? Look at how they are stored with such precision and such respect when there is only one Book to be read.

These *stupid* people. Look at them, their faces lowered to these pages, studying only the life of this world, preparing to rise within it, to rise in their unbelief to power they will use against his brothers and sisters. So often he has asked himself why do these kufar have so much power? Why have they been given all that they have?

But look, Bassam, at what they have. They have eyes yet they do not see. They have ears yet they do not hear. And from their mouths come only seductions and boasts and lies. And do not forget Yunis 10:88, "'Lord,' said Moses, 'You have bestowed on Pharaoh and his nobles splendor and riches in this life, so that they may stray from Your path.'"

Bassam's heart pounds inside him but his legs no longer feel too light and his hands are steady. The woman at the desk, how she glanced upon you as if *you* were a student at this best school; to be included in this, something that would make Ahmed al-Jizani proud. Because why do you prepare to write to your honored mother and not your father? His tired eyes lecturing you of jihad. His newly purchased thawb loose upon him. The clothing he buys with his dirty money working for the kufar. And their jahili king selling himself and their kingdom as well, allowing their holy lands to be occupied, blocking the route of the Prophet, peace be upon him, to the farthest mosque in Jerusalem.

Khalid was educated and he was Bassam's older brother, but he was weak, too. Perhaps even weaker than himself. If the kufar had not been allowed to spread its dirty music across the borders, its cigarettes and autos and televisions, its noise and its speed and its distractions. If the king had not allowed it into the birthplace of the Prophet, Allah's blessings and salutations be upon him, would not Khalid still be alive in Khamis Mushayt? Would not their mother have been spared her grief? For accept this, too, Bassam, there is no guarantee Khalid was spared either. Yes, he would give a cold man his coat, but his mind was given over to these people, was lost to these people.

The kufar couple are sitting at a small table. They face one another. The woman's foot rests on the man's bare knee, and he reads as if he is not this close to a woman, as if this means nothing. He is large. He is an athlete of some kind, and Bassam has practiced often against men his size, many times with Imad. The hand on the forehead, the jerking backward, the thrusting into the skin below the ear. He could do it now. He could walk into their area, stand a meter behind the man, pretend he is looking at the high window and its afternoon light, the 'Asr prayer coming soon, very soon. She may look up at Bassam and smile again, so warmly as before, and he would strike, the blade pulled from the boy's neck before he even feels the hand upon his forehead. The blood that must come. Her screams. Her eyes the eyes of one who can now see. Her ears that can now hear.

Bassam's heart is pushing hard in his chest. He opens the notebook, puts the pen from Florida to the right side of the page.

O Dear Mother, ya umma al'aziza, I said to you I would write but I have not written. For this I am apologizing. Muta'assif.

Mother, what I have done, Insha'Allah, I have done for the Creator. This is a great honor. I hope you are well pleased.

Bassam stops writing. His father, he sees him laughing so immodestly. Sitting against the tapestried wall of the outer building with his brothers, with Uncle Rashad, laughing at one of his jokes. Bassam as a boy, he walked into the room, his father and uncle still laughing, Ahmed al-Jizani's eyes wet and shining as they saw him, the joy there, an added happiness that he was here, his youngest son of so many. And the years that followed. His only son not to go to university. Those days with no end in rooms of lessons he soon forgot and the sitting and sitting he could not forget—why go to university when the streets and teahouses and souqs and malls are full of educated men with no jobs? Why go to university only to race on the highway and smoke on Mount Souda with educated men who, if they have work at all, it is for those such as Ali al-Fahd? Why, Father? And what will you think of me soon, Father? Will you be proud? Will you be ashamed? Ashamed you could not see what was in your own home. A *chosen* one? A chosen *shahid*? Or will you disown me, Father? Are you so blind and deaf, you no longer truly *believe*?

The black kafir woman coughs. It is time for prayer, time to leave this temple of false idols and pray with his brothers. And if Tariq has not turned off the haram movie, Bassam will do it for him. He will pick up the television and throw it into the street. He knows he is strong enough to do this. He can feel it with each breath, with each breath given to him by the Mighty.

He reads what he has written. He does not know how to sign it. What final word for her when there is not even one for his father?

Far away there is muffled laughter. He must hurry back and pray. He writes:

YOUR SON,
MANSOOR BASSAM AL-JIZANI

I n a Wal-Mart south of Bradenton, April pushed a cart up and down the aisles and filled it with things for Franny: a deep green bedspread, three pair of shorts, two cotton dresses, one she'd love because it had smiling yellow suns against blue; she picked out two bathing suits, a pair of flip-flops, a packet of underwear, and four pairs of ankle socks with purple stitching at the hem. She bought her a sand bucket and shovel and a pair of goggles. She wanted to get her a new toy chest for her room. And maybe a soft chair for kids. But they couldn't look new. None of this should be in her room looking too new.

She was hungry. It was after one and it occurred to her she'd had nothing all day but coffee. She pushed her cart into the fast-food area near the big tinted windows and ordered a hot dog and Diet Coke and she sat in an orange booth and ate too quickly. She regretted telling Lonnie she'd let him take her to dinner. Leaving the club, she knew she wanted to go shopping for Franny, then work on her room until it looked better than it ever had. But Lonnie was so cheerful and upbeat after quitting the Puma, he wanted to take her out to lunch on a beach somewhere.

"I need to get ready for tomorrow, Lonnie. Can you just drive me back home first?"

He'd looked guilty for thinking of himself, but she felt as if she'd just used him and owed him something.

"Maybe later?" she'd said.

"Dinner?"

"Okay."

She had the rest of the afternoon ahead of her, but first she had to find a furniture store. There was that big mall in Bradenton. Franny liked it because of the Play Place in the food court, the netted pit of hundreds of plastic balls, Franny sliding down the red chute into them, disappearing as if she were underwater.

At a table on the other side of her cart, a man kept looking at her over his sandwich. He sat across from his wife and daughter, both heavy, the woman's bra strap creasing the flesh under her shirt. His face was pink and shaved smooth, and he looked away from her looking back at him. April may have danced for him but couldn't remember. She stood and crossed the room to throw away her hot dog wrapper and half-empty cup. She knew he was watching her, his face on fire that his nightworld and dayworld were here in the same place at the same time. It was as if she were electrified, could walk over there, put her hand on his shoulder, and make his heart stop. It was a power she did not want. A fame she'd like to shed.

Out in the bright parking lot, she pushed her cart over the asphalt past all the glaring cars. She hoped she'd be able to get the furniture in her trunk, that whatever she bought would be small enough to fit into the only space she had.

ARIQ'S SHOES ARE no longer near the entrance. The room is darkened and quiet, the television off, and Bassam can hear them through the wall. Their voices are low. They are preparing for prayer. He places his notebook upon his bed and leaves quickly, allowing the door to close and lock behind him. He will perform his ablutions in Imad's room, and he knocks upon the door. "Imad? Tariq?"

Imad greets him. His face is damp. He smiles downward at him and steps to the side, and as Bassam removes his shoes, he hears the voice of the Egyptian, he hears Amir.

"Mansoor?"

It has only been ten days but the Egyptian has changed; his face is shaved as usual and there are the dark lines he applies beneath his eyes, but he appears thinner, his skin olive-yellow, his eyes darker, and he smiles at him and approaches and grasps his hand and kisses both his cheeks. "Assalaamu 'alaykum."

"Wa 'alaykum assalaam."

Amir keeps his hand on Bassam's shoulder, regards Tariq standing near the bed, Imad. "Everyone is here now. And the rest are where they should be. Have you been fasting?" He asks this in a way Bassam has never heard before, not as a commander, forever monitoring him, doubting him, but as gently as would a friend.

"Yes," says Imad. And so Bassam does not have to say no, he has not been fasting.

"Good." Amir steps to the bed and opens a leather briefcase. It has brass fasteners and they snap open on the springs and he lifts the case's cover and removes three sealed envelopes. Bassam thinks how he must mail his letter to his mother. He must mail it.

"Brothers," Amir hands one to each of them. There is no writing on its face, nor on its back. "Tomorrow, Insha'Allah, is the last day, and you will open these. Read these instructions carefully and follow them." He looks to each of them. The light of the lamp is in his eyes, and Bassam can smell his cologne, the same as before and now even stronger, but this is not the Egyptian with whom he has lived and traveled these months. Forever watching over each detail of each movement, of each plan, of each place they have lived. Forever watching *them*. This is the Egyptian Bassam saw for only one moment when he pulled the Cessna's stick and they rose so steeply into the sky, *Allah is great, Allah is great*, his face so expectant of the joy to come, his reward everlasting.

"We are just moments away, brothers, Allah willing. But you must be vigilant and you must help one another and be strong. After tomorrow's morning prayer, read these and follow them. I will see you the next morning in the matar, Insha'Allah. Now hurry, finish your ablutions and we will pray together. Then I must leave."

They have pushed the second bed aside and there is room for two rows of two, Tariq and the Egyptian Amir, then Imad and Bassam. Imad has lighted the incense, and how fitting that the direction in which they pray has the television at their backs, Makkah so far away but not far away, simply through the walls of this hotel and over the square of the best school and its high walls that cannot protect them, over the loud and dirty streets of the kufar, through their homes of false idols and over the sea on which sail tankers of Saudi oil, over the shores of England and France and Germany, over the heads of their women who laugh and smoke and drink and tempt believers away from where he travels now, through Spain and Italy and Greece, its wine-drinking kufar, its women naked on beaches he turns away from, through the Balkans where thousands of Muslims were massacred and the West watched, then over the Mediterranean he has never seen and blood-soaked Palestine the Zionists occupy, his brothers and sisters living in camps since they were born, the holy city occupied by Christians and Jews, their polytheistic temples and churches, their worship of Ezra and the Messiah as if there is not One Lord, then south through Egypt and Sudan and across the Red Sea to the beaches of the kingdom where as a boy he played and swam with his older brothers, his mother and aunts and sisters in full abayas on blankets beneath umbrellas, and years later he and Khalid and Karim would drive there in their auto built by the far enemy and laugh and make silly jokes about nothing, even later sitting so closely together on a mirkaz in one of the restaurants on the water, eating fried fish and yogurt, again talking about nothing because they were nothing, because they were adrift on the sea of unbelief and none of them had even begun to prepare for the hajj, nor would they now, though the shahid is exempt, the shahid is exempt, and Bassam is nearly there, passing the two hills of Safa and Marwa and the eternal springs found by the faith of Abraham's wife to the Al-Haram Mosque and its stone Ka'bah built by the hands of Abraham and his son and how can Ahmed al-Jizani not be proud? How will he not be so very proud?

But Bassam's mind is wandering and he must not allow it. They have already performed two raka'ats, and he knows he recited the prayers and words of praise with the others though time has left him, he has stepped into non-time, and how can this not be a sign from the Holy One Himself? This feeling he is nearly a spirit, he is already nearly a spirit in this world of flesh and a constant love of it. How happy he will be to rid himself of it. How joyous!

Now they are sitting, Imad's shoulder touching his. His hip and his knee. He and Imad with their very important task. Amir and Tariq with theirs. His heart thrusts inside him. The camel races in the Empty Quarter, how the sand rose and blew over the tourists. He must forget this. He must let go of all thoughts of home for he will soon rise toward the only certain home there is. He is behind in reciting with his brothers the tashahud, and he begins it quickly to himself, then joins them.

Amir is gone. The room is quiet. Imad places his envelope on the lamp table. He sits upon the bed.

"You both should be fasting."

Tariq holds the envelope to the light, his eyes becoming narrow.

"Yes," Bassam says. "You are right." And there is no bad feeling as before, no feeling that Imad is stronger than he and more disciplined and more prepared, that he is more deserving of this honor given to each of them. He looks at Imad sitting upon the bed in his polo shirt. Its back is wrinkled from his rest and his arms are thickened from exercise. And Tariq, look at him attempting to read the letter through the envelope, forever restless, a man Bassam has known since they were boys and they kicked the ball back and forth to each other in the dusty street, how Tariq would always keep it in the air before him, never letting it touch the ground.

"Brothers." The room becomes blurred. There is only the light from the lamp and the shadows of his friends. "I have such a love for you. I have such a love."

﹀ ﹀ ﹀

APRIL STOOD IN Franny's doorway and tried to see her room as the inspectors would; the rug was vacuumed and the bed was made with the new bedspread. Behind the closed doors of the closet her dresses hung on hangers, her other clothes put away in the bureau April had dusted. The chest was bigger than she thought. It was painted yellow with white daisies, and in the store, among trunks of dark walnut and polished maple, it had looked like a cheerful child stuck in a roomful of adults and April couldn't help but think of Franny. She set it at the foot of the bed and filled it with all of her toys. Even the new bucket, shovel, and goggles fit. She placed the Barbie dollhouse on top, the pink clashing with the yellow, but it all looked less perfect that way so she left it.

The beanbag chair was more of a problem. It fit just under the window, but it was shapeless and too big and its faux-leather cover gave off a new-chemical smell. She was still sweating from carrying it and the trunk up the stairs. Jean had come out of her house in her loose sundress, her hair matted on one side, her eyes puffy from sleep.

"April, let me help you."

"I've got it, thanks." April had hugged the trunk to her chest. Every few steps she rested the bottom on a stair and it would have been easier with Jean but the poor woman breathed hard just uncoiling the garden hose. It was nice of her to ask, though.

Last night, when she and Jean were eating dinner together in Jean's kitchen, rain falling against the window panes, April had felt cared for. Jean drank wine and April had water and it was almost like being with Stephanie again. They didn't talk much but it wasn't uncomfortable. And now April would rather stay in and eat with Jean again, make her something this time.

Franny's room had never looked this good. Why did it take this for April to finally throw away the cardboard box she'd been using for Franny's toys? The same one she'd bought for their move down here? Why this to get her to buy something to sit in and a nicer bedspread? To clean and organize her daughter's room better than ever before?

She could ask the same thing about this whole place, though. The furniture was Jean's—the gilded mirror hanging in the living room, the lamps and stools, the bed and bedside tables in April's room; it wasn't *April's* home in the first place. Just an in-between for where she'd been and where she was going. Franny's real room was downstairs. The one she slept in four to five nights a week, the one she got tucked into.

Every night that week after Jean had finished it, April had walked into Jean's house three hours before sunrise and crept to Franny. She pulled back the perfect comforter and lifted her daughter up and carried her out the door up the stairs to her room. With one hand April had pushed away clothes and toys and a tablet and crayons and laid Franny onto her bed. And so what if she woke and started to cry? So what if April had to lie down with her awhile under the sheet and hold her till she slept again?

Then Franny woke her three hours later ready to play, dress, and eat, and April had gotten up. She made coffee and poured Franny some cereal. She tried to be cheerful and listen to Franny talk about Dipsy and the boat she dreamed about or her list of favorite colors starting with yellow. But after only a half hour or more April would have to put in a Disney movie and lie down on the couch and wake up minutes later, it seemed, to the blank screen and Franny poking her arm with her finger. "Mama, can I go play with Jean now? Mama?"

So why not leave her to sleep there anyway? Let her be loved by a woman with nobody while April got some rest and Franny was happy?

A knock at the door, Lonnie standing there smiling on the other side of the glass.

For Maghrib they prayed separately, and now Imad is in one of the restaurants breaking his fast and Bassam has started his. He has purposely missed the night meal and will eat, Allah willing, tomorrow morning after Fajr. The entire last day he will fast, and after nightfall he will take only enough nourishment to reserve his strength for the morning after, which, Insha'Allah, will begin with a final meal.

Lying upon his bed, there is again a thrusting of his heart at the thinking of this, the final meal of Bassam al-Jizani. But it is not fear. Or, it is not entirely fear. It is readiness. It is the engine that must be in a condition to take him where he must go, for there is a calmness; the awareness of his fate approaching has lifted him away from noise and loud movement and trouble and worry. It is not unlike gazing into a fire, how everything falls away, how you stop thinking of all that has been done and must be done and should have been done differently by everyone, especially yourself.

There is the calm, and there is the clarity. How clear everything is: the ceiling above him, the round cast of light upon it from the lamp, its rough surface applied there by workers lost in their unbelief; the wooden cabinet built by more kufar, the polished scratches along its front and sides, the television it holds, surely an invention of Shaytan himself, for look at how Tariq stands there with the remote control device pushing the button so quickly, the screen a jumble of color moving pictures celebrating nothingness. And still, still Bassam would not stop him if he were to press the Adult button once more. Is this not so, Bassam? For even in the strength from prayer, your weakness remains. It is there in your desire for Tariq to press the button.

Tariq, his restlessness will not distract him. He has always been this way. He has never needed purity to perform his task. Khalid was the fastest, but after his death, it was Tariq, restless, distracted, always smoking.

"Bassam?"

"Mansoor."

"Mansoor?"

"Yes?"

"I'm going to buy a woman."

"What?"

"I'm going to buy a woman."

"When?"

"Now. Tonight. Tomorrow I will fast with you and Imad, Insha'Allah."

Bassam's heart beats more strongly. He wishes for Tariq to be lying. And he wishes for him to be speaking the truth. "Imad will not like it."

"I do not care, Bassam. I have already called this escort service. It was easy. She will be here very soon, Allah willing. Do you want to share her?"

"No."

"This is your last opportunity, Bassam. Aren't you curious? Don't you want to know what it's like?"

"I will find out in Jannah, Insha'Allah."

"But take this bounty from the kufar, Bassam. It is something the Holy One would not deny us. He deemed me to find the telephone number from the book."

"Or it was Shaytan, Tariq."

"No, Bassam. We have left our homes, our families, everything behind for the Creator. He wishes for the shahid to take a bounty."

"Take it then."

"Yes." Tariq closes the television cabinet. "But where will you go?"

"Out. I will go out."

Tariq nods his head and moves to the bathroom. He makes no supplications for entering the toilet, and Bassam can hear the slap of cologne, can smell it.

A woman. Here. A kafir who will do it for money. April who danced as Spring, how she pulled back so quickly when he touched her above her qus. And it's true, he would like to sit with her once more. Not in that rented box in that evil place, but here in his room in this last hotel in this northern city.

A knocking. Bassam begins to stand, his heart thrusting. Imad? No, beyond the corner of the wall, Tariq's voice. His clumsy English. And now a woman's voice. Look at how she walks into the room. She could be one of the white students from the best school. In the bathroom's light her hair is long and shining, brown and blonde at once, her eyes green, her legs uncovered from her short dress to her high heels.

"I thought it was just one, sweetheart."

"He is leaving."

"Really? I can do both of you for two-fifty." She smiles directly at Bassam. It is playful, even respectful. She is like Kelly the trainer, and he says nothing and he does not move.

"Bassam?" Tariq says in their language. "Stay. She likes you. Stay."

He smiles at the kafir woman. "Please, wine? Whiskey? We have minibar."

"First you have to pay me, sweetie. If it's just you, he has to leave."

Leave. *Leave*, Bassam. *Go*.

She holds a leather night bag over her shoulder. In its side pocket a silver cell phone shines. She still smiles, looking to each of them, but the playfulness has been blown from her by the cool wind of business. It is difficult not to look at her nuhood behind her blouse, at her hips and uncovered legs.

Bassam hears his voice say, "Two-fifty is too much."

"One of you is one-fifty. I think that's a good deal."

"Two hundred." Bassam's breath is high in his chest, his legs have become thin reeds.

"Two-twenty."

"Okay," Tariq says. "That is good. That is good. Please, for sitting down." He moves to the lamp table between their beds. His sealed envelope lies beside the Book beside his clip of money, a brass clip he purchased in Dubai, and he pulls free the bills and pushes them into the whore's hand. She licks her finger and counts it quickly and efficiently. She smiles once more and pushes the money into her purse and how easy it would be to kill her now. Does she not know this? Does she not think of this? And the calmness and the clarity, where did it go? What is this shattered glass inside him?

Tariq is pouring wine from a small bottle from the mini-fridge. She unbuttons her buttons, and removes her shoes. How different it is to watch her do this when Bassam has not been drinking. How like a boy he feels. How dry is his mouth as she lets drop her shirt and brassiere. How damp are his hands and forehead as she unwraps her short dress and lays it over her purse and cell phone and money. She is completely uncovered except for her undergarment which is black and covers her backside. She walks slowly to the glass Tariq has filled. And restless, distracted Tariq, unbuttoning his shirt so quickly.

She drinks. Bassam can only look at her nuhood, small, smaller than those of April. Tariq is unclothed, lying there upon his bed. Bassam cannot look at him. She smiles into his face. She smiles and lowers her wine and walks to him. She views Tariq. "You don't need any encouragement, do you? Put on some music, sweetie."

But she says this as one moving sentence, and Tariq's English, he does not understand and does not move. In their language, Bassam says to him, "Music, Tariq. She would like music." And he would as well. And for the lamp to be off. For the room to be lost in shadows and noise, like the club for men in Florida.

"Where are you from? Is that Arabic?"

"No." An intelligent whore. An educated whore. Music enters the room from the radio. It is not loud but still too loud. It is music he knows and it enters him as she touches his chest and begins to unbutton his shirt. It is the music of Khalid, David Lee Roth, this music for racing on the Road of Death, his loud screaming, his hat for cowboys, how Khalid loved it, and Bassam is hard and above the smell of Tariq's cologne is her smell, cigarette smoke and mint, woman's perfume and cosmetics. She smiles and looks him directly in his eyes. Her skin is smooth. She has more years than he and now her hand rubs him over his pants. On the bed behind her Tariq waits, his own hardness a thing Bassam sees and does not wish to see, and the electric guitar of David Lee Roth pierces him like a sword, the drums kick at him. No being has ever touched him where she touches now and he sees his body gone, evaporated. He will be given a new body. One untouched. And Khalid was never given this opportunity.

Khalid.

She frees him from his pants. She stands and pushes down her black undergarment. Bassam is ashamed of his hardness exposed for Tariq to see, and he covers himself but Tariq watches only the young kafir woman. Her hair above her qus is like the black whore's, a thin shaved line. And she turns and lifts her clothing and reaches into her purse. Her naked rear is exposed to them.

"Bassam," Tariq says in their language, "do you want to go first? You are older, you should go first."

"It's rude to tell secrets, boys. English, please." She tosses to Tariq a small square package and she opens hers and kneels before Bassam. "Take off your clothes, honey. Come on, I won't bite." She pulls down his pants and he lifts one leg, then the next. How weak he is. How so very weak. Thirty or thirty-one years, this is what she has, and the skin of her back is smooth and Bassam touches it with fingers that shake. She rolls the rubber skin over his hardness, her face only centimeters from it. His legs are trembling.

"Go on, Bassam," Tariq says. "I wait."

"What'd he say, sweetie? Huh? You want to tell me? Do you?" She leaves the socks upon his feet, rises and pushes his shirt past his shoulders, Bassam's throat and face burning. *This is too much. This—* "Tariq, please. Close the lamp. And the *Book*, remove it." Now the music is finished and a man speaks loudly, selling a product, Ford trucks. The room darkens and Tariq carries the Book to the closet, making a supplication before closing the door. She pushes against Bassam's chest, makes him lie down upon his bed. And she is a professional, such a professional. Where did she acquire the small bottle she opens now, pouring the liquid onto her hand, rubbing it along his hardness? Then she touches herself with it, wipes her hand on the bedcover, and more music begins, the kicking drums, the piercing guitar, the singer's voice forcing its way out of the radio and over their sealed envelopes into Bassam's head to where he has disappeared. He makes the du'a to be said before lying with a woman, one he has never made: *In the name of Allah. O Allah, keep Shaytan away from us and keep Shaytan away from what you have blessed us with.*

How soon and how fast he is inside her. Completely inside her. She begins to rise up and down and she calls to Tariq, calls him to her. Bassam closes his eyes. He holds her hips, feels the skin and beneath it her muscle and beneath that, her bones. How long will she possess this? How many years will she be given by the Creator before she will burn? For now a sadness opens itself inside him, a cool darkness where lies so much: his father and his brother, his mother's cries, her cries for Khalid and the cries he knows she will have for *him*, Allah willing. Allah willing. These ripples of heat pricking across his skin, this fire lit and now burning. Her fire pushing onto his, his into hers. "That's it, sweetie. That's it. Come here. C'mon."

There is Tariq's leg touching his own. The woman makes sucking sounds and Bassam opens his eyes and look how in the near darkness she does as did the pale whore. He closes his eyes, the sadness receeding for there is only her fire pushing onto his, his pushing so deeply into hers, and Bassam sees the black whore, her qus, feels her now on top of him as he goes as deeply into her as this. Then she is Kelly the trainer, her fingers touching him as he exercised. And now she is April, her baby's scar, her larger nuhood and long dark hair, her eyes like those of a girl from home, the flames inside him rising higher, higher. He could have had a good girl from a good family that in another's fate he would have married, the Shawfa and Milka and Shabka, the Haflat al-Henna, his bride's hands and feet decorated with henna, the flames rising and rising, the wedding celebrations he would have had, the dowry he could never have afforded himself, never, not as Bassam al-Jizani, a poor stock boy with only his father's name he would never equal, except now, except now, bringing it lasting respect, not empty status, not envy, his flames now the whore's flames, all of his thoughts and deeds descending, then gathering, then rising so hotly up and into the woman's fire, a sound escaping him, a sound he has never before made and it shames him, his seed not in the whore but gathered in the reservoir of rubber, and the radio is too loud, a kafir woman singing, and this woman keeps moving for she does not know.

He opens his eyes. The bathroom's light is behind her. Her face is difficult to see as she continues sucking. Tariq, his head back.

"Get off. Please, get off."

She stops. "Already, sweetie? Already?" She lifts herself from him and releases Tariq and lies upon his bed and opens her legs and Bassam rushes into the harsh light of the bathroom. *O Allah, I take refuge with You from all evil and evildoers.* He pushes closed the door. He locks it. His reflection there in the glass, he cannot look. He is sweating and his legs are weak and he pulls the reservoir from him and wraps it in tissue from the toilet and pushes it into the container for trash. He hears the bumping of Tariq's bed against the wall, the kufar music from the radio, the whore's cries of pleasure. And do not lie to yourself, Bassam. You would like to watch her do this. You would like to open the door and see more, to feel more. You would like to rest and do it with her again. The way Tariq does it now, on top. Your body has been dirtied, but it is a cooling fire and already you wish to burn again. For listen to her, her cries come from Shaytan himself, his dark joy at weakening you. Seducing you with the life of this world when less than one hour before you were in a state of purity, a state befitting a shahid. Could Shaytan be more joyous at this moment?

But no, Bassam, calm yourself. Calm yourself. We have only taken a bounty from the al-Adou al-Baeed; the Book, it is written clearly— *women are your fields.* This whore is simply the shadow of a taste of what is to come, Insha'Allah, as the women of Jannah will lie with them on soft couches in lush gardens watered by running streams. And there will be no kufar music playing, no whores, no money, but Bassam's eternal flesh inside their eternal flesh. Allah willing, forever.

The bumping has stopped. Tariq speaks. The music has once again become men selling products. As he and Tariq have just been sold this one. That is all she has been, Bassam. A drink of vodka or beer when you were living among them, or a health shake Imad buys at these gyms after exercising.

The radio becomes silent. Bassam presses his ear to the door. The whore's voice is close by, and he can hear her dressing. He hears the zipper. But he does not wish to hear any more, nor can he see her. She has made him do this, and if it would not harm their plans he would take his razor knife and push her to the floor and cover her mouth and cut her throat, let her bleed her dirty blood onto the carpet, let her body lie there while he and Tariq sleep comfortably on their beds whose sheets would have to be changed because of her and what she made them do.

Again she laughs, says, "Your friend."

He pushes aside the shower's curtain. He turns on the water as nearly hot as it allows. Is she *laughing* at him? Does she think he is a *boy*? He steps inside and pulls closed the curtain. She must leave their room. She must be gone when he is through, but if she is not, it will be difficult to control himself. It will be difficult, and he is grateful for the cleansing water, for the hot rain that extinguishes fires and leaves only ash, wet and black.

∨ ∨ ∨

UNDER THE FLUORESCENT light of Publix, April pushed her cart. Inside it was romaine lettuce and vine-grown tomatoes, bags of pears, apples, and a slim crate of clementines. There were carrots and a box of raisins and a package of almonds. There was sliced cheddar cheese and smoked turkey and ham and Ritz crackers. She was buying what she and Franny always bought, nothing to hide here, nothing to change.

She hadn't wanted to go out and told him so, told him she hadn't showered yet and still had to buy groceries, that she didn't know what time these people would be here in the morning and this just isn't a good time, Lonnie.

"You have to eat, don't you?" He stood there in an ironed short-sleeved shirt the color of bananas, his damp hair combed back from his face. He was looking right at her with the steady warmth he'd always given her at the club. Just a friendly face.

It was a marina restaurant on Sarasota Bay, one of the places April had applied to with Franny, and as soon as they walked in April wanted to leave. She followed the hostess, who led them through the air-conditioned cool, the linen-covered tables only half-full, out to the patio bar and the table Lonnie had reserved.

But the patio was nice. There were small tables under the last of the sun, most of them full, a woman singing on a platform just under the thatched roof of the tiki bar. She had long dark hair and wore white and she was singing something in Spanish, a keyboard player keeping time beside her. April sat down and looked at the piers of white boats, the sun shining off Sarasota Bay. She closed her eyes, saw Franny holding her arms out to her in Tina's office.

She stood.

"You okay?"

"I'm sorry, Lonnie. I have to go."

In the health food section, she opened a protein bar, cookies and cream, and ate it slowly. It's what she and Franny did. She grabbed a peanut butter chocolate for her and dropped it into the cart.

Lonnie had driven her home quietly, as if he were deeply ashamed of himself. She didn't mean to embarrass him, but to care right now about how he felt was beside the point. Back in front of the house he'd gotten out fast to come around and open her door. She was going to have to deal with him soon, wasn't she?

Before leaving for here, she knocked on Jean's door and asked if she needed anything, had she eaten? She said she hadn't, but she wasn't feeling too well, and behind her on the counter was a mug, her cat licking a tea bag on a spoon.

April put the protein wrapper on the clementines where she would see it and not forget to have the girl ring it through. It's how she and Franny did it. How they always did it.

In the dairy aisle, April opened a pint of milk and drank. It was cold and cow-sweet. This too would be rung up empty, then thrown away, the cashier dropping it into the wastebasket under the register, the virtuous feeling this gave April every time, that she was a good citizen, an honest person who worked hard and did the right thing without ever being told to, her daughter happy and well-fed and cared for. So why now, standing before the bright shelves of milk and cheese and yogurt and butter, did she feel like a liar, one about to be found out and then punished?

THE BEDSIDE LAMP burns once more and Tariq is dressed and sits beside the window he has opened, his feet resting upon a chair. He is smoking, blowing it into the darkness. The room is cool and there are the smells of the smoke and the whore's perfume. On the desk is the glass of wine she did not drink and Bassam, his towel wrapped tightly about his waist, thinks of Imad seeing it and he takes the glass and pours it into the toilet, the red swirling in water.

He rinses it and carries it back to the minibar cabinet.

"Bassam, did you like it?"

"No."

"No?"

"She is a whore, Tariq. A kafir whore. She is fortunate I did not kill her afterward."

Tariq smiles. Look at him sitting there with no modesty like a kafir:

his feet with no socks, smoking his cigarette. No longer distracted, no longer restless.

"What is funny, Tariq? Do you think I am joking? I will go find her and kill her now, Allah willing. I will do it."

"Bassam, you liked it. I know you liked it."

"My body liked it, Tariq. I did not."

Bassam grasps his khaki pants and makes the du'a for dressing. *All praise is for Allah who has clothed me with this garment and provided it for me, with no power nor might from myself.* He secures the button of his pants. He pulls over his head the polo shirt from the drugstore in Del Ray Beach. He picks up from the floor his soiled clothing and carries them to the closet and shuts them inside.

"Think how much better will be Jannah, Bassam. Insha'Allah. Just *think* of it." Tariq pushes his cigarette into the small wine bottle, the smoke rising.

"Do not be proud, Tariq. We must be vigilant now."

"I am not proud, Bassam. I am prepared, that is all. I am ready." And he rises and passes Bassam, touching him lightly upon the shoulder.

I am ready. How *different* they are. Tariq has lain with a whore and now he is ready to leave this world. But why did you lie with her as well, Bassam? How could you have felt so stongly in the presence of the Holy One in one moment and then succumbed to the worst of this life in the next?

The door closes, the shower runs, and Bassam knows he has lied to him. He would not kill the whore, he would not. What he wants with her is more time. What he wants with her is more and more of what she sold to him, for it was over so quickly. And there are so many ways of doing it, are there not?

He looks at their remaining money beside the beds, and Al-Khaliq help him, for he wishes to count it, to see if there is enough to buy her once more. Or to buy another one. One even prettier. But he will not be able to bring her here. Imad will return soon, Insha'Allah. Allah willing. Allah willing. What is he thinking?

He looks downward at his mattress. Its cover is wrinkled slightly but that is all. There is no other sign of what happened here. No sign of his seed being wasted. So why does he wish to waste it again and again? For a *feeling*? A simple physical sensation? Or is his soul as tied to the earth and all its pleasures as strongly as a kafir's?

Cliff, at the convenience station, over sixty years and he has bleached hair and smokes the entire day and wears gold around his throat and wrists, the inked markings there of women and their hips and naked nuhood, the cross of Mary's son, the names of kufar women he has lain with, one of them burned away by a lighted cigarette. Cliff, who called him Sammy. Cliff, who has certainly lain with many, many women in this world. His face and body an ugly map of his lostness, his nothingness, his unbelief.

What, Bassam? Do you want to stay here, is that it? Do you wish to smoke and drink and lie with whores and non-whores like the tall girl who smiled at you today? The girl who certainly at this moment is taking her boy inside her, pulling his precious seed from him? His strength? For that is what they do, do they not? These kufar women? Even the kind ones like Gloria, like Kelly, especially the kind ones— they take from you your power, your physical strength, yes, but also your ability to think clearly, to receive the Word of the Creator, to see and accept His signs.

Bassam grasps the bed's cover and rips it from the mattress. He throws it into the corner. He sits. On the table, the sealed envelope from their commander. To all of them. Here, and across the river, and in the two cities to the south. Look how many thousands of kilometers from home they have come. Look at all the work and preparation, the training and practice, the fasting and prayer. Do you think this is wasted, Bassam? Do you think one brief thrusting into one kafir whore will waste this? Are you not ready to do what must be done? Are you not?

He pulls open the bedside drawer. He removes his razor knife. It is gray and metal and always he has liked the weight of it in his hand. But he has not always liked what they have planned to do with these, has he? A kafir businessman, yes. But a woman? A friendly woman—he has been *blind*. For look at how weak he is now. Look at what the white whore and Shaytan have done to him.

He pushes the button, the blade revealing itself. It is silver and very short and shines in the light from the lamp. It is so sharp it cuts paper and it will cut flesh easily, Insha'Allah, it will cut through it very fast, and after all is done, Allah willing, from the highest rooms he will witness what happens to these jinn on the Last Day. He will watch them beg for their souls. He will watch them kneel before the Judge and the Ruler and tear at their faces and prostrate themselves and beg and beg, but for them only will be the everlasting fire and what joy Bassam will feel, Allah willing, as he watches these whores fall from the bridge into the flames. As he watches them fall.

He retracts the blade, drops it onto the holy book of the kufar, and he pushes shut the drawer.

¥ ¥ ¥

S HE HAD TO talk to him through a video screen. Her own son. She had to sit in a chair in front of a TV with him looking back at her in his jail clothes and talk to him on a telephone in the narrow, loud hallway where many others sat in front of similar television screens talking to their loved ones too.

She'd never seen him look so bad. Even when he had to come live with her away from his family, even then. It was his eyes. The will she'd seen in them his entire life. That undying determination to get done what had to get done, to get through what had to be gotten through. It was there in his low-slung eyes when he was little and pushed one toy into another, when he was bigger and walked off to the school he hated, when his voice was changing and he closed his bedroom door to her and whatever man she was giving herself to, when he was grown and carried all of Eddie's tools onto the sunporch each evening and then back out every morning, when he married that

Deena—even then, standing before the justice of the peace in the county courthouse with only her mother and father and Virginia as witnesses, Alan in a jacket and tie she'd bought him, his pregnant bride in a plain cotton dress, he had that look, that this was another thing to take on and he was going to take it on and get *through* it.

But looking at him this afternoon on the television monitor looking back at her, she saw him in a way she never had. His shoulders were slumped and he kept looking away from the camera like he wasn't sure where he was or what he was supposed to do now or if she was even there on the other side.

He'd taken a long breath and let it out. *I was trying to do something good, Mama. I was trying not to think of my*self.

You never do, honey. You never did.

On the drive home she began to cry for him, this boy she'd raised to take on everything so *alone*. Why couldn't he have just called the police? Why couldn't he have asked *her* for help?

But why would he? Lord, why would he? When she thought of their past together, so much of it was with AJ as a tag-along—to her work, to the barroom or pool hall with whomever she was with, as a young third-wheel she'd put in front of the TV while she carried on with Eddie or the men before him in the kitchen or the bedroom.

Then Eddie gone and his vodka too. How quiet the house got, AJ working nights at the drugstore in the clothes she ironed for him. She'd smoke and flip through the channels, not really watching, just waiting, it seemed. But for what? Weeks and months of this, and she was smoking so much she couldn't breathe. Had to get that tank. And then that woman on TV, that pretty woman Virginia's age talking about her assault, about two men who'd bound and gagged and "violated" her for a day and a half. Virginia doesn't remember how she escaped or what happened to the men, only that the woman went on to describe years of drinking and promiscuity. "You'd think I wouldn't want any man to touch me. But I was trying to fill an emptiness only the Lord can fill. Only Him."

Virginia began to weep.

The following Sunday she walked into a Catholic church. Seated in half the pews were well-dressed families: husbands and wives and kids. The walls seemed to be made of dark wood and stained glass, and suspended high above the altar was Jesus on the cross. The priest was young, his dark hair combed back from his face. He was handsome and spoke of the evil among and within us, and it was like putting words to the name of something you'd seen or used for years but had never known. There was the feeling she was being gently lifted and placed on the right path, one she could only stay on by letting go of the wheel.

You need to sell my truck, Mama.

But she wouldn't. She had two CDs worth plenty and tomorrow she'd cash them in and hire a lawyer.

And she'd get him out of there. With God as her witness, she would do whatever she had to for her son. For her one and only son.

MONDAY

THE ROOM IS darkness. Bassam touches his chest. He touches his face. He turns upon his side and pulls up his knees, his legs whole, his arms—still here.

The shower runs. Tariq's bed is empty, and the red light of the clock radio casts dimly: 5:03. Your last full day, Bassam. Allah willing, your last full day. He makes his supplication for waking: *All praise is for Allah who gave us life after having taken it from us and unto Him is the Resurrection.*

Bassam pulls the covering away. He sits and turns on the lamp and his eyes narrow at the light. He closes them and prays the morning supplication: *We have reached the morning and at this very time all sovereignty belongs to Allah, Lord of the world. O Allah, I ask You for the good of this day, its triumphs and guidance, and I take refuge in You from the evil of this day and the evil that follows it.*

Water runs in the pipes in the walls. The brass clip is empty, their remaining money lying upon the two sealed envelopes. Bassam lifts his and rips it open, his fingers shaking as they did with the whore he fears now has ruined him.

It is several pages photocopied, and it is both a comfort and an admonition seeing his written language from home.

The Last Night

1. *Make an oath to die and Renew your intentions.* Bassam rubs his eyes. He sits more erectly. *Shave excess hair from the body and wear cologne. Shower.*

2. *Make sure you know all aspects of the plan well, and expect the response, or a reaction, from the enemy.* Bassam's heart begins to beat more quickly. He breathes deeply through the nose and he wipes more sleep from his eyes.

3. *Read Al-Tawbah and Anfal and reflect on their meanings and remember all of the things that Allah has promised for the martyrs.* Yes, yes.

4. *Remind your soul to listen and obey all divine orders and remember that you will face decisive situations that might prevent you from 100 percent obedience, so tame your soul, purify it, convince it, make it understand, and incite it. Allah said: "Obey Allah and His messenger, and do not fight amongst yourselves or else you will fail—"*

Imad last evening, his shouts, his anger at the smell of perfume, Tariq proud and with no fear shouting back at him as if Imad were Karim, lost and with no knowledge of the Truth. "It was a *bounty* and nothing else, Imad! Leave me alone. Only Al-Khaliq is my Judge!"

"Tariq, is *this* how you prepare? Is it? And Bassam, you as well? *You?!*"

Bassam could not answer and there was the slamming of their door, the slamming of Imad's. Tariq laughed.

"Be quiet, Tariq. Say nothing, please. Nothing."

—and be patient, for Allah is with the patient.

Their fighting, their smoking, their purchasing a woman who

could well have been police, how easily they could have been stopped, detained, *exposed*. And Bassam feels as if he is a small child entrusted with something precious to which he has no right.

The water stops in the pipes. But this letter, written to him by whom? One of their commanders, perhaps even Abu Abdullah himself, may Allah bless him. Bassam imagines him sitting in the central tent, writing it to them so far away. This holy man. This holy warrior whose words Bassam continues to read slowly and with great care.

Purify your soul from all unclean things. Completely forget something called "this world" or "this life." The time for play is over and the serious time is upon us.

The words become difficult to see; Bassam's eyes burn and he wipes at them.

The time for play is over.

All is known, all is forgiven.

That is what his sheikh is telling him. He knows where he has sent them to live. He knows what they have faced here. And so wisely he has given them these instructions with only one day remaining, so there will be no further time to waste, no further time to be led astray. Abu Abdullah's eyes. His *belief* in them! His *love* for them!

How much time have we wasted in our lives? Shouldn't we take advantage of these last hours to offer good deeds and obedience?

Yes, yes. Bassam sits back in his bed. He covers his bare legs.

Keep in mind that, if you fall into hardship, how will you act and how will you remain steadfast and remember that you will return to Allah and remember that anything that happens to you could never be avoided, and what did not happen to you could never have happened to you. This test from Almighty Allah is to raise your level and erase your sins.

Erase your sins. He has *not* lost his place in Jannah, he and Tariq and Imad chosen through Abu Abdullah by the Creator Himself. Have you forgotten this, Bassam? Have you forgotten everything ever taught to you by good and holy men? He must simply perform his task and, Insha'Allah, all is guaranteed. He must pray for this. He must pray.

The bath door opens. There is steam and the smell of soap and from it Tariq appears. He is fully dressed, his polo shirt tucked tightly into his pants.

"Tariq. You must read this. You must read it, and no more fighting, brother. No more arguing. You must read this, and then we pray Fajr with Imad."

Imad answers the door. His room smells of incense.

"Sa'bah al-khair, Imad."

"Sa'bah al-khair."

"Imad, let us say Fajr together."

"I have, Bassam. It is nearly sunrise."

"Have you read the letter?"

"Yes. Have you?"

"Nearly half, yes."

Imad regards him. Tall, large Imad. His shaven face. His deep eyes which no longer hold anger but something else. The eyes of Karim when he first felt the change, standing in the street in his kufar clothing, looking from Imad to Tariq to Bassam, their thin, pure bodies, their full beards—his eyes like Imad's now, saddened at this new distance between them. To these eyes, Bassam says: "The time for play is over, Imad. I know this, brother. Tariq knows this as well."

Hot tea and sugar and a baked good with berries and nuts. Bassam ate this just before the sky lightened outside the hotel window and the sun made the brick buildings a reddish brown, the color of the dust he would sweep from the shop of Ali al-Fahd. That other life. It is like one he heard in a story, a boy with no future in this world or the next. *You should feel complete tranquillity, because the time between you and your marriage in heaven is very short. Afterward begins the happy life.* Together he and Tariq had prayed. Now Tariq reads the letter in the chair near the window, his lips moving, his tea steaming. Bassam sits on the bed. The kafir girl who brought their food was young. She wore the hotel uniform of black pants and white shirt, and as Bassam signed for their meal, she spoke of the weather, the beautiful day.

"Yes," he had said, "it *is* beautiful." And he smiled at this kafir who did not even know she was in the presence of two who would be in Jannah, Allah willing, in less than thirty hours.

Yes, it *is* beautiful.

And Tariq said to her thank you as well in his poor English and he stared at her backside as she left. But Bassam did not. He did not. Today is the last full day and it will be, Insha'Allah, a day of prayer and fasting. He does not even wish to leave this room, but he must if his mother is to receive his letter. And was it enough? Is there anything more he should say?

No. Let his fate say everything. Let what he has done, Insha'Allah, be delivered to them as the good news that it is.

"Tariq?"

He holds the pages closely to his face.

"Tariq, is it about the Last Night?"

"Yes." Tariq's voice is as before racing, as before the whore.

"Are you well?"

"I wish we were going now, Bassam. I cannot wait one more day."

"Yes, but you must. Read the words of the Creator: 'And be patient, for Allah is with the patient.'"

"But, Bassam?"

"Yes?"

"Are we strong enough?"

"For patience?"

"No, for what we must do. What if they are stronger?"

"Allah willing, they will not be, Tariq. They do not have belief in the Holy One so they will fail. Read number 10." Bassam unfolds his letter, his eyes reading from right to left, the ancient way, the only way. "Remember the words of Almighty Allah: 'You were looking to the battle before you engaged in it, and now you see it with your own two eyes.' Remember: 'How many small groups beat big groups by the will of Allah.' And his words: 'If Allah gives you victory, no one can beat you. And if He betrays you, who can give you victory without Him? So the faithful put their trust in Allah.

Do you, Tariq, put your trust in Al-Qudoos?"

"Yes."

"Then, Allah willing, we will have victory. It is not for you to fear or not to fear. It is out of your hands."

Tariq stares at Bassam a moment longer, his eyes on the future perhaps. Perhaps that. Bassam leans back against the bed's headboard, Tariq's, the noise it made last evening. Again, a bad dream receding. He continues to read:

Check your weapon before you leave and long before you leave. (You must make your knife sharp and you must not discomfort your animal during the slaughter.) The artery. How Bassam must immediately find it. The blood draining so quckly from the unbelieving brain, Insha'Allah. How little the kafir will feel then anyway, how his resistance will diminish as well. Bassam's heart is beating more forcefully now. Yes, give me strength, Al-Aziz. Please, give me resolve.

Bassam rises and from the closet shelf removes the Book. *In the name of Allah.* It is worn, a paper copy purchased by Amir in Pakistan. A simple black. Inside it, everything. *Everything.* Bassam places it beside him, presses his hand to its cover.

In the room, there is only the slow turning of pages, the cooling air from the vents, this rising readiness inside him. Their emir advises them now in which supplications to utter upon leaving this room, upon entering the taxi, upon entering the matar. With each word, Bassam can feel his soul become cleaner, with each word he feels it turn more directly to the Holy One, to the Compassionate and the Merciful, the Mighty and the Loving. How *blessed* is Bassam!

There is more to read, but he does not wish for these instructions to be completed so soon. Now is the time for movement. His body can no longer lie still. He will mail the letter home to his mother. He will ask the concierge where is the postal office and, Allah willing, he will mail his letter home.

∨ ∨ ∨

A PRIL HAD BEEN standing at her bedroom window so long she went to the kitchen for a chair and carried it down the hall and sat where she could see the street. It was early September on the Gulf Coast, but the morning air looked smoky, the way August did up north. Her apartment had never been so clean and her hair was dry from the shower she'd taken at seven. She'd dressed and undressed three times, finally settling on what she would normally wear—shorts and sandals and a cotton top.

Since coming south, she'd never been up this early. She watched two of her neighbors in shirts and ties get in their cars and drive past. A little later she watched a young mother in a business suit and running shoes lead two kids into a van, buckle them in, and turn in the opposite direction. Three teenage boys pedaled by on bikes. None of them wore a helmet and all three had backpacks strapped on. Not long after, an old man walked a dog down the sidewalk. The dog was small and had a short tail and it stopped at the palm tree and sniffed the trunk, then lifted its leg and pissed on it. In the sunlit haze, the palm fronds looked blue.

April may have seen some of these people on a day off, but if she had, she didn't remember it; how different the street looked to her now. These past months she'd been on it mainly when people were inside, at dinnertime when she'd climb into her car for the club, then at three in the morning when she'd pull into the driveway, her feet aching, her eyes burning from all the smoke, cash in her pocket. It was like seeing the neighborhood for the first time and she felt hopeful because from here it looked affluent and clean and full of tax-paying contributors to society.

And that's what she was, wasn't she? Wouldn't the inspectors see that too? She imagined her daughter drawing in a sunlit kitchen with a heavy, warm woman who wanted nothing to do but take care of this young girl in her house, a house that looked just like Jean's; that's who she was with, somebody as loving and alone as Jean Hanson.

Y Y Y

A S A BOY many times Bassam had a dream that always was the same. Ramadan was over and the entire family was celebrating the Eid al-Fitr. His mother and aunts served baby camel in a pot of cracked wheat covered with cinnamon, cardamom, and saffron, and in the courtyard his father and uncles danced to the beating mirwas, tablah, and daff. Earlier the children were given gifts: silver Bedouin jewelry to be worn modestly by his two sisters; for his thirteen brothers were knives and swords carved from wood, a fine carpet for Adil, a shining brass mabkhara for Rashad. Bassam received nothing, yet in this dream he did not care.

In his dream, he was apart from and above his family and their celebration. He was with them yet he was somehow not with them. He ate the food but he did not taste it. He saw the laughter but he did not hear it. His mother embraced him but he did not feel it. No, there was instead the feeling they were celebrating *him*, not simply himself, but him through the Sustainer. That he, shy Bassam, had done something to bring them all closer to Allah, that there were no gifts for him because he *was* a gift. To his family. To his clan. To his kingdom.

Still a boy, he would wake from this dream early for Fajr and feel like a fool, for he was ashamed of his lack of humility, *him* who had never done anything special, who had trouble with his studies, who never concentrated during prayer and who only wanted to kick a ball to his friends. Who was *he* to have this dream?

Remember that you will return to Allah and remember that anything that happens to you could never be avoided, and what did not happen to you could never have happened to you. These words inside him as he walks under the sun among the kufar. Such a comfort is fate, his own blessedly foretold to him. For that is what that dream was, Bassam, a foretelling.

He nearly feels pity for these people. Look at them walking so quickly on a mid-morning Monday, these men in neckties with their cell phones pushed to their ears, these women out in the streets, talking so importantly with one another like the two before him. Look at them speak as they cross the busy street, closed containers of coffee in their hands. So many of these people rushing and rushing. Would they rush so if they knew what awaited them?

He, too, waits for traffic and crosses, walking slowly, taking all the time necessary. A van of workers passes close by, the driver from his open window shouting at him. Bassam regards them as they go. On the van's roof, a ladder, a red kerchief tied at its end and flapping wildly. There is the feeling he cannot be harmed. There is the feeling he is firmly aboard a large craft that cannot be stopped. He feels a supreme peace and from this feeling he would like to do something good. *Shouldn't we take advantage of these last hours to offer good deeds and obedience?* Today there is very little anger toward these people. They have no iman so they will fail. And this mission, Insha'Allah, will be the first victory among many.

A young woman stands at the bottom of the stone steps of the postal office. She is small, her hair short, and Bassam disciplines him-

self not to look at her backside in her tight pants. Before her is a
baby's carriage. She regards the six or seven steps. She regards her
carriage, a deep blue, its frame silver and bright under the sun.

Bassam pushes the letter into his rear pocket. He approaches her
just as she bends forward to grasp the carriage and lift, her nuhood
visible in her brassiere, the gold chain and cross of Mary's son. "Miss?
Allow me to help please." And he smiles into her face, which appears
startled. But what does she see? She sees a young man, clean and
shaved, his clothes ironed by himself before leaving the fine hotel
where he is staying, an expression upon his face of pity and a desire
to do only good. She too smiles and thanks him and together they
carry the baby's carriage up the stone steps, Bassam grasping the front
wheels and walking backward, the woman holding the handle, and
look at the baby, Bassam. Look at him look at you. No fear in his eyes.
Just a question, or does he even question? Is he so new, he has yet no
questions?

"Thank you very much."

"Yes." He lowers the carriage and pulls open the glass door and
now he does look at her backside as she enters. *O Lord, I ask You for the
best of this place, and ask You to protect me from its evils.* He follows her
and her baby into the postal area. There is a long line of kufar. Men
and women. A television in the upper corner, this CNN Amir would
often watch in their many motel rooms here. The story now of a fire
in the West, trees and homes burning in the smoking winds. And he
sees above the postal windows this country's flag. It hangs behind a
glass frame, the very flag flown on the military base of Khamis Mushayt, the very flag hanging from the tall post above the buildings built
by Ahmed al-Jizani. How is it possible that the flag of the kufar has
come to hang in the land of two holy places? And though he has not
seen it, it surely hangs in the American compound in Riyadh among
the executives who come for their oil. It hangs from the tanks in the
desert where they killed hundreds of thousands of Iraqis. It hangs in
the hearts of the Zionists in Palestine. It hangs here in every school
where children like this baby before him are taught to hate the believ-

THE GARDEN OF LAST DAYS 479

ers. And why did it not hang in Bosnia? Why did the kufar do nothing as thousands and thousands of their Muslim brothers were lined up and shot or were held down to have their throats cut while their mothers and sisters and daughters were violated, their sacred mosques burned to ashes? Where was this kufar flag then? Surely it was folded tightly in the pocket of Milosevic himself, for where there is an enemy of Allah, is it not clear there too is this flag behind its glass on painted walls above the heads of government bureaucrats? And now Bassam does not wish to give them his money. Why should he pay them to deliver this important letter back to the birthplace of the Prophet they have occupied?

But this anger, it is distracting. He closes his eyes and makes the du'a for it. *I take refuge with Allah from the accursed devil.*

He breathes deeply through the nose. The kafir whore, her uncovered hips beneath his fingers, her rising and falling. *Already, sweetie? Already?* As if he is a boy. As if they are all boys. He opens his eyes once more. The line moves slowly. At the nearest window an old man purchases stamps. His hair is white and his back is hunched from the pull of the earth and he leans hard upon his walking staff. Soon he will die and soon they will burn, Allah willing. All must be turned back to the Creator; these people will fail because the Holy One will deem it so. There is no need for Bassam to be distracted with this anger. He must return to a state of purity and good deeds, that is all, for Shaytan is at work, is he not? How happy would be the dark angel to see them fail. How happy he would be to further strengthen the unbelievers and protect them and keep them.

You should feel complete tranquillity, because the time between you and your marriage in heaven is very short.

Yes, Insha'Allah, yes.

From his rear pocket Bassam retrieves the letter. It is warm from his body, and he wishes to send that warmth directly to his mother. Her laughter when he was small, her smell—perspiration and cinnamon, garlic and silk—how so often she would embrace him and hold his face between her hands. She will pray for his soul, he knows this. For she, too, like Ahmed al-Jizani, does not understand the true meaning of jihad. Or perhaps she once did, but no longer. Slowly she is being pulled into the ways of the far enemy, but how can jihad be only a struggle within when the Creator has so clearly shown us His enemy without?

The baby cries. The old man walks slowly from the window. The baby continues crying, and the young kafir mother bends forward and lifts him from the carriage and lays him against her shoulder. Her voice is quiet. Bassam does not hear her words, only the ceasing of the baby's cries. The baby's head, look how large it appears for his small neck. He has difficulty holding steadily, but he looks once again at Bassam. His eyes are blue, and they stare at him in their blueness as if he knows his thoughts.

The line moves more quickly now. A man dressed in a suit approaches the window. A large woman walks to the next, and soon a kafir in athletic clothing is summoned to the third. The man's shirt has no sleeves and his shoulders and arms are uncovered, the muscles there much larger than even Imad's. *But are we strong enough, Bassam? What if they are stronger?* Surely Bassam and his brothers are weaker than this man. But in body only, Bassam. In body only.

He is hungry. But there will be no midday meal. Already he is looking forward to the greater hunger, the emptiness that only the Sustainer can fill. And he wishes he began fasting days ago with Imad. But instead of this, what did he do? He drank alcohol and let his lust lead him and now he has lain with a whore and can only pray he will fight tomorrow, Allah willing, as did the pious early generations. He can only pray that his love for the Creator will be stronger than any kafir like this man and others like him.

O Allah, protect me from them with what You choose.

The line begins to move, and Bassam follows the mother and her now silent and sleeping child.

＊　＊　＊

THE PROTECTIVE INVESTIGATOR'S name was Marina, an unfortunate first name, Jean thought, in a place full of boats. But she was pleasant enough, sitting on the edge of the sofa beside Jean, nodding respectfully at Jean's answers to her questions with the detached warmth of a nurse.

"So she sleeps here every night?"

"No, just on the nights her mother works."

"And that's five nights a week?"

"Sometimes four." Jean sipped her ice water. The woman wrote something on her notepad. She was short, with olive skin and a man's haircut, her khakis tight at her hips. She hadn't touched her water.

"What time does she get home every night?"

"Oh I don't know really. I'm asleep."

"But you said she used to carry her daughter upstairs. What time did she do that?"

"Around three or three-thirty, I suppose." Jean's face burned. Most of the women's questions were about April, but she began to feel scrutinized in a place she'd been hiding.

"May I see the room?"

"Certainly." Jean led her down the hall to Franny's bedroom, stepping to the side as the woman walked in ahead of her. Jean watched her look at the bed and homemade quilt, the stuffed animals, posters, and curtains; was she taking in how clean and neat the room was? The love and care obviously at work here? What else could she be jotting down in her notebook?

The woman looked up, neither smiling nor frowning, and a weight began to press on Jean's chest: What if she denied them anyway? What if what she saw wasn't quite enough?

"May I see your room, please?"

"Of course. It's that one."

Marina DeFelipo thanked her. Jean didn't know if she should follow her or not. Would that look like she was hovering, trying to distract her from seeing something? But she couldn't just turn and walk away either; it may seem as if she didn't care what was put in her report. She stayed in the doorway.

The woman took in Jean's mahogany nightstands, the matching reading lamps with the tasseled shades, the half-empty water glass, and the paperback Jean bought last week in St. Armand's Circle, *Anxiety: The Cure*.

"Do you suffer from anxiety?"

"No." Heat tightened the skin of Jean's face and throat, this lie so obvious. "Well, panic, I would say. I sometimes get these attacks."

The woman nodded slowly, taking her in more fully now: the loose jowls under her jaw, her fleshy bare arms and massive sundress, the varicose veins in her calves, the slippers she was still wearing. "Are you getting treatment?"

"No." Jean looked away, the weight pressing harder against her chest. A cool sweat broke out on her forehead and upper lip, the back of her neck. "It's not that bad, really." She walked quickly to the window and parted the curtain. She was thinking of the hospital Friday night, of ripping off the wires and leaving the pills in the bedsheets.

"You should get some help for that, Mrs. Hanson. Anxiety is a common problem. May I see your bathroom?"

"Yes, please, follow me." Jean moved down the hall quickly because moving helped; her breath seemed to come more easily, the weight on her chest easing up a bit. She didn't wait for the woman this time; she knew she was going in there to look for medications; in the mirrored cabinet she would find some for her blood pressure, another to lower her cholesterol, some aspirin to thin her blood. But nothing for anxiety or panic. Nothing that would make her look like a liar.

While the woman was inspecting the bathroom, Jean picked up both water glasses from the coffee table. Her vision blackened as she stood, her heart fluttering. Now she could see clearly again, but there was more cold sweat she wiped away with the back of her arm, her skin cool.

"Are you all right?" Marina DeFelipo stood at the end of the hallway. There were the beginnings of gray along her hairline, and she had put on glasses with silver wire rims.

"Yes, I just haven't been sleeping well." Jean moved around the counter. She rested the water glasses in the sink. She could feel the investigator watching her and she'd had quite enough of this, she who'd done nothing wrong. "Are you going to interview April now?"

"Yes, thank you." Her eyes lingered on Franny's drawings on the wall, so many of them crooked houses under bright suns.

∨ ∨ ∨

IT WAS ONLY one inspector, the same woman who hadn't let her see Franny, and April was surprised she'd gone into Jean's first. She was down there a long time. Now she stood in April's living room looking at the dusted row of Disney movies under the TV, her notepad open.

"How is she?"

"She seems very nice."

"No, my daughter. Your tests. Please, how is she?"

The woman looked steadily at April. "She shows no real signs of having been abused. I'll be seeing her again, however."

April nodded, her eyes filling. She turned and walked past the peninsula into the kitchen. *Thank God, Thank God, Oh thank God.* But she didn't like how the woman didn't ask to see her daughter, just informed her she would. Nor did April like the hope in her that this woman had taken note of her tears.

"May I see her room, please?"

April led her down the hallway. She stepped to the side to let her in, and it felt as if she were showing her a lie.

The woman looked at the made bed and the Barbie dollhouse at the foot of it. She looked at the new beanbag chair. She walked over and tested the latch on the window.

"This is kept locked?"

"Yeah, the AC's always on."

The woman glanced at the poster of the moon over the ocean and she opened the closet and took in the hanging dresses and tops, Franny's pink backpack on the floor, her new flip-flops lined up neatly beside her old ones. She peered inside and looked in both corners. She turned and smiled. "Is this where she plays a lot? Here in her room?"

"And downstairs with Jean. She's there every morning."

"Until you get up."

"Yeah, that's about ten."

"Jean said eleven."

"Between ten and eleven." April's face hummed. She tried to smile but couldn't.

"Does she know what you do?"

"Jean?"

"Your daughter?"

"I've told her I'm in show business."

"Does she know what that means?"

"I tell her I dance on a stage."

"What did she see Friday night?"

"Just women in a dressing room. Just, you know, women."

She nodded. She kept her eyes on her, and April saw Mary, her good sister Mary, who never broke a rule and never would. And should she tell the woman now that she didn't even work there anymore?

"May I see the rest of the home?"

"Please."

April stood to the side and let her go look herself. Yesterday she'd put the ironing board and iron in the closet where they never went, she'd hung her clothes on hangers and dusted off the bureau and bedside table. She'd straightened the stack of magazines and vaccumed the carpet and washed the windows. Now she heard the closet door slide open. Her leather pocketbook was on the floor beside her bed. It was zipped shut. All that money from the foreigner she hadn't deposited yet. Today was her first chance to do it. Would the inspector look inside it? *Could* she?

But now she was a shadow moving down the hallway, smiling at April as she found the light switch and stepped into the bathroom and opened the medicine cabinet.

"Do you own any weapons? Firearms?"

"No, never."

"Do you have a boyfriend?"

"No."

The woman closed the cabinet. She parted the shower curtain and looked at the gleaming tub, Franny's bath toys lined up along the porcelain, her Barbie mermaid sitting at attention.

ᵛ ᵛ ᵛ

Bᴇᴛᴡᴇᴇɴ ᴛʜᴇ 'Aꜱʀ and Maghrib prayers, Imad and Tariq take the opportunity for one more exercise session in the hotel's gym. Imad urges him to go as well, but Bassam has not been disciplined enough and knows his muscles will be sore tomorrow, Insha'Allah.

"I have not finished the instructions. You two go, Imad. What you need from me are speed and resolve, and these things I already have."

Imad in his sweat suit they purchased at a Target in Boynton Beach, Tariq in his—they stood in the hotel corridor like two boys on their way to play a game in the streets. Imad nodded his acceptance, and now it is a joy to be alone. In the quiet of the room, still darkened by the drawn drapery and lighted only by the bedside lamp, Bassam feels the beckoning opportunity to study and to pray and to better prepare himself.

His mouth is dry, but he will not drink water. His hunger has returned, but he will not think of food. He sits back upon his bed and takes up the final instructions for the shuhada', these words the only nourishment he needs.

Do not forget to take a bounty, even if it is a glass of water to quench your thirst or that of your brothers, if possible. When the hour of reality approaches, the zero hour, wholeheartedly welcome death for the sake of Allah. Always be remembering Allah. Either end your life while praying, seconds before the target, or make your last words: "There is no god but Allah, Muhammad is His messenger."

Afterward, we will all meet in the highest heaven, Allah willing.

Bassam can no longer lie still. He refolds the instructions and pushes them back into the envelope. He stands and walks back and forth between the beds and the television cabinet and minibar.

Do not forget to take a bounty.

Tariq, could he have been correct? Was it allowed, even encouraged, for them to take this whore? And so they could do it again, could they not? Something to quench their thirst?

No, *no*, this is weakness. No, he must wait. This time tomorrow, Insha'Allah, he will have been in Jannah for hours.

So *close*. They are so close!

Upon the table beneath the curtained window are what Imad purchased this morning, the cans of cream for shaving, the two bags of disposable razors. Bassam should shave his body now, in the bath. He steps toward the table. But no, the instructions are for the last night and it is still day. He should have gone with Imad and Tariq to the gym. He could exercise lightly. No, he was right; this would only make his muscles sore and slow.

He steps to the window and parts the draping. Outside, sunlight upon the new brick walls of the hotel. Down below the courtyard, its trees full and green. He wants to go there. He wishes to be under this sun, walking, moving his body. But then he will be among the kufar. He will be among them and all their distractions.

No, Bassam. Calm yourself. Make an ablution and pick up the

Book and read from Al-Anfal and Al-Tawbah as instructed. Read the words of the Holy One.

And yes, it calms him. Yes, it fortifies him. But so early in the sura, Bassam reads it as if for the first time:

Your Lord bade you leave your home to fight for justice, but some of the faithful were reluctant. They argued with you about the truth that had been revealed, as though they were being led to certain death while they looked on. These words refer to the Prophet, peace be upon him, and the victorious Battle of Badr, but Bassam also sees Karim, hears again his words defending the Zionist/Crusader alliance as if they truly are fellow People of the Book, as if they are not corrupting polytheists and unbelievers. And Ahmed al-Jizani, Bassam sees his father as he sat against the wall, his elbow upon his raised knee, his tea steaming in the clear glass he held, his eyes on his youngest son. "And if it comes to fighting, it is only for defense, Bassam. A fard kifaya."

But jihad is *not* a collective duty, it is fard'ayn, a *personal* obligation. An *eternal* jihad against apostates near and far. And have they not read the words of Allah? Is it not clear whom He favors most? Those who stay home in comfort and make excuses, or those who leave and *fight*?

But this pride in himself is wrong, the heat of shame rolling upward through his face. All this is not for *him*, but for the Creator, for the Judge and the Ruler, for the All-Knowing and the Merciful. And Bassam must be more respectful to his own father. Yes, he may not be destined for the highest rooms with his son, Insha'Allah, but he is the builder of a sacred mosque, the father of fourteen children, the husband of Bassam's dear mother, and is it not promised to the shahid that his sacrifice will erase the sins of seventy members of his family as well? Is it not? And yes, if Bassam is forced to slaughter, Allah willing, he must dedicate it to his father. He will dedicate the first spilled blood to Ahmed al-Jizani.

⌄ ⌄ ⌄

THEY WERE LATE. Marina said one o'clock but it was already fourteen past. Three times cars had driven up Orchid, the sun reflecting off their hoods and windshields, blinding her just before they drove by.

April leaned against her Sable. The trunk was hot against her lower back, and her mouth was dry and her heart seemed to be pounding in her empty stomach. Jean had waited with her awhile, but then got a little faint under the sun and went inside for her straw hat. April was sweating and thirsty, but she didn't move.

A dog barked. A door opened and shut. She was squinting and needed her sunglasses.

A white car turned onto Orchid, then a dark blue van. The sun hit the chrome and glass of both and April held her hand over her eyes. The first car was Marina DeFelipo, and she was alone and April was already out of the driveway and walking fast down the sidewalk to the van pulling to the curb. It was new, its side windows tinted, and a woman sat behind the wheel, and as she put the gear in park, April was already at the rear passenger door jerking on the handle. There was a clicking noise, then a whimper, her eyes filling, the dark glass a smear. She kept jerking on the handle but only the front passenger window rolled down.

"Let go so I can unlock it." A polite voice but firm, and April let go. She wiped her eyes and pressed her face to the glass. She cupped her hands to her temples, and there she was, locked in a car seat in a white dress, smiling at her and waving, her curly hair bouncing, her legs kicking, her feet in new white shoes.

∨ ∨ ∨

J EAN SAT AT the patio table, her cheeseburger untouched, the bricks warm beneath her feet. The mottled light of sundown lay over her garden, and in it sat Franny and April across from her, Franny in her mother's lap talking about how there were good toys and a sand box and a little pool she swam in. Her hair was clean and curly, her face unmarked, her eyes as clear blue and lit with as much joy and curiosity as they'd ever been. How was it possible to feel any greater happiness than this?

Jean raised her glass and sipped her Cabernet. She'd wanted champagne but couldn't tolerate the thought of leaving Franny for even that one errand. And how good it was to sit here behind these walls among the hibiscus and bougainvillea and frangipani, the gate latched, all officials gone, the three of them safe. Now Franny slid off her mother's lap and walked around and climbed up onto Jean's. A welling caught itself in her throat and she pulled her close, this strong young body. This strong, unharmed, miraculous body. "Oh I'm so happy you're *home.*"

"Yeah, I didn't like that I couldn't come home."

"We didn't either, honey."

April said, "Remember what I told you, Franny? They wouldn't let us see you. It's because of what *I* did, honey. Not you."

April looked as if she might cry again, one bare knee drawn up to her chest. Her hair was pulled back and she wore little makeup and she hadn't eaten much of her food. Before, Jean would've felt uncomfortable holding Franny like this in front of her, as if she were stealing something. But not now. April was looking at them both like they went together, one essential to the other.

Franny was eating a tomato slice from Jean's plate. Jean kissed her, could smell her hair. Some kind of floral shampoo. It's not what April used, and it smelled wrong to Jean, as if Franny had been someplace so very far from them. Someplace foreign.

THE SUN HAS set, and for their night meal they have ordered from the hotel's room service: chicken and rice, yogurt, though it is sweetened, salad with extra cucumbers they will mix with the yogurt, bread and tea. And if they were not breaking their fast together in Imad's room, would they keep the kafir server from entering as does Imad? Would they have been so pure?

But again, there is no resentment inside Bassam as he wonders this. He is grateful for Imad's steadfastness. And when they are seated around the table, a third chair carried from their room by Tariq, they lower their heads and make the supplication for fast-breaking. *The thirst has gone and the veins are quenched, and reward is confirmed, if Allah wills.*

In the name of Allah.

Bassam's first bite is of the rice. It is too moist with butter and he wishes for saffron. But he must be grateful for this food, and he must not think of himself or the pleasures found in the life of this world. They eat quietly. Tariq, as always, eats too quickly, pushing the bread into his mouth behind the rice. Imad ignores him. He regards Bassam across the small table. He smiles directly at him. It is the smile he gave when they said together their bayat so many months ago in Khamis Mushayt, a love for him borne from the greater love for the Creator.

"In the morning, Insha'Allah, you and I will fight like Ali and Ubaydah, Allah rest their souls."

"Yes, Allah willing." Bassam lowers his eyes out of respect, and again, the thrusting of his heart, the rising pride inside him that he has been called to fight like the heroic cousins of the Prophet, peace be upon him.

He bites into the chicken cooked by the kufar. Do they know whom they are feeding tonight?

Tariq reaches for his tea. "And I will fight like Hamza, Insha'Allah."

"Yes." Imad looks at him and he nods as if he sees already that this will be true. "Allah willing, yes."

But it is as if Bassam's blood has grown cooler by two or three degrees, the fear he begins to feel now. The inescapable fear before battle. But what is this fear? Surely it is not of death.

No, it is the fear of failing and remaining here in this life. That is this feeling. The fear of living.

∀ ∀ ∀

L ONNIE PULLED HIS truck up to the curb in the dark. He looked out his open window at the marine supply across the street. Behind the plate glass, the store was in blackness but a fluorescent light glowed behind the sales desk, hooks of life jackets hanging above it in shadow. Had he ever noticed that before? And April's light on in the bedroom of her daughter. Before driving home, he'd sat in his truck across the street watching it like a creep. Over the top of the garden wall hung a flowering vine, the richness inside brimming over.

How could he have ever thought she'd be up for a night out?

He was happy for her. He was. And he wasn't stupid. He knew when a woman was interested and when she wasn't and April was *not*.

Lonnie got out of his truck and closed the door and unlocked the squat rental he couldn't afford much longer. The AC was on too low. The place was dark and smelled damp as a swamp, and Louis's call today, his voice tense and teasing, "C'mon, Lonnie, I'll be open soon. What *else* you gonna do? What else you good at but knocking people's lights out?"

                                ∨ ∨ ∨

F RANNY FELL ASLEEP while April read to her, her daugh-
       ter's head on her shoulder. Now they both lay under the sheet
       and new bedspread, Franny on her side, her small back curled
against April, and she hadn't washed or brushed her teeth but she
wasn't leaving. She reached up to the wall switch and flicked off the
light.

   In the darkness, that woman who'd insisted on lifting Franny out
of the van herself, and the look in her eye, some kind of resignation
at having to hand her over. And Marina's voice: "You'll have to take
some parenting classes. Reach out to some resources we have here.
Work on becoming less isolated."

   Isolated. She was, wasn't she? Always had been. How was that going
to change? Did anything or anybody ever really *change*? Lying here
with Franny safe beside her, it felt like an intercession from God,
but what had she done wrong other than to trust the wrong woman

to watch her? What had she done to deserve the last two days? She was out of a job now. Yes, she had money, but it wasn't enough. She couldn't just quit working and buy something. Not yet. She needed more. A hundred thousand. Two hundred thousand. It would take time, but she was disciplined enough to do it. She *had* to do it, didn't she?

You do it for this. The drunk foreigner's fingers on her. His bad English. Trying to say *flesh*. Is that why she did it? Because she *liked* it?

No, he was wrong. What she liked was doing it so well, finding something she did better than other women, many of them beautiful women, but not as smart as she was. Not as forward-thinking as she was. She did it because of the money, yes, but also because it made her feel like more than just anyone. It made her feel she could do something not many others could.

She still hadn't deposited the money he'd given her. Tomorrow it would go into her account. Tomorrow, if the weather was good, she and Franny would go to the bank and then the beach. And Jean, maybe she would want to come along too.

TUESDAY

I T IS STILL quite early, the lobby of the hotel empty, its red carpet soft beneath their feet. They walk together with their luggage to the desk of the concierge. There are two kufar, a man and a woman. She is African and beautiful, her hair quite short, her lips red with cosmetics. She smiles brightly at them all, but Imad ignores her and hands to the man their plastic room cards.

"Did you enjoy your stay?" says the woman. Imad does not look at her, and surely, this is a distraction from Shaytan, but Bassam smiles and says, "Yes, thank you."

Again she smiles so brightly and it is difficult to ignore her large nuhood beneath her blouse and buttoned jacket, Shaytan working harder now, and the dark kafir in Florida, what she showed to Bassam.

"A taxi?" She looks to Tariq and Imad, who say nothing, who stand at the polished counter waiting for the receipt out of habit, for surely there is no need for it.

Her smile, it has not diminished, but there is the tightness of a business transaction across her features, the lovely face of another whore. Bassam says: "We have telephoned for it, thank you."

And it is here. Beyond the glass, a yellow auto pulling to the curb outside. The brick wall of the building across the street sits in a pink and golden light, and now the bellman approaches them. He is as young as they, his hand outstretched to take their bags.

"No." Imad moves past him, Tariq as well, and is it weak of Bassam to smile at the boy and say, "No, thank you very much"?

The driver is not Morrocan or Pakistani or Indian, as so many here are—he is a white kafir, a short and heavy man who wears a bright green cap and opens the trunk lid for their luggage.

Imad remains there with his bag, and it is clear to Bassam he is making a silent du'a before entering a transport. Tariq hands to the driver his duffel and so then does Bassam.

"Logan?"

"Excuse, sir?"

"Logan Airport?"

"Yes."

The man's face, it has lines in it beneath two or three days of no shaving, white and silver, and there are small broken veins across his nose and upper cheeks.

"What airline?"

"Yes, the airport."

Forcefully the man closes the lid. "What *airline*, sir? United? American? Delta?"

"American."

Imad and Tariq are seated in the rear, their supplications completed. The driver pulls aside newspapers and Bassam sits and pulls closed the door and makes his own invisible du'a: *In the name of Allah and all praise is for Allah. How perfect He is, the One Who has placed this transport at our service, and we ourselves would not have been capable of that, and to our Lord is our final destiny. All praise is for Allah, All praise is for Allah, All praise is for Allah. Allah is the greatest. How perfect You are, O Allah, verily I have wronged my soul, so forgive me, for surely none can forgive sins except You.*

The man drives fast and recklessly. The streets are nearly empty of other vehicles. In the rose light the sidewalking areas hold few kufar, but an old woman walks her animal before a furniture shop, a dog who walks quickly and sniffs the concrete.

A radio plays. Kufar talking loudly. There is the smell of coffee, a white covered cup of it in a holder beneath the radio. The ashtray is full of ash and smoked cigarettes, and from the rear mirror hangs the cross of Mary's son. Taped beside the driver's photo is a small painting of her, rays of light shining from around her uncovered head as if she were holy, this mother of nothing but a messenger these polytheists worship.

Bassam looks away. *There is no god but Allah. Allah is all we need. He is the best to rely upon.*

A black kafir dressed in soiled and ripped clothing stumbles along. At his feet a discarded newspaper, an empty bottle. There is a restaurant for Indian food, its sign a bright yellow plastic. There is a restaurant for food from China, yesterday the kafir in the doorway, the music she made from her stringed instrument—beautiful, the work of Shaytan.

The driver speaks. He says more loudly than the loud talk on the rado, "You boys going home? Where you from?"

He views Tariq and Imad in his rear mirror. He looks to Bassam.

"We are students."

"I figured that. Engineering, right?"

Bassam says nothing. The car rumbles over steel tracks. He looks out his window and in the hazy air between low buildings, a train approaches. It is far away and will take time to arrive here, but his heart begins its thrusting. *Allah is all we need. He is the best to rely upon.*

"I've met a lot like you. You come here for your educations, then go back to help your own people, right? You gotta respect that. Kids nowadays, I'm telling you, they're in it for themselves. Number One, know what I mean?"

Bassam nods to his question, or the sound of it in his voice, for he is not listening to this kafir who reminds him of Cliff in Boynton Beach. The same inked markings on his bare arms upon the wheel, the same evidence in his face of a life of drinking, but he is warm, friendly, and Bassam does not wish to like him, even for this short ride. Even for this.

They speed onto a low bridge over water. A river separating two parts of the city. And now the sun begins to show itself, its light reflecting off the bottom floors of the many office buildings on the other side. Some are quite high, the sky beyond them a deep and cloudless blue. Bassam begins to sweat. He feels it come out on his forehead and behind his neck. And look at the lighted sign for oil, Bassam. It is larger than some buildings, another monument for these kufar to worship: CITGO.

The windows are open. Cool wind fills the auto. It is the angels calming him. It is the mala'ika keeping him steadfast.

Now they are in city streets and there is more traffic and the driver turns left and travels down a boulevard of tall trees. The buildings they pass are made of brown stone or gray stone or brick, green vines growing thickly up their sides. The radio talk has become music, not the stabbing electronic the young listen to, but something softer, a man and woman singing together, two lovers, and Bassam is grateful when the kafir turns it off.

Imad says in their language, "Bassam, is he going the right way?"

The driver looks briefly at him in the rear mirror.

"Sir," Bassam says, "is this the best way to airport?"

"I've lived here my whole life, pal. I'd better know where it is."

A yellow cargo truck looms up and the driver turns sharply, his coffee spilling outward from its container, Bassam leaning.

"Fuck you!" The driver yells this from his window, but he does not seem as angry as his words, more like a man expected to perform a role so he is performing it.

"Bassam, what does he say?"

"Don't worry, Imad. He knows where he is going."

There are traffic lights and stops and many more autos on the streets. Now they are driving beside the river they have crossed. The sun shines more directly upon it, and on this side are green parks of trees, many kufar jogging, men and women, some on roller blades Bassam saw so much of in Florida, others on bicycles. Always this drive to keep their bodies strong so that they may live many, many years, pleasuring themselves as long as possible.

"What're you? Electrical? Mechanical? That's what most of you study, right? Computers too. We can't forget that."

"Excuse me?"

"What're you taking up in school?"

Does he ask what he studies? Yes, he must be asking this. "Medical." Bassam does not know why this is his answer. There are no doctors in his family.

"Yeah? Medical school? Whereabouts? Over to Harvard?"

"Yes, Harvard."

"Impressive. Very impressive. How 'bout your friends?" The kafir regards them in the mirror, more respect in his eyes now, subservience even. Yes, Bassam can see it, a humbling of himself, his descent to his social station away from where they are rising. And Bassam wants to tell this noisy kafir the truth, that their true titles are far more exalted than that of doctor who does nothing but tend to the living.

His mouth is dry. At the airport he will drink water, Allah willing. "Yes, medical too."

The driver nods his head and seems to drive faster, as if he is now carrying very important people. They descend into a tunnel. Its light is a dull yellow that makes the day too bright when they enter it once more and then they are in city streets and there are many autos and the shops' doors are open, their electric signs lighted in the early-morning air that smells of concrete dust and garbage and gasoline. There is a hospital, a large parking garage. A police officer stands beneath the canopy of a restaurant, a container of coffee in his hand, and his eyes stare briefly into Bassam's. He closes his and makes the du'a for entering a village for he has never been to this part of the northern city and he must remind the angels to remain with him, to guide and protect them: *O Allah, Lord of the seven heavens and all that they envelop, Lord of the seven earths and all that they carry, Lord of the evils and all whom they misguide, Lord of the winds and all whom they misguide, Lord of the winds and all whom they whisk away, I ask You for the goodness of this village, and I take refuge with You from the evil of this village, the evil of its inhabitants and from all the evil found within it.*

At a traffic light, the driver brakes suddenly, the cross of Mary's son swinging. The kafir drinks from his cup. Once again he nods his head. "You guys goin' home for a visit?"

"No." Why do you tell him the truth, Bassam?

"A few days off?"

"Bassam," Imad says, "what is he talking about?"

"Nothing. He is nothing." He turns to the kafir. "Yes, we are visiting friends."

"That's good."

The light becomes green and the driver pushes gasoline into the engine. Soon they are passing an outdoor market, men in soiled aprons handling vegetables and fruit, fish laid out on ice, their bodies slit open a dark pink, the smell of it—fish and damp cardboard and something rotten from days before, rotten and stepped over in the street. And when they enter another tunnel, this one longer and darker, some of its lights broken or blinking with little power, Bassam sees the souqs from home, how during prayers he would lie down beneath a covered table away from the muttawa and smoke one of Khalid's Marlboro cigarettes and watch the smoke rise. It may as well have been smoke from his own burning soul.

Just meters ahead is the light of this day. He closes his eyes: *La ilaha illa Allah wa Muhammad ar-rasulullah.*

They merge into the sunlight behind many autos. The driver accelerates and they are on an overpass and on the other side of it are brick buildings, apartments Bassam can see, small balconies attached. There are grills for cooking meat, flower boxes, outdoor plastic furniture. Over the railing of one is clothing drying in the early sun, and on the roof is a large sign, a photographed woman looking directly at him, smiling with seduction, a glimmering stone on her finger.

"Bassam," says Tariq from the rear, "look at the sky."

It is the same uninterrupted blue he had seen over the clouds when they flew here from Florida. Surely, a sign. Surely, the angels at work for them.

And Imad speaks quietly the words of the Prophet, peace be upon him, whenever he would receive pleasing news, "All praise is for Allah by whose favor good works are accomplished."

"American, right?" The driver looks briefly at Bassam.

"Yes, American." Now they are nearing the airport, its control tower visible beyond concrete overpasses and the traffic of buses and autos. Beyond it, in the deep blue, a passenger jet descends and to the south another rises steeply. It is as if there is no moisture in Bassam's mouth and never was. His heart is beating erratically inside him, and he breathes deeply, and *please, Mala'ika, calm me, keep me patient, steadfast, and tranquil, for truly, Insha'Allah, I am less than three hours from entering Jannah.*

There is no god but Allah, and Muhammad is His messenger.

"You guys travel light. Christ, whenever I go anywhere I pack a whole trunk. And the wife is worse than me." The kafir laughs though Bassam is not completely certain what he said. But it no longer matters for the taxi pulls up beneath a sign for American and the kafir pushes a button on his price machine, the red numbers like those of the hotel clock in their last room, like all the clocks of all the motels, the red numbers stating the price. The Egyptian would try to negotiate this number downward, and will he be as joyful and at peace as he was two evenings ago? Is he already here?

"Thirty-two seventy, please. You need a receipt?"

"No." Bassam pushes two twenty bills into his hand, knows it is customary to give a gratuity, but all the money he gave freely in the South in the small black room. His drunkenness, his weakness.

The kafir places two coins into Bassam's palm, then a note of five and notes of one, and in the care with which the driver does this, Bassam can feel his hope for some to be given back to him.

Shouldn't we take these last hours to offer good deeds and obedience?

Bassam gives the kafir the bill of five. The driver looks him in the eyes and smiles the satisfied smile of a surprisingly successful transaction, but in that green cap of a boy he looks foolish, and doomed. "Thank you, sir. You have a good trip now."

He exits the auto and retrieves from the trunk the duffel bags of Bassam's and Tariq's. The kafir drives back into the roadway, and Imad is already walking ahead of them, his cell phone pressed to his ear for the call to Amir, Tariq close behind. Bassam wants to call to them to wait, to remember their instructions and to say first a du'a for place, but they have entered the revolving door and in the turning glass he sees briefly his reflection, his narrow shoulders and ironed clothing, his smooth face, his bag hanging beside him. Then the door opens and his reflection is gone, a sign of his fate, yet another sign of his blessed Al-Qadr.

A family moves quickly past. The woman holds an infant and the hand of a young boy who hurries beside her. The man carries a girl. Her head rests upon his shoulder and her eyes are open and her thumb is inside her closed mouth.

O Lord, I ask You for the best of this place, and ask You to protect me from its evils. Bassam waits for the glass to swing open once more, and then he follows this American family into the matar.

The line for tickets is short. Very soon they are standing before a kafir who, behind the long counter, asks for their names and their destinations.

"Los Angeles," says Bassam.

"Name?"

"Al-Jizani."

"Spell it, please." The kafir is older than they and tall, his shoulders rounded downward beneath his shirt. He wears the eyeglasses of the aging, the sort that is only half as high so he may look at them over the lenses. Bassam spells for him his family name, as well as Imad's and Tariq's, though these are no longer their names.

"ID, please?" The man briefly regards their driving licenses from Florida, and he thanks them without looking in their eyes. "Checking baggage?"

"No thank you."

And the kafir directs them to their gate and prints their passes, and when he hands them to Bassam, how strange it is to receive these from a large and aging kafir who does not even know, Allah willing, he has given three shuhada' their tickets to Jannah.

But the gate. They must first pass through security at the gate.

"Bassam, Tariq," says Imad, "this way." And he points to the area so close by, a short line there as well, men and women dressed in business clothing, an old couple, and the young American family. Imad is nearly smiling. He stops and says, "Stay calm, brothers. Al-Aziz is with us. Make your du'a for meeting the enemy."

They walk slowly. There is a Starbucks coffee shop, four or five kufar waiting to be served. There is a shop for newspapers, books, and magazines, again the colors of bare flesh. Bassam looks away to the broad back of Imad before him. Beyond are the matar security guards in their white and black uniforms and their sensors and X-ray machines. Again, the dryness of his mouth and throat, the need for water, and now the need to relieve himself. "Tariq, Imad, please."

The bathroom area is large with a long row of many sinks before a mirror, and Bassam enters the privacy of the enclosed walls and locks the metal door. He lowers his pants and sits. There are the sounds of water running in the sinks, footsteps upon the floor, the flushing of toilets, the main door as it opens and closes. A hand dryer is activated.

A kafir answers his ringing cell phone, speaks into it. "Yeah, I'll be in Denver tonight."

These people and their assumptions. How they never invoke the Holy One when discussing the future, how it is simply believed by them they control their own destiny and no one else.

Bassam reaches for the paper. Above the dispenser are scratchings from a pen, the drawing of a man's erectness and his seed leaving it, a telephone number beneath. The whore, her rising and falling onto him. Again, his weakness, the feeling he has just begun to know women in this world, and now he must leave.

This *cursed* place! Everywhere a temptation. Everywhere a stronghold for Shaytan.

Bassam cleans himself and flushes the toilet. *Allah, forgive me.*

His bag beside him, he washes his hands a very long time, the water quite hot. The mirror begins to fog slightly and in it is his face, the nose and mouth of his mother, but the eyes of his father, the eyes of his father when his belief was still pure, when Bassam had only ten or eleven years and his father returned from the hajj. The family compound was filled with joy, his mother and aunts cooking and passing out gifts and offering praise to the Creator. Bassam's uncle Rashad had slaughtered a goat and a sheep, donating the meat of the goat to two poor families outside Khamis Mushayt. And Bassam and his brothers ate the roasted sheep with the men in the outer building. His father had never looked so young to him, so strong and free of his worries. His beard appeared darker, his eyes shone, and he sat straight but with humility, and when his eyes passed over Bassam, Bassam felt his father's love pass through him straight from the Creator, for his father had made the holy pilgrimage to Makkah. His father, Ahmed al-Jizani, was now a hajji.

"Bassam." Tariq appears in the glass. "Imad waits for us. And do not forget. Act calmly."

Bassam nods his head. There are three other men at the sinks, two white kufar and one Asian. Each in the shirt and tie of a businessman.

Each washing his hands. Each in his own thoughts. And why does Tariq call him Bassam and not Mansoor as he did earlier? Has Bassam not changed since they were boys? Is he the same youngest son of Ahmed al-Jizani, forever in the long shadow he casts? Is this what Tariq sees? Why does Tariq not call him Victorious?

Bassam splashes his face. No, Tariq calls you Bassam because he has always done this. *You must stop looking for negative signs. This is only the work of Shaytan. Do not forget the mala'ika who guided you here. Allah is all we need. He is the best to rely upon. He is the greatest.*

Once again in the matar, the same noise as before: the voices of announcers over the system, the rings of cell phones—one nearby, a musical tune—the rolling of luggage wheels and the clicking of women's shoes upon the floors and throughout all of this is talking, incessant talking.

A hand squeezes Bassam's shoulder. Tariq nods and smiles as if Bassam has just told him a funny story. "You look too serious, Mansoor."

"Yes, all right." The smell of Tariq, his cologne, his shaved face and washed hair, the hotel's shampoo. Their knives are each in inner pockets inside the carrying bags. They are allowed, but now is the test. Now is the test.

A woman has carried her child through the X-ray doorway, and the guard beckons to her husband, who holds a girl. He follows.

Imad places his bag on the moving beltway. He takes a plastic bowl and puts into it coins and his watch with its silver band, one Bassam knows he purchased in Peshawar. He holds his pass, and the guard, his belly protruding, his pants too long, he motions Imad forward. The X-ray doorway of course remains silent, but Bassam's heart thrusts now inside his head for he is watching the woman guard who studies the screen of what is shown in the bags. She is of middle age, and she has changed the color of her hair to blond and she chews gum, her eyes narrowed upon her work. Tariq is now called to enter, and surely Imad's bag has passed through and still the woman's eyes do not change.

Yes, Bassam can see it, Imad grasping it and walking away from them.

Bassam places his bag onto the beltway. There are only a few coins remaining in his pocket and he wishes he had given them all to the driver so he might avoid this extra step. He takes the gray bowl and drops into it his coins. His watch is plastic and glass and he leaves it upon his wrist. And look, Bassam, Tariq is walking away with his bag now as well.

Bassam's heart slows slightly, but his breath is shallow, his tongue thick. He prays he does not appear the way he feels.

"Come through, please." The kafir regards him. He looks quickly from his face to his shoes as if he is sorting pomegranates, putting the new here, the old there, and he is bored with his duties and has been for a very long time.

Bassam passes through.

"Have a nice day, sir."

"Yes. Thank you."

There it is, his bag exiting the machine and rolling down to his waiting hand. No kafir speaks to him. No kafir stops him. He squeezes tightly the handle and he begins walking. There is a calmness, a warmth and a lightness in his arms and legs and face and heart, as if he is water that these twenty-six years has been contained in a vessel and now the vessel is broken and what he viewed before as himself has spilled free and there is no fear at the sudden lack of clay walls to hold him.

"Sir? *Sir?*"

There is no god but Allah. Bassam turns. It is the kafir guard. He smiles and holds forth the container of loose coins. "Don't forget this now."

"Yes, thank you." Bassam releases his breath he did not know he was withholding. He steps forward and allows the man to pour the money into his cupped hand. *All praise is for Allah by whose favor good works are accomplished.* Then Bassam turns and joins his brothers, who await him in the crowd.

⌄ ⌄ ⌄

LONNIE WOKE AT noon. He found he was out of coffee and drove into town. The inside of his truck was hot, and the AC wasn't cooling it off fast enough, and he rolled down his window, the air smelling like palm fronds and newly turned dirt. He needed to buy some groceries. Get something in the fridge. He thought of April dumping him to go shopping. He could've gone with her. Felt pathetic for thinking that.

At the corner of Osprey and Ringling, he stopped for the light, a car pulling up beside him, its windows open, the radio on. He heard the word *hijacked*, then more words. The woman behind the wheel was shaking her head, her mouth half-open. She stared into the empty intersection.

He turned on his own radio.

"Sweat is dry and feet are in the sand
If there were only water—"

He ejected the tape, found a news station, but they were all news.

Adrenaline. That old dangerous friend. Such a gush of it, his arm and legs as light as razors, and it was like the whole club had erupted into a hundred open pockets, yet there was nowhere for him to go, no one to defend.

v   v   v

AJ COULD ONLY think of Cole.

No, he kept *feeling* him. His small body on his lap, his feet knocking against AJ's shins while they ate together somewhere. Or lying down beside him reading him a book, his son's head against AJ's arm. How could his father *not* be with him right now? How could he not be there in their hurricaneproof house, his rifle loaded, guarding the door from whoever these people were?

Did his son know about this? Did Deena? Was she letting him watch it on the TV? AJ hoped not. Lord, he hoped not, and sitting here beneath the tiers in his orange clothes on an orange bench bolted into an orange table, watching hell come to pass in a room full of bad men, it occurred to him he should pray. But with so much suffering, where should he start? My God, where should he *begin*?

Then the tower collapsed into its own rising plume, and one of the men laughed. Some sonofabitch was *laughing*.

⌄ ⌄ ⌄

I T WAS A day of celebration. It was a day April and Franny and Jean had planned to spend together, and they did. After a breakfast of pancakes down in Jean's, Franny sitting on two gardening books at the peninsula, her voice high and cheerful, April had gone back upstairs and made turkey and cheese sandwiches. She wrapped them in foil and placed them in the beach bag with clementines and pears, three carrots, and the box of Ritz crackers. Her kitchen was washed in sunlight and she hummed a song she knew but couldn't name.

This morning, waking up beside Franny, the room was lit from outside the color of roses. There was her sleeping daughter's leg over hers. If April had ever prayed before, she couldn't remember when or why. But in that moment she felt blessed by something large and loving, far away but close too. She pulled Franny into her and kissed her cheek. She thought of her mother. Imagined her waking up in that empty house. Supposedly happy. Smoking alone in the kitchen while her coffee brewed. Today April would call her. She and Franny both.

But first, the beach.

It was Tuesday morning in mid-September and only a handful of people had come. Most of them were on the main beach and not here, the palm fronds flicking in a warm beeze, Franny and Jean making a sand hill. Jean wore her straw hat, sunglasses, and a blue bathing suit she covered with an unbuttoned overshirt. April could see the varicose veins behind her knees and down her calves, the liver spots on her gardener's hands. Franny kept filling the bucket and dumping it in front of Jean, Franny's high, nearly breathless voice telling her what to do with the sand and where to put it.

April couldn't go look for work in Miami, not that far. Tomorrow she'd drive up to Tampa and check out that national chain. See what the house fees were. Ask about the clientele.

Because look how happy Franny was with Jean. They couldn't leave her.

At ten before three, April pulled into the bank's parking lot. Jean looked hot and tired on the passenger side, though she was still upbeat, turning around to talk to Franny about the Slush Puppie she planned to get her after this errand, the iced coffee she was going to buy herself. But her color wasn't good. She'd worn that sun hat all day but her face was pale and sweaty and April left the engine running, the AC on high, and ran across the hot asphalt with her pocketbook full of money.

The bank was cool and smelled like polished wood and coins. One man was at a teller's window, the rest empty. He turned and gave her the once-over, his eyes lingering on her breasts beneath her top, and she ignored him and set her pocketbook on the counter and pulled out the cash. She began to count it. She'd spent some on the Chinese food with Lonnie, more on the new things for Franny's room, more for groceries. But there were still sixty-four one-hundred-dollar bills.

Six thousand four hundred dollars. The foreigner's fingers on her. His hair already thinning. His cigarette smoke rising above them.

There was a fifty and a few twenties and she folded them and pushed them into the front pocket of her shorts and filled out a deposit slip. The man was gone. April went to the window where he'd been. The rest of the tellers were counting money, closing up. It was a woman her age or younger, a curl of blond hair at her neck, her skin a golden mocha. And it was like being Stephanie, seeing a younger, prettier girl who could leave all this and make some real money if she dared to, if she had what it took. April said hi and pushed the cash and deposit slip under the glass, never feeling more proud of who she was or how much money she'd made on her own.

The girl turned to her keyboard. From the side she looked older, her mouth downturned. She typed in April's account number and counted the money quick as a machine, but she looked like a drooping flower.

"Long one?"

"Yep." The girl shook her head. She stacked the money and began dividing it into thousands. "I can't believe we stayed open. The whole country should stop just out of respect." She slipped a band over ten hundreds, reached for another. "My uncle worked in one of those buildings. My mom's been calling his cell phone all day."

"What buildings?"

The girl stopped counting. She turned toward April, the stool squeaking. The whites of her eyes were pink. "You haven't *heard*?"

"No, what? I haven't heard what?"

She turned and looked over her shoulder, then back at April, her expression almost angry. "Are you serious? Do you really not know what's just *happened* to us?"

＊ ＊ ＊

THE DAYS AND nights of television. The images she wouldn't let Franny see. It was September and maybe it was time to find a preschool for her, but April couldn't even think of driving her off and leaving her somewhere. There was the feeling she'd been given a great gift while others were robbed of everything.

She called home a lot. Just to hear her mother's voice. She even called Mary in Connecticut. They talked a long while about their kids, how much they loved them, Mary's voice breaking. She said they should come visit them soon. "Please, April. *Soon.*"

April spent her mornings with Franny and Jean at the beach. After, they'd share a lunch down in Jean's kitchen or in the shade of the mango on the Adirondack chairs, Franny on one of their laps, and in the afternoons, after a bath to wash off the sand, April would lie down with Franny on her bed and read her a story and sometimes she'd fall asleep with her. She'd curl up around her, her nose in her damp hair.

There was the feeling she was in a temporary state of grace, one that could not last long, and she knew she should drive up to Tampa or down to Venice to look for work.

One afternoon in late September, she slid out of Franny's bed and went into the kitchen. She poured cold coffee into a cup and heated it in the microwave. She pulled the phone book from its drawer and opened to the yellow pages, but when she opened to the E section, there was Entertainment—Children and Family, then the phone numbers of animal trainers, puppeteers, and clowns. Below that was Entertainment—Others, nothing but Exotic Dancers and Escort Services, and she closed the book and carried her coffee to the living room.

She would call, she would have to, but not now, maybe tomorrow morning when the manager or owner would be around. She flicked on the television. It'd been days since she watched it. How many times could people see such terrible things over and over again? There had to be something else. And there, in a row of photographs of men, all dark, all young, was him; for a moment she couldn't remember his name—Mike, no, *Bassam*. And he looked at her as he'd first looked at her, like he had important things to do but first he had to make time for this, just this.

Then there was the blue sky and the tall sunlit buildings and it was clear who the others were and she punched the Off button and threw the remote to the couch.

There was his face as he stared between Retro's legs, his lips parted, his eyes dark and almost fearful. There were his fingers on her. On her scar from Franny. There was his cigarette smoke and all his money, and her face burned and she stood quickly and rushed into the kitchen. She just stood there.

Jean was probably napping, but April wanted to go wake her and tell her. But Jean's face, her eyes that no longer bore into her with such judgment, and now April didn't want to tell her. She didn't want to tell anyone.

Late that afternoon, when Franny was down in Jean's garden helping her aim and spray the hose, Louis called from the club. His voice was thick and raspy. He told her he'd just given her name to the FBI, that they were talking to anyone who'd had anything to do with any of them. "And you had one of them in the Champagne, didn't you, Spring?"

She didn't say anything, felt her lips against the receiver.

"Spring? Didn't you?"

The next morning the sky was too gray for the beach. April had made more coffee and was about to call the club in Tampa when the phone rang. It was Jean. She spoke in almost a whisper, "Some men from the FBI are coming up to talk to you." April could already hear them outside her door. They began knocking. She thanked her and asked if she could send Franny down and she hung up and let them in.

They were older than she was, their shirts ironed crisply, their ties just the right length. They all wore wedding rings and each had a handgun clipped snugly to his belt. Franny stared at one of them as April held the door open for her and told her she'd be down soon. At the bottom of the stairs, Jean waited, her eyes on April's, the dark light of distrust back in them.

April offered the agents coffee but they politely said no. Two of the men stood at the peninsula. The oldest-looking one sat in the chair across from her on the couch, a pad and pen on his lap. His hair was combed back over his bald spot and there were laugh lines etched around his mouth, but his eyes were a cool gray.

He asked her how long she'd worked at the Puma Club, the shifts of her average workweek, then that Friday night and the approximate time when she went into the Champagne Room.

She told him, thought of Franny in Tina's office as she said it.

"What did you do for him?"

"What do you mean?"

"What services did you perform?"

"I danced."

"That's all you did?"

"Yes, that's all I ever do."

"Did he ask for sex?"

"No. And he wouldn't have gotten any." A wave of heat rose into her face.

"But I understand you spent over two hours with him."

"That's right, we talked too."

"What about?"

"I don't know. He was drunk. He didn't make a lot of sense."

"Were you drinking as well?"

"Yes, you're supposed to in the Champagne. But I wasn't drunk."

He nodded, wrote something on his pad.

She was barefoot and wearing shorts and she could feel one of the agents staring at her.

"I understand that was a rough night for you."

April nodded. His tone was patronizing, and she didn't like it. She looked away from him. There was Tina's empty office, the bright empty dressing room, the empty darkness under the stage, her screams lost in it. She made herself look back at him.

"But you're all right now."

"Yes."

"Good." He wrote more, as if something had just been verified for him. "What did he say that didn't make any sense?"

"I don't know, he talked about truth and lies. He said none of what we did was allowed."

"He was instructing you."

"No, he wasn't instructing me."

"But how did he say it?"

Now they were all looking at her, the oldest one's eyes on her eyes, like she knew something she wasn't telling and should, but more, it was as if she had no right to know what she knew, that she'd gotten this knowledge wrongly.

"He said it like he hated us. You know, you could tell he hated us."

"Who? You dancers? Or Americans?"

"No, all of *us*." She waved her arm in the air to encompass the men in her house, but her last word hung between them and she felt outside of it, not that she wasn't hated too, but that she had somehow been banished from the rest.

There were more questions about him, about anything else he may have said or done, but soon it felt to her as if they were talking in a wide floating circle. As they were leaving, the oldest one placed his card faceup on her kitchen counter like an unpaid bill. They thanked her for her time and stepped out into a soft rain. She waited for them to drive away, then she went down to Jean's, the steps warm and wet. The television was on, Franny sitting cross-legged on the rug in front of it, a plate of cheese and crackers on her lap.

Jean was pulling a bowl from the dishwasher. April wiped her feet on the mat. The television's bright colors spilled over her daughter and Jean's cat lying beside her, and Jean straightened and pushed a strand of hair from her face. She was flushed in the cheeks and when she looked over at April she no longer looked distrustful but sad and slightly impatient, as if whatever she was here to tell her, then please, let's get it over with.

They sat on the edge of Jean's bed. The cat had followed them, and he stretched out behind them on the bedspread, his tail lightly flicking April's back. There were vacuum tracks in Jean's carpet. It felt thick and soft under her feet.

"I danced for one of them."

"Who?"

The rain tapped the window. From down the hall came Franny's laughter. April turned to Jean, could see in her eyes that she knew but wasn't saying so. "The hijackers."

Jean nodded. She looked away. "I read that some of them had been seen there, April. I was hoping—"

"What?"

"I don't know."

"No, Jean, what?"

"I hoped you'd had nothing to do with that."

"I didn't. I just danced for one of them." There was the small smoky Champagne Room, his eyes on her face and breasts, his money scattered across the sticky cocktail table.

"What did they ask you?"

"What he was like."

"What *was* he like?"

"Like a boy. Just some drunk and lonely boy."

"Are you in any kind of trouble?"

"No, why would I be in trouble?"

"My show's over." Franny stood in the doorway. There were cracker crumbs on her shirt, and she'd been smiling, but now she wasn't, her eyes moving from April to Jean, then back to April. She looked close to making some kind of important decision.

The next day the sun was back, and before they drove to the beach April told Jean she had a quick phone call to make. Would she mind waiting for her with Franny down in the garden? In the kitchen she opened the yellow pages and found the club in Tampa. She pressed the numbers and waited, her eyes on the number in the ad box, a silhouette of a naked woman lying across it as if it were a bed.

The rings were long with little space between them. She could feel her pulse in her palm. She looked out the kitchen window down into the garden. Near the cedar boxes of hibiscus and allamanda, Jean and Franny were hopscotching over the terra-cotta brick work. First Jean, heavy on her feet, then Franny, the sun on her hair.

"The Golden Stage, a Gentlemen's Club." It was a woman's voice. April pictured her standing in a pink entryway. Behind her was the hum of a machine, maybe a vacuum cleaner, a man shouting something, and she imagned a big windowless room that would soon darken and fill with more men.

"Hello?" The woman's voice sounded so young and hungry to please. Outside, Jean sat in one of the Adirondacks breathing hard and Franny was hopping on one leg, trying to hit each brick with her foot.

"Hello?"

It was as if April had just woken a long venomous snake and now it was slithering past her and Franny and Jean. She opened her mouth to speak but there came a click in her ear, then the dial tone.

She hung up.

She closed the phone book and placed it back into its drawer and slowly pushed it shut. Maybe she would try again later. Maybe tomorrow.

She picked up her beach bag and walked outside. The day was early and bright. From the landing she could smell the mango leaves, could see Jean's garden spread out before her. And she hurried down the stairs to join them, her friend and her daughter, waiting for her down there under the sun.

∨ ∨ ∨

FOR TWO YEARS Deena had done her best, one weekend a month packing up Cole and driving the eight hours north and west to the farthest end of the panhandle here to Santa Rosa. She had to stay in a motel in Milton, or Pensacola. Pay for a room she couldn't afford. And that did something to him. Her going to all that trouble. Those first visits she held the phone to her ear and stared at him through inch-thick glass, her hair finally her own, her eyes sometimes welling up. She'd sit Cole on her lap and let him talk though Cole never understood that the voice he heard was his daddy on the other side of the glass, and he'd look away from him and talk to the man on the phone instead.

After seven years he's in Open Population, him and seventy-nine other men on bunks in the barracks just off the rec yard. He's got a locker and pictures on the wall of his son, and his job assignments are no longer in food service scraping slop after slop from plastic trays, or in the laundry room washing out the sweat and piss and dried semen of lowlifes.

For a while he worked in the law library cataloguing books. Then the trustee there saw his head for numbers and for two years he's been a math tutor in the ED helping men learn what nobody ever taught them before, or they were too damned smart to listen to. Some of them call him Teach. Sometimes they come up to him in the rec yard or when he's just lying on his bunk and ask him to help them with their GED or to send a budget back home to their wife or girlfriend or to give them the probability of getting an ace in a deck when three have already been played. Some of them just come up and ask him things because others call him Teach, and they think he knows more than the others.

One asked him about God, if he believed in him, and AJ shrugged and said, "Man, I just hope he believes in *us*."

Once or twice a year now Deena will drive Cole to see him. Her husband stays back at the motel, and for a while AJ preferred it that way, didn't want to lay eyes on him. But it's different now. He no longer pictures her fucking him in their bed in their house she sold anyway. He no longer pictures him reading Cole a book at night, helping him with his homework, throwing a ball to him under the sun, this man Deena met at the Walgreen's where she got her old job back. She wrote to him how it felt good to be working again, that she'd lost weight and one afternoon a computer salesman came in for ballpoint pens and they got to talking.

After the divorce papers she stopped writing letters about herself, just sent along pictures of Cole, the latest of his team photo from Little League. AJ's son was the skinny one in the back row, his uniform shirt tucked tightly into his pants, his ears sticking out beneath his cap.

But he looked happy. That was the thing. His son looked happy, and cared for.

On Wednesdays, after the two-thirty head count, AJ sits in a corner of the mess with two dozen short-timers and they talk about how they're going to live when they get out, how they're going to avoid coming back. Ray Brown, the leader, a man who for years stuck a gun in people's faces and took everything from them, said he wrote letters to all his victims, even if they were dead. He wrote letters and asked forgiveness.

The letters help with parole too, but for so long AJ couldn't even imagine writing anything. He shouldn't've done what he did, he knew that. But who brought her there in the first place? And then when he'd seen and read who else was there that night, that she may have danced for one of *them*—well, it was too much.

It's three o'clock on a Friday in September, job assignments done for the day. AJ's sitting against the wall in the rec yard. Tomorrow he'll get a new student, a young con in a wheelchair. He sees him at the edge of the basketball court now, a dark-skinned kid with dead legs lighting a cigarette, a bunch of short-timers playing a loud game of full-court in front of him. At the exercise station some of the younger ones do push-ups and chin-ups, the free weights hauled out of here last winter after somebody smashed an iron plate into another's face. All this rage all the time. AJ just doesn't feel it anymore. He doesn't feel much at all really. But he looks forward to the small things, sleep after lights-out, a good piss, hot coffee, then teaching, sitting down with another man beside him and laying out the rules of numbers for him, how to create a problem and how to work it out.

And this isn't so bad, this concrete against his back, the sun high and in his face. In this heat he can smell the sap on the other side of the chain link and concertina wire, can see the thick stands of slash pine and loblolly and red cedar. He knows the Blackwater River is somewhere beyond that and that it flows twenty miles south of here to the Gulf, fresh water into salt, all that water flowing out to more water, our bodies made of it. He sees him and Cole on a boat fishing together, laughing together. And once again, there's the little girl, how he held her and sang to her and lay her down asleep. For a moment he doesn't remember her name, but then it's there in his head, like a prayer.

The unit will be quieter now. He'll sign out a pen and get his notebook from his locker. He'll lie down on his bunk. He does not yet know what he'll say or if she'll ever receive it or even read it, but she's the one he must write to. And he'll write to his son after that. Tell him more than he has in the past.

The kid in the chair tosses his cigarette. He wheels himself away from the game and stops near the chain link and stares through it to the trees.

٧ ٧ ٧

I T WAS THE waiting that did it, that crept up on her and pressed against her chest and reached in with a cold hand and squeezed her heart. But then something truly horrible happens and you're still here. More fortunate than so many others. Blessed by fate.

But, still here.

After April and Franny moved, there was one other tenant, a young man from Haiti who spoke poor English and played his music too loud and had over many friends. They stayed late, speaking in French and drinking, laughing and sometimes yelling, and after two months of this, Jean worked up her nerve and asked Jean-Paul to leave.

She didn't need the money. Again, it was to fill the awful silence of the house.

April's face as she sat beside Jean under the mango. She hadn't worked in weeks and was darker than ever from their mornings at the beach, but she looked tired, her eyes missing something that had been there before, a kind of confidence. Franny was inside watching a movie, its bright blues and reds reflecting off the window.

"Do you miss working, April?"

"I miss the money. But I can't go back to that."

"Good."

"I just can't separate it anymore."

"What?"

"Me by day and me by night."

"What're you going to do?"

She shrugged and ran her fingers back through her hair, not knowing that in only days her mother would call from New Hampshire, her true mother, the one who'd raised her and was Franny's grandmother. She would call to say she was moving to a condo. Did April want to buy the house for cheap?

Jean still had the letters and Franny's drawings, the ones she'd drawn here and the two she sent in the months after April drove her north. As a housewarming gift, Jean had sent flowers from her garden. She clipped hibiscus and frangipani, the red stars of ixora and the orange petals of her bougainvillea. She wrapped all this in damp leaves from her mango and jacaranda trees, and she bought baby's breath and florist's paper and bundled it all and boxed it and drove to the post office and mailed it off to New Hampshire, a place she'd never been.

She imagined mountains and farms, snow and pickup trucks.

Over a year ago, the last letter. In it April said she was working in a realtor's office, that she met someone and was getting married. She included a school picture of Franny, this striking eight-year-old girl with long hair, the curls gone, the blond too. But her eyes were the same, still bright, still warm, still so curious about the world and her place in it.

On the back was April's handwriting: *Franny, 3rd grade, she still talks about you and the garden!*

But did she? She'd been only three. Was it possible? Jean didn't think so, but she hoped it was true.

Her room was as she'd left it. Some nights when Jean couldn't sleep, when her breathing seemed to come with difficulty and she broke out in a sweat, she'd go into Franny's room. She'd lie on her smaller bed and close her eyes and rest. She'd see their mornings together, hear Franny's voice again as she talked about her dreams from the night before. Jean would see and hear other things—Harry smiling at her from behind his reading glasses, her father's hand gripping the handles of his medical kit, that conscientious inspector, the way she stood in Jean's room and studied her, searching for flaws when that's all she'd ever been, a jumbled bundle of them.

Jean takes her newspaper and a glass of Shiraz, old Matisse following her outside. It's sundown, early spring. In a week, God willing, she'll turn seventy-seven. How had this happened? How had she outlived everyone she came from? She didn't always feel well, but the attacks were over; if something terrible was going to happen, then there was very little you could do about it anyway. This she knew now. Why *wait* for it?

She sipped her wine. There was a photo in the paper she had to see again. She set her glass down and slipped on her reading glasses. His head was shaved and he wore the white-brimmed hat of the Marine Corps. She'd seen so many of these pictures, all of young men staring resolutely into the camera and their own fates, the Stars and Stripes behind them. But this one's expression was neutral, as if he were lying in wait and did not want to be seen, not yet. And it was him. It was April's polite bouncer, and Jean's heart flattened out in her chest. Was he one of the thousands? There were the words "active duty" and "past ties to the community." Like so many, he'd enlisted because he wanted to *do* something, but he was one of those here who'd actually "brushed shoulders" with one of them and could not forget it.

And he had gone back for a third time.

She folded the paper and set it in her lap. Outside the walls a car drove by, one of Jean's neighbors she didn't know. She would work on that. She was sure good people lived here, as they did everywhere. If she opened her gate and invited them in, wouldn't they come?

The wine spread out warmly in Jean's chest. She breathed deeply. She could smell mango leaves and hibiscus, palmetto and hyacinth and trumpet vine. There was the damp soil of her new plantings, its dark scent indifferent and ancient and enduring.

She stared at her garden and tried not to think of anything. Just to see it. Its beauty here for as long as she was, as long as she cared for it.

A lizard flitted over the brickwork into the ferns. One of them trembled, then went still. The cat just stared after it as if she were through chasing things. Then another fern moved, and Jean's cat shot into them and she couldn't see her anymore, just heard her, her frantic search in the garden.

ACKNOWLEDGMENTS

I am grateful to the following people who were most generous with their time and expertise: Professor Peter Whelan of Francis Marion University, Parkie Jones, Gale Brunault, Robin Pearson Cogan, Lieutenant Blair Waller of the Sarasota County Sheriff's Deptartment, Rema Badwan, Joel Gotler, Rick Taylor, Gunner Davis, Kerrie Clapp, my brother Jeb Dubus, Bill Cantwell, Stephen Haley, Jim Champoux, and Joseph Hurka; Pin Print technician Shannon Conrad, and JoEllyn Rackleff, press secretary at the Florida Department of Corrections.

I am deeply indebted to the Guggenheim Foundation for its support. And I thank my agent, Philip Spitzer, for his patience and good cheer, as well as my tenacious and persevering editor, Alane Salierno Mason. Finally, I thank my wife, Fontaine, for the gift of her faith.